Early Praise for

WAGES OF EMPIRE

"Masterful storytelling will keep you furiously turning the pages of this compelling historical WWI novel. A winner!"

–Andrew Kaplan, New York Times Best-Selling Author of *Blue Madagascar* and the *Homeland* Novels

"The characters, historical and fictional, come to life on the page as the storyline drives relentlessly forward. Bravo!"

–Matt Coyle, bestselling author of the *Rick Cahill* novels

"*Wages of Empire* is a gripping adventure set during World War I...an exciting ride through this intriguing period of history."

–Penny Warner, Author of *Dead Body Language* (optioned by Marlee Matlin for TV/Film)

"Compelling novel with global insights . . . offers history buffs a thrilling ride."

–Sujata Massey, internationally bestselling author of *The Widows of Malabar Hill*

"A finely wrought and lovingly researched novel that brings history and historical figures to life. The next best thing to a time machine!"

–Kenneth Wishinia, Award-Winning Author of *The Fifth Servant* and *From Sun to Sun*

"A must-read blockbuster for history buffs of all ages. The novel's masterful storytelling will leave readers wanting more."

–Chanticleer Book Reviews – 5 Stars – Best Book

"A beautifully written tale . . . exhibits seamless research in illuminating unforgettable historical and fictional characters . . . a tour de force!"

–Professor Ronit Meroz, Dept of Jewish Philosophy and Talmud, Tel-Aviv University, Israel

"An engaging history lesson as contemporaneous as the morning newspaper, but far more enlivening."

–John Bennison, Rel.D - Lead Teacher: Pathways Faith Community

"This superb historical novel is a must read . . . directly relates to issues we face today."

–Rizek Abusharr, Emeritus Director General of Jerusalem International YMCA

"Cooper has made this period of history come alive. It is a treat to read."

–Rabbi David Zisenwine, Ph.D. Professor Emeritus of Education, Tel Aviv University

"A Young Indiana Jones–style adventure."

–KIRKUS reviews

"Story is gripping and the characters that he describes come alive through his skillful writing. I couldn't put it down!"

–Rabbi Gordon Freeman, Ph.D., Rabbi Emeritus, B'nai Shalom, Walnut Creek, CA

AWARDS

CIBA 2022 Rossetti Grand Prize for YA Fiction
CIBA 2022 Hemingway First Place Honors for Wartime Fiction

Wages of Empire
by Michael J. Cooper

© Michael J. Cooper

ISBN 979-8-88824-186-8

Cover photograph derived from Old City Jerusalem, Temple Mount (undated, post 1910); Photo credit: (c) DEIAHL, Jerusalem—Used by permission from the Protestant Institute of Archaeology.

Published by

ĸ köehlerbooks™

3705 Shore Drive
Virginia Beach, VA 23455
800-435-4811

WAGES

OF

EMPIRE

MICHAEL J. COOPER

VIRGINIA BEACH
CAPE CHARLES

Also by Michael J Cooper

Foxes in the Vineyard

The Rabbi's Knight

In loving memory of

Bill Gottfried

brilliant mentor and generous friend

To learn the age-old lesson day by day:
It is not in the bright arrival planned,
But in the dreams men dream along the way

—James Elroy Flecker, *The Bridge of Fire*

AUTHOR'S NOTE

Wages of Empire is a novel set in the first months of World War I, inspired by actual historical events, and peopled with factual as well as fictional characters. While the novel generally adheres to the historical timeline, there are a few departures for purposes of craft and continuity as noted in the list of characters at the end of the book, and I beg the reader's indulgence for these digressions.

Wages of Empire traces the fictional journey of Evan Sinclair into the intrigue and brutality of the Great War, weaving multiple storylines to paint a portrait of the initial explosion of the conflict in Europe. The book also expands the canvas to reveal the growing attraction of the colonial powers to the land bridge at the crossroads of Europe, Africa, and Asia, with an intensifying interest in the Middle East. Here the war would be fought for control of the Suez Canal to the west and the rich oil reserves of Arabia to the east, with the diadem of Jerusalem as the ultimate prize.

While some observers at the time referred to the Middle East Front as a "sideshow," there is ample evidence to suggest that this particular bit of real estate was a central aspiration of Kaiser Wilhelm II. Indeed, one of the novel's central themes is the kaiser's obsession with Jerusalem, on full display during his visit there in 1898 when he initiated major building projects and had himself crowned "King of Jerusalem." And these machinations were only a prelude to his invasion of France by way of Belgium in 1914, igniting the European theater of the Great War.

At its core, *Wages of Empire* holds up a mirror to current conflicts in the Middle East that are the direct descendants of the promises made and broken during and after the Great War for Civilization.

This map is not drawn to scale and is provided for the
reader's general orientation as to the approximate borders
of empires and countries, along with the approximate
location of capitals and some significant sites as they
were at the beginning of the Great War.

Map illustration by Scott Schiller/mapsbyscott.com

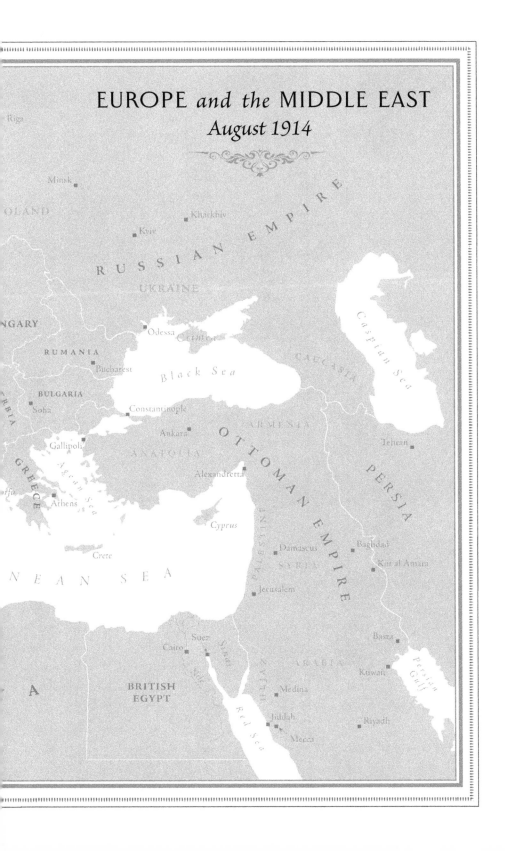

EUROPE *and the* MIDDLE EAST
August 1914

Riga

Minsk

POLAND

Kharkhiv

Kyiv

R U S S I A N   E M P I R E

UKRAINE

NGARY

Odessa

Crimea

Caspian Sea

RUMANIA

Bucharest

Black Sea

CAUCASIA

BULGARIA

RBIA

Sofia

Constantinople

ARMENIA

Tehran

Ankara

O T T O M A N

GALLIPOLI

Gallipoli

ANATOLIA

PERSIA

GREECE

Aegean Sea

Alexandretta

orfu

Athens

Cyprus

PALESTINE

E M P I R E

N E A N   S E A

Crete

Damascus

Baghdad

SYRIA

Kut al-Amara

Jerusalem

Suez

Basra

Cairo

Sinai

ARABIA

Persian Gulf

Kuwait

A

BRITISH
EGYPT

Nile

HIJAZ

Medina

Riyadh

Red Sea

Jiddah

Mecca

PROLOGUE

·❖·

April 18, 1911
Jerusalem

THE TEMPLE MOUNT was shrouded in darkness. It was the dead of night yet sounds of digging echoed within the Dome of the Rock.

Gunter von Wertheimer knew the sounds well—the steady scrape of a shovel, the bite of a pick, and the whisper of soil poured from full panniers.

Cloaked in a hooded robe, he stood in the shadow of the shrine and looked up at the sky. Among the bright points of stars, the constellation of the scorpion hovered over the Dome, the sharp stinger formed by a bright star the Arabs called *Lasa'a,* poised to strike.

As the digging continued, another sound whispered out of the darkness.

"It's time."

He knew the voice was that of his friend and fellow archeologist, Rahman B'Shara, a hulking shadow in the darkness.

"You know what you must do," said Gunter.

"It's strange, though," Rahman murmured. "When Walker first came, I thought he was like the others—just another greedy treasure hunter, anxious to get his hands on the golden vessels hidden beneath the Foundation Stone. But once I joined the dig, I couldn't believe how quickly it was progressing."

"Do you still believe he'll break through in the next few days?"

"No. He'll break through in the next few hours."

"Because of the spiritualists and clairvoyants he hired?"

"More likely, it's the unchecked access he's had to dig for the last two weeks. Walker has a keen sense of which Ottoman officials to bribe—starting with the Turkish governor." Rahman turned, stepped past Gunter and whispered, "There's no time to lose."

"Good luck, my friend."

"Why do I need luck?"

"You know that better than I. His guards are well armed."

Rahman smiled, his white teeth flashing in the starlight. "We have something more powerful than their guns."

"Indeed. We have the power of the Temple."

"In the end, yes, but I was speaking of a power of *this* world—the power of the mob."

"And what a mob!" Gunter agreed. "Thousands of pilgrims in Jerusalem for the Feast of Nebi Musa! When they hear the Temple Mount has been desecrated by treasure hunters, Walker won't need to enter the Temple to experience divine wrath."

"Yes! The faithful will be quick to avenge this outrage." Rahman bolted away, disappearing into the darkness.

Gunter knew he was heading to the Muslim Quarter beyond the northern edge of the sacred precincts. After a few seconds, he heard his voice calling out, echoing among the narrow lanes.

"Sacrilege! The Frengi are breaking the foundation stone! Sacrilege!"

Within seconds, two armed Turkish guards with torches shot out of the shrine and sprinted in the direction of Rahman's voice.

Gunter flattened himself against the smooth tiles and watched as they came to a stop, apparently despairing as they heard the words Rahman was shouting.

"Arise to vengeance! The Turks have given over the Holy Mountain to the greed of infidels. Avenge the sacrilege! Arise!"

The guards ran back into the shrine and within seconds, Gunter heard the anxious voice of Montagu Walker.

"We must get out of here double quick! Hurry! Take whatever you can carry!"

As he waited in the shadows beneath the arches of the arcade, Gunter knew that Rahman had been the one best suited to infiltrate Walker's scheme—to expose and stop him. Walker had hired Rahman as his consulting archaeologist to give his treasure hunt the patina of a legitimate excavation—Rahman, who could trace his ancestry in Jerusalem back for a hundred generations.

Though Gunter had also been born in Jerusalem, he was the son of German Templers, and never completely trusted by the local population; suspected of working for the Germans, or the Ottomans, or both.

But Gunter served no colonial empire. He, like Rahman, was a Guardian of the Temple Mount, an order that traced its origins to a time before the holy mountain had a name, a time cloaked in the shadowed silence before history.

A line of flaming torches appeared along the northern border of the Temple enclosure. Shouts of execration filled the air.

Walker and his crew tumbled out of the Dome of the Rock, struggling with heavy sacks, shovels and picks that scraped and clattered on the paving stones.

"Leave that stuff!" Walker shouted. "Run for your lives!"

They rushed headlong away from the mob, frantically clawing past one another.

Gunter knew they were making for a gap in the southern border of the enclosure.

The mob surged forward in pursuit, the light of a thousand torches beneath the black sky.

Walker was finished.

The passages and chambers within the Temple Mount would remain sealed, as they had been for a thousand years.

But Gunter knew that others would come—drawn by the power and mystery of Jerusalem. And he also knew that the Guardians of the Temple Mount would be watching, and they would never rest.

CHAPTER 1

June 11, 1914
Cedar City, Utah

EVAN SINCLAIR was in no hurry to get home.

Finding refuge in a pickup game of baseball after the last day of senior year, he stood in center field amid patches of parched grass and tufts of saltbush, shirtless in the summer heat of the high desert. The dry ground shimmered beneath the late-afternoon sun, and from somewhere a chorus of cicadas whined, the sound sustained and rising.

He squinted at the distant contest between pitcher and batter, framed by the rickety wooden backstop and the Pine Valley Mountains. His team was ahead by two runs with two outs in what both teams had agreed would be the last inning.

"C'mon! Get this guy out," Evan said in conversation with himself since no other player was within a hundred feet of him.

Nearly two years had passed since his mother's death, and bereft of her touch, home had become little better than a boarding school with a strict live-in tutor. In addition to the regular high school curriculum, Evan matriculated under the unbending tutelage of his father in ancient Greek and Classical Latin.

He was in no hurry to get home.

Pushing sun-streaked hair out of his eyes, he relished the simplicity of baseball and the camaraderie of his friends—welcome relief from the oppressive loneliness and static mental labors he faced at home.

And once the game ended, he wouldn't be going home, but to the dry gulley a quarter mile from the house—there to enjoy the quiet solitude of practicing with his sling.

And tomorrow, graduation . . .

As a prank, he had formally requested that his diploma be issued under the name "Pancho Villa." His father hadn't been amused. Nor had he been pleased to discover blank college application forms crammed into a box in the hall closet. Despite Evan's best efforts to the contrary, he had done well enough to gain admission to college. But there was the small matter of the application.

"Let's finish this!" Evan pounded a fist into his worn leather glove and bent at the waist, resting his hands on his knees. He imagined he was in the vast green outfield of the Polo Grounds in upper Manhattan, where he had fallen in love with baseball and with the New York Giants on a hot summer day in 1912, soon after he and his parents had arrived in New York City by steamship and before leaving by train for Utah. His mother, in the early months of pregnancy, had elected to stay close to the electric fan in their hotel room.

On entering the Polo Grounds, Evan's breath had caught—the sweet smell of the freshly mowed grass and the vast sweep of green stretching into the recessed shadows of center field. The majestic glory of the green cathedral was further enhanced by the great pitcher, Christy Mathewson, winning the first game of a doubleheader against the Boston Braves.

His father, not wanting to leave his mother alone all day, insisted they forego the second game of the doubleheader, but Evan's baptismal experience was complete—reborn a new convert to the religion of baseball.

The memory of that day was one Evan cherished—the last time he could remember a sense of easy friendship with his father.

In his imagination he was now playing center field for the New York Giants against the Boston Braves, with Christy Mathewson pitching. Framed by the huge green stadium on either side, with the first and second decks rising two hundred feet into the sky and filled with spectators, Mathewson stood unmoving—the batter also still but for the bat waving slowly like a cobra, waiting to strike.

"Throw the ball, already," Evan muttered as he picked a stone off the ground and tossed it aside.

Finally, the pitcher reared back and threw.

The batter swung and Evan heard the sharp click of contact between bat and ball—the white dot arcing upward against the blue sky.

Tracking the ball's flight, Evan uncoiled and began to run, shouting, "I got it!" as he skirted clumps of weeds and gopher holes. He raised his glove, caught the ball, and without breaking stride, trotted in, pausing briefly near second base to acknowledge the thunderous applause from the capacity crowd at the Polo Grounds.

"Nice catch," Mike Cope said and raised his glove.

Evan threw him the ball. "Yeah, good game."

"You wanna have a soda in town?"

"No. I gotta go home." Evan stuffed the glove into his haversack.

"Hey, buddy, finals are over. We're done!"

Evan shrugged. "My father . . ." He left off, not needing to elaborate.

"Your dad is so strange," Mike said, shaking his head.

Evan bristled at the characterization, even though he largely agreed with it. He missed the version of his father he had glimpsed that day at the Polo Grounds.

"Have you asked him about our trip to Moab?"

"Yeah—no problem."

"Good! See ya tomorrow."

"Why? What's tomorrow?" asked Evan, deadpanning. "Oh! You mean graduation?" He shrugged. "Not sure I can make it."

"Too busy conjugating Latin verbs?"

"Yeah, that's it exactly!" Evan said and struck off into the desert.

He was soon well away from the ball field, the ground-heated air fragrant with the pungent smell of sage and parched earth—the trackless waste dotted with manzanita. Still shirtless, his faded canvas haversack hung over his right shoulder and swung as he walked. His face and arms were deeply tanned while the skin of his broad shoulders and long torso were of a lighter hue and freckled. The cicada's song had ended, and the only sounds were those of his footsteps over the dry ground and the sibilant whisper of the late-afternoon breeze cooling his body.

He stopped walking and closed his eyes as thoughts of his mother's death rose in his mind. They often did when he was alone. The memories stabbed through his heart; the anxious dread in her eyes with the too-early birth pains, the fear in his father's voice as he guided the automobile through the night, the asphalt road illuminated by the headlamps from Cedar City to the hospital in St. George, the weak cry of the sister he would never see, his mother's blond hair radiating out on the hospital pillow after she had died, and the emptiness of leaving St. George without her.

He exhaled a sigh and resumed walking until he reached a deep ravine. He descended a stairway of boulders into the dry riverbed with its pavement of coarse gravel dotted by smooth stones. Rounding a curve in the gulley, the silence was broken by a sudden rasping hiss that brought him up short—a barn owl huddled in the shadow of a rocky cliff. The owl rotated its white, heart-shaped face, following him with its small eyes as he skirted by.

After a few minutes, he saw his goal—a large beavertail cactus cascading down the gulley wall with bright magenta flowers.

He stopped at a distance of about fifty feet, tossed down his haversack, unhitched the clasps and took out his sling—a strip of sheepskin seven-feet long. He examined the stitches that secured the quarter-pound lead weight to one end, and with his pocketknife, cut away a few trailing threads. As he worked, he thought about Ned Lawrence.

Ten years Evan's senior, Lawrence had taught Evan how to make the sling when they'd met during his father's first sabbatical year at the Carchemish digs in Northern Syria. Lawrence, already a working archaeologist, had shown Evan how to cure and split the sheepskin to make the leather supple, how to select stones of the proper size and shape, how to grip the sling, how to launch the stone, and how to use the weighted end like a South American bola.

Evan had already mastered the sling's bola function as evinced by dozens of amputated dried-out flesh pads and faded cactus flowers that lay scattered on the riverbed. That part hadn't been difficult. But slinging stones was challenging.

He fitted a rock into the sling's apex and began to spin it. As the sling rotated faster and faster, he thought about what Lawrence had told him about the connection of the sling to the Balearic Islands, how men of the islands had served the Roman Empire as a special division of hoplites.

The sling blurred. Releasing the lower, unweighted strap, the stone flew forward, though far wide of the mark, missing the cactus by at least ten feet. He picked up another rock. Again, he whipped the sling about. This time the stone slapped into the ground at his feet.

As stones flew—occasionally in the direction of the cactus— his mind was crowded with thoughts. *I will not go to college in the fall. Maybe I'll run away—volunteer to fight for Pancho Villa and the revolution in Mexico. Or maybe I'll hitch rides to Blytheville, Arkansas and try out for the Giants' farm team . . .*

Finally, a stone hit the cactus with an audible pop.

"Yes!" he shouted and pumped his fist in the air. "The Balearic hoplite strikes," he bent down and picked up another rock.

As evening fell and the desert cooled, his missiles began hitting the cactus with regularity—stone after stone. And the air rang with his triumphal shouts.

✻   ✻   ✻

"Where the hell is he?" Clive Sinclair said aloud as he set water to boil on the stove. "He should have been home hours ago!"

Leaving the kitchen, he went to the living room, which also served as foyer of the small house. He opened the front door and looked out through the screen, already adorned with lacewings, past the porch and dusty front yard into the desert. *Where the hell is he?*

Still dressed in the dungarees, khaki shirt and boots he had worn for work, Clive turned from the door. Regarding the mahogany clock on the mantelpiece, he took the watch from his pocket and checked the time, then opened the glass lens over the clock face and pushed the minute hand back three minutes to eight o'clock. Closing the glass, he was surprised at how loud the smooth metallic click of the copper clasp sounded in the silence of the house.

His eyes rested on the photograph next to the clock, taken at the outdoor bus terminal in Jarablus on the day that they had left for Beirut—the first leg of the return trip to England, before continuing his sabbatical in the United States.

"Almost two years now." He lifted the photograph off the mantelpiece and looked at Janet—her hair the way he loved it, gathered in a single braid over her shoulder. Leaning closer, he saw that a fugitive strand had escaped the braid and lay along her cheek. He looked into her steady eyes, her mouth smiling. He saw the same happiness in his own and Evan's face as they stood on either side of her. And in the glass over the photograph, he saw the weary solitude of his own reflection. "Now Evan is avoiding me and we're still in

Utah," he said with a sigh. "My love, in this land of long shadows, you were the bridge between us. Evan and I are now like two solitary and unmoving pinnacles--in vague proximity but no longer connected."

He thought back to the night of her death—the onset of early labor, the pain rippling through her belly, the fear gripping their hearts, and the same unspoken prayer; *Please, God, not again!*

But the pattern was sadly familiar; Janet had miscarried twice in Mesopotamia, and the long drive through the night from Cedar City to St. George was fraught with the specter of a recurrent nightmare. As he drove, checking the time and counting the miles to the hospital, he realized that his notions of time and distance had yielded to a primal force that kept its own measure—in the ebb and flow of the birth pains and in the sound of Janet's breathing. In the end, the baby had been born in the hospital, marked by a single weak cry followed by silence.

And Janet?

"We're trying to stop the bleeding."

But the bleeding wouldn't stop.

Clive took off his wire-rim spectacles and dried his eyes.

In the kitchen, the teakettle was shrieking. He turned off the fire, and the shrill whistle fell silent.

And in that silence, he heard a voice.

Out in the desert, someone was shouting.

He stepped to the front door and stood listening, looking into the crimson desert.

There it was again.

Someone calling for help?

And in the space of one terrible moment he realized it was Evan. He sprinted out of the house, past the low picket fence, and across the road. Threading a path among clumps of sagebrush, he was guided by Evan's sporadic shouts, his heart gripped with fear as he catalogued lethal denizens of the high desert—cougars, diamondbacks, recluse spiders. A final shout led him to a bluff above a dry wash.

To his relief he saw that Evan appeared unhurt. He paused to catch his breath and watched him fit a stone into what looked like a sling and spin it round. Then he saw the target—the remains of a huge flowering prickly pear cactus on the far wall of the gulley with ragged fragments of the plant scattered on the ground.

He watched as Evan released a stone with such force that it tore through the cactus' pulpy flesh and rattled among the boulders along the gulley wall.

As Evan shouted for joy, Clive shouted from the bluff, "What in the name of heaven are you *doing*?"

Clearly startled, Evan turned. "Just . . . practicing with my sling, sir."

"I can see that." He picked his way down the steep embankment and nodded in the direction of the cactus. "And *that's* your target?"

"Yes, sir."

Clive approached the wounded prickly pear, shaking his head. Apart from the fragments and flowers scattered on the ground, dozens of stones were embedded in the flesh of the plant's remaining pads, with jagged wounds where stones had grazed it.

"Have you *completely* lost your mind?" he asked, struggling to control his anger. "Do you realize that this cactus may have been a hundred years old? Do you realize that you have destroyed an ancient living thing?"

"Sorry," Evan offered weakly.

"He's *sorry*," Clive repeated in the direction of the cactus. "And there's *this*." He produced an envelope from his jacket pocket. "Have we forgotten about your application to the Branch Normal School?" His voice rose as darkness fell. "I *distinctly* remember that you were going to take care of this."

"I did," Evan replied quietly.

"What?" asked Clive putting a hand up to his ear.

"I said I did!" shouted Evan. "I decided not to fill it out! I don't want to go there!"

"And what do you *intend* to do?"

Clive turned and paced silently as he looked up at the darkening sky, night taking hold of the desert, the air cooling. "Where's your shirt?"

"In my haversack."

"Put it on. You'll catch cold."

Clive watched Evan kneel, pull his shirt out of the haversack, and angrily stuff in the sling. "Where did you get that?" he asked.

"I made it. Ned Lawrence showed me how in Carchemish. He told me it's a Balearic sling."

"As in the Balearic Islands?"

"Yeah."

At least an appropriate historical connection, Clive thought as he felt his anger ebbing away. "So long as you're a minor, it's my responsibility to direct your choices. I'll discuss the matter of your application with my colleagues at the college and see to it that you'll be allowed to tender a late application. This application." He held up the envelope. "Understood?"

Evan shrugged as he buttoned his shirt.

"And after graduation tomorrow, you'll begin looking for a summer job."

Evan barely nodded as he picked up his haversack. Clive wasn't sure if it was resignation or resistance he saw in Evan's shoulders.

They walked in silence through the twilight toward the lighted porch.

Clive's heart was heavy as he wondered how he might repair things—how they might return to just being father and son.

Reaching the house, he mounted the two wooden steps illuminated by the porch light shining through a cloud of lacewings and a few clumsy June bugs. He put his hand on Evan's shoulder. "You want some dinner?"

"Sure."

"How about soup? We have vegetable and tomato."

"Tomato."

"Okay. Go wash up."

As Evan turned toward the bathroom, Clive spoke again. "And, Evan . . ."

"Yes?" he replied without turning.

"There will be no more tutorials—we'll just talk."

"About what?"

"Whatever you want. And that trip with your friends to Moab in August?"

Evan turned. "I can't go?"

"No. I want you to go. It's a good way for you to enjoy your summer break."

They ate standing together in the kitchen—soup with saltine crackers. They spoke about baseball, the civil war in Mexico, and the rising tensions in Europe.

Clive thought the evening went well.

CHAPTER 2

June 11, 1914
Ionian Sea

MONTAGU WALKER didn't need a clairvoyant to find the village of Gastouri on the island of Corfu. He studied the map fluttering in his hands as he leaned against the yacht's polished wooden railing, shirtless in the morning heat. Turning his face into the wind, he scanned the island's green eastern shore as the white hull of the yacht sliced through blue water toward land.

A few years before, he had required the services of a clairvoyant—to guide his excavation of the Temple Mount in Jerusalem. But he didn't need one now. He knew exactly where to find Kaiser Wilhelm. And he didn't need a clairvoyant to know that the road back to Jerusalem began with the kaiser since only with his patronage would he and his partner, Clarence Watson, be able to finish what they had started. Only with the kaiser's support could they hope to enrich themselves with the Temple Mount treasures.

"There!" Walker pointed. "Make for that jetty."

Folding the map, he watched Watson guide the thirty-foot yacht in a wide arc toward the fairway. An expert sailor, Clarence was also Walker's closest friend. They had served together during the Second Boer War while still in their teens, an age when most sons of English gentry were tucked away at university. And at the Battle of Modder River, a special bond was forged between them when Watson braved enemy fire to rescue Walker, who lay wounded on the veld, tortured by heat and thirst.

After the war they parted ways—Watson for the yacht racing circuit while Walker plunged into London's social whirl. But after a few years a chronic shortage of money brought them back together and they joined forces to hunt for treasure, starting in Jerusalem.

Walker smoothed his dark Van Dyke beard as he leaned against the railing, looking landward. Their excavation on the Temple Mount had not ended well. Narrowly escaping an angry mob, they had left their Arab diggers to their fate and slipped out of Jerusalem. Unfortunately, Turkish customs authorities at the port of Jaffa had detained them, impounding and searching their baggage, only to find nothing. There was nothing to find—the treasure hunt having ended prematurely. But they had come close, and Walker was anxious to return to Jerusalem—which is where Kaiser Bill came in.

Walker thought about the aborted excavation with a twinge of regret. Although, they had nothing to show for all the time, money, and effort, they *had* escaped with their lives. He recalled how he had calmly denied all accusations, reassuring the customs agents that any misunderstandings could easily be clarified in the comforts of Watson's well-appointed yacht lying at anchor in Jaffa Harbor. There all questions would be answered over a sumptuous dinner followed by fine cigars, glasses of good port, and, if they wished, female companionship. The agents agreed to pursue the investigation under the suggested conditions and allowed them to row out to the yacht to prepare for their arrival. Needless to say, Watson had the yacht under full sail well before the appointed hour, making for open sea.

Thereafter they continued to work together, conducting a number of diving expeditions for sunken galleons off the Spanish coast. While these ventures rarely yielded any actual treasure, Walker became adept in eliciting political and financial support from the powerful and wealthy. However, an audience with no less a personage than the kaiser would be a crowning glory. While Walker wasn't one to be overawed by nobility, the kaiser was not just another noble—he was the eldest grandson of Queen Victoria. Moreover, like Charlemagne, Wilhelm fancied himself as Holy Roman Emperor, and like his Crusader ancestor Frederick II, saw himself as King of Jerusalem.

"Certainly a chap with a taste for titles," Walker murmured as the yacht moved toward shore. "I would never have had the sand to proposition the kaiser—to think he actually sent for us!"

The yacht picked up speed and white caps danced over the water. Walker leaned against the railing with sea spray cooling his bare skin. He raised his arms high over his head and shouted into the wind, "I am Siegmund, son of Wotan, flying through the tempest to join my illicit bride in Valhalla!" Lowering his arms and closing his eyes, he listened to the sounds of water drumming against the hull, and the sail snapping in the wind. He began to loudly hum Wagner's "Ride of the Valkyries."

Feeling the boat slow, he opened his eyes and saw that Watson had tacked into the wind, coming into the fairway by a stone jetty.

"Siegmund!" Watson called out, laughing, "When you get back from Valhalla, set the fenders—that stone jetty will ruin the hull!"

"I'm not Siegmund anymore, old boy," Walker said as he readied the fenders and dock lines. "Now I'm Parsifal, coming to the Grail Castle for an audience with the wounded king, and with his withered arm Kaiser Bill is certainly wounded."

In anticipation of their meeting, Walker had gathered all the information he could about the man known for his arrogance, intelligence, and quick temper. He also knew that the kaiser was nearly as British as he was German, having spent summers throughout his childhood and adolescence with his English family on the Isle of Wight. There, spoiled by his grandmother, Wilhelm raced yachts with his uncle, Edward, Prince of Wales before he became King Edward VII, and played chess with his cousin George, eight years his junior and now King George V. Over the years, he'd remained close to George, and still referred to him as a "very nice boy," and in private conversations, they still used their childhood nicknames, Georgie and Willie. They had last met at Edward's state funeral in 1910 where Wilhelm met another cousin, Nicholas II of Russia. Having taken an instant liking to the czar, and in keeping with the family's fondness for diminutive terms of endearment, he'd taken to calling him Nicky.

Walker watched Watson furl the sail and considered how bizarre it was that the nations ruled by these cousins might soon be at war with each other. And in preparation for that war, Willie had built a formidable navy that many believed was the direct result of his wish to impress Georgie and Nicky. Turning, he saw they were nearing the jetty where half a dozen men stood waiting.

Armed men.

"Who the hell are *they*?" asked Watson as he secured the sail to the mast.

"The kaiser's personal guard, I shouldn't wonder," Walker replied before ducking into the cabin to grab a clean white shirt.

Back on deck, Walker watched Watson pull on the flywheel of the Evinrude outboard, and he heard it cough into life. Then, beneath Watson's steady hand, the boat bowed in and docked.

Walker tossed a midship line to one of the guards, who looped it over a cleat. Watson cut the motor, and once all the lines were made fast, they stepped onto the jetty.

"Which of you is Montagu Walker?" a guard asked in a heavy German accent.

"I am."

"His Imperial Majesty awaits you at the Achilleion."

"Certainly. Mr. Watson and I are honored—"

"No. Only *you*."

Walker bowed his head. "As His Majesty requests." Glancing back at Watson, he raised his shoulders. "Sorry, old boy."

The guard led Walker from the quay, across a stone bridge arching over the dirt shore road, to a paved carriage road where a yellow horse-drawn stagecoach waited. Two Rheinland heavy draft horses stamped and shook their long manes as Walker climbed in.

The carriage lurched forward and moved up a sloping hill, switchbacking through groves of oleander flush with pink and white flowers. All the while, Walker's heart pounded as he quietly hummed the "Ride of the Valkyries." But as the minutes passed, with turn after turn up what Walker now saw was a steep cliff face, he wondered how much longer the trip would take.

Finally, a looming edifice of white marble came into view, the carriage came to a stop by a cast-iron gate, and a guard opened the door.

"His Majesty awaits you in the garden," he said and nodded toward the gate.

Remembering that Kaiser Bill was very self-conscious about his withered left arm, Walker made a mental note not to stare. Passing beneath an archway of twining wisteria bedecked with heavy clusters of blue-scarlet flowers, he saw Wilhelm striding toward him, arrayed in the uniform of a British admiral, his chest studded with shining medals.

Walker dropped to one knee and bowed his head. Above him boomed the kaiser's voice, speaking with a perfect British accent.

"Montagu Walker, is it?"

"Yes, Your Imperial Majesty," he replied, still kneeling.

"Oh, do get up man! We have much to discuss and little time. I leave soon for the Norwegian fjords."

"Yes, sire." Keeping his eyes down, he rose to his feet.

"And stop averting your eyes!"

"As you wish, sire." Walker raised his head and looked directly at the kaiser. Above his medaled chest, Wilhelm's eyes shone an amazing blue. His light-brown hair was almost blond and brushed smartly to the side. Beneath his handlebar moustache, he was smiling.

"That's better! Walk with me, Montagu!"

Out of the corner of his eye, he saw that the kaiser's useless left arm rested on the hilt of his sword. "Your summer palace is most impressive, sire."

"My summer palace is in Stuttgart. This place serves me during the digging season. The island is *rich* in antiquities, Walker—mostly Byzantine, though I've unearthed a few Roman and Greek artifacts." The kaiser continued speaking as they followed a path winding through the smooth expanse of a green lawn studded by classical statuary and tall palm trees toward a towering bronze statue set on an equally massive marble pedestal—the lithe but muscular figure of a helmeted man with spear and shield overlooking the Ionian Sea.

That must be Achilles, Walker thought as the kaiser came to a stop and fixed him with his eyes.

"As you, Walker, I have a great love of archaeology! This is an area of common interest I wish to discuss with you."

One of the news articles he'd read mentioned Wilhelm's particular interest in one of the Imperial Regalia at the Hapsburg Treasure House in Vienna. "Does His Imperial Majesty refer to the Spear of Destiny?"

"Actually, no." The kaiser's eyes narrowed. "But, tell me, what do you know of the Spear?"

"I know it was used by the Roman guard Longinus to pierce the side of Our Lord. I know that whosoever possesses the Spear holds in his hand the destiny of the world—"

"So some believe, but there are a number of lances revered as the Spear—one in Krakow, another at the Vatican, a third in Armenia, and, of course, the one in Vienna. In your opinion, Walker, which is the true Spear?"

He sensed the kaiser was testing him. "Your Imperial Majesty, I know with a certainty that the true Spear rests upon a bed of red velvet at the Imperial Treasury in Vienna. I've seen it with my own eyes."

"Have you, now? And how do you know that's the one?"

"By its history, sire. This is the spear that passed from Longinus to generations of Roman soldiers until it came to Emperor Constantine the Great, who believed in the Spear's power, keeping it ever with him as he won many battles and rebuilt Rome. From Constantine, the Spear passed to the Merovingian Kings and in this manner to Charlemagne, who also knew its power, vanquishing all who rose against him as he built his empire. Since Charlemagne, every Holy Roman Emperor has prized the Spear, keeping it at the Hospital of the Holy Ghost in Nuremberg. Only when the usurper Bonaparte rampaged across Europe to claim it, was the Spear moved to Vienna for safekeeping."

"Your knowledge impresses me, Walker." The kaiser turned and looked past Achilles and out to sea. "So, it would appear you've heard that I plan to take possession of the Spear."

"I've heard such rumors, sire."

"The rumors are true! After all, the Spear along with *all* the Imperial Regalia are mine! They are the rightful property of the Holy Roman Empire and should have never left the Fatherland. The Habsburg Emperor has no claim to any of them—not the crown, the scepter, the orb, nor the Spear." Wilhelm put his right hand over his heart. "They belong to *me*, but, as I said, that's not why you're here."

Thank God, thought Walker. *I would hate having to poke around Vienna for a rusty spear tip!* Hoping to change the subject, he nodded over the lawn, statuary and flowers. "Strikingly beautiful palace and grounds, Your Majesty."

The kaiser nodded toward the bronze statue towering above them. "You've undoubtedly noticed the many images of Achilles—hence the name of the palace— Achilleion. The Austrian Empress Elisabeth had quite the fixation on Achilles and built this place in his honor. After her death it stood empty for quite a few years until I acquired it. Would you care to guess why I was so keen to have it?"

"Something to do with Achilles, your majesty?"

"*Everything* to do with Achilles—invincible except for his heel—as I'm invincible except for this!" He lifted his left arm from its resting place on his sword hilt. "*My* Achilles' heel, which is another reason I want the Spear—some say it has the power to heal."

"Sire, it would be an honor to acquire the Spear for you," Walker said even as he cringed at the notion.

"As I just told you, I have others about that business."

"Then, why am I here, sire?"

"Finally something you *don't* know." Wilhelm nodded toward a marble bench. "Sit with me, Walker."

Once seated, Wilhelm looked out to sea and began to speak, softly and almost to himself. "I uphold a tradition of Holy Roman Emperors that began with Charlemagne a thousand years ago. Like Charlemagne, and like Frederick before me, I am the Holy Roman Emperor. When I entered the Holy City of Jerusalem at the turn of the century as a guest of the sultan, I also claimed the title that Frederick bore, that of King of Jerusalem. The Ottomans didn't care as long as I was willing to prop up their nominal control over what they believe to be their empire. And as for Jerusalem, Walker, I know the Holy City holds a special place in *your* heart."

"It does, sire! It's my greatest wish to return and continue my exploration of the Temple Mount."

"*That* is the reason you're here! It is, indeed, for the sake of Jerusalem and the full flowering of the Holy Roman Empire that I have summoned you."

Walker bowed his head, overjoyed that the kaiser was giving him exactly what he most desired. "Sire, I am unworthy of such a high honor."

"On the contrary, you are the first person since the twelfth century to excavate the Temple Mount!"

"Thank you, sire. I gladly accept whatever task Your Imperial

Majesty sees fit to give me."

"That is well." Wilhelm patted him on the shoulder. "Regarding Jerusalem, I knew that my British and Russian cousins were much alarmed when I entered the city. It was no secret that they had their own designs in the Holy Land. But understand this—the love I have for my young cousin, King George, is such that I don't begrudge him his holdings in Africa, Egypt, India, and Asia—likewise my cousin, Czar Nicholas with his vast Russian empire. I respect their claims out of my love for them, and to honor our royal grandmother. But *I too* deserve a place in the sun! And that includes Jerusalem!"

"But you must know, sire," Walker began, choosing his words carefully, "They were also alarmed at the buildings you commissioned in Jerusalem; the hospice named for your royal wife, and the Dormition Abbey upon Mount Zion—"

"You've seen the abbey?" Wilhelm asked.

"Yes—an edifice of great beauty, nearly finished when I was last there."

"Did you hear any talk of its resemblance to the Aachen Cathedral?"

"No, sire."

"You will soon enough!" Wilhelm said with a sly smile. "You see, my dear Walker, I determined that the Dormition Abbey should resemble Charlemagne's Aachen Cathedral, because just as Aachen was the center of the First Reich under Charlemagne, Jerusalem will be the center of my Kaiserreich!"

"Kaiserreich, sire? I don't understand."

"It's like this—due to the efforts of my royal father and the great statesman, Otto von Bismarck, toward the end of the last century, I inherited a unified Germany—the Kaiserreich—the flowering of the Imperial German State, also known as the Second Reich. But I will push beyond it!" The kaiser leaned toward Walker and whispered, "The day approaches when I will add all of Arabia and Mesopotamia to my empire, with the diadem of Palestine and the crown jewel of Jerusalem! And on that glorious day we will have forged the next manifestation of the Holy Roman Empire, the Third Reich—a German State that will thrive for a thousand years!"

Wilhelm patted Walker on the knee and stood up. "I'm putting a good deal of trust in you, Mr. Montagu Walker, and I require assurance that I can rely on you completely—that you will follow my orders without question."

"I swear my undying fealty to Your Imperial Majesty," Walker said and got to his feet. "What else would you have me do, sire?"

"I will tell you what you can do."

✻ ✻ ✻

After his audience with the kaiser, Walker was accompanied by two of the kaiser's personal guards and conveyed by carriage toward the sea.

Coming in view of the jetty, Walker saw Watson's yacht tipping lazily in the swell.

The kaiser's personal guards led Walker over the stone bridge, stopping when they reached the jetty, leaving Walker to go forward alone. Advancing over the smooth paving stones of the quay, he saw that there were a few soldiers sitting with Watson playing cards. He heard one of the guards call out something in German and the soldiers immediately stood up and left the quay.

Upon seeing Walker, Watson stood up. He opened his mouth to speak, but no words came.

Walker lifted the pearl-handled pistol one of the guards had just given him and pointed it at Watson.

"Sorry, old boy."

CHAPTER 3

June 17, 1914
Jerusalem
The German Colony

GUNTER VON WERTHEIMER hadn't slept well, and he didn't know why. With coffee cup in hand, he stood in his undershorts, looking over his desk cluttered with papers. He took a drink and sighed. Something was amiss—for one thing, there wasn't anywhere to put his cup. With his free hand, he pushed aside a newspaper and made room.

At thirty-six, Gunter was an archeologist with École Biblique and spent every weekday with his colleagues, Rahman B'shara and David Nathanson, at the school's dig site next to the Temple Mount.

He leaned over his desk, pulled open the two double-pane windows, pushed aside the peeling green shutters, and opened the room to morning light and cool air from the garden. *That's better, but something's still not right.*

His eyes fell on the newspaper next to his coffee cup on the desk, a month-old copy of *Norddeutsche Allgemeine Zeitung.*

That was it—something in the newspaper . . .

He scanned the front page and there it was—a short article below the fold. The lead was nondescript enough: *Exhibition of Germanic Art to be held in Berlin.* Scanning down, he found what had disturbed him—*His Excellency, Kaiser Wilhelm II has invited His Majesty, Emperor*

Franz Yosef of Austria to attend this exhibition in person on a State Visit as guest of honor, and in gratitude for the emperor's forthcoming loan of the German Emperors' holy relics to the exhibition.

"That's it!" Gunter nearly shouted. "Wilhelm is up to something, and it has *nothing* to do with Germanic art and *everything* to do with the Spear of Destiny. I'm certain of it!"

"Who are you talking to?"

He looked up from the paper and saw his wife Rachel framed in the study doorway, beautiful in her crème-colored robe, her brow furrowed with concern.

"Sorry, darling—just talking to myself."

She flashed a smile and turned back to the kitchen. "The carriage should be here in about fifteen minutes. You might want to get dressed."

"Why? Do I need to impress the driver?" he called after her.

Closing the window, he caught a glimpse of himself in the glass, the reflection unforgiving in the morning light; his blond beard needed trimming and his hair was tousled. Stepping to the washbasin, he splashed his face with water, brushed his teeth, wetted his hair, and gave it a good brushing, all the while thinking about the kaiser and the Spear of Destiny.

Gunter had seen the Imperial Regalia on a family trip to Europe after finishing high school in Jerusalem. Even after twenty years, he vividly remembered the pointed tip of the Holy Lance—dull brown metal offset by a short golden sleeve shining in the dim light of the imperial treasury at Hofburg Palace.

He'd later read firsthand accounts of Wilhelm's obsession with the Spear, starting with his state visit to Jerusalem before the turn of the century. At the time, the kaiser had been quoted as saying that it was "a crime against God" to allow the Spear to remain outside the borders of Germany, and he'd spoken about regaining it—"to harness its power for the future destiny of the Fatherland."

Gunter was certain that this exhibition of Germanic art was merely a ruse to obtain the Spear, and he hoped the Austrian Emperor wouldn't fall for it.

He buttoned up his sun-faded khaki shirt, tucked it into his white trousers and checked himself in the mirror. Taking his coffee cup off the desk, he glanced out the window and saw that the lane beyond the garden wall was empty.

"The carriage isn't here yet," he announced to his wife and daughter as he stepped into the kitchen to refill his cup.

"Wonderful," said Rachel, who sat next to Tirzah at the kitchen table. "We'll be able to review a few more spelling words." She looked to Tirzah, who waited for the next word with her pencil poised over a notebook.

"Mischievous."

Tirzah wrote down the word, then spelled it out loud.

"Perfect," said Rachel and read out the next word, "Descendant." Looking up at Gunter, Rachel whispered, "How are you feeling?"

Once Tirzah had successfully spelled out the word, Gunter replied, "Exhausted."

"Hey!" Tirzah protested. "That word isn't on the quiz!"

Rachel laughed. "That's enough review, darling. The carriage will be here soon. Get your things ready."

Gunter watched Tirzah leave the kitchen. Like Rachel, she was dark-skinned, and her long golden-brown hair was gathered in a single braid down the middle of her back. He couldn't help but smile at her school uniform—a long-sleeved white blouse and long black skirt—the modest garb of an orthodox Jewish young lady.

While not orthodox, and not even identifying as Jewish, Tirzah was considered fully Jewish according to Rabbinic Judaism, which determined that the mother's religion wholly determined that of the child, and Rachel was of Yemenite Jewish ancestry. Gunter was always pleasantly bemused to see Tirzah dressing the part on school days because, in order to attend the Evelina de Rothschild School for Girls in West Jerusalem, she was required to wear the uniform.

"Rough night?" Rachel asked.

Gunter nodded. "Sorry I disturbed you." Not wanting to burden her with his thoughts about Kaiser Wilhelm, he changed the subject. "Any students today?"

"Two young Turkish soldiers."

"Really? What language are you teaching them—English, Arabic? Rachel shook her head. "Hebrew."

"That's odd!" Gunter was barely able to conceal his alarm, concerned that the Ottomans were looking for ways to infiltrate Zionist groups in Palestine, just as they'd done with Arab and Armenian nationalists.

"They both just graduated from that American high school in Constantinople, and when they showed up here—each with a beard, fez, and Turkish Army uniform, it was so incongruous—hearing them speak English like a couple of American boys."

The sharp ring of the carriage bell sounded from the lane. "Tirzah!" Gunter called out. "The carriage is here!"

"I'm ready!" she shouted and ran out of her room carrying her book bag. She gave Rachel a hug before bolting down the narrow hallway that led to the backdoor, the only way in or out of the house.

Gunter picked up his leather attaché case. "See you this evening, darling." With his free hand around her waist, he kissed her cheek. But as he followed Tirzah out the door, Rachel pulled him back.

"You're not getting away that easily," she said with a low growl and kissed him softly on the mouth. "Be home for dinner by six, okay?"

He crossed the back porch to a path carpeted by pine needles, and stepping through the weathered green front gate, saw Tirzah already seated primly in the heavy carriage drawn by two muscular draft horses. Once he was seated next to her, the coachman snapped the reins and the carriage lurched forward.

The fact that Rachel was teaching Hebrew to the Turkish soldiers added to the agitation he already felt about the kaiser's intentions.

"Are you alright, Aba?" Tirzah asked as the carriage reached the end of the lane and turned onto Bethlehem Road.

"Yes, darling. I just didn't sleep very well last night."

A train whistle shrieked, and he glanced toward the station on Hebron Road where a column of black smoke rose into the air—the morning train for Jaffa about to depart.

As the carriage moved along Bethlehem Road, Gunter pointed. "Do you see this paved section of road that leads into town, darling?"

"Yes. I've wondered about that . . ."

"I don't think I've ever told you, but this part of the road was paved a few years before you were born—"

"Why?"

"So Kaiser Wilhelm and his wife could visit the German Colony in their motorcar. Back then, there were very few paved roads in Jerusalem. We also didn't have any electric lights or running water."

"Really?"

"Jerusalem was just a small dusty town, but all that changed before the kaiser's visit. The Turkish sultan appointed a new governor to bring Jerusalem into the twentieth century. I was twenty-one, and still living here with my parents. All of us in the colony worked for months to make decorations and presentations to welcome the kaiser and his wife to Jerusalem." Even as he spoke, Gunter couldn't believe he'd been so naïve.

The coachman drew reign as they reached Mamillah Road to allow for a flock of goats to scamper across.

In the relative quiet, Tirzah asked, "Where will you be working today?"

"Same as yesterday—Rahman, David and I will continue to excavate along Robinson's Arch by the Wailing Place of the Jews."

"How long have you known them?"

Gunter paused to consider. "I've known Rahman for fourteen years, starting when we began graduate studies at École Biblique, the same year you were born. I've only known David for a few years."

"May I help with the dig when I'm on holiday?"

"I'm counting on it."

He left off speaking as the carriage lurched and rattled forward, climbing a low hill through the small commercial section of West Jerusalem.

Nearing the school, Gunter saw about two dozen girls milling about by the black wrought-iron gate, all dressed like Tirzah with long sleeves and long skirts as prescribed by Orthodox Jewish custom.

The coachman drew rein and Gunter jumped out to help her down.

"Goodbye, Aba. See you after school," she said and joined a clutch of her school friends, talking excitedly and laughing as they entered the school grounds.

Gunter paid the coachman a few extra piasters to reserve the ride home, and the carriage rattled away as a bell sounded. A heavy-set school guard closed the gate.

Gunter paused to look through the bars at the now-empty schoolyard. He and Rachel were delighted with the school and its full curriculum of Jewish studies along with the best secular education in Jerusalem.

He turned and continued down Prophets Street toward East Jerusalem. Damascus Gate soon came into view, its crème-colored limestone spires and crenellated battlements beneath a clear blue sky. The cool morning air dispelled the last vestiges of the lassitude Gunter felt after his troubled sleep.

Joining the foot-traffic converging on Damascus Gate, he passed a half dozen fruit sellers tending makeshift stalls and beggars in threadbare robes on either side. He entered the Old City through the open left half of the gate, the other closed and painted with the Turkish crescent and star. Once through the shadowed gatehouse, he stepped into a patch of warm sunlight bathing a cobblestone lane bounded on both sides by outdoor cafés, with the Armenian Quarter to his right, and Muslim Quarter to his left. The lane sloped downward, giving way to a descending stone staircase.

Cutting through an alley, he neared Rahman's house and saw him descending the stone steps leading down from the veranda, his large frame filling the staircase. His mane of black hair was only partially tamed by a purple fez, and his full black beard was cut short. Like Gunter, he wore a khaki shirt and white pants.

"Good morning, my friend—" Gunter began in greeting.

"Shh!" Rahman raised a finger to his lips. "I must speak with you."

"What is it?"

"Over here," he whispered and stepped into a stone alcove partially hidden beneath a large caper bush. Once there he said, "Montagu Walker is coming back."

"That English treasure hunter? When?"

"Soon."

Gunter sighed. "Last time he certainly gave us cause for concern—digging on the Temple Mount. But in the end, he was like all the others—inept and greedy."

"Maybe this time not so inept. This time he'll have a patron—Kaiser Wilhelm."

Gunter suddenly felt dizzy, and his heart began to pound. *Now it all makes sense—the rising tensions in Europe, the kaiser's attempts to acquire the Spear of Destiny, and with the help of Montagu Walker, Jerusalem's Temple Mount.*

"Are you alright?" asked Rahman.

"No. I'm not alright. None of us are. I believe the kaiser intends to start a war."

CHAPTER 4

June 21, 1914
Manchester, England

CHAIM WEIZMANN eased his son's bedroom door closed and turned to see his wife, Vera, coming down the hall in her robe and slippers.

"Is Benjy asleep?" she asked.

"I think so." At forty, Weizmann was of medium height, with delicately chiseled features and dark hair receding before a high forehead. He had come far from his native village of Motol, a backwater hamlet in the western Russian Empire. Now a British subject, he was equally committed to his vocation—chemistry—and to Zionism. Recently named chair of the Biochemistry Department at Manchester University, he was also a member of the Executive of the World Zionist Organization.

Vera peered at the book in his hand and winced. "Rilke? He's seven years old! Why not a nice *children's* book?"

"I'll have you know that Rilke's use of myth is very appealing to children—"

"Please!" She shook her head and quietly opened the door to peek in.

"It's also an opportunity for him to hear good German."

"I'll say this for Rilke," she whispered and drew the door closed. "He certainly puts Benjy to sleep." She nodded in the direction of the library, where their houseguest, Asher Ginsburg waited. "I set out tea for you and Asher, and I told him he shouldn't even *think* of returning to London tonight. The spare bedroom is ready, and I put out towels."

"You should sleep now, *Frau Doktor*," Weizmann said and stroked her hair. He loved the way she wore it, smoothed back and gathered in a bun at the nape of her neck. "Don't you have an early clinic tomorrow?"

"I do." She kissed him, then turned and headed down the hall.

"Bonne nuit ma princesse lointaine," Weizmann called after her.

She stopped and turned. "Princesse lointaine? You haven't called me that since Geneva." She stepped back toward him. "I had always meant to ask you—why did you call me 'my distant princess'?"

"My way of flirting with you." Chaim shrugged. "Unlike the other girls, you were particularly quiet—and better looking."

"But that didn't stop you from leaving—for England of all places, and you didn't even speak English!"

"In Geneva I was only lecturing on chemistry, but in Manchester I knew I'd also be able to do research. And don't forget, I didn't leave until you agreed to marry me."

"Yes, but that took another four years!"

"I had to established myself here and you had to finish medical school."

"Well, at least we're together now." She closed her eyes and nestled in his arms. "So good to no longer be distant."

"But always my princess."

She kissed him again and stepped away. "Good night, sweet prince."

✻ ✻ ✻

Weizmann hesitated in the library doorway looking at Asher Ginsberg, who sat reading in an armchair by the hearth. Twenty years his senior, Ginsberg's unflinching critique of Zionism had informed and shaped his own ideas over the years. His brand of Cultural Zionism supported settlement of the land of Israel but stressed the importance of core Jewish values—compassion, truth and justice—especially when dealing with the Arabs of Palestine. Cultural Zionism also stressed the rebirth of Hebrew as a living language and central to a new Jewish national identity.

At fifty-eight, Ginsberg was a slight man with oval wire-rim spectacles, a high forehead, and a short graying beard. He was widely known under his pen name, Ahad Ha'am, meaning "one of the people," but to close friends and family he was still Asher. He had been living in London for the past six years, managing the English headquarters of the Wissotzky Tea Company.

As Weizmann stepped into the library, Ginsberg looked up. "Is Benjy asleep?"

"He is," Weizmann said and put the poetry book on the table next to the tea service Vera had prepared. "Rilke works every time!"

"Rilke? Why not some nice Hebrew children's poems by Bialik?"

"Exactly what Vera tells me, Asher. You are and remain my moral compass!"

"I'm very glad to be your moral compass, Chaim." Ginsberg smiled as he accepted a cup of tea from Weizmann. "This is *Wissotzky* tea, yes?"

"I wouldn't *dare* serve you anything else!"

"In that case, we'll drink to my successful struggle to establish Hebrew, rather than German, as the language of instruction at the Technikum—the first Jewish institution of higher learning to be built in Palestine!"

Weizmann raised his cup of tea and settled into an armchair. "To

Hebrew!" He took a sip, then asked, "But wasn't it understood that the language of instruction would be Hebrew?"

"So I thought. I was completely surprised when some wealthy Jewish-German board members insisted it be German. Until that point everything had gone smoothly. My employer, Ze'ev Wissotzky, provided a hundred thousand rubles to purchase the land in Haifa and hire an architect. Plans were drawn up and approved—everything by unanimous agreement. But about this, they wouldn't budge!"

"What were their reasons?"

"At first they wouldn't give any! I argued that it was crucial for a Jewish institution to use the language of the Jewish people—how else to contribute to the rebirth of Hebrew?" Ginsberg produced a tin of Navy Cut cigarettes, took one, tapped it on the armrest, put it in his mouth, and began patting his jacket pockets in search of a match.

Weizmann took a matchbox from his pocket and lit Ginsberg's cigarette.

"Things got very heated." Ginsberg sat back and exhaled a plume of smoke. "In a private conversation with a Jewish-German board member I learned that the reason for their demand was direct pressure from the German government—from Kaiser Wilhelm himself! I couldn't believe the kaiser had time for that sort of thing."

At first Weizmann said nothing. He reached into his jacket pocket and took out his pipe and tobacco. Shaking his head, he filled the pipe bowl and tamped down the tobacco. "It really makes no sense—the kaiser intervening about the language of instruction at some Jewish technical school in Palestine . . ." He lit his pipe and took a few puffs. "But in the end, you said it was decided that Hebrew *would* be the language of instruction."

"Only after months of mishigas! They wouldn't budge. I wouldn't budge. They offered an idiotic compromise—Hebrew would be allowed as the language of instruction, but *only* for gymnastics and drawing." Ginsberg drew on his cigarette and sighed out the smoke.

"The whole project seemed headed toward collapse, but I had one last gambit. I met with the Technikum instructors and told them what was going on, and they voted to go on strike—refusing to teach unless it would be in Hebrew. And after a few days the board voted again, and, thankfully, a narrow majority picked Hebrew!" He took a final puff and crushed out his cigarette. "But, as I said, this whole episode made me very uneasy—the manner in which Kaiser Wilhelm inserted himself into the negotiations . . . it was *unsettling*."

Weizmann nodded. "Perhaps a harbinger of things to come."

"What do you mean—*things to come?*"

Weismann raised his shoulders. "I also have an uneasy feeling about this . . ."

CHAPTER 5

June 21, 1914
Mecca
Ottoman Province of the Hejaz

FAISAL BIN HUSSEIN completed morning prayer and kissed his wife and four sleepy children before leaving his apartments within the walls of the Holy Precinct. Tall and slender, he wore a long robe of white silk, his brown head cloth was bound with cords of scarlet and gold, and his black beard accentuated the pallor of his face. Moving quickly over smooth paving stones, Faisal crossed the shadowed square toward his father's quarters, the air cool on his face. He glanced up to see the first rays of the rising sun illuminating the Kaaba—the most sacred site in Islam, originally built by the Prophet Ibrahim himself with help from his son, Ismael.

For millions of the faithful, a visit to the holy precincts was a once-in-a-lifetime pilgrimage, but for Faisal, it was commonplace. This was his home.

He knocked on his father's door, which was opened by a servant, and stepped in. "You summoned me, Father?"

"I summoned you an hour ago, my son," Hussein said in gentle rebuke as he rose from his seat on a light gray divan. He placed his hands on Faisal's shoulders, kissing him first on the left, then on the right cheek. Dressed in an embroidered gown, Hussein bin Ali Al-Hashimi, the sharif and emir of Mecca, had a full white beard and piercing dark eyes. His head was crowned with a dark turban, his face long and finely drawn, his eyebrows bushy. Though a full head shorter than his son, his bearing reflected a confidence in his breeding—thirty-seventh in the line of direct descent from the Prophet Mohammed. "What delayed you?"

"My apologies, Father. I received your note while at prayer, and came as soon as I finished, pausing only to kiss my wife and little ones."

"That is proper and praiseworthy, my son. I am pleased that you honor your family in this manner. Now that you are all back in Mecca, I'm delighted to be able to see so much of you and your beautiful children. It is well said that grandchildren are Allah's way of compensating us for growing old."

"And we are blessed to have you in our lives, Father. My Azza tells the younger children that you never run out of hugs or cookies."

Hussein laughed. "I can't believe she's eight—already a lady!" He brought his hands to his chest and took a deep breath. "It delights my soul to see how your family grows. How I wish your dear mother had lived to see your beautiful children . . ."

"I know how much you miss her, Father."

"You were but three when she left us, and at only twenty-eight—in the flower of her youth, and so very beautiful! But more than that, she was intelligent—she spoke four languages flawlessly and was very good with numbers. She also provided wise counsel, helping me maneuver with the Ottomans, which has never been easy!" Hussein sighed. "Like Victoria, she was a queen and the mother of kings!"

"The mother of kings?" Faisal raised his eyebrows. "None of us are kings, Father—not Ali, Abdullah, nor I."

"*Not yet*, my son, but I foresee a time when the three of you will join in the leadership of our people. It is for that reason I summoned you this morning." He extended a sheet of paper toward Faisal. "Peruse this dispatch, my son—sent by the chief of the German general staff, Count von Moltke to his foreign ministry. I'm interested in hearing your impression."

Faisal saw that it had been translated into Arabic and read it aloud: "*Once we have a pact with Turkey, we will arouse the fanaticism of Islam. Since the Turkish sultan is also the caliph of Islam, he will promote Islamic fervor among the seventy million Muslims in British India, and the sixteen million Muslims of the Nile basin. An insurrection against the British in India, Egypt, and the Caucasus is of utmost importance. This will wreak havoc with British interests throughout the Raj, Arabia, Syria, and North Africa. And regarding the latter, when war comes with England, the Egyptians serving under their British masters will rise up against them, disrupting all communications, railways, and port installations, making the Suez Canal inoperable. The signal to begin these actions will be a frontal attack on the Canal by thirty thousand Turkish troops with seventy thousand Bedouins under Hussein, whose cooperation we expect.*"

Faisal was stunned. "Is that your intention, Father? To join in an attack against the British at the Suez Canal?"

"No. That's Moltke's wishful thinking."

Faisal shrugged. "And what is this war they speak of, Father? Europe has been at peace for half a century."

"It's a cold peace, my son, and one that won't last." Hussein placed the paper on a side table. "This confirms my suspicions about Germany's designs in Arabia. They have already constructed a railway from Berlin to Constantinople, and it's well known they hope to reach Baghdad, and eventually the port of Basra."

Faisal stood up and studied a large map hanging among rich tapestries along the walls of his father's study. "This will give Germany petroleum to fuel its navy and easy access to their colonies in East Africa."

"You are correct on both counts, my son. The extension of the railway to Baghdad and Basra will be a loaded pistol pointed at British interests from Egypt to India. It's been known for years that there is a lake of petroleum beneath the sands of Mesopotamia, but useless without transportation for shipping. The railway will solve that problem. This is why the British, along with the French and Russians, grow more anxious with every meter of German rail laid toward Baghdad. They know the completed railway will strengthen Germany and shift the balance of power in the entire region!"

"Given all this, my father, is it not to our advantage to forge closer ties with the Turks and Germans?"

"I've considered this very issue, my son, and find that I am of two minds on the subject. This is the reason I wish to speak with you as I determine how to proceed. You should know that I have been in contact with the British General Kitchener in Cairo—"

"But Father, we are citizens of the Ottoman Empire. This is high treason!"

"Yes, and punishable by death."

Faisal's breath caught with the terrifying realization of the danger this posed to his family. "If these are the stakes, Father, shouldn't we remain loyal to the Turks?"

"I've been maneuvering with the Turks all my life—mainly arguing for self-rule, which was the reason the sultan placed us under house arrest in Constantinople for fifteen years." Hussein fixed his eyes on Faisal and added, "I'm certain you recall it was an accommodating confinement; our villa on the shores of the Bosporus was more a pleasure palace than a prison, and the sultan's royal guards more our servants than sentries."

"True," Faisal said and sat next to his father. "And my brothers and I were expensively educated during those years."

"And in the end, the sultan appointed me grand sharif and we returned here to Mecca." Hussein patted Faisal on the knee. "Given this, I might agree to our continued loyalty to the Empire. However, why do you suppose the Turks treated us so well despite my proclivity for stirring up trouble in the Hejaz?"

"Clearly, they don't want to be accused of mistreating a descendant of the Prophet, fearing a violent reaction throughout the Hejaz, especially in the holy places."

"That is exactly the leverage I use to challenge Constantinople—pushing back against their plans to take full control of the Hejaz, forcing them to cancel the general conscription they sought to impose, frustrating their plans to remove me from my position. Our *bloodline* is our leverage!"

"Since you've been so skillful in maneuvering with them, Father, why not continue? And with war on the horizon, we'll have even more leverage—all the more reason we should remain loyal to the Turks."

"It's not the Turks that concern me as much as the Germans, my son. Should war come, it's very likely that there will be an alliance between Turkey and Germany—and it is Germany that concerns me."

"Why?"

"Kaiser Wilhelm." Hussein sat back and sighed. "I met him twice in Constantinople, and on both occasions, I found him to be quite unbalanced—either angry or arrogant—usually both. And in every conversation with him, he did all the talking and was always boasting."

Faisal could see that his father was growing agitated as he spoke of the kaiser. "But why should we endanger our families and our fortunes because of him? He's only one man!"

"He is one man who's very *dangerous*!" Hussein shouted and hit the side table next to the divan with such force that it toppled over. "He's an affront to everything we cherish. In the Holy City, he declared himself *Holy Roman Emperor* and had himself crowned *King of Jerusalem*. He directed that an entire section of Jerusalem's Old City wall be removed so he could ride into the Holy City on a white steed like a conquering hero."

While Hussein spoke, Faisal worried that his father's hatred of the kaiser might lead him to turn against the Ottoman Empire. And that could spell disaster for the entire family. Faisal drew a deep breath and said, "I understand, Father, but the kaiser commands a powerful army with a growing array of weapons. Is this not so? Why forego the advantages of such an alliance? Why not stay safe and remain loyal to the Ottomans?"

"Because the Ottomans have become the kaiser's *puppets*! The caliph and the Young Turks don't seem to care that the kaiser strikes at the very heart of our faith, but I do. He makes a mockery of Islam! Do you know that German agents are even now spreading the lie that the kaiser converted to Islam and is now a devout Muslim? And when war comes, if Germany, with the help of Turkey prevails, he will rule over an empire extending from Europe into Asia. And in that vast empire, it will be Kaiser Wilhelm we'll have to contend with. This is the reason I sent your brother, Abdullah, to meet with Kitchener in Egypt."

Faisal felt a stab of jealousy—that his father sent Abdullah as emissary to the British. But remaining composed, he asked, "What came of the meeting?"

"Not a great deal, which wasn't surprising since I'm not yet ready to support the British." Hussein moved closer to Faisal on the divan. "I see and appreciate your caution, my son, and I share it. For the present, we must discretely explore the situation with the British without straining our relations with the Turks."

As Faisal listened to his father, his heart filled with dread, and he began to despair of finding any argument to dissuade him from making such a traitorous arrangement against the Ottomans, yet he took some solace in the feeling of his father's hand on his shoulder and in the calm reassurance he heard in his voice.

"My son, I know that the notion of turning against the Ottoman Empire frightens you. It frightens me also. But if we remain loyal to Turkey in alliance with Germany, and if this unholy alliance is victorious in the coming war, the Ottoman Empire will remain intact as a German vassal state, and we will find ourselves with two masters—the Turks *and* the Germans with Kaiser Wilhelm reigning as a self-appointed *King of Jerusalem*. And we will *never* know freedom."

Faisal drew a deep breath. "I understand, Father. And if, on the other hand, Great Britain and her allies win the coming war *with* our support, the Ottoman Empire will be dismantled. In that eventuality, is it your hope that England will reward us with our own sovereign land?"

"It is, my son—but *only* if we're able to make a clear pact with them, which I believe is a favorable calculation. Because the British are masters of India and Egypt, and also masters of the seas—just as we are masters of the desert. When war comes, and it will, the Turks allied with Germany will face the combined might of England and her French and Russian allies, along with support from England's vast empire—Australia, Ireland, New Zealand, India, Canada—even from her former colony of the US. With such an alliance, along with our contribution of an Arab revolt against the Turks stretching from Mesopotamia to the Hejaz—I'm certain that the Ottoman Empire will vanish like a cloud chased by a storm."

Hussein sat forward and added in a low voice. "General Kitchener made verbal promises of British support when he met with your royal brother in Cairo. Moreover, he was recently elevated to the position of British secretary of state for war and transferred to London. In this role, his words carry even more weight." Hussein paused and fixed Faisal with his eyes. "But I see that your mind is still clouded by doubt, my son."

Faisal couldn't help but blurt out, "Father, it is well known that the Germans are formidable in battle!" But even as he spoke, he saw Hussein nod and stroke his beard, a mannerism he recognized as a sign that his mind was made up. Faisal closed his eyes in despair and felt his father pat his shoulder, as if to comfort him.

"It is good that you are judicious and careful, but consider this . . ."

He waved a hand at the map hanging among the tapestries. "How much aid will be forthcoming to Turkey from Germany fighting on two fronts in Europe?"

"I'm . . . I'm not certain . . ." he stammered.

"Then I will tell you—none! I doubt they'll spare *any* troops or equipment, and this will assure victory for England and her allies in Arabia. And if we are allied with England, this will also be *our* victory!"

"But is it possible you are mistaken, my father?"

In response Hussein raised his shoulders and asked, "Is it not written that it is better to die on your feet than to live on your knees?"

That's what I needed to hear. Faisal thought, and with the release of held breath, he said, "I support your decision, my father. Tell me what you would have me do."

"My agents in Amman and Damascus are creating contacts with the secret societies that look to us, the Hashemites, to lead the Arab revolt. These Arab patriots include many a diverse people— from the shopkeepers of Amman to the intellectuals of Damascus. When the time is right, I will have you meet with them."

Faisal's despair gave way to his father's will, and his heart filled with anticipation of freedom from Ottoman oppression. Kneeling, he took his father's offered hand and kissed it. "I will do all you ask."

As Faisal spoke the words, he felt a thrill of excitement. His heart pounded wildly, like the beating wings of a caged hawk about to be released, about to take flight.

CHAPTER 6

June 21, 1914
Cedar City, Utah

AS HE HAD PROMISED his father, Evan set out to find work the day after graduation and landed a job at Cedar City's only filling station, owned and operated by Bob Pitney. The pay was good at twenty-five cents an hour, as were the hours of six to noon. Plus, he could have up to three free bottles of Hires Root Beer per shift.

Though there were a few hundred motorcar owners in town, many continued to get their fuel and oil from the livery stable, and the pace of work at the filling station was pretty slow. Apart from learning to do repair work with Bob, Evan pumped petrol, cleaned windshields, serviced tires and tubes, and checked and filled motor oil. But there was usually plenty of time between customers to sit in the office beneath the slowly rotating ceiling fan, drinking cold root beer, and reading *The Deseret Evening News,* which regularly arrived a day late from Salt Lake City.

On an already warm summer morning, Evan headed into work as the sun rose over the Pine Valley Mountains. He coasted on his Sunbeam bicycle through the sleeping streets of Cedar City, the silence perfect but for the sound of the rubber tires gliding over the smooth dirt road, a steady and reassuring whisper.

He leaned the bicycle against the filling station's whitewashed cinderblock sidewall, pleased to see that the paperboy had already delivered. He picked up the newspaper, stepped to the office door, fished the key out of his pocket, and let himself in.

The single room felt warm and stuffy, still holding some of yesterday's heat. He left the door open and pulled the ceiling fan cord. The blades began to rotate, stirring the stale air. He tossed the paper onto the wooden desk in the sparsely appointed office, took a bottle of root beer out of the small dusty icebox in the corner, and sat down.

The newspaper was filled with lurid stories of the chaotic Mexican Revolution. Reading like the unfolding chapters of a serialized book, it was the highlight of Evan's day, and he couldn't wait for the next installment. Though he did delay the pleasure, first checking the sports section on the newspaper's back page.

Looking at the National and American League standings, he ignored the new Federal League, which was in its first season. Like many baseball fans, he considered it illegitimate, an "outlaw league." Looking at the real standings, he smiled. *Great! The Giants shut out the Reds six to nothing and they're in first place by two games. Hopefully, we'll make it back to the World Series, and this year we'll win!*

He pried the cap off the root beer, took a drink, and turned the newspaper over to the front page. *Now for the news from Mexico!*

The revolution, now in its second year, was actually pretty confusing—presidents rose and fell, generals came and went, warring factions fought pitched battles, and there was endless political intrigue with charges and countercharges of corruption. While nothing seemed to happen in Cedar City, the daily eruption of news from Mexico was captivating. And beyond that, Evan's passion for adventure was fueled by the singular character of Pancho Villa.

It was mainly his striking appearance—the large moustache and sombrero, the sash-like bandoliers full of bullets strapped across his chest, and the occasional photograph of Villa mounted on a white steed and commanding a fierce cavalry or brandishing a rifle while mounted on a new Indian motorcycle.

Evan took another drink and began to read an article about how Villa's peasant army was preparing to move down from the north in order to converge on Mexico City with Zapata's forces from the south.

As he read, he yearned for something more than being an observer of history already made—he wanted to be part of history in the making. He daydreamed about joining the revolution. Cedar City felt like a parched riverbed that even the backwaters of time had abandoned. But the Mexican Revolution was a roaring current only a two day's journey south. He had already mapped the route—a bus to El Paso and a short walk across the border would bring him to Villa's home state of Chihuahua, where he would find the northern revolutionary army.

He turned a page and saw a story that brought him up short.

Huerta's Federal Army is rapidly deteriorating with reports from government sources that the dictator will soon abdicate. According to these sources, Huerta is actively seeking to get out of Mexico with roughly half a million marks in gold as well as paper currency. Reportedly, he is negotiating with the German government for asylum.

"Damn!" he said aloud. "Looks like I might miss the revolution!"

When a gray Ford Model T pulled up to the filling bay, he stepped outside.

"Fill it up, please," said the lady behind the steering wheel.

"Glad to, ma'am," said Evan. He used the pump to fill the calibrated glass cylinder on top of the gas dispenser, and once there were four gallons in the cylinder, he stopped the pump, opened the Ford's tank, opened the petrol valve and let gravity fill the tank.

"Check your oil, ma'am?" he asked.

"No need. Bob checked it a few days ago."

"How about I clean your windshield?"

"Please do! I must have killed a thousand lacewings on the drive down from Salt Lake City."

As he worked, Evan cursed under his breath, *Damn! Mexico doesn't look like an option for me anymore. But one way or another, I'm leaving. No way I'll be starting college in the fall.*

"That will be thirty-six cents, ma'am," he said.

The woman handed him a half-dollar. "You're such a dear, keep the change."

"Thanks, ma'am. Drive safe now." He waved and the Ford rattled off.

The morning was well on, and Evan knew that Pitney, who lived in a bungalow behind the filling station, would soon come by to relieve him. According to the thermometer on the Red Crown Gasoline sign nailed to the doorjamb, it was already over a hundred degrees. Evan went back inside, took a long swig of root beer and sat back down to read.

Flipping through the pages, he found a headline:

AUSTRIA'S ARCHDUKE FRANCIS FERDINAND ANNOUNCES STATE VISIT TO SAREJEVO, BOSNIA

Who cares? he thought and continued to flip through the paper. *Maybe I'll go to France and use some of the French I took. Lord knows I can't communicate with anyone in classical Greek or Latin—anyone living that is. But, if I want to travel, I'll need my passport. I should find it . . .*

He stopped at another article.

GERMAN OCEAN LINER SS BISMARCK TO LAUNCH—KAISER WILHELM II TO CHRISTEN SHIP TOMORROW

He read further.

The kaiser has doubled the size of the German fleet to 38 battleships, making it clear that the German navy isn't just patrolling the coastline. It is directly attempting to rival Great Britain—

"How'd it go today, Evan?" Bob Pitney asked as he stepped through the office door, his suspenders hanging loose at his sides.

"Real quiet, Mr. Pitney—just one customer."

Bob nodded toward the door as he placed one suspender, then the other, over his shoulders and hiked up his pants "You can head out now, Evan—least I can do after working you three hours extra last week."

"Thanks, Mr. Pitney!" Evan said as he stood up. "Sure you won't need me?"

"Naw. All we have today is Ron Bigelow this afternoon to git new tires for his Baker Electric." Bob shook his head. "He's a damn fool—putting good money into that 'lectric vehicle. Any half-wit knows that the future of the automobile is with the gasoline engine!" Bob nodded at the newspaper on the desk. "You done with the paper?"

"Yes, sir. Looks like the revolution in Mexico is almost over, and the German Kaiser is building up his navy."

"Seems to me that the kaiser wouldn't be buildin' his navy if he wasn't fixin' to use it." Pitney scratched the stubble on his chin and frowned down at the paper.

"That's what I think, too," said Evan as Pitney turn a page and bent to read.

"An' lookit' this here . . ."

Evan peered around Pitney and saw that he was reading the story beneath an artist's drawing of a huge stone building with a tall tower perched on a high hill.

BUILDING OF KAISER'S

AUGUSTA VICTORIA HOSTEL ON
JERUSALEM'S MOUNT OF OLIVES COMPLETE.

Glancing at the text, Evan saw that the hostel had been under construction for ten years, and during that time the kaiser had also completed two other prominent buildings in Jerusalem—Christ the Redeemer Church within the Old City and the Dormition Abby and bell tower on Mount Zion.

Pitney tapped the photo of the hostel with an index finger blackened by grease. "Nice place . . . I reckon the kaiser's fixin' to move in."

As the German kaiser, the notion of him living in Jerusalem seemed preposterous, but as Evan scanned the article, the following words jumped out: *the kaiser's construction projects have transformed Jerusalem, dominating the city . . .*

Evan felt uneasy as he headed toward the door. "See you tomorrow, Mr. Pitney."

As he pedaled toward home, his mind was crowded with thoughts. *Bob's probably right—the kaiser really does want to use his navy. And with all that building, Jerusalem must be important in what he's planning.* Evan pedaled faster. *But whatever the kaiser's plans are, if there's going to be a war over there, that's where I should go! And since I'll be home early, I'll have time to look for my passport.*

The empty driveway told him that his father wasn't home yet. He took a few envelopes from the mailbox and leaned his bicycle against the side of the house. As he mounted the porch steps, he flipped through the mail—a couple of bills and an intriguing pink envelope from England addressed to his father, the sender's name embossed in shining gold on the back—Gertrude Bell.

He let himself in, tossed the mail on the low table by the divan, and went straight to the roll-top desk in his father's study. *I'm not sure I actually have a passport, but if I do, it'll be in here.*

He began checking each of the half-dozen drawers above the

writing surface of the desk until he found a worn, brown British passport. Opening it to the first page, "Name of Bearer" was listed in neatly printed black ink as Clive Robert Sinclair. Below that it read, "Accompanied by his wife (maiden name)," followed by "Janet Ann Stewart." And this was followed by, "And by children" with his name, "Evan Jonathan Sinclair."

Evan frowned. *Mom and I are listed in Dad's passport! Does that mean we don't have our own?*

He checked the other drawers but found nothing.

Without a passport, I'll just have to figure out a way—maybe with my high school diploma. He replaced his father's passport, closed the desk, and headed to the kitchen.

Passing through the living room, he caught another glimpse of Gertrude Bell's pink envelope on the low table by the divan. He remembered her from the dig in Mesopotamia—his father had called her "a human contradiction," claiming that people either loved her, or hated her, or both.

He went into the kitchen, took a round of cheese from the icebox, and began slicing it for sandwiches as he continued thinking about Bell. She had often been at tea when he had been obliged to join his parents—chatting with his mother about the latest fashion in ladies' hats, or arguing with Clive about women's suffrage, which he supported and she vehemently opposed, or arguing with the dig leader, Charles Hogarth, about different artifacts, or jabbering in fluent Arabic with the servants.

He heard Clive's motorcar in the front drive, the ratcheting sound of the brake, and the sound of the engine rattling into silence—then the slam of the car door, the whistling of his father's favorite Scottish tune, the thumping of his boots on the front porch, and the bang of the screen door.

"Evan?"

"In the kitchen!"

Dressed in dusty khaki drill with a sun-bleached fedora, Clive dropped his battered brown briefcase by the kitchen doorjamb. "I'm parched! Anything to drink?"

"There's lemonade in the icebox, and you've got some post in the living room—a letter from Gertrude Bell."

Clive left the kitchen and after a second, Evan heard the bang of the screen door.

After pouring himself a glass of lemonade, he poured another for his father and brought it out to the porch.

"Here you go, Dad."

"Thanks. I'll just be a few minutes."

Returning to the kitchen, Evan put together a couple of sandwiches, and after covering his father's with a tea towel, he sat at the kitchen table and began eating as he thumbed through a dog-eared copy of *All Story Magazine* featuring "Tarzan of the Apes—A Romance of the Jungle."

He was certain that the magazine story was far more interesting than Gertrude Bell's letter.

CHAPTER 7

June 21, 1914
2 Polstead Road
Oxford, England

THOMAS EDWARD LAWRENCE asked, "When can we get back to Mesopotamia?

Leonard Woolley stretched and yawned. "If we don't do a convincing job with this report, there won't be any going back."

The two were working late into the evening at a large circular table under the light of a tall kerosene lamp. In their early twenties, they had spent the previous few years working together on archeological digs and geographical surveys in Ottoman Syria, most notably excavating the Hittite city of Carchemish.

The dig was funded by the British Museum, but they quickly understood that they were also spying for British Naval Intelligence. Beyond unearthing and cataloguing the ruins of Carchemish, they monitored German agents in the region, along with the construction of the Berlin-to-Baghdad railway.

When tensions between England and Turkey rose over the Suez Canal late in 1913, they were tasked with a new mission—to conduct an archeological and geological survey of the northern Sinai and the Arabah deserts. Though under the auspices of the Palestine Exploration Fund, the survey also served British Intelligence in anticipation of an Ottoman attack on the Canal; when the desert became a battlefield, the British would need accurate maps with clearly marked hills, valleys, villages, and wells.

Lawrence and Woolley had completed the survey a few weeks before and were now back in England—confined to an Oxford cottage until they finished the formal report. Sitting at the kitchen table cluttered with papers, they dressed as they had in the desert—short trousers, undershirts, and well-worn Oxford University tweed jackets.

The kettle began to shriek.

Lawrence stood up and cut the fire on the stovetop. Deeply tanned, his yellow hair was well ruffled, brushed to the side with a hint of a part. Beneath a high forehead his piercing gentian blue eyes were slightly red-rimmed from too many hours writing and too few sleeping. "I believe we've done a smashing job with our narrative, along with our delightful drawings and photographs," he said as he poured hot water into the teapot.

Woolley sighed. "But after wandering about in the desert like the Children of Israel, they've stuck us here until we finish this damned report. It's like house arrest."

"Or university." Lawrence sat down in front of a stack of papers. Glancing at Woolley, he asked, "Are you still working on that map of Ain Kadeis?"

"Yes, and I'm stuck here . . ." Woolley rotated the map for Lawrence to see. "Weren't there some hills a few miles to the south?"

"Yes—steep hills above the wadi. Do put them in!"

Woolley bent to the task as Lawrence continued speaking. "You and I know that Kitchener believes this is the only way to make the survey look legitimate, to convince the Turks we weren't spying on them, but I don't believe they're that naïve. They likely suspected all along that it was just a military game."

"And if there's going to be war, it's pretty clear which side they'll choose. The Germans have embraced them for years with arms sales, the railway, and plenty of scratch."

"Still, we *have* produced a solid report, replete with archeological, geological, and Biblical references," said Lawrence as he poured tea into two chipped cups.

Woolley shrugged. "Perhaps they *will* reserve judgment a bit longer, perhaps even remain neutral—"

"Not bloody likely!" Lawrence took a drink, then asked, "What shall we call it?"

"How about *A Geological and Archaeological Survey of the Sinai*?"

Lawrence winced. "Let's go for something a bit more Biblical! How about *The Wilderness of Zin*?"

"Whatever we call it, Kitchener wants it PDQ."

"I *do* love it when you talk military like that, Lenny! What does PDQ mean?"

"Pretty damn quick. K wants it ready for the printer in a week."

"We'll be lucky to finish this in a month!"

CHAPTER 8

June 21, 1914
Cedar City, Utah

CLIVE SINCLAIR finished off his lemonade and put the glass down on the weathered boards of the front porch. The wicker chair creaked as he sat back and drew the blade of his penknife along the edge of the envelope. He removed the pale pink stationary of Gertrude's letter and a perfumed fragrance wafted into the warm air. From somewhere out in the desert came the sustained song of a male cicada.

He began to read.

> *British Embassy, Constantinople*
> *May 12, 1914*
> *Dearest Clive,*
> *Your letter with the sad news about your beautiful Janet's*
> *passing was waiting for me when I arrived here from Sidon on*
> *10 May. I feel dreadful not knowing and only responding now—*
> *almost two years since her death. I recall her so very fondly from*
> *our long conversations and teas together in Carchemish—such*
> *a vivacious, intelligent, and lovely person! I know it's beyond*
> *my power to console you, especially so long past the time of*
> *your sharpest grief. I would, nonetheless, offer some sweet*
> *words tendered by my affection for you. I can think of no better*
> *expression than lines from my translation of Hafez. So, my dear*
> *Clive, across the miles between us, and the centuries since they*

issued from the quill of Hafez—
Art thou with grief afflicted, and with the smart
Of absence, and is bitter toil thy part?
Thy lamentations and thy tears, oh Heart,
Are not in vain!
Where is the extinguished lamp that made night day
Where is the sun?

I so regret that our correspondence lapsed, starting I suppose
when you went to America for your sabbatical. Given your
departure from Carchemish and, indeed, from the Levant, I
suppose neither of us felt we were still on "the same page."

From what I glean from the Geographic Society, American
Indian petroglyphs yield very little comprehensible information
(though your intellect and energy may have already altered that
estimation!) In any case, I do apologize for being remiss and for
not endeavoring to stay in touch during this time, which for you
has proved so very unhappy.

As to my most recent travels, two years of journeying
between Constantinople, Damascus, and Baghdad have
been both arduous and astonishing. My very latest foray was
especially gratifying: With a generous gift from my father, I
was able to assemble a caravan of seventeen camels. Led by
a wonderful guide, we set out from Damascus last December
and went by way of El Hamad and Wadi Sirhan, then south to
Jebel Shammar, east to Hayil, north to Karbala, and finally to
Baghdad.

I offer the itinerary that you might trace my journey in your
memory (and perhaps in an atlas). I returned to Damascus,
thence to Constantinople, and after another fortnight here, I'll
return to England.

What amazing adventures, dear Clive! I was able to document
a line of wells that have never appeared on any European map!

I also catalogued information about the Bedouin tribes ranging between the Hejaz Railway on one flank and the Sirhan and Nefud Deserts on the other. The Howaitat Bedouin are especially impressive, and my stay in Hayil proved most informative concerning the Rashid house. If and when hostilities arise in the region, the War Office should be very interested in these details! Though, given the unpleasant interactions I've had in the past with the "old men of Whitehall," I'm not encouraged that they'll deign to hear anything a woman has to offer.

But I look forward to giving you and Ned Lawrence a full accounting whenever we meet again since you both share my love of the Levant. The desert is such a glorious and terrible desolation! The hypnotic texture and sweep of endlessly rolling dunes, the sudden slabs of sandstone rising so very high against the sky, the beautiful perfection of a lonely purple flowered terebinth, and at night, the sky so vast and crowded with stars!

And, when might we meet again? I imagine you're sabbatical is coming to an end, and you'll soon return to British shores. I'm certain your son, Evan, is yearning for home as well. I remember him in Carchemish as a boy, though by now he's no doubt grown into a fine young man. I'm sure that for him as well as for you, Janet's passing has been a frightful blow.

With sincere condolence, dear Clive, and warm regards to Evan.

Gerty

He refolded the pages of the letter and replaced them in the envelope. Settling back in the wicker chair, he stared out at the desert. Though the sun was setting, heat rose in waves from the parched brown earth. The male cicada, apparently having found a mate, had ended his song. The air was still and fragrant with sage.

He got up and went back into the house.

❁ ❁ ❁

Evan was still at the kitchen table reading "Tarzan of the Apes" when he heard the screen door close. Expecting his father to come to the kitchen, he marked the page and closed the magazine. He considered confessing his plans to leave home, but knowing his father would have a tantrum, he decided to say nothing.

Entering the living room, Evan saw his father leaning against the mantelpiece with Bell's letter in his hand. "Bad news?" he asked.

"Not at all. Miss Bell is fine. After a lot of travelling in the desert, she's back in Constantinople and will soon return to England." He took the family photograph from the mantelpiece. "Remember the day we left Carchemish? A happier time . . ."

Evan's heart filled with sadness as he studied his mother's face in the photograph. "Who took this?" he asked.

"Ned Lawrence—an accomplished photographer, among his other talents."

"You first met him in Carchemish?" Evan asked.

"Long before that. I first met Ned in the South of France during the summer of '08—he'd just finished a bike trek from the Channel all the way to the Mediterranean!"

"Wow! How far is that?"

"About a thousand miles. Here, I'll show you." Clive turned, sat on the divan, opened the large atlas that rested on a low table, and flipped through the pages. "We met here at Les Baux, a small village on an olive-sandalled mountain north of Montpellier."

Evan sat next to his father on the divan and studied the map.

"I had stopped my motorcar on the edge of a precipice when I first saw the shining edge of the Mediterranean. I was enjoying the view when I heard someone from the mountain above me shouting, Tha'lassa! Tha'lassa!"

"The sea, the sea!" Evan laughed. "Ned quoting Xenophon . . ."

"Yes, and very loudly! He startled an eagle on the opposite hill! Not in the least *silent, upon a peak in Darien!*" He patted Evan on the knee. "I'm happy you remember the source. Your classical education has apparently left a residue of some appreciation."

"I always appreciated Xenophon, Dad—soldier and historian. *The March of the Ten Thousand* about the Greek army stranded in Persia—now *that's* a great story—every bit as good as anything I've read of Tarzan."

"Now you go too far!" Clive said in mock anger. "How dare you compare Xenophon to the King of the Apes?"

"Sorry, sir," Evan smiled, and for the first time in a very long time, he felt at ease with his father. *I'm glad for that—I want to leave on good terms.*

"It turned out we were both heading to the old port city of Aigues-Mortes."

"So you gave him a lift?"

"I offered, but he refused—completely understandable considering how far he had already come—within sight of the Mediterranean and just before the final descent. So, he hopped on his bicycle and disappeared down the hill. I followed in my touring car. By the time I got to Aigues-Mortes, he was splashing about in the Mediterranean—the happiest I ever saw him. The day was perfect—sunny and warm with a light wind. I joined him, and afterward, we explored Aigues-Mortes together, a lovely old town huddled along narrow streets. Then we had a nice dinner at an outdoor café."

Evan felt an unfamiliar respect for his father's enterprising spirit. "And then you parted ways?"

"No. He was planning to complete his bicycle trek with another thousand miles back to the Channel, but he decided to join me on a detour to the hills above Nice to look for a mysterious little pyramid—"

"A *pyramid?* In France?" Evan cut in, not sure he had heard correctly.

"That was the reason I'd made the trip. Having read about it, I wanted to see the pyramid with my own eyes. It was so anachronistic—that's what attracted me—the strangeness of it, the mystery."

Evan located Nice on the map. "Here?"

"Actually, a few miles inland. Outside this village—Falicon."

Evan wondered why his father hadn't ever told him about this before. "What did you know about the pyramid?"

"Only a few tantalizing lines in a guidebook apparently drawn from a combination of local lore, rumor, and speculation. It wasn't really known who built it and when. The more likely theories were that it was built by Roman legionnaires who practiced the cult of Mithras during the later Empire, or that it was built by Knights Templar returning to Europe after the fall of Acre at the end of the thirteenth century. Anyhow, when Ned heard where I was going, he wanted to come along, so we tied his bicycle to the back of my automobile and by nightfall we were in Nice. The next morning we drove into the mountains, parked at a little hotel-restaurant outside Falicon, got directions from the innkeeper, and set out on foot to find the pyramid—which took hours! It was high on a hill overlooking Nice to the south, with the Mediterranean stretching to the horizon."

"Was it a real pyramid—like at Giza?" Evan asked.

"Not at all! Barely Giza in miniature, and badly weathered—by time and tourists who had picked away at it over the centuries—missing its apex and only about twenty feet high. Nonetheless, it was impressive—so remote and enigmatic. Plus, it straddled a deep cave the locals called *Bauma des Ratapignata*—Occitan for 'cave of the bats.' Someone had left a strong rope secured to the stone, which allowed us to rappel down. We followed the cave as far down as we could without a torch and managed to see some stalactites with a central pillar and a very worn inscription."

"What did it say?"

"I made a rubbing, though it's largely undecipherable. Would you like to see it?"

"Boy, would I!"

Clive pushed up from the divan. "I have it hidden in my edition of Xenophon's *Anabasis*." He opened the book. "Along with this photograph of me and Ned."

Evan couldn't help but smile; there stood Lawrence—disheveled and squinting, next to the taller and well-dressed Clive. "Who took this?"

"Ned had a remote cable for the shutter release."

Evan moved his attention to the pyramid, the stones fitted together with a few jagged gaps where caper bush and flowers grew at odd angles. Low to the ground, he saw the dark maw of the cave. "I'd very much like to go there with you."

"Me too," said Clive and carefully unfolded a sheet of thin paper. "This is the rubbing I made of the inscription, such as it is. Can you make out the two triangles?"

"Is this one equilateral?"

"It is."

"And this is an inverted triangle below?" Evan asked, pointing.

"The wide apex angle is just under one hundred and twenty-eight degrees."

"Which makes it obtuse." Evan smiled. "Like me. And the script?"

"When it comes to the script, we're all obtuse. The letters I could make out seemed to be Paleo-Hebrew. But I've yet to find anyone able to decipher it—which compounds the mystery." Clive refolded the rubbing and placed it along with the photograph back between the pages of the book. "It's every bit as incomprehensible as the petroglyphs here in Utah." Clive replaced the book on the shelf and turned to Evan. "Did you make any lunch?"

"I made you a sandwich and there's more lemonade in the icebox."

Once back in the kitchen, Evan picked up his magazine. He was anxious to finish his Tarzan novella, and as Clive sat down to eat, Evan asked, "Do you mind if I finish reading my story?"

"Go right ahead."

Evan went into the front room where he sat on the divan and put his father's battered fedora on his head.

Before long Clive joined him. "The hat suits you," he said, and when Evan reached up to take it off, Clive was quick to add, "No. Keep it. I have another."

"Thanks, Dad," Evan said and tugged down on the brim.

Clive headed for the front door. "Let's go for a walk."

"Are you kidding? It's a hundred degrees out there."

"I've got something to show you," he replied and to Evan's surprise, added, "And bring your sling."

With the sun a hand's breadth above the horizon, they set out over the desert, the heat rising in waves from the gravel pavement.

"This way," Clive said and led the way along the dry riverbed where there was little vegetation other than patches of beavertail cactus and an occasional scraggly cottonwood.

Evan wondered where they were going as they traversed the dusty watercourse. Rounding a bend, he saw something that looked like a fat scarecrow in the shadow of the ravine. "What's that?"

"That, my young squire, is a quintain—a fixed target with a knight's shield."

"That's not a shield, it's a garbage can cover."

"Indeed, it is! Shall we splinter a lance, Sir Evan? Try hitting it with a stone from your sling."

"From here? It's at least fifty yards away."

"Ma foi! Never have I given ear to such folly! Come, brave squire, lest I smite you with my quarterstaff. Take a shot. A nickel if you can hit it."

"I won't do it for less than a dime."

"Done."

Evan bent down, picked up a piece of black flint and placed it in the apex of the sling. After a half dozen rotations, he cut the stone loose and it shot through the air, hitting the target dead on with a resounding clang.

"Well shot, good squire!" shouted Clive. "You're clearly well practiced."

"You owe me a dime, my lord," Evan said and picked up another stone.

"Put it on my tab. See if you can do it again."

After the debt had mounted to two dollars, Clive shouted, "Enough! You've exhausted the grant. Whatever you do now is gratis."

Evan was pleased to show off, repeatedly hitting the garbage can lid as Clive watched, sitting cross-legged in the gravelly talus of the riverbed. But as the sun set over the sagebrush flats, his arm tired and he was relieved when the battered lid fell to the ground.

Clive climbed to his feet. "Good shooting, son. Let's go home."

With banners of clouds gleaming crimson along the western edge of a gunmetal sky, they walked together through the desert.

Evan sighed as his father began whistling the melody Evan had heard so many times over the years. "What's that tune?" he asked.

"'Brian Boru's March.'"

"Didn't you sing that to me when I was little?"

"Yes. When I put you to bed. I'm surprised you remember."

"I also remember that I didn't understand a word."

"Neither did I. It's Gaelic, one archaic language I never got around to learning."

"How did you come to know it?"

"Just as with you, my father sang me to sleep with it, as my grandfather had done with him—a family tradition going back for generations."

"Any idea what the words mean?"

"Some of them." Clive stopped walking and began singing, "*Ó neart an chatha go neart na síochána. On bhith dhiaga beannacht an ghrá . . .*"

Evan listened, smiling up at the stars beginning to emerge in the darkening sky.

Once Clive was done, he spoke the translation. "From the strength of battle to the strength of peace. From a divine world, blessings of love."

"When we get back to the house, could you write that down for me?"

"Happy to do it."

They walked on in silence until the porch light came in view. Even from a distance Evan could see the June bugs crowding around.

They mounted the steps and opened the door.

"I'll bet you're looking forward to starting school in September."

"Sure, Dad," said Evan.

But despite a renewed appreciation of his father, Evan had other plans.

CHAPTER 9

June 28, 1914

Sarajevo, Bosnia

WE HAVE FAILED! The Archduke Franz Ferdinand still lives.

The thought burns within my heart as I lean over the railing of Lateiner Bridge where the River Miljaka flows beside the Appel Quay. I curse and spit into the river. All the months of planning have been for nothing.

Grabez approaches from his position down the road, joining me on the bridge. "Gavrilo," he whispers, "what happened?"

"The idiot, Muhammed did nothing as the motorcar passed by him."

"Were they going too fast?"

"No. He simply failed to act. He's not one of us, Grabez. He should never have been included. So, it fell to Cabrinovic, who acted as a patriot and showed resolve. He struck the percussion cap against a lamppost, just as we had practiced. Then he threw his bomb directly at Ferdinand's motorcar."

"Did it fail to explode?"

"No, but the driver sped up and the grenade exploded behind the royal carriage, injuring some spectators and damaging the motorcar behind that of the Archduke."

"And what of Cabrinovic?"

"He took his cyanide tablet and jumped into the river—a true patriot."

"When we remember the fathers of Greater Serbia, the name of Vaso Cabrinovic will be honored forever."

"Yes, but sadly, the Archduke is probably on his way back to Austria. We have nothing to show for all the months of planning. Nothing."

"Should we return to Serbia?"

"Not yet. We remain here until we hear from the others."

I check my timepiece. It is almost eleven o'clock. The day is warm, and I ate no breakfast this morning. My next meal was to have been the cyanide tablet, which is still in my pocket. "Do you want to get something to eat?"

"No, Gavrilo. I should return to my station."

With that, Grabez walks off the bridge and back down the street. I watch him go. I cross the Appel Quay to a lane leading away from the river. I look up at the street sign and cannot help but laugh—Franz Joseph Street! The bastard's father! What bitter irony!

I go to the food store of Moritz Schiller on the corner and push the door open. The little bell sounds. I order a sandwich with kulen and Vojvodina ham. In the weeks we have been in Sarajevo, I have found the sandwiches here quite good.

I leave the shop and eat my sandwich standing on the street, but with our failure, it tastes like sand in my mouth. I throw the sandwich in the garbage. Across the Appel Quay, I can see Grabez walking back and forth. Suddenly, he stops. He is looking down the boulevard in the direction of city hall. Something is happening.

I turn and cannot believe what I am seeing!

The convoy of the Archduke has returned! Directly in front of me the motorcar of the mayor is turning from the Appel Quay onto Franz

Joseph Street. Behind is the carriage of the Archduke! I grab at the pistol in my pocket. Everything is happening too fast. I am so close. My hand shakes. I fear I will miss my chance.

I hear someone shout at the driver.

"Fool! This is the wrong way! You should stay on the Appel Quay!"

The motorcar comes to a stop within a few meters of where I stand. The driver struggles with the gears to reverse. I see the silly white helmet of the Archduke dressed in his white uniform. He is looking right at me. Beside him is his wife, Sophie, also in white with a pretty, wide-brimmed hat.

I take the pistol from my pocket. I see the fear in their eyes.

It is well they should be frightened.

The motorcar begins to move.

I raise my hand and shoot. And again I shoot.

※　※　※

Carnac Plage
Brittany, France

CHAIM WEIZMANN was drying his hands after washing the dinner dishes, when he felt his wife, Vera, hugging him from behind.

"Do you realize this past week has been the first real vacation we've ever had?" she whispered.

"What about last week in Paris?" Weizmann asked as he turned and kissed her. "Wasn't that a *real vacation*?"

In the lingering warmth of evening, they were both barefoot and in their swimwear, standing together in the small kitchen of their rented villa at the seaside resort of Carnac Plage in Brittany.

"A real vacation?" she laughed. "With your daily meetings with French Zionists and Lord Rothschild? And always in a three-piece suit?" She stepped back and smiled up at him. "Look at you now! Look at us—this is how people dress on a real vacation—in these scandalous French swimsuits, sleeveless and leg-revealing!"

"Truly shocking!" he said and kissed her again.

As usual, Vera's dark hair was smoothed back and gathered in a bun at the nape of her neck. He bent and brushed her neck with his lips, then nodding toward their son's small bedroom, he asked, "Is Benjy asleep?"

"No. He's waiting for you to read to him."

Weizmann picked a book off the kitchen table and stepped toward the bedroom.

Vera looked at the book and grinned. "Again with sedation by Rilke?"

"I'll make it up to him tomorrow night with Bialik's poems for children."

"No you won't. Have you forgotten? I'll be putting him to bed on the train to Zurich. You'll be getting off in Paris—to meet with Rothschild." Vera sighed. "Again."

"I'm sorry, darling, but you know how important it is to secure funding for the university in Jerusalem. Rothschild can meet our goal with one stroke of his pen." He raised his shoulders. "And in two days I'll join you and Benjy in Zurich . . ."

"I understand, Chaim. I'm just afraid to lose you to His Lordship for an entire week."

"Two days—that's all. Then I'll join you at our hotel in Zurich. I promise."

Vera nodded, rose up on her toes, kissed him on the cheek, and frowned. "You feel warm." She placed her hand on his forehead. "Are you all right?"

"I'm fine—just . . . tired."

"Would you like me to draw you a bath?"

"That would be lovely!"

"I'll put some lavender oil in the bathwater. Perhaps His Lordship's generosity will be proportional to your fragrance."

CHAPTER 10

July 29, 1914
Paris

WEIZMANN KISSED Vera and Benjy goodbye, took his valise, and jostled by passengers, stepped onto the platform at Gare de Lyon. As the train to Zurich pulled away, he waved and blew kisses.

He checked his pocket watch and saw that it was one o'clock. Scheduled to meet with Rothschild at seven, he hoped to check into the Royal Saint-Michel early and get some rest. *Vera was right*, he thought as he left the platform, *I do have a fever*.

As he entered the station, a roaring wave of noise washed over him.

What's going on here? He pushed through the crowd, gripping his valise tightly in his hand. Outside, the situation was even worse. He tried to hail a coach or cab but there was such a struggle for every conveyance, he gave up and decided to walk. Crossing the boulevard, he wondered, *What happened to the peaceful Paris we enjoyed last week?*

But he knew what happened. On the train there had been talk of the assassination of the archduke of Austria-Hungary in Sarajevo, apparently by a secret Serbian organization. As a result, Austria-Hungary was threatening to declare war on Serbia. *That must be it . . .*

Once he was well away from the station, he put down his valise and wiped the sweat from his brow. *I do feel terribly hot—my head hurts and my body is aching—clearly a case of the grippe.* He picked up his valise and continued walking.

The near-deserted Parisian streets were quiet and soothing, but he still felt poorly and wasn't relishing the prospect of walking two kilometers carrying a heavy valise in the summer heat to the hotel. As he passed Jardin Du Luxembourg he began to sneeze. *I'm in no condition to meet with Rothschild.*

The hot sun conspired with his fever to create a sense of intolerable heat. Beneath his suit jacket he was sweating. Looking into the park, he squinted against the sunlight and saw a bench in the shade of a chestnut tree. *I'll rest there until I feel better.*

Reaching the bench, he took off his fedora and saw that the lining of the crown was dripping with sweat. He placed the hat on his valise to dry. Taking off his necktie, he opened his collar, took off his suit jacket, and lay down on the bench using his folded jacket for a pillow. Turning his head, he looked through half-opened eyes at the deserted winding paths among the well-manicured hedges and lawns of the park. He closed his eyes, crossed his arms over his chest and listened to the sound of a light breeze rustling the leaves of the chestnut tree.

He thought back to their visits to the garden the week before— the beautiful and symmetrical flower beds, the Luxembourg palace at sunset, the marionette theater, and most of all the carousel—Benjy riding around and around on a big white elephant.

Almost dreaming, he recalled how delicious it had been to sit on a bench next to Vera with his book of Rilke's poetry while Benjy joyfully rode on the elephant, around and around, exactly like the lines of the poem Rilke had written at that very spot;

Under the roof and the roof's shadow turns
This train of painted horses for a while
In this bright land that lingers
Before it perishes . . .

And now and then a big white elephant . . .

With a start, his eyes shot open. He sat up and looked around. In a sudden panic he wondered why the park was deserted. The question screamed in his brain as his heart pounded. *Why would the French be so concerned that Austria-Hungary is threatening Serbia?*

Then he remembered and a cold fear clutched at his chest. *Serbia is allied with Russia, Russia is allied with France, and Austria-Hungary is allied with Germany. Is it possible that tensions are already rising between France and Germany? Does Paris already imagine the enemy at her gates?*

He shook his head and realized he had slept, but for how long?

He snapped open his timepiece. *My God, I've been asleep for two hours!* It was almost three o'clock.

He stood up and felt weak—fatigued with shaking chills. He put on his fedora, and with his jacket over his arm, he picked up his valise and left the park.

Reaching the hotel, he sneezed as he pushed through the door and sneezed again as the bellman took his bag. He glanced up at the wall clock.

Half three. Plenty of time to reschedule my meeting with Baron Rothschild.

At the registration desk, he announced, "Professor Chaim Weizmann to check in."

"Certainly, Professor. It's a pleasure to have you with us. Sign here please." The desk clerk rotated the guest book and pushed it toward Weizmann.

He signed the ledger and sneezed.

"Monsieur does not feel well?" the clerk asked.

"A summer cold." Weizmann sighed and placed his fedora and jacket on the desk. "I should like to send a telegram."

"*Certainement, Monsieur.*" The clerk placed a smooth sheet of buff-colored paper on the desk.

Uncapping his fountain pen, Weizmann began to write.

To your eminence, Lord Baron Edmund de Rothschild,

I offer my profound apologies to Your Lordship, and beg your indulgence, but I am currently indisposed with a bad case of the grippe, and in no condition to meet this evening. I hope we might reschedule for tomorrow, preferably in the early afternoon, if convenient for you.

    With my sincere apologies and profound respect,
      Chaim Weizmann, PhD
      Chair, Department of Organic Chemistry, University
      of Manchester, Member of the Executive,
      World Zionist Organization

Weizmann pushed the paper toward the clerk, and asked, "Do I pay for this now?"

"Not necessary, Monsieur. It will be included with your room charges." But, apparently seeing the name of Rothschild as recipient of the telegram, the clerk's eyes grew wide, "Truly? This is for the baron?"

"Yes, and I hope he might receive it with dispatch. Will it be sent by wireless?"

"No, no, no Monsieur. I will *personally* carry this to the baron by taxi!"

"At what cost?"

"None, *Monsieur!* I will do this service for you at no cost." The clerk fluttered with excitement and moved away from the desk.

"But, tell me, how do I arrange to draw a bath in my room?"

"No arrangement is necessary, Monsieur! Each of our rooms has access to the most modern gas water heaters. The bellman will demonstrate for you."

"And, one more thing," Weizmann said as loudly as he could since the clerk had opened the hotel's brass front door and was about to leave. "I saw a crowd of anxious people at the railway station today. Is France worried about war with Germany?"

"No, no, no Monsieur—a minor diplomatic ruffle to be smoothed over by some consular tête-à-tête." He raised the telegram. "I will deliver this now to the baron!"

Weizmann sighed as he followed the bellman into the lift, hoping the baron would deign to reschedule. He simply had to secure his support—without it, the Hebrew University project was finished.

The bellman closed the lift's cast-iron gate with a metallic clatter, and the lift lurched upward as Weizmann's thoughts remained with the baron.

Unique and flamboyant, Rothschild was a bundle of contradictions; though an ardent Zionist, he disliked the organized Zionist movement and especially hated the congresses and meetings with the debates and speeches. On the other hand, he was very generous in supporting many of the Zionist projects in Palestine.

That's what Weizmann was counting on. But for the present all he wanted was a nice bath followed by uninterrupted sleep.

Once the bellman had shown him to his room and demonstrated how to fill the bathtub with heated water, he departed. Weizmann pulled the drapes closed, stripped off his shirt, kicked off his shoes, and stepped out of his trousers. Lying back on the bedspread, he closed his eyes against the muted daylight and soon fell asleep. When he awoke, the room was dark. He switched on the light and checked his timepiece. It was already half six. He hoped Rothschild had received his note.

He willed himself off the bed and filled the tub.

Partially restored after his bath, Weizmann was already in his favorite striped pajamas when the room door shook with impatient knocking.

He pulled on his robe, opened the door, and found himself in the presence of Rothschild. In his late sixties, the baron had a full white beard and a mane of white hair. He was exquisitely dressed, and a bright diamond pin glittered in his dark scarlet cravat. Behind him was a large entourage.

"I heard of your condition, Dr. Weizmann," Rothschild announced and stepped into the room. The entourage hovered at the door.

"How good to see you, Baron, please, come in," he offered weakly as Rothschild, arms akimbo, stalked about, examining the accommodations. His previous meetings with Rothschild had taken place at the baron's palatial office, and for those meetings, Weizmann had dressed impeccably. Now he was barefoot and in his pajamas.

"I don't see that Professor Weizmann has any tea!" Rothschild announced in a commanding voice. "Please see to it that a pot of Wissotzky mint tea with lemon is delivered to this room *immediately*!"

A member of the entourage rushed off, and Rothschild swung the door closed. He turned to Weizmann and held out an envelope. "While we wait for your tea, Professor, *this* should make you feel better."

Weizmann opened the envelope and almost swooned as he stared at a check made out for the sum of forty thousand pounds sterling. His heart began to beat wildly. "Lord . . . Lord Rothschild," he stammered, "your generosity—it's astounding!"

Rothschild chuckled as he shrugged out of his greatcoat and draped it over a chair in the room's foyer. "I trust this will cover the Hebrew University library."

"Nearly so, Baron Rothschild. Thank you so very much!"

"*Nearly so?*" He swung about and faced Weizmann. "Did you say *nearly so?*"

"Yes, Baron, but that isn't a problem. Other benefactors will—"

"*Other benefactors?* That's quite out of the question! After all I've spent on the university, some *frier* will come along with a few miserable francs and share the glory?" He shook his head vigorously.

"No!" He tapped a finger on his chest. "If you need more money, you come to me!"

"I will, Baron Rothschild. I will. You have my word."

Rothschild sat on one of the plush couches in the foyer. "This Hebrew University will be a great center for light and learning, Professor. From Jerusalem, knowledge will radiate out to the uttermost edges of the earth. The very *idea* of going to others . . ." He sat back, crossed his arms, fixed his eyes on Weizmann, and frowned. "I suspect sir, that you are something of a Bolshevik!"

"One is always *someone's* Bolshevik, I suppose," Weizmann struggled not to smile as he sat across from the baron.

Rothschild laughed heartily, sat forward, and slapped Weizmann on the knee. "You're no Bolshevik, Chaim! You may be a Russian, but you're too fond of money to be a Bolshevik!" Rothschild shot to his feet. "You will have your university in Palestine, and I will endow it. But now, you must rest."

"I will, Baron, thank you." Weizmann also stood up. "I should think I'll be quite myself tomorrow."

"That's what I'm afraid of," Rothschild replied, as he took his coat, a smile playing on his lips. "I would prefer that you remain at rest."

"Sir?"

"You're always going about making *speeches*." Rothschild flapped his thumb and fingers together a few times, apparently to indicate the act of speaking. "Always making speeches!" Rothschild headed for the door. "You attract too much attention. I'd prefer if you'd stop making speeches."

"Baron," Weizmann replied, "be so kind as to give me the combination to your safe and I promise not to make any more speeches."

"As I said, Chaim," Rothschild chuckled. "You're no Bolshevik!"

He began to reach for the door handle, then stopped. "What's that sound?"

They both heard it—shouting from the street below.

Weizmann went to the paned-glass door overlooking boulevard Saint-Michel. He released the latch and pulled the door open. He and Rothschild stepped out to the iron-grille balcony. A crowd was moving along the boulevard beneath the bright electric carbon arc lamps. Their shouting filled the air.

"On to Berlin! On to Berlin!"

Rothschild leaned over the balcony railing and called down. "What's the news?"

"France will soon be at war with Germany!"

As Weizmann looked down at the crowd, his breath caught as Rilke's words rose in his mind.

> *Under the roof and the roof's shadow turns*
> *This train of painted horses for a while*
> *In this bright land that lingers*
> *Before it perishes . . .*

CHAPTER 11

August 5, 1914
2 Polstead Road
Oxford, England

T.E. LAWRENCE APPROACHED the cottage door carrying a box of groceries. Turning to the side, he knocked with his elbow. When Leonard Woolley opened the door, Lawrence stepped forward and announced, "It's begun."

"Where? How?"

"Belgium," Lawrence said and put the box on the kitchen table. "The Germans are moving through Belgium toward France. They completely ignored Grey's ultimatum and our compact to defend Belgium's neutrality—a *scrap of paper* they're calling it"

"What about Downing Street?"

"There are resignations in the cabinet—Morley among them. But Grey and Churchill are standing firm, and there's a crowd outside Buckingham Palace singing 'God Save the King.'"

"And the Turks?"

"Still officially neutral."

Woolley lifted a thick manuscript off the table. "And our opus here—*The Wilderness of Zin*? Will this *keep* them neutral?"

"I doubt it—with the Berlin-to-Baghdad railway, Krupp artillery, German arms, and German ships, the Sublime Porte is in hock to the kaiser up to the tassel on its fez."

"But Kitchener is so sure it will keep us in their good graces . . ."

"It may buy some time but thank God we're done with it!" Lawrence exclaimed. "We should start packing."

"Whatever for?"

"What else? To join the fight!"

Woolley tossed the manuscript onto the table where it landed with a thud. "So, if Turkey joins the war with Germany, all our work—what's the *use* of it?"

"The *use of it* my dear Woolley? Have you forgotten the glowing letter Newcombe wrote to the War Office about our survey?" Lawrence lifted a sheet of paper from the cluttered table and read, "*I am pleased to inform you that all roads and wells have been marked on a new map. The survey of southern Palestine is complete—from Beer Sheba in the north to the approaches to Aqaba in the south—all carefully mapped by the surveyors and explorers of the Palestine Exploration Fund.*"

"That's *us,* Lenny—the surveyors and explorers of the Palestine Exploration Fund! If and when we face off with the Turks in the Sinai and the Arabah deserts, our forces will know where to find roads and wells—all because of our survey!"

"But K is still expecting us to tinker with the final draft!"

"I disagree—we're done with it!" Lawrence shot back. "Now we get into the fight—I've already been to the induction center."

"And?"

"They told me I'm too short."

"You're joking."

"I suppose they're right. At five feet, five inches, I'm positively dwarfish—"

"Like Lampy the garden gnome?"

"Precisely, Leonard, but it's probably for the best because, after that rejection, I went over to Whitehall and spoke to people in MO-4, the geographical division of military intelligence. *They* don't think I'm too short. What about you?"

"I agree. I don't think you're too short."

"No!" Lawrence laughed. "I mean, where are *you* planning to go?"

"MO-4 would be a good fit for me as well. That, or the Royal Artillery—"

"Artillery? What a bloody waste of your talents, Leonard! If you'd like, I'll get you an interview at MO-4."

"That would be great, but I just want we get into the fight before it's over—by Christmas, they say."

"Christmas? What year?" Lawrence stepped to the grocery box on the counter. "Whatever the case, this calls for a toast!"

"With what? Tea?"

"No, silly man! I picked up a few cold bottles of Vim Tonic—a delightful cordial and perfect for a toast!" He opened a bottle, handed it to Woolley, and then opened a second bottle for himself.

Woolley raised his bottle. "Who shall we toast?"

"God!" Lawrence exclaimed. "Because He put us on an island!"

"And Churchill," Woolley added. "Because he gave us a navy!"

"To God and Churchill!" they exclaimed and drank down their bottles of Vim Tonic with a flourish.

CHAPTER 12

August 6, 1914
Mecca
The Holy Precincts

FAISAL KNOCKED on the door of his father's royal apartments within the holy precincts. A servant opened the door, stood to the side and bowed.

"O my father!" Faisal greeted Hussein as he stepped forward, his long white cotton robe grazing the smooth blue tiles of the study. "I came as soon as I received your summons."

"Thank you, my son!" Hussein rose from the divan. "I am happy to tell you that the time for your journey to Amman and Damascus has arrived."

Thrilled with the opportunity for action, Faisal bowed his head. "I am grateful for the chance to be of assistance, my father. When would you have me leave?"

"This very night since the war in Europe has begun. Soldiers of Germany are, even now, moving through Belgium. Though the Turks have not yet broken their neutrality, we must act quickly." Hussein gestured. "Please, sit with me now."

Barely able to contain his excitement, Faisal sat by his father on the divan. "What is my charge?"

"You will seek out contacts with the secret societies in Amman and Damascus to determine if they will be loyal to me when I declare our rising up against the Turks."

"Yes. I recall we spoke of this."

"There's more, my son. Once in Damascus you will go to the palace where you will convey a letter from my hand with personal blessings to Djemal Pasha, governor of Greater Syria, requesting that he give you lodging as his house guest—"

"What?" Faisal blurted out. "You would have me stay in the house of Djemal while I contact the Arab nationalists he seeks to exterminate?"

"Calm yourself and hear me out, my son!"

But Faisal couldn't calm himself. "You would have me conspire with the nationalists under the nose of Djemal Pasha—who many call Djemal the Butcher?"

"Silence!" Hussein thundered. "Is it not written that Allah gave us two ears and one tongue so that we might *listen* more than we speak? Therefore, listen!"

Faisal fell silent and nodded, though his chest filled with rage.

"What you say regarding Djemal is true, my son. However, of the three Young Turks ruling the Empire, he is the most reasonable. Because of him Turkey remains neutral. Enver Pasha, who was once a military attaché in Berlin, advocates for Turkey to join with Germany. Only Djemal has stopped this from happening."

"I understand, Father." Faisal struggled to compose himself. "Please continue."

"You will praise Djemal for keeping Turkey neutral and ask that he continue."

"I will."

"And you will appeal to him as governor of Greater Syria for Arab self-rule—"

"Self-rule?" asked Faisal as his confusion increased. "After six hundred years of Ottoman domination, you ask that I appeal to Djemal for self-rule? Isn't it likely that his reply to me will be the gallows?"

"Not with the respect he holds for my office. Indeed, I'm certain he will appreciate your candor. Understand, my son, this is *precisely* the moment when we might have leverage—courted as we have been by the British and the Germans—all looking to us for support. Do you require any further proof than that dispatch I showed you from Count von Moltke counting on us to assist in the attack on the Suez Canal? This is the leverage we now *have*, and it is *now* we must test it!"

"But, Father, what of your talk of assurances from the British?"

"That remains just talk—with no assurances in writing, my son. We must maintain all options and constantly gauge where we stand with the Turks and with the British."

"But what of your distrust of the kaiser?"

"That is, indeed, a major concern. However, if Djemal prevails and Turkey maintains her neutrality throughout the war, we'll never have to deal with the kaiser, and Djemal will be in a position to reward us for our continued loyalty. So we must tread carefully and keep all opportunities open. It is for this reason I charge you to appeal to Djemal for Turkish neutrality and for Arab self-rule with absolute respect."

"I understand, Father. I will be careful of my speech when I deal with him."

"And you won't refer to him as Djemal the Butcher?"

"Not to his face, Father."

"Good!" Hussein clapped Faisal on the shoulder. "I know how servile and flattering you can be, my son! I will also provide gifts from our house to his: jewel-encrusted daggers and my own prized hunting sea-eagle—rarely used in falconry. You will measure his response to our petition. Your brother, Abdullah, will be doing the same with the two other pashas in Constantinople. Also, Abdullah will apprise General Kitchener of the need for clear and written British assurances. In this manner we will carefully determine our course."

"But what of the Arab revolt, Father? Is *that* not our goal? Faisal asked.

"The revolt is one possible option and remaining with the Ottoman Empire without the kaiser is another. For now, we remain loyal citizens of the Empire. The only imperative is that we proceed with utter discretion."

"But if I stay at Djemal's palace, how can I possibly connect with the secret societies?"

Hussein leaned toward Faisal and spoke in a low voice. "In your retinue will be some of my most trusted retainers. They will have coded messages to the underground leaders hidden in their sword hilts and sewn into the lining of their cloaks and shoes. They will secretly contact the Arab nationalist leaders in Amman and Damascus to meet with you safely and discretely. You will learn who among them is in favor of revolution, and who will swear allegiance to me if the Turks ally with Germany, and I decide to lead the rebellion with the support of the British. You will inform the nationalists that I will require an oath of loyalty to me as spokesmen of the Arabs along with a clear protocol including boundaries of the Arab state that will rise from the ashes of the Ottoman Empire after the revolution."

"I realize the value of examining all options, my father, but please tell me which path you actually prefer."

"That depends, my son. If Djemal prevails and the Ottomans remain neutral throughout the war, we remain loyal to the Turks. On the other hand, if the Ottomans ally with Germany, we likely revolt and put our faith in Great Britain."

Faisal was frustrated by his father's ambiguity. "So, you remain of two minds?"

"I have only one mind, my son; I seek that which is best for the Arabs and for our family. I know that you view my actions with some confusion. Indeed, it is confusion I wish to engender! Only this will keep the Turks off balance and away from an alliance with Germany. This confusion will also encourage the British to a greater generosity toward us. We are like a bride with an enviable dowry; we have only to bide our time and allow our British and Turkish suitors to vie for our affections!"

CHAPTER 13

August 6, 1914
Jerusalem
The German Colony

GUNTER VON WERTHEIMER kissed his sleeping wife and daughter and set out for work before dawn. Tirzah was on summer holiday and had been working with him at the dig site near the Temple Mount almost every day. But on this particular day she would be spending time with her mother and getting some extra sleep.

Gunter eased the back door closed and drew a deep breath, relishing the cool morning air. He had cancelled the carriage service during the summer, preferring a daily brisk morning walk. Pausing, he looked across the Hinnon Valley as the Judean hills emerged from the dawn mist ignited by the sun rising over the Mountains of Moab.

Descending into the valley, his thoughts turned to the troubling possibility of Walker excavating on the Temple Mount as part of the kaiser's sinister machinations in Jerusalem. He blew out a deep breath, relieved that there was still no sign of Walker.

Pushing away those thoughts, he considered his current research paper, looking forward to showing it to Rahman. Since it dealt with Robinson's Arch and the portico at the southern end of the Temple Mount, he knew that Rahman would find his conclusions of interest; the paper offered strong evidence that when sacrifices were offered at the Temple during Christ's ministry, the portico would have held the stalls for selling birds and animals along with the tables of the moneychangers.

He froze in mid-stride. *Did I remember to take it?* Kneeling, he opened his briefcase and saw the paper wasn't there.

Damn! I must have left it on my desk!

Since it would take only minutes to retrieve, Gunter quickly retraced his steps back to the house. Entering quietly, he was surprised to see Rachel in her robe, drinking coffee and reading a newspaper in the kitchen.

"Good morning, darling."

Rachel's head jerked up, her eyes wide. "Gunter!" She gulped a breath of air, her hand over her heart. "You startled me! I thought you had left."

"I did. Why are you up so early?"

"Two men from the German consulate came by to speak with you. You just missed them. But why are you back? Did you forget something?"

"Yes—a research paper," he said and ducked into his study.

Once he was back in the kitchen, Rachel said, "That's not the only thing you forgot!"

He stopped in midstride. "What else?"

"You forgot to kiss me goodbye."

"No, I didn't—I kissed you while you slept. But now that you're fully conscious, I'm happy to do it again." He bent and kissed her, then asked, "What did they want?"

She shrugged. "Some administrative matter. I told them they could find you at the dig site. One of them left a card." She pointed with her cup. "It's on the counter."

Gunter picked up the white business card. *Dietrich Wunderlich, Assistant des Konsuls—Konsulat des Deutsches Kaiserreich, Jerusalem.* "This might be about the grant I've been waiting for. If I don't see them at the dig, I'll pop by the consulate on my way home." He stuck the card in his shirt pocket and took a step toward the door, then paused. "Are you feeling alright darling? You look a bit pale."

"Just tired."

"Why not go back to sleep?"

"I should be fine after another one of these." She raised the coffee cup. "Besides, now that I'm up, I'll see if I can roust Tirzah."

"What are your plans?"

"Your basic mother and daughter day—shopping in West Jerusalem, shopping in East Jerusalem, followed by high tea at the Austrian Hospice rooftop terrace in the Old City."

He decided to tease her. "Why not drop by the Church of the Flagellation? It's only a block away! For a few beshlik, the monks will be happy to give you a flogging!"

"No thanks, just afternoon tea."

"Since you'll be in the neighborhood, why not pop by the dig site and lend a hand?"

"I prefer flagellation," Rachel smiled and waved.

Gunter left, walking quickly to make up for lost time.

Entering the Old City by Jaffa Gate, he was surprised to see a large crowd gathered outside the Grand New Hotel—everyone standing in total silence, apart from someone speaking, though he couldn't hear what was being said.

"What's going on?" he asked someone on the edge of the crowd.

"The war's begun in Western Europe!"

"What's happened?" Gunter gasped, his heart pounding.

"Germany invaded Belgium. The hotel manager is introducing the American consul who just received a dispatch by wireless. We're about to hear more details."

Working his way through the crowd, Gunter saw the consul standing in the hotel doorway, reading from a paper in his hands.

"Following the refusal of King Albert of Belgium to allow Germany to violate his country's neutrality on August 3, Germany declared war on Belgium and France, and France declared war on Germany. On August 4, German troops invaded Belgium, and Great Britain declared war on Germany for violating Belgian neutrality. Also on August 4, the United States declared its neutrality. This morning, we were informed by the German consul general . . ."

Gunter pressed forward, straining to hear.

" . . . all male German citizens of military service age are to proceed immediately to the nearest German consular facility to be conscripted. The consul general also wishes to convey that a German supply ship, the *Kronburg*, is waiting at anchor in Haifa Harbor, and that conscripts will receive free transport to Germany by way of the Dardanelles."

The news struck Gunter like a hammer. He was certain that the men from the German consulate had come for him—coming early, expecting to find him at home.

He lurched away from the crowd and raced down the terraced lane leading to the dig site. But after a few seconds, he skidded to a stop. *What am I doing? They're no doubt waiting for me there!*

His mind raced as he faced his life in shambles. He was resolved that he would do everything in his power to avoid returning to Germany. *I won't follow the dictates of a deranged narcissist, and fight in his criminal war of aggression!*

Taking the first opportunity to turn off the main thoroughfare, he moved toward the Muslim Quarter. The mounting dread he felt was in stark contrast with the quiet terraced steps and the cool air of the previous night that still lingered in the shadows of the labyrinthine stone lanes.

I've got to find a way to speak with Rachel and Rahman, but how?

He was certain that German authorities were watching his house as well as the dig site.

He glanced at his timepiece. *Just past eight o'clock.*

He knew that Rahman was already at the dig site, and would be there all day, only returning home to the Muslim Quarter that evening.

But Rachel and Tirzah planned to go the Austrian Hospice for afternoon tea. I could meet them there!

But looking down at his shirt and shorts, he knew he looked too conspicuous.

Sweeping his gaze along the small storefronts lining both sides of a lane in the Muslim Quarter, he saw a tourist shop. In addition to carved olivewood nativity figurines and hammered copper souvenir plates, they also sold quaint articles of Arab dress.

He bought a Bedouin robe and headscarf. Retiring to a changing room, he put them on over his white shirt and shorts. He also bought a leather bag. After he transferred his books and papers from his brief case into the bag, he hid the empty brief case under a pile of rugs. Slinging the bag over his shoulder, he left the shop.

Next stop was an apothecary where he bought a pair of brown-tinted spectacles.

Forcing himself to walk slowly, he sauntered into a coffee shop, sat at a table in a remote niche well away from the lane, and considered that he was probably overreacting. He couldn't believe that the German consulate would be sending officials after every German of draft age. But then he remembered that he wasn't just a German of draft age; he was a noncommissioned officer who had served with the German Expeditionary Force in China during the Boxer Rebellion. *That's why they're looking for me!*

He decided that he would go to the Austrian Hospice earlier than afternoon tea, since Rachel and Tirzah might go there for lunch. He had to speak to Rachel and decide what to do.

When a waiter came by, he ordered tea.

He passed the morning trying to review research papers, though he found it difficult to concentrate as he fretted about the possibility of being sent back to Germany.

When another patron began smoking a nargileh with clouds of noxious smoke, he picked up his papers, placed them in his bag, paid the bill, and left.

Heading toward the Austrian Hospice on Via Dolorosa, he found himself among crowds of Christian pilgrims marking the trail of tears that Jesus traveled from the house of Pilate to Golgotha. Threading his way through the crush of pilgrims, he reached the hospice, ducked in through the stone archway and mounted two flights of steps—the contrast stark between the noisy lane and the pristine silence of the hospice.

He walked down a pillared hallway, through the café, and out to the garden terrace. He scanned the tables for Rachel and Tirzah. They weren't there—not yet.

Passing back through the café, he checked for them in the elegant sitting room, but they also weren't there. *It's still early,* he reasoned.

Standing among the empty tables and overstuffed chairs of the sitting room, he took a moment to relish the stillness, and to study the paintings of Austrian aristocracy that covered the walls. The only portrait he recognized was that of Emperor Franz Josef. According to a framed letter memorializing his visit in 1869, he saw that Franz Josef had been "the first crowned head of a Catholic country to visit Jerusalem since the Crusades."

Knowing that his Bedouin robes were likely to create dismay and confusion among the café staff and patrons, he approached the counter, and in his best Austrian High German, reassured the staff that he was the scion of a wealthy sheik just returned from studying in Vienna. He then ordered strudel and coffee, which he brought out to the terrace garden. Sitting at a table above the teeming lane below, he sipped his coffee as a few patrons arrived for luncheon, then for afternoon tea—reassured by the waiters about the Bedouin in their midst who spoke perfect *Österreichisches Hochdeutsch*.

As he waited for Rachel and Tirzah to join him, he again tried to review and edit his research papers, but soon gave up, finding it impossible as he looked up every few minutes to see if they had arrived. He picked at the strudel but had no appetite.

As the hours passed, his concern about Rachel and Tirzah increased, his mind racing with anxious thoughts. Knowing that Rachel wasn't shy about giving voice to her thoughts, he worried that she may have had an altercation with a consular agent and may have been arrested by a Turkish constable. Or perhaps, they were being detained by the consular agents to leverage his cooperation.

He shook his head. *Stop fretting!* he told himself. *They may have simply decided to eat somewhere else and are already back home.*

He had to get word to Rachel—that they find somewhere to hide, somewhere secure for long-term shelter. *But where? What about Cairo? No—as a German national, the British would consider me an enemy alien.*

A waiter came by, informed him that the kitchen would be closing, and asked if he wanted anything. He ordered another coffee.

As evening approached, he despaired of meeting Rachel and Tirzah, and considered how he might connect with Rahman. *Perhaps he'll be able to help me get them out of the house. He might also know of a good place to hide.*

A muezzin from a nearby mosque began the haunting call to evening prayer—his voice floating over the rooftops of the Muslim Quarter. At the same time the bells of Christian churches began to ring. He knew that Rahman would soon be leaving the dig site to return home.

He paid the bill and left the café. As darkness took hold of the Old City, he descended the stone staircase to a now deserted Via Dolorosa where lamplighters were moving along the lane, and merchants were taking in their wares.

He made his way to Rahman's home, hoping he would already be there. Quietly mounting the stone steps to the veranda, he eased the gate open and stepped quietly forward. He could hear Rahman's wife, Fatima, working in the kitchen and speaking to their nine-month-old son, Mahmoud. There was no sign of Rahman. Not wanting to disturb Fatima, he waited in the shadows as night fell.

Finally, he heard footfalls on the mural steps. He took a step forward, then hesitated, his eyes fixed on the veranda gate.

The footsteps grew louder, the gate opened, and two men stepped onto the veranda.

❋　❋　❋

It was well after sunset when Rahman B'Shara had finally left the dig site for home. He had lingered longer than usual, half expecting Gunter to show up, though hoping he didn't—not with German guards hanging about.

Rahman hadn't felt any particular concern earlier that morning when two officials from the German Consulate had come by, politely asking to speak with Gunter. But that was before he heard the news about Germany at war—news that spread through Jerusalem like a wildfire. And that had been before four men in suits and dark-tinted glasses appeared at the dig site and stood about, looking out of place.

Rahman worried that Gunter might show up before they left. But they never left, and were still there when Rahman finally departed, which was somewhat reassuring since he reasoned that, if they had already apprehended Gunter, they would have pulled the guards.

Lanterns, hanging from iron brackets on the limestone walls, cast lonely islands of yellow light on the smooth cobblestones as

Rahman darted in and out of the labyrinthine alleyways to avoid being followed.

Before reaching home, he saw two men on the corner, smoking and engaged in animated conversation. One of them called to him, "Mas il-cheer, ya Rahman!"

Recognizing his brother-in-law, he called back, "Ya Mahmoud! Walk with me!"

"Why are you so late today?" Mahmoud asked and crushed out his cigarette.

"Extra work at the dig site."

"How is it with your little son, my nephew and namesake?" asked Mahmoud.

"Your nephew—yes, your namesake—no."

"Really! I'm honored that you chose to name him after me!"

"Believe what you wish, Mahmoud, but you know that he was named for your dear father, not you!"

Mahmoud laughed and slapped Rahman on the back as they climbed the mural steps leading up to the veranda.

At the top of the steps, Rahman froze. Peering into the shadows at the edge of the porch, he saw a Bedouin with flowing robes. "Bagdar a'sadek, ya sidi?" he asked as he pushed open the gate, gripping the dagger he wore at his side.

"Rahman, it's me!" A whisper rasped out of the darkness.

"Gunter?"

"Yes."

"Alhamdulilah! Thank God you're here!" Rahman motioned toward Mahmoud. "You know my brother-in-law, Mahmoud."

"Of course," Gunter replied, anxious to speak with Rahman. "Pardon me, Mahmoud, but I must speak with Rahman in confidence."

"I understand," he replied without hesitation. "I'll look in on my sister."

Once Mahmoud had gone inside, Rahman gave Gunter a powerful hug. "I was so worried about you. You've heard the news about the war—"

"Yes."

"I must tell you, my friend, two men from the German Consulate came to the dig site asking about you, and after they left, there were German guards there all day."

"I know. They're looking to impress me into the German army."

"But you were born *here*."

"That doesn't matter. I'm of German parentage and therefore a German subject. Don't you recall when I did my compulsory military service at the turn of the century?"

"But now, aren't you a bit too . . . *old*?"

"Hardly. They're taking everyone under forty-five. But, as I've told you before, I had a bellyful of war during the Boxer Rebellion. I'm done fighting for the kaiser and his Imperial Germany!"

"What can I do to help?"

"I believe Rachel and Tirzah are at our house in the German Colony. I need to get them out of there. Will you come with me?"

"No," Rahman said.

"What are you saying? You won't help me?"

"You must stay here!" Rahman said. "I'll go! If they're watching at the dig site, it's certain they're watching your house." He walked Gunter back into the shadows. "I'll find a way to bring them here and make sure we're not followed. And once you're together here, we'll shelter you until the time is right to . . ." Rahman left off speaking, hesitating.

"Until the time is right to access the portal?" Gunter whispered.

"Yes. But, have you and Rachel told Tirzah about our secret calling?

"Not yet."

"Perhaps it's time to tell her."

"Perhaps it is," said Gunter.

"Let's go inside and tell Fatima what's going on. Then I'll bring Rachel and Tirzah here."

"Rahman, I can't begin to thank you—"

"No need to thank me, my friend. From what I understand, this war will likely have three fronts—Western, Eastern, and Middle East. We need you here on this front."

CHAPTER 14

August 6, 1914
By Rail from Paris to Zurich

CHAIM WEIZMANN sat on the bench seat, crushed against the window and barely able to move—one of twenty people in a compartment designed for six—the train filled beyond capacity.

An hour had passed since they had reached the outskirts of Zurich. Beyond the hedgerows and houses, he was able to see the late-afternoon sun hanging low in the western sky. Having managed to extricate his timepiece from his waistcoat pocket, he held it in his hand and consulted it frequently. He saw that it was six o'clock. *Little wonder we're over three hours late with all the extra stops in France to pick up passengers. I've never seen such desperation!*

The window darkened as they passed through a tunnel, and he could see his own reflection in the window along with the other passengers crowding around him. *This is more like a convoy of refugees!* he thought, then realized. *This* is *a convoy of refugees!*

He sighed and closed his eyes. *Vera has been waiting such a long time, especially with a fidgety seven-year-old like Benjy!*

To his relief, the train slowed, and the steam whistle shrieked. Bells rang and steam rose as the train neared the Zurich station. When the crowded platform came into view, Weizmann anxiously searched for the faces of his wife and son.

Lurching to a stop, the train exhaled a last breath of steam, and he saw them—Vera on the platform, not twenty feet away, holding Benjy's, hand.

Their eyes met. She smiled and waved.

As the compartment emptied, he grabbed his valise off the overhead rack and joined the crush of passengers leaving the train, pushing impolitely forward as he was pushed from behind. "Sorry," and "Excuse me," he said again and again until he finally squeezed out of the car and stepped onto the platform.

Vera met him, hugging him fiercely with her free hand. Then, just as fiercely, she kissed him. "Darling!" she shouted over the noise of the crowd. "I was so worried! Worried you weren't on the train, worried I wouldn't be able to find you!"

"Let's get out of here!" he shouted back.

Vera took his valise. "Take Benjy—he's missed you terribly!"

Picking Benjy up in his arms, he whispered, "Hi, Mr. Seven-year-old!" His mouth near Benjy's ear. Hugging him close, he threaded a path through the crowded terminal and out to the broad concourse leading to the street. He turned to look for Vera but couldn't see her in the throng swarming out of the station.

❀ ❀ ❀

Vera anxiously searched the crowd leaving the train station before finally spotting Chaim and Benjy on the sidewalk by the street. Reaching them, she smiled and shouted, "I can't tell you how good it is to see you holding Benjy!"

"Probably as good it feels!" He hugged Benjy and gave him a kiss.

"May I please get down now?" Benjy asked and struggled to free himself. "I'm not a baby, you know!"

"Sorry." Chaim lowered him to the walkway and looked up at Vera. "How far to the hotel?"

"Twenty minutes by taxi. I'll flag one down," she said and took a step to the curb.

"Wait! Before we leave the station, shouldn't we buy our tickets for the return trip to Paris so we can get back home?"

"I already looked into that!" she shouted as she hailed a taxi. "Travel in that direction is only for the military—"

"What are you saying? We're marooned here?"

"Yes! According to the British Consulate, we are!" she shouted back. As a bright red Ranault slid to the curb, she bent down to shout a question to the driver, "Könnten Sie uns bitte ins Hotel St. Gotthard bringen?"

"Bestimmt! Steig ein."

"The St. Gotthard?" Weizmann exclaimed, as they piled into the back seat, Benjy between them. "That's top of the line!"

"It's worth it! I wanted hot running water, and they're one of the only hotels in Zurich that have it. Besides," she added with a smile, "I know you're *dying* to take a hot bath after that hellish train ride." She patted Chaim on the knee. "You'll thank me later."

"I'll thank you now!" he said and gave her a kiss on the cheek.

Vera finally allowed herself to relax as she looked out the window and admired the evening sky streaked with scarlet pinions of clouds. The cab gathered speed and maneuvered down *Bohnhofstrasse*. She patted Chaim on the knee and said, "And the St. Gotthard is only for one more night. Tomorrow we leave for the Rhone Valley."

"The Rhone Valley? But that's so far from Zurich! Shouldn't we stay *here* so we'll be able to get a train back to Paris when it becomes possible?"

"Not according to the British consul."

"But this is *insane*! We're just going to stay on *vacation*?"

Concerned about how their conversation affected Benjy, she

patted Chaim on the shoulder. "Calm yourself, darling. There's a war raging *elsewhere* in Europe, not *here!*"

"But, who goes on vacation at a time like this?" he asked, nearly shouting.

"The British consul for one, along with his wife and children. But it's hardly a vacation, Chaim! The consul wants all British nationals together for group transport back to England when it becomes possible." She began to stroke Benjy's head, her eyes fixed on Chaim, silently conveying the fact that his anxiety was affecting their son.

Seeming to suddenly understand, Weizmann patted Benjy on the knee. "Mommy is just telling me everything that's been happening when I wasn't with you. It all seems fine to me." He looked up at Vera and mouthed the word sorry.

Relieved that he had calmed down, Vera continued speaking gently to Benjy, and to let Chaim know the arrangements. "Mommy found out that the British consul and his family were on vacation by a big lake when all this mishigas began. He's staying there with lots of other nice English people, and they want us to join them, because they're having so much fun! Then, we'll all go back to England together!"

"That's great, Mommy!" Chaim said and put his arm around Benjy's shoulders.

As the taxi sped through the darkening streets, Vera closed her eyes against the feeling of panic clawing at her heart. The pandemonium she had seen at the train stations, in Paris and Zurich, fresh in her mind. She knew the same panic was sweeping through much of Europe. She breathed out a sigh and stroked Benjy's head, remembering words from a poem she had read when putting him to bed—not one by Bialik as she would have preferred, but one by Rilke—about the merry-go-round, which Benjy insisted she read.

And on the lion whitely rides a young boy
clinging with his little hands
while the lion shows his teeth . . .

The words conjured up a haunting image, a harbinger of things to come.

CHAPTER 15

August 6, 1914
Jerusalem

RAHMAN LEFT THE WALLED CITY beneath a full moon, hoping he would find Rachel and Tirzah at home in the German Colony, and that he would be able to rescue them without being seen by the guards. He spotted a taxi parked on the dirt road outside Damascus Gate. He climbed into the back seat and said, "The German Colony."

"An address would help."

"Go south on Bethlehem Road. I'll tell you when to stop."

The driver accelerated down Sultan Suleiman Street, headed west along the northern face of the Old City wall and crossed into West Jerusalem before turning south.

Looking out the window with the night air cool on his face, Rahman saw how the full moon illuminated the empty fields on both sides of the road. Entering the colony, he leaned forward. "Stop here please."

He got out of the taxi, leaned in through the window and whispered, "Extinguish your headlamps but keep the motor running. I'll be back within the half hour—"

"You know this will cost you."

Rahman pressed some coins into the driver's open palm. "Those are three silver francs. When we're back at Damascus Gate, I'll give you a five-franc silver coin."

"Kwayis, ya zalami!" the driver exclaimed and flashed a smile.

Rahman entered a narrow alley bounded by high walls and shadowed in darkness. He moved quietly forward, reaching Gunter's backyard before the alley opened into the main road. There he stopped and listened.

He could hear the voices of two men whispering to each other in German. Peering out from behind the wall, the street looked deserted in the moonlight, but in the shadows beyond the road's edge, glowing tips of two cigarettes flared and faded in the darkness.

From the alley, he slipped into Gunter's backyard and mounted the steps. The glass of the upper part of the back door shone with a faint light. He tapped on the glass and waited. When there was no response, he tried the door. It was locked. He tipped up a flowerpot next to the door, where Gunter kept a spare key. Fitting it to the lock, he opened the door.

"Rachel!" he whispered into the half-light, "Rachel, are you awake?"

"Rahman?" she whispered in reply and stepped from the shadows. "Thank God! Is Gunter with you?"

"No. I wouldn't let him come. He's been avoiding German consular staff all day."

"They're right outside," she whispered. "They've been there since morning."

"Is Tirzah awake?"

"Yes."

"I have a cab waiting on Bethlehem Road. Take some things—"

"Everything's ready. I'll get Tirzah."

He waited at the back door. Rachel and Tirzah soon emerged, each carrying a small suitcase. He quietly closed and locked the door. Peeking out of the alley, he saw that the guards were still smoking on the main road. Turning, he whispered, "Follow close behind me."

Keeping to the shadows, they were soon on Bethlehem Road where the taxi idled. As Rachel and Tirzah got into the backseat,

Rahman sat next to the driver. "Keep your headlamps dark and turn around." Before the driver could protest, he added, "I'll tell you when it's safe to light them."

Ten minutes later they were walking through Damascus Gate into the Old City. Reaching Rahman's home, they mounted the steps and found Gunter waiting on the veranda. "Thank God!" he exclaimed as Rachel and Tirzah rushed to greet him.

Rahman watched as Gunter gathered them in his arms, his face wet with tears.

Fatima, with baby Mahmoud in her arms, appeared at the front door waving them in. "Come in! Come inside! I'm so glad to see you!"

Rahman beamed with happiness as he watched Fatima hug Rachel and Tirzah.

"I'm so pleased you're safe!" said Fatima. "Gunter told me about the guards."

"They were on the street in front of their house. We easily slipped out the back."

"And we're so happy to have you staying with us!" said Fatima

"Thank you, dear sister," said Rachel as she sat down with Tirzah and Gunter in the front room. "Thank you for opening your home to us."

"This will be *your* home as long as you need refuge," Fatima said, "and there will be no need to thank us, because we are one family and what we do for each other is as natural as breathing."

"Nonetheless, we're grateful," said Gunter. "What of sleeping arrangements?"

Rahman nodded toward the front door. "I'll be sleeping on the veranda—"

"No you won't!" Gunter objected. "I won't put you out of your own home! *I'll* sleep on the veranda."

Rahman smiled at him. "I *prefer* sleeping outside during the summer."

"You'll be here on the divan, Gunter," Fatima said as she paced with Mahmoud over her shoulder. "It's very comfortable. I'll sleep in the guest room with my little friend here, and Rachel and Tirzah will share the main bedroom."

"This won't be for long," Rahman said. "We're going to need a more secure long-term option . . . elsewhere . . ." He left off speaking, certain that Gunter, Rachel, and Fatima would know he was alluding to finding shelter within the hidden chambers of the Temple Mount. Rahman saw Rachel register her understanding with a slight nod to Gunter. He also saw that Tirzah was confused—looking back and forth between her parents.

"What aren't you telling me?" she asked them.

Rachel rested her hand on Tirzah's shoulder and said, "Darling, we'll speak about this tomorrow morning. You know I've been feeling poorly all day. I need to rest."

"Yes." Rahman nodded. "We've all had a challenging day. After a good night's rest we'll be better able to face tomorrow."

"You most *definitely* need some rest, darling," Gunter said to Rachel. "You look quite spent. Right to bed with you!"

Rahman saw that Rachel's face was indeed flushed, and perspiration glowed on her forehead. She didn't look well. In his heart, he felt a gnawing apprehension.

✸ ✸ ✸

Oxford, England

As Lawrence and Woolley neared the railway station, they were confronted with a recruiting poster plastered to a large circular red mail drop.

"I think he's pointing at you, old boy." Lawrence nodded toward the arresting image of Kitchener, with blazing eyes and guardsman's mustache, his gloved hand pointing: YOUR COUNTRY NEEDS YOU.

Woolley shook his head. "No, he's clearly pointing at both of us—accusing us of not remaining in Oxford to endlessly tweak our report."

Lawrence laughed and asked, "When's our train for Paddington?"

"Half-seven."

Like most young Oxford men, their hair was brushed smartly to the side, and they wore rumpled trousers, white shirts open at the collar, and tweed jackets. And like most young Oxford men on this particular day, they were off to exchange one uniform for another.

"It's quite remarkable," Lawrence said as they took their place in the ticket queue. "Even before Kitchener's scolding, enlistment was brisk—thousands springing to arms with a positively medieval ardor."

Woolley sighed. "I'm already having second thoughts about taking a commission in the Royal Artillery."

"At least you'll get right into the action! I'm still smarting that the army wouldn't have me, slight and delicate as I am."

"As delicate as a mongoose . . ."

"No matter." Lawrence raised his shoulders. "Hogarth is certain they'll offer me a commission in MO-4, and I do hope it comes soon. I feel rather ill at ease with you and two of my brothers already enlisted—"

"MO-4 is exactly where you *should* be, Ned. It's where *I* should be as well."

"I'll put in a good word for you," Lawrence said as they reached the ticket booth. "I believe I pay this time."

"No you don't. You paid last trip. This one's on me."

They crossed back through the station to the platform where a great black locomotive idled, steaming and seething like a horse at the pickets. They boarded, found their compartment and settled in.

Woolley pulled a folded newspaper out of his jacket pocket.

"Any news?" asked Lawrence.

"More of the same—heavy fighting in Belgium."

"That's it? Just *Fighting in Belgium*? No details?"

"The censors are clearly hard at work," said Woolley. "It does leave a bit of a void, though, which is why they print so many rumors."

Such as?"

"Here, for example." Woolley leaned forward and read, "*All of Edinburgh is abuzz with stories of Russian troops, numbering in the thousands, who reportedly landed in Scotland on their way to reinforce the Allies in France. The Laird of Duddingston Manor claims that a division of the czar's army trampled his hedgerows. A railway porter at Waverly station insists that he worked for hours to sweep the platform clean of snow from their boots.*"

"Snow?" Lawrence laughed. "In August?"

"Or this one: *A Mrs. Crimmons of Hastings claims she saw two men walking along a bluff by the Channel. They had odd bulges in their coats and gave her evil glances, all the while speaking in a foreign tongue, which she believes was German, though she couldn't be certain.*"

A shrill conductor's whistle sounded, and the train lurched forward.

"I shouldn't wonder that there *will* be spies about," Woolley said. "The Germans know they'll need every advantage if they hope to win this."

"There will no *winning* this war, Lenny," Lawrence said as he turned from the window. "I can't see either side strong enough to overrun and occupy the other."

"The Germans seem to be rolling through Belgium—"

"For now, but mark my words—the war in Europe will soon become a stalemate. The *real* war will be in Arabia. That's what *I'm* up for!"

"What are you *thinking*, Ned? The Turks aren't even in this—"

"They will be. The Germans will make sure of it. We both saw their overtures to the Turks in Carchemish. It's as clear as the mustache on Kitchener's face. Kaiser Bill looks at the empires of his English and Russian cousins, and it drives him mad with envy. What does *he* have? Can you even name one German colony?"

"Sure. Cameroon."

"All right. Can you name another?"

Woolley screwed up his face in thought. "German East Africa?"

"That's my point. Germany has been pretty much out of the colonial game—landlocked and late to the table. Which is why I'm convinced that the German offensive in Europe is a distraction—"

"Are you *daft*? How can you say that the war in Europe is a *distraction*? As if they're not in earnest!"

"They're in *deadly* earnest! But for Germany, the real prize lies elsewhere."

"In *Arabia*?" Woolley asked derisively.

"Where else?"

"Oh, do come off it, Ned! If anything, Arabia will be a sideshow!"

"Don't be so quick to scoff—"

"The war is in Europe!"

"I grant you that the *battlefields* are now and will generally be in Europe. But after the fighting, the imperial feast will be purely colonial. *Really*! What bits of territory will change hands in Europe? But the Ottoman Empire is finished, and all of the Levant—from Mesopotamia to Palestine—will be up for grabs: If Germany wins, Kaiser Bill will grab it! If the Entente wins, they'll divide it up."

"Really, Ned!" Woolley stretched out in his seat and smiled. "Your oversimplification of this business is alarming."

"The truth is often simple, old boy. Do you think it was an accident that Kaiser Bill went off to Palestine a few years back and declared himself *King of Jerusalem*? Do you believe that the railway the Germans built from Berlin to Baghdad was a lark? My dear Leonard, it's no secret that every player in Europe has been salivating over the possibility of carving up the Ottoman Empire like some delicious

Christmas goose, just dripping with oil. *That's* where the real war will be—on the sands of Arabia, fighting over all that oil!"

"Your romance with the Levant is getting the better of you, Ned. Any fighting in Arabia will be a sideshow—a sideshow of a sideshow—nothing more."

"Think again, old boy—more likely, the next Crusade!"

CHAPTER 16

August 7, 1914
Cedar City, Utah

FOR CLIVE AND EVAN, the long summer days began before dawn. Through the night, the desert gave up its heat, and the morning wind that stirred the kitchen curtains was deliciously cool. Father and son sat together over breakfast, talking quietly about events in Europe, or baseball, or were silent and content to listen to the dawn chorus of the canyon wrens that nested in the eaves. To Clive's relief, there were no arguments, and to Evan's relief there were no tutorials. After cleaning up they parted ways for their respective places of work; Clive by automobile to Parowan Gap, and Evan by bicycle to Bob Pitney's filling station.

❀ ❀ ❀

Why the hell am I still here? Clive wondered as he drove through the high desert for another day of cataloging the Ute petroglyphs along the high canyons.

I certainly remember why we came—the dream of having a new baby in a new land. But that dream died with Janet and the baby . . .

The ribbon of blacktop stretched into the distance as he gripped the steering wheel and spoke to her as if she sat beside him in the motorcar. "I'm haunted by your absence, Janet. I can't find a place in the house where I don't see you, feel your presence. Is that a reason to stay or a good reason to leave? I also find myself holding onto Evan too tightly. He wants to stretch his wings—to be his own man—as he should."

Alone in the automobile, he began to sing "Brian Boru's March"—the few lines of the Gaelic he remembered. Stopping midway, he cursed, "Damn it! I promised Evan to write it down and completely forgot! I'll do it this evening . . ."

The sun rose over the shoulder of Mount Nebo—the beauty of the snowcapped triple peaks a refreshing distraction. *And the irony of this Mount Nebo—named for the original across the Jordan and north of the Dead Sea.* For the hundredth time he whispered in English, then Hebrew, the divine injunction to Moses, who had only glimpsed the Promised Land from Mount Nebo before dying there. "I have shown it to your eyes, and there you shall not pass." He breathed out a sigh, and said to Janet, "Your death ended that glimpse of our promised land, my darling, leaving me in this desolation."

Then, why are you still here? she asked, her voice in his mind.

"I made a commitment to the university for another year, and I enjoy working with the Ute guides. As I often told you, *Ute* means 'upper people' in their language—"

Indeed, she cut in. *You mentioned that very often—and they're called that since they've always lived in the high caves of the canyons.*

"There's also a quiet nobility about them, an aloofness . . ."

Like you? she asked.

He smiled at the memory. "You always did consider me aloof. Our friend Gunter had a good German word for that—*Luftmensch*—pretty much describes me and the Ute. Perhaps that's why I feel a kinship with them, why I've enjoyed working with them in the warm silence of the canyons, cataloguing the petroglyphs while they traverse the narrow ledges, clearing loose rock from the high cliffs."

So, what's changed?

"I've grown disenchanted."

Why?

"I can't find any meaning in the petroglyphs. I yearn for a language I can understand, a mystery I can solve. I need a key, but there is none. And the Ute understand no more of the cliff drawings than I do! It's as if they've been orphaned, cut off from their forebears by the unbroken silence of these undecipherable cliff drawings. For all the rocks they clear from the cliffs, there's no Rosetta stone to touch their ancestors."

He turned off the road at Parowan Gap, a deep notch in the hills surrounding Cedar Valley, the canyon walls still in shadow.

And what of my ancestors? He asked himself. *What of the Sinclairs of Rosslyn? What of Scotland?* He parked the Buick beneath a cloth canopy next to the shack that was his office. *My country is at war in Europe and I'm six thousand miles away studying meaningless cliff drawings.* He shook his head and shouldered his haversack.

"Why am I still here?"

❄ ❄ ❄

Evan rode into work on his bicycle as he considered that there were only a couple of days before he and Mike were supposed to leave for Moab. He also considered the fact that he didn't want to go. As the filling station came into view, an epiphany formed in his mind. *This is my chance to leave with no drama. Dad will think I'm just away on the two-week trip, and I'll tell Mike that Dad wouldn't let me go.*

Though he hadn't decided exactly where he would go when he left Cedar City, the opportunity was there, and as he coasted to a stop, he reminded himself to get his back pay from Bob. Wherever he was going, he'd need money.

After parking his bicycle in its usual place against the filling station's sidewall, he approached the office door, picked up the newspaper, and let himself in. He pulled the cord to turn on the ceiling fan, tossed the newspaper on the desk, and sat down, equally excited to check the baseball scores and to find out what was happening in Europe. He'd lost interest in the Mexican Revolution once it had become a civil war.

Looking at the National League standings, he saw the Giants were still in first place with a four and a half game lead over the Chicago Cubs. "Excellent!" he exclaimed to the empty room.

Through the open door he heard the sound of a motorcar rattling along the dirt road. Thinking it might be a customer, he stepped to the front window and watched a Model T pass by and disappear down the road.

As silence returned, he noticed a large bluebottle fly buzzing and tapping against the inside glass. Since no one bothered cleaning, a host of dead flies lined the windowsill, and those suspended in corner cobwebs moved like languorous marionettes in the slow breath of the ceiling fan.

He returned to the desk, anxious to read the latest installment about the rising tensions in Europe. Still standing, he turned the newspaper over to look at the front page.

GERMANY INVADES BELGIUM,

the headline screamed in bold three-inch letters. "Wow!" he whispered and scanned the lines below.

ENGLAND FORCED TO FIGHT,

and below that,

ALL CHANCE FOR SETTLEMENT OF GIGANTIC STRUGGLE ENDED BY DEVELOPMENTS OF TODAY.

"I shouldn't be surprised, but I am," he said aloud. "Everything over the summer led to this."

He looked up at the Prudential Insurance Company calendar tacked to the wall by the desk. Beneath the quiet gaze of the calendar girl with her sailor suit, pink cheeks, and Mona Lisa smile, he had marked the days with each of the rapid-fire events beginning with the assassination of Franz Ferdinand and his wife in Sarajevo.

Reaching up, he took down the calendar, then pulled open a desk drawer where he had saved the months of June and July. He placed them in order on the desktop and swept his eyes over his notes.

"So, how did we get from the day of the assassination on June 28 to here?" But he already knew the answer. "This spider-web of alliances, agreements, threats and ultimatums—it's managed to trap all these countries into this war!"

He blew out a breath as he squinted at his crowded notes filling the days of July into early August. Then, taking the newspaper, he scanned the bulletins beneath the headlines, jotting notes on August 4 and 5, speaking as he wrote. "Germany attacks Belgium, Austria-Hungary declares war on Russia, Serbia declares war on Germany, Montenegro declares war on Austria-Hungary, and England declares war on Germany."

He put down the pencil and stared at his crowded notations in slack-jawed amazement. "Gosh!" he whispered. "In one week, seven European countries are at war!"

Glancing again at the newspaper, two other bulletins caught his eye—one was a quotation of the British foreign secretary, Edward Grey, "The lamps are going out all over Europe. We shall not see them lit again in our time." The other was a short sentence: "The first members of the British Expeditionary Force are beginning to arrive in France." Placing an asterisk on August 5, he wrote them down along the bottom of the calendar.

He stood up and tacked the calendar back on the wall.

Turning, he looked out the window, but the sleepy quiet of early morning couldn't staunch the strange feelings that gripped his heart and made it hard for him to catch his breath.

Feeling dizzy, he sat down, leaned forward on his elbows, closed his eyes, and covered them with his hands. It seemed that every bit of news about the European war added another brushstroke to the portrait of a gathering storm. Staring into the darkness, he was at once horrified and excited by the emerging portrait of vast armies gathered beneath heavy clouds lit by lightning and ordinance—a dark and blasted landscape that mocked the bright warmth of summer— the image of a conflict already being called the "Great War for Civilization."

He opened his eyes, but the image remained. He could see it in the print of the newspaper, in the face of the calendar girl, in the gasoline pumps standing like sentinels beyond the window, and in the empty husks of dead flies swaying in the cobwebs.

The portrait was nearly complete.

The only detail missing was his own face.

CHAPTER 17

August 7, 1914
Pless, Silesia

MONTAGU WALKER had traveled with the kaiser from Berlin to what was already being called the Eastern Front. There, all was quiet—in stark contrast with the Western Front, where pitched battles raged throughout Belgium and Alsace.

At the kaiser's insistence, Walker attended all war briefings. Indeed, he accompanied the kaiser everywhere, having become a fixture in the royal entourage since the incident with Clarence Watson on Corfu.

This particular occasion was an inspirational speech to be delivered in the kaiser's honor by the eccentric Austrian, Guido von List. The title, "Superiority of the Ario-Germanic Nation," gave Walker a good idea what to expect.

The mess tent, cleared of tables, was filled with neat rows of chairs, and the canvas sides were raised in the warmth of late afternoon to admit a light breeze. Sunlight threaded through the branches of the surrounding pine forest.

When the kaiser was introduced, Walker, wearing a three-piece-suit, rose to his feet, applauding along with scores of German Army officers and enlisted men. The applause grew louder as the kaiser strode confidently into the tent, his shoulders bedecked with golden braid, his chest with shining medals. He wore a decorative *pickelhabe* similar to the spiked helmets worn by the half-dozen generals in his entourage, except that the kaiser's spike was larger than theirs.

As the applause continued, the kaiser took his place in the front row flanked by his generals. He acknowledged the acclamation with his right hand raised to the level of his spiked helmet, moving his hand slightly back and forth in what struck Walker as a distinctly papal gesture. After a minute, he waved his hand, and the adulation stopped.

As a protocol officer stepped to the lectern, Walker's thoughts turned to Clarence Watson. He felt no guilt about killing his old friend; his death, though regrettable, was a casualty of the war, and there were thousands of deaths every day—Watson's just happened to have been one of the first.

The protocol officer announced that the evening would begin with the kaiser's proclamation to his Eastern Army.

With resounding applause and cheering, Wilhelm strode to the lectern and signaled for silence. He then read his proclamation in a booming voice. "The spirit of the Lord has descended upon me because I am emperor of the Germans. I am His sword—the instrument of the Most High! Woe and death to all who resist my will! Woe and death to those who do not believe in my mission! Woe and death to the cowards! Let them perish with all enemies of the German people! God demands their destruction. Remember that you are a chosen people, and God, through my mouth, commands you to execute His will!"

Sustained applause followed, and the kaiser returned to his place of honor in the front row. He acknowledged the adulation with a bow and sat down.

The officer then introduced Guido von List. Walker found the recitation of List's avocations intriguing—playwright and champion rower, mountaineer and journalist, avid hiker and poet, high priest of Wotanism, and founder of the High Armanen Order.

After his introduction, List, who was of short stature, took his place next to the podium so as not to be hidden by it. His appearance, though diminutive, was striking—sharp eyes burning behind wire-rim spectacles, a huge bushy beard, and an even more exuberant moustache. A rebellious shock of gray hair was barely controlled by a jaunty black beret. Walker guessed he was in his late sixties.

The lecture began with List effusively thanking and praising the kaiser.

From where he sat, Walker had a side view of List and an excellent view of the kaiser. He watched Wilhelm nod his approval as von List completed his homage.

Walker knew enough German to understand List's opening remarks, but once the actual speech began, he was lost. Apart from unfamiliar vocabulary, List's explosive delivery was distracting. He spoke in torrential spasms, alternating between shouting and whispering, pleading and cajoling. Constantly in motion with manic energy, he strutted back and forth, arms swinging. On a few occasions, he stood ramrod straight with head back and arms at his sides, raging with his hands clawing the air, then suddenly bending his arms at the elbow with his fists clenched tightly beneath his bushy gray beard. One oft-repeated word was clear—*Übermensch*, which Walker knew meant "the superman."

A fool who struts and frets upon the stage! he thought as he watched List's gyrations.

Unable to understand much of the speech, Walker shifted his attention to the kaiser, studying his reactions to the histrionics. He noticed that the kaiser's face, like those of his generals, expressed rapt attention and agreement. But the kaiser reacted to some of List's more bizarre gesticulations and comic posturing with barely suppressed laughter. His generals, on the other hand, maintained fixed expressions of attentive respect.

Watching the kaiser, Walker felt a sense of camaraderie with his benefactor. *We're cut from the same cloth—he's as good a confidence man as I am . . .*

Once the lecture was over, Walker watched as the kaiser congratulated and spoke at some length with List. Finally, he stepped away, caught Walker's eye, and nodded toward the exit, where Walker met him.

"I've got to get out of here," the kaiser whispered though clenched teeth. "Come, let's enjoy an invigorating walk."

Leaving the mess tent, they made their way among the ordered white tents of the mountain encampment. The sun was nearly set, though the evening was still warm. Two of the kaiser's personal bodyguards followed at a discrete distance.

Once clear of the tents, the kaiser stopped and turned. "Have a cigar, my dear Walker—my own brand."

"Thank you, Your Excellency." He took one of the two cigars proffered by the kaiser and thought, *I can't get over his British accent— it's as if I'm speaking with an English king*! He studied the cigar band, sporting the likeness of a younger version of Wilhelm, bounded by gold braid and bold red and blue stripes. Neatly embossed red capital letters proclaimed, *WILHELM II KAISER*. Passing the cigar beneath his nose, Walker was genuinely impressed. "Lovely aroma, sire!"

"A Turkish blend." The kaiser bit off the tip and spat it out.

Walker produced a box of matches and lit the kaiser's cigar, then his own.

"So, how did you like our speaker?"

"Certainly compelling, but . . ." Walker shrugged.

"Don't judge the man by his appearance," Wilhelm murmured with a chuckle. "No one knows more about the wellsprings of German culture than List." He motioned with his cigar toward the west where purple clouds bannered the sky. "This way," he said and walked forward as he continued speaking. "His notion of Aryan racial and cultural superiority—Armanism, as he calls it—resonates with people of the Kaiserreich. Have you ever heard of the Aramanen Futhark?"

"I haven't, sire."

"It's the ancient language of our homeland."

"What homeland, Your Excellency? Bavaria, Prussia?"

"Neither. List contends that the *original* homeland of the Ario-Germanic people was further north—an island nation known as Thule, which disappeared thousands of years ago, like Atlantis. List knows much about Thule—he claims the Aramanen Futhark was the basis of their language—an alphabet, though far more than mere letters! Apparently, the Aryan priesthood of Thule used the Futhark's ancient symbols for divination and magical incantations, or so List believes . . ."

"What do *you* believe, Excellency?" Walker asked as they entered a pine grove.

"What do I believe? Do I believe that the Germanic people are superior to all other races? Do I believe that non-Aryans are fit only to be slaves? Do I believe in the code of racial purity that List espouses? Do I believe that List is insane?" The kaiser paused and turned to face Walker. He puffed on his cigar, the tip glowing a bright orange. "What I *personally* believe is of little consequence. What matters is what the *people* believe. And the people believe that List is a true prophet, a clairvoyant—able to conjure up a proud history and a powerful religion. Because of this, he is valuable to our purpose."

"How so, Your Excellency?"

"His notion of an Ario-Germanic Herrenrasse—this idea that we are a master race—is very useful. It will serve to motivate the masses in the difficult days ahead. Because of this, I have retained List as an adviser—my own personal Rasputin!" The kaiser chuckled at Walker's look of disbelief. "What is it, man? Should only my royal cousin, Alexandra, have *her* Rasputin and I be denied?" he laughed. "Besides, List has already proved his usefulness. It was *he* who urged me to acquire your services."

"He *did*?" Walker asked. "Does List consider me an Aryan?"

"He does, indeed."

"But, my liege, you know that I'm English."

"Don't be quick to scoff. In these matters, List is actually quite diligent, even scientific. Have you heard of phrenology?"

"No, Your Excellency."

"It's the study of the human skull. According to List, the very shape of the skull tells much about the nature of the man." Wilhelm stepped toward the cliff edge where several wooden benches were arrayed.

The overlook point offered a dramatic view of the western sky, the crimson clouds above a brooding forest. Flashes of light preceded the dull thud of artillery in the distance. The kaiser's two bodyguards emerged from the grove and stood, fidgeting by the trees, trying to look inconspicuous.

Wilhelm tossed down his cigar and crushed it out. "I suggest you do the same—there may be snipers about." He sat on a bench and motioned Walker to join him. "You've no doubt heard about the ancient human skulls recently discovered in Asia and Africa. Scientists use the shape of these skulls to determine the various species of ancient man. Like this, List uses phrenology to determine who is a member of the Herrenrasse. In this manner, he determined that you are of Aryan stock."

"But sire, he never saw me before today—"

"Not so, Walker! He and his scientists have studied your photographs for years."

"My photographs, Your Excellency?"

"Quite a few were taken during your troubles in Palestine. List is certain about your good standing as an Übermensch. Indeed, that's why you were chosen. Though it was your excavation in Jerusalem that brought you to *my* attention!"

"Please, sire. Don't remind me of that fiasco. I came away with nothing—"

"Tosh, tosh—I'll have none of it." Wilhelm waved away his

protestations. "You were the first European in seven hundred years to excavate the Temple Mount! Robinson, Warren, and all those vaunted British archaeologists with their permits and their academic airs—they nibbled away at the edges. But *you,* Walker—*you* had the gall to go straight for the heart of the Holy Mountain! Because of that brazen impudence, *you* are the single person on earth with firsthand knowledge of the caverns beneath the foundation stone."

"Granted, sire, but why is that important?"

"Why is that important?" The kaiser laughed. "Tell me, Walker, are you a member of the Church of England?"

"Nominally, I . . . I suppose I am . . ."

"And who is the head of the Anglican Church?"

"The King of England, sire—your royal cousin, George, the fifth of that name."

"And who was the first king to head the Church of England?"

"Henry VIII, sire. But what's that to the matter?"

"Just this—because Henry VIII would not be bound by the dictates of Roman Popery, my little cousin now sits at the head of the Anglican church." The kaiser placed his right hand over his chest. "I am the Holy Roman emperor of Germany! Why should I be shackled to Rome? Let the *pope* have Rome. Let my cousin *George* have London. *I'll* have another capital for my empire." Wilhelm turned his face to the lavender western sky and drew a deep breath. "*Jerusalem* will be my capital, Walker, and my palace will be built upon the holy mountain—the very spot you know so well."

"But, my liege, the Turks are masters of Jerusalem—"

"The Turks are masters of *nothing*!" the kaiser snapped. "They exist to serve *me*! So List assures me, and so I am wont to believe. The Turk, like the Arab, the Jew, the African, the Chinaman—they are all lower races—Üntermenschen—apelings! According to the precepts of Aramanism, I tolerate them only so long as they serve me. The time draws near when I will assume my place in the sun—on the throne of the Holy Germanic Empire in Jerusalem with all of Palestine and Arabia at my feet. And on that glorious day, the Übermenschen will serve me or cease to exist!"

For a moment, Walker was taken aback by the kaiser's outburst and said nothing. Indeed, he feared that the kaiser was just as unbalanced as List, perhaps more so. But he knew he must play along if he was to benefit from his position. And that called for flattery and pragmatic engagement. But mostly flattery.

"A *glorious* strategy, Your Excellency," Walker exclaimed. "However, it's well known that the British and French have their own designs in the region."

"That's fully expected and precisely why we must quickly win the war in Europe! By God, we don't seek to permanently occupy France, England, or any of our neighbors. However, we must have *leverage*. Let the British and French keep their lands and their colonies throughout Africa and the Far East. But when we prevail in Europe, the Turks will yield their empire to me! All the Holy Land will be mine—from the Nile to the Euphrates with an anointing of Arabian oil and the diadem of Jerusalem as my capital!"

"*Brilliant*, sire! And what role would you have me play to achieve this magnificent result?"

"I am sending thousands of advisers to the Ottomans—particularly to Palestine—under the guise of helping them. You will be among those advisers." The kaiser patted Walker's knee. "You were a military man. I know of your distinguished service in the Boer War. You will work with the Turkish military and see to it that neither the British nor French get so much as a toehold in the region. In particular, you will see to it that they never gain Jerusalem. In this you will be aided by List."

"But sire, I am told that List has never been to the Holy Land, while I have. How would he presume to aid me?"

"In two ways. First as a clairvoyant—you used one when you

plumbed the secrets of the Temple Mount, and List possesses such abilities. The second is this: List is aware of certain individuals who serve as *guardians* of the Temple Mount. These adepts foiled your efforts three years ago! They were unknown to you then, and they are unknown to you now. But with List's help you will find them!"

The kaiser put his arm around Walker's shoulder and drew him near. "List will convince these guardians to join our cause. In this manner we will unlock the secrets of the Temple Mount and secure Jerusalem as capital of a great German Reich, insuring our hegemony for a thousand years!"

"I rejoice in the chance to serve Your Majesty! When do I leave for Jerusalem?"

"Tomorrow. My staff will review all the details with you and List this evening, but one thing I will tell you is this: you'll be based at the hostel I established on the Mount of Olives in the name of my dear wife—the Kaiserin Augusta Victoria Hospice. From there you will oversee my interests throughout the region, especially in regard to Jerusalem's Temple Mount. Because, before I build my palace there, you will have the unique honor of excavating three thousand years of history. And you will not merely uncover history, Walker, you will make history!"

The kaiser smiled. "I will, of course, occasionally join in the work because, as you saw on Corfu, I very much enjoy the thrill of discovery, and this dig will be one of *unparalleled* discovery! Think of it! You will have all the time and resources you require to plumb the greatest secrets of the Temple Mount! We'll unlock unspeakable treasure and divine powers to serve the Großdeutsches Reich, and this time there will be nothing furtive about it. You will operate under my authority—the most powerful patron and ruler of the world, the Holy German Emperor and King of Jerusalem!

Walker found himself swept up in Wilhelm's grand vision. He

was on his feet, facing the kaiser, his heart pounding in his chest. In the fading evening light, he could see the kaiser's eyes shining as he continued speaking.

"War is a historic opportunity for bold action, Walker, an opportunity not to be missed! Here in Europe, I have no doubt that we will soon prevail. And when the Entente sues for an armistice, Jerusalem and the entire Near East will be firmly in my grasp."

Walker could scarcely believe his good fortune. After all the years of scraping by, he was now at the center of power. "I understand, sire, and I will do my utmost to fulfill my role."

"And you will have a *major* role, Walker. Guido von List has foreseen it."

CHAPTER 18

August 8–9, 1914
Cedar City, Utah

EVAN LEANED his bike against the side of the house after his last day of work. Stepping onto the front porch, he saw a piece of paper tacked to the doorjamb. He pulled it off and read, "Meeting in St. George after work. Don't wait for me to eat."

Good! He'll be gone for hours!

He went into the kitchen, his mind crowded with everything that needing doing before he could leave home early the next morning. He poured himself a glass of cold lemonade and took a drink.

He'd already received his back pay from Bob Pitney and left on good terms—with an open offer to work at the filling station once he returned from his trip to Moab, and whenever his college schedule allowed. But he knew that he wouldn't be going to Moab, and he wouldn't be going to college.

While he was relieved to have the ruse of the trip, he felt awful about it—ashamed of lying to his father and ashamed of lying to Mike about his father not letting him go. He was even ashamed of lying to Bob Pitney. But the opportunity of leaving without an ugly argument with his father was worth it—giving him about two weeks before his father would suspect anything.

He wandered into the living room and stared at the family photograph on the mantle. His mother stood between him and his father, beaming into the camera with steady eyes.

She wouldn't be happy with the way I'm leaving—she'd want me to at least leave a note with an explanation and an apology. And with Dad gone to St. George, I'll have plenty of time to do that.

He headed to his bedroom, rummaged through the closet and found a duffel bag. He stuffed in a blanket, his haversack, and a few changes of clothing. Dropping to his knees, he groped beneath the bed for his Balearic sling and the cigarette tin where he kept his money. He stood up and stuffed the sling into the duffel bag.

Glancing at his desk, he noticed his baseball glove resting on a thick tome of *The Works of Flavius Josephus*. For a second, he considered bringing both, but shook his head. *That's crazy—I won't need either—besides, I need to travel light.* Reaching out, he took his copy of *All Story Magazine* and put it in the duffel bag. *That qualifies as light reading.* He picked the cigarette tin off the floor and added the money he had just received from Bob Pitney.

Remembering that he didn't have a passport, he figured that he might be able to use his high school diploma for identification. He carefully folded it, took his French notebook off his desk and placed the diploma between its pages.

Now for that letter to Dad . . .

He took a pencil and, sitting on the edge of his bed with his French notebook, he thumbed past his notes to a clean page. He was about to begin writing when his breath caught at the sound of his father's motorcar in the front drive.

What the hell?

He dropped the notebook, pushed the duffel bag and cigarette tin under the bed, and darting into the living room, he grabbed a leather-bound copy of Pagninus' *Chaldean Lexicon* and sat on the divan just as his father stepped through the door.

"I'm glad to see you're reading something more edifying than *All Story Magazine!*" Clive said as he dropped his briefcase by the door.

"Have you already eaten?"

"No. I just got home." He put the book to the side and tried to steady his breathing. "What happened to your meeting in St. George?"

"Cancelled," Clive said as he went to the kitchen. "What do we have to eat?"

"There's some leftover macaroni and cheese in the icebox, and canned tuna in the pantry." Still trembling, Evan followed his father into the kitchen.

"Great! Get the tuna along with a can of green peas and a bag of potato crisps, and we'll have all the makings of your mother's signature tuna casserole."

Evan's mind was racing as he plied the can opener. *I'll get up real early and write the note before I leave . . .*

"When are you leaving with your friends to Moab and the Arches?"

"Early tomorrow morning."

"Will you be back in time for the start of the semester?"

"Sure! We'll only be gone for two weeks."

"What about your job at the service station?"

"Today was my last day."

Clive placed his hand on Evan's shoulder. "You've worked hard this summer, and you certainly deserve a break before school starts. Just promise me one thing . . ."

"What's that?" Evan asked, trying to sound natural.

"Don't kill any more cacti," Clive said and mussed up Evan's hair.

"I promise," Evan said as he struggled to tamp down feelings of guilt.

Over dinner, they spread out the pages of *The Deseret Evening News* and spoke of the war in Europe, the German advance into Belgium, the French mobilization, and the arrival of the first members of the British Expeditionary Force in France.

"I read that the BEF troops are buying their own tickets for the ferry across the English Channel," Evan said between forkfuls of tuna casserole. "Once they reach France, they go by train, motorcar, or by foot to Maubeuge—that's the BEF concentration point near the Belgian border."

Clive sighed. "It's strange, really, at this distance, watching this insane disaster slowly unfolding."

"Now that England's in the fray, will we be going back?"

"I hope the fray will end before we have to consider that. I suppose I haven't gotten past the unreal nature of it all yet. I'm still hoping to pick up tomorrow's newspaper and read how the old men of European governance will meet at a fine hotel in Zurich to settle this over brandy and cigars—"

"It's gone beyond that, Dad!" Evan said, raising his voice more than he intended.

"I know," Clive said and breathed out a sigh. "But as I read about the young men shipped off to the front, I keep thinking about Abraham's binding of Isaac—the careful preparations for the sacrifice—only these young men are being bound in Sam Browne belts and cross straps. "I'm still hoping Abraham hears a voice that stays his hand."

"This isn't some Biblical allegory, Dad!" Evan nearly shouted. "People are dying! Look at what Germany is doing to Belgium! Don't you think they'll do the same to France and England?" He was immediately sorry that he'd raised his voice. The last thing he wanted was to have an argument before he left.

"Do you really believe war is the answer?"

Evan shrugged, determined to control himself. "It doesn't matter what I believe or what you believe. We can talk about making a better world once Germany is defeated. That's what people are saying—that this can be the war to end all war."

"I'm sorry, son, but I'm a bit skeptical about that notion. This war, like *every* war is a war to end war, until the *next* war."

"Okay, Dad." He lifted the pitcher. "How about a cease-fire and more lemonade?"

❊   ❊   ❊

Evan awoke well before dawn. He lit a candle, and taking pencil and paper from his desk, he began to write.

Dear Dad,
By the time you read this, I'll be far away.
I know you wanted me to start college this fall, but the war in
Europe has given me another direction. After all, I am a British
subject, and thousands of Englishmen my age are choosing this
path. Great Britain didn't start this war, but we must put an
end to it. With our friends and allies under attack, we have no
choice but to come to their aid. I hope you'll understand my
decision.
*   I'll write as soon and as often as I'm able.*
*   Love, Evan*

He quietly dressed and slid the cigarette tin stuffed with money into the pocket of his trousers. Carefully holding the note to his father, he picked up his duffel bag, and with his free hand, took the candle to light his way to the living room. Once there, he placed the candle on the mantelpiece and put down the bag. He put the note in the center of the coffee table, where it would be easily seen. Then he picked up his bag, blew out the candle, and groped in the darkness for the front door. He eased it open, pushed the screen door, and quietly stepped onto the porch.

The night wind off the desert was cool on his face. He paused for a moment to look at the sky. The russet blush of sky over the Pine Valley Mountains heralded dawn though the western sky was still dark and bannered with stars.

He silently closed the front door, then eased the screen door closed and stepped off the porch. He began walking, his duffel bag over his shoulder.

When he reached the main road outside town, he kept walking—north to Salt Lake City—listening for the sound of automobiles from behind, hoping to hitch a ride. All the while, he found himself whistling "Brian Boru's March."

※　※　※

Clive awoke in the predawn darkness, thinking he had heard the sound of the front door closing. Realizing that Evan was leaving for Moab, he got up to say goodbye. Also, he'd written down the words he knew to "Brian Boru's March" and wanted to give it to Evan before he left.

He lit a candle and went to Evan's room. It was empty, the bed neatly made. He rushed to the front door and stepped out to the porch. "Evan!" he called out into the dark emptiness of the desert. "Evan!" he called again. But the only reply was the sound of the wind whistling through the dry saltbush. His candle guttered and went out.

He went back inside and closed the door.

He might have left a note, he thought and lit a lantern. He checked the living room, the kitchen, and Evan's room, but found nothing. Disappointed and saddened, he drew a deep breath and went back to bed.

Little did he know that when he had opened the front door, a gust of desert wind had lifted Evan's note off the living room table and delivered it into the darkness beneath the divan.

CHAPTER 19

August 12, 1914
Jerusalem

GUNTER STOOD at the front door watching Rahman B'shara roll up a pallet on the veranda while his ten-month-old son, Mahmoud, sat on a nearby blanket clapping his hands. From within the eaves, Gunter heard doves murmuring. He looked up at the sky, a delicate blue and pink iridescence framed by the dark silhouettes of roofs and domes. Morning was breaking over Jerusalem. He prayed that the cool morning air would ease Rachel's fever.

Within a few days of their arrival at B'shara's home in the Muslim Quarter of the Old City, Rachel had developed severe fatigue and fever. Suspecting that she was coming down with the flu, Fatima recommended that Tirzah be separated from her mother and moved into the guest room. Rachel would remain in the master bedroom where Fatima would attend her, wearing a cloth to cover her nose and mouth to avoid the contagion.

Gunter stepped away from the front door and went to check on Rachel. After putting on the face covering Fatima provided for him, he pushed open the bedroom door and peered into the half-light. The white muslin curtain over the window next to the bed swelled and moved in the morning breeze. As his eyes accommodated in the weak light, he saw that Rachel was sleeping, her breathing unlabored, her eyes lightly closed.

He went to the bedside. Looking down, he resisted the desire to smooth a strand of dark hair away from her forehead. She opened her eyes and smiled.

"Boker tov, my love," she whispered in Hebrew, her eyes shining.

"How are you feeling, darling?"

"Better. Where's Fatima?"

"Asleep on the cot at the foot of your bed."

"The poor dear was up half the night caring for me." She drew a deep breath and asked, "Who was that doctor who saw me yesterday?"

"Abraham Musayaf—an old friend of Rahman. He lives near the Nathansons in the new West Jerusalem Jewish neighborhood, Nachalat Shiv'a. He'll be back later this morning to look in on you."

"I had such an awful headache. What did he give me?"

"He calls it his special concoction—sodium salicylate, sodium bicarbonate, tincture of opium, and champagne—but it's mostly opium and champagne!"

"It certainly did the trick! I feel ever so much better." She lifted her head, then winced. "Mmm, my head still hurts. Perhaps I shouldn't get up yet."

"There's no reason to get up, darling. It's just past dawn. Go back to sleep. I'll check on you later."

He eased the bedroom door closed, took off his face covering, and went out to the veranda where Rahman stood, holding Mahmoud in his arms.

"Sabach il hir, ya sahbi," Rahman greeted him.

"Sabach il noor, Rahman! I still feel guilty that you're sleeping out here."

"If I'm still out here in December, *then* you can feel guilty. How's Rachel?"

"Much better. It's probably a bout of influenza—hopefully, a mild one."

"In'shala!" Rahman murmured and glanced uneasily at the lane below. "Let's go inside. We *know* the Germans are looking for *you*, and the Turks may soon be looking for *me*." Carrying Mahmoud, he led the way into the house. "Last evening I saw a group of Turkish recruits tied together like criminals. It looks like a general mobilization."

"But the Turks are still neutral—"

"For now, but when they do enter the war, it'll likely be with Germany."

"Why are you so sure?"

"Isn't it obvious? Jerusalem has been filling up with Germans for months—military personnel, bureaucrats, engineers . . . while British nationals are all but gone."

"But the Anglican Cathedral and the British Boys' School are still open."

"For now, but the Turks have been coercing the schoolboys to spy on their teachers and parents!"

"You're serious?" Gunter asked and followed Rahman into the kitchen.

Rahman nodded as he took a bowl of strained white leben from the icebox and put it on a tray. "Last week one of the boys told a Turkish constable about a *canon* in front of the altar in the Anglican Cathedral!"

"Some kind of prank?" Gunter asked as he poured black coffee from a brass decanter into two white porcelain cups.

"Part prank and part misunderstanding." Rahman carried Mahmoud into the front room and sat with him on the divan.

"But why on earth would the British have a cannon in the cathedral?"

"Canon with one 'n,' as in His Holiness, *Canon* Hitchens." Rahman laughed and placed a bib under Mahmoud's chin. "A squad of Turkish troops was dispatched with a team of workmen to look for the *cannon*."

"Please tell me you're joking."

"I wish I were! The workmen started digging with pickaxes and shovels in front of the altar to find the *cannon*, while Canon Hitchens was yelling, 'But, *I'm* the canon you're looking for!'"

Gunter threw back his head and laughed. "Did he manage to stop them?"

"No. The soldiers had their orders. They forced the workmen to continue digging until a government official arrived and—"

There was a knock at the door and Gunter shot to his feet. "It's Dr. Musayaf," he said after peeking through the curtain. Lifting the latch, he opened the door. "Good morning, Doctor. Please, come in."

"How's Rachel?" Musayaf asked as he removed his tan fedora, which matched his linen suite. In his late thirties, he was clean-shaven and his neatly trimmed, dark hair had a salting of gray. "Did she sleep well?"

"Thanks to you, yes. She seems much better this morning."

"Wonderful! Is she already awake?"

"She was earlier," said Gunter. "I'll check and be right back." He went to the bedroom door, knocked lightly and whispered, "Rachel? Fatima?"

When Fatima opened the door, Gunter whispered, "Good morning."

"You don't have to whisper, she's awake."

"I heard you had quite a night." He nodded toward the front room. "Dr. Musayaf would like to see her."

"Perfect timing—we just finished washing up."

Gunter returned to the front room. "Now is a good time, Doctor."

"Thank you." Musayaf took his black bag and turned down the hall.

Once he was gone, Gunter began to pace.

"You're as nervous as an expectant father," Rahman remarked over the edge of his cup. "I'm sure she's fine."

"I hope so!"

"Don't worry so much—you said she felt better."

"You're right. Besides, I'll know soon enough."

Dr. Musayaf's face was ashen as he stepped into the front room.

"What is it?" Gunter asked, finding it suddenly hard to breathe.

"She's developed a high fever with red spots in her mouth and on her tongue—"

"But I just saw her!"

"They must have just come up, along with the fever." Musayaf paused and said nothing for what seemed a long time before he spoke again. "It's smallpox."

"Oh, God!" Gunter crushed his eyes shut and breathed out his despair. Fixing Musayaf with his eyes, he asked, "Are you sure?"

"I'm afraid so. There have been a number of cases in the German Colony, and Rachel told me she's never had alastrim—"

"What's that?" Gunter asked, as a cold fear clawed at his chest.

"A case of mild smallpox that would have protected her. She also doesn't remember ever receiving calf lymph vaccine, and I can't find any vaccination scar—"

"Will she survive?" Gunter blurted out, almost pleading,

"I hope so." Musayaf placed his hand on Gunter's shoulder. "We'll know more within the next few hours." He paused and added, "I'll do everything in my power to help her and keep her comfortable."

"Thank you, Doctor." Gunter suddenly felt dizzy. He sank onto the divan and put his hands over his face. As he struggled to catch his breath, he heard Musayaf speaking.

" . . .and I'll inform the Turkish sanitary authorities—"

"Please don't!"

"I'm sorry. I'm required to notify the sanitary authorities about every new case."

"But they'll send her to the pest-house!"

"No, they won't!" Musayaf replied firmly. "She'll remain here under quarantine, and Fatima will tend to her since she had cowpox five years ago and is protected."

Mahmoud began to cry. Rahman stood up, put him over his shoulder and began to pace as he patted him on the back.

Musayaf's eyes moved between Gunter and Rahman "I need to know if anyone else has been in contact with Rachel in the last two days."

Gunter exhaled a trembling breath. "I looked in on her this morning, but I wore a face mask and didn't touch her."

"You'll also need to be quarantined." Musayaf turned his eyes to Rahman. "What about you? Have you been in direct contact with Rachel or Fatima?"

"Not with Rachel for days, and not with Fatima since she started caring for Rachel yesterday." He raised his shoulders and added, "We thought it best to avoid contact if Rachel had influenza since I'm taking care of this guy." He nodded at Mahmoud in his arms.

"That's good. Continue to avoid all contact with Fatima. Anyone else?"

"Our daughter, Tirzah," said Gunter. "We've kept her away from Rachel for the last two days."

"How old is she?"

"Fourteen."

"Alright, then." Musayaf said and drew a deep breath. "This is what we need to do: I'll inform the Turkish sanitary authorities, then I'll return here to look in on Rachel."

"What will you be looking for?" asked Gunter.

"Are you sure you want to hear?"

Despite a growing sense of dread, Gunter nodded.

"I'll be checking to see if the spots in Rachel's mouth will have grown into small blisters filled with fluid. If they have, we'll see if the blisters spread to her face, arms and legs, hands and feet. Most importantly, we'll see if her fever goes down as the rash spreads . . . or not."

"And, if the fever doesn't go down—what then?"

"Then it won't bode well for her. In the meantime, you should cover all windows and lights in her room with red cloth—so the smallpox rash won't scar."

"When will you know if she'll be alright?"

"By tomorrow." Musayaf picked up his black bag and, looking from Rahman to Gunter, added, "When I return to check on Rachel, I'll administer calf lymph vaccine to all of you."

"But you said that Fatima is already protected," said Rahman.

"Protection from smallpox by having had cowpox is almost absolute for about three years, but then decreases. Since she had cowpox about five years ago, I'll give her the calf lymph vaccine just to make sure." He looked at Gunter and said, "Once I inform the Turkish sanitary authorities, they'll place a perimeter around the house—"

"A what?" asked Gunter.

"A perimeter—to establish the quarantine. So no unauthorized person might enter."

"Or leave?" asked Gunter.

"Or leave," Musayaf replied. "We've established that Fatima is at low risk of becoming infected, so she'll stay here to care for Rachel. Now, about the rest of you . . ."

"Don't we all have to remain here?" asked Gunter.

"No. It's early enough in the incubation period for everyone else to be placed in isolation elsewhere for eighteen days."

"I want to stay here with Rachel," said Gunter.

"I thought you would." Musayaf nodded. "But you must have no contact with her as long as she's ill."

"Will I be able to speak with her?"

"Of course. But only with a face covering and from a distance of about six feet."

"And what about our daughter, Tirzah?"

"She'll require eighteen days of isolation and quarantine. That can be provided at the Italian Hospital that's being built in West Jerusalem. Even though it's unfinished, there's a wing of rooms we use for isolation and observation. I'll arrange a room for her there, and if she's okay by the end of the eighteen-day incubation period, isolation ends."

"And once she's out of isolation, where can she go?" asked Gunter. "I assume she won't be permitted to come back here."

"Correct. The quarantine here will be in place for a full month. She'll have to stay elsewhere for a week or so—perhaps with the Nathansons?"

"Could you speak with them on our behalf?"

"Of course." Musayaf turned to Rahman and continued, "About Mahmoud, the situation is more complicated . . ."

As the doctor spoke to Rahman about issues of feeding, isolation, and quarantine as they related to ten-month-old Mahmoud, Gunter's thoughts returned to Rachel. Even though Musayaf had mentioned the quarantine restricting any movement in or out of the house, Gunter believed that, somehow, he would be able to access the healing power of the Temple Mount on Rachel's behalf. But he wasn't sure when or how.

"Gunter?"

"Yes?" He felt Musayaf's hand on his arm and realized he was speaking to him.

"I was just saying that you should make sure that Tirzah packs a bag with everything she'll require for the few weeks she'll be in isolation and observation."

"Of course." Gunter nodded.

"Good," Musayhaf said and placed his hand on Gunter's shoulder. "I'll do everything I can for Rachel, but I know this will be a terribly difficult and frightening time, and my heart goes out to you."

CHAPTER 20

August 16, 1914

Mediterranean Sea

Off the coast of Palestine

MONTAGU WALKER leaned against the iron railing of the cruiser's foredeck, watching the prow cleave a path through the water toward Jaffa harbor. Time had not eased the bitter pang of frustration after his escape three years before—his glorious quest for treasure reduced to a frantic scramble to survive. But now he was back, and this time would be different—because with the full support of Kaiser Wilhelm, he wouldn't have to bribe corrupt bureaucrats. His heart raced in anticipation of serving the kaiser and excavating the Temple Mount.

Facing into the wind, he could see the breathing tide etched in white lines of breakwater as they neared land. Along the shore, he could make out the low pink limestone buildings of Jaffa, and beyond the grey haze shrouding the horizon, the ramparts of the Judean hills mounted upward to Jerusalem.

His reverie was interrupted by Guido von List, who appeared like an apparition at his side, sunlight glinting off his wire-rimmed spectacles, the wind stirring his wild beard. "We'll have lunch in Jaffa, Herr Walker?" he asked in heavily accented English.

"Yes, Herr von List, and dinner tomorrow in Jerusalem!" Walker shouted to be heard over the drumming of the ship's engines.

"It is a long journey?"

"We'll set out tomorrow morning by carriage or motorcar. The ascent through the mountains will require the better part of a day."

"And the accommodations the kaiser has made for us . . . they are satisfactory?"

"The Augusta Victoria is well beyond satisfactory—a hostel with the most modern appointments and luxurious amenities. It was almost completed when I was here three years ago. It sits on the Mount of Olives with spectacular views of the Old City. I assure you, Herr von List, you'll not be disappointed."

"You have many acquaintances from your previous sojourn in Jerusalem?"

"Not really, since the circumstances of my departure were . . . unfortunate."

"*Unfortunate?*" List gave a little laugh. "Is that how you describe your departure? You were nearly lynched! I certainly hope our current sojourn will be more dignified and successful."

"As long as we don't inflame the local population—"

"Don't presume to lecture me about the *local population*," List said sharply. "The sooner we establish ourselves as their masters, the better. These apelings must be made to comprehend that they exist to serve us. Only their service to the kaiser guarantees our beneficence toward them. They must have no illusions in this regard—because when the kaiser rules his empire from Jerusalem, this manner of dealing with the *local population* will be the coin of the realm."

"I understand, Herr von List," Walker replied, choosing to be agreeable, though he silently considered that List had no idea of the firestorm that could be ignited by insulting the Arabs' religious sensibilities. He smiled at the old man—wondering if List would live long enough to witness the kaiser's vision—a vastly expanded Holy Roman Empire ruled from Jerusalem. He couldn't believe that the kaiser would entrust the securing of Jerusalem to one so old and frail as List. He knew there had to be a contingency plan. He wondered what it was and who else was involved.

"It would appear that our mission is of some importance," he began smoothly.

"That, my dear boy, is an understatement."

"Given this, has the kaiser not seen fit to bolster our numbers, or does the entire enterprise rest upon our shoulders?"

"Be assured, Herr Walker. With prudent foresight, Kaiser Wilhelm has enlisted the counsel of others. For one, there is Jorg Lanz von Liebenfels, a wise gentleman of rich experience, who may assist us in the future."

Walker was intrigued. "Who's Liebenfels?"

"Up until a few years ago, he was a Cistercian monk, extensively schooled in the Scriptures and all doctrines of Orthodox Catholicism."

"But is this not diametrically opposed to everything you believe?"

"That's what Liebenfels *was*," List said sharply. "He has long come to understand the supremacy of the Aryan people among the nations of the world. Indeed, he was one of the two founding members of the Order of the New Templars—*Ordo Novi Templi*—dedicated to reclaiming Aryan racial purity and our rightful dominance in the world."

"New Templars? But, Herr von List, the Knights Templar were devoutly Catholic. Does Liebenfels cling to vestiges of Catholicism?"

"Not at all. He views the Aryan as God's chosen race, with Christ as the embodiment of Aryan perfection in human form. As for the Templars, he replaced their religious code with a pure Aryan priesthood."

"And how will he support our activities in Jerusalem?" Walker asked.

"We will discuss that if and when the need arises." List snapped. "For the present, understand that Liebenfels is not my equal, he's my disciple."

"I see, and if I may ask one more question . . . you mentioned that Liebenfels was one of *two* founders of the Order of the New Templars. Who was the second? You?"

"Perhaps. Perhaps not." List raised his heavy eyebrows and smirked. "We should prepare to disembark."

❁ ❁ ❁

Jerusalem

Fatima peered at Gunter through the half-opened bedroom door. "Rachel does not wish for you to see her like this." Her voice, faint and ragged with fatigue, was edged with sadness. "It is better that you do not come in."

"I must see her," Gunter whispered, insistent.

She raised her lantern and saw that Gunter's cheeks above his cloth face covering were streaked with tears. As Dr. Musayaf had suggested, the lantern was wrapped in red cloth and cast a dull red light so that the smallpox would not pit and scar. But Fatima knew that Rachel was beyond such concerns. She knew Rachel was dying.

Only three days had passed since the first lesions had appeared on her forehead and hands, but they had quickly spread and coalesced with swelling and hemorrhaging into the skin, the mouth, and the throat with the spitting up of blood—the appalling pestilence exploring Rachel's form, claiming her.

Dr. Musayaf had told Fatima that nothing could be done to stop it. He could only name it—purpura variolosa, black smallpox.

Musayaf also provided nostrums to make Rachel comfortable

along with the gentle bathing of the face and eyes with boracic lotion, the application of thin linseed poultices covered with Vaseline, and the use of cooling ice—so scarce in the heat of a Jerusalem summer. But despite all this, Rachel was dying, and she knew it.

Fatima wished that Rachel might be spared that terrible knowledge, but Dr. Musayaf had said that despite the severe incapacitation and disfigurement, the mind remained clear to the end.

Fatima heard the rough staccato of Rachel's coughing and her heart clenched. She so wanted to weave Rachel a comforting invention of hope, of recovery, but she couldn't. Because from black smallpox no one recovers.

"Please, Fatima, allow me to speak with her!" Gunter pleaded at the door.

"Of course, Gunter." Her voice softened. "I'll take the lantern with me and leave the room in darkness as Rachel prefers. You may stand in the doorway and speak with her. Take all the time you need," she whispered and disappeared down the hall.

※　※　※

"Rachel?" Gunter called softly from the doorway. "Rachel?"

"Yes, my love." Her voice, a faint whisper in the darkness. "I would that you take my hand, but you mustn't. Promise me you won't come in . . ."

"I promise," he said and leaned against the doorjamb, listening to her labored breathing, and her voice speaking out of the darkness.

"I was dreaming just now. I was with our little Tirzah in the garden by the tree in the front yard. It was morning, but not early—the sun peaking over the garden wall—warm and golden, though the air was still cool, and so sweet, with that smell of the sleeping earth and the pine trees in the morning, and the smooth stones you painted white, and Tirzah placed to border the garden all around, and so many butterflies . . ."

"Was I there with you—in the garden?" Gunter fought to control his voice.

"Oh, yes, my darling!" she said and exhaled a short laugh. "You were working at your desk and got up. You pushed open the window casements to lean out, smiling and watching us in the morning." Rachel paused, breathing deeply. "Tirzah was picking tomatoes for our breakfast. It was like a treasure hunt— our little girl among the butterflies." She paused again, then asked, "Tell me, my husband, is it morning now?"

"No, my love, it is night."

"When will morning come?"

"Some hours from now," Gunter said, knowing that the time to access the healing power of the Temple would come with dawn. But he also knew that Turkish guards maintained the quarantine around the house and patrolled the Kidron Valley. Nonetheless, he hoped to convince Rachel to try, to allow him to help her reach the portal, to enter and be healed. He began by asking, "How is it with you, my love?"

"I'm tired, but there's no pain. The nostrums and Fatima's care are a great help."

He continued urgently in a hushed voice. "Listen well to me now, my love. We might get past the sanitary authority guard, and then to the portal. It's the only way—"

"No," she cut him off. "You know that this is not why the portal exists!"

Gunter shut his eyes against the tears. "Please reconsider. Let me bring you—"

"No," she said, her voice sharp, splitting the darkness. Then, softly, "I beg you, darling, leave off from speaking thus. I am an adept no less than you. I would not risk our calling for this—to strive to save my life only to reveal the portal? We are sworn to guard it, to protect it! Therefore, speak no more of it. Besides, I will be there soon enough."

"But, what of Tirzah?"

"I leave her to your keeping." She paused and drew a deep breath. "Now I will sleep, perhaps to dream. I should like that—to dream of us in the garden, in the morning."

CHAPTER 21

August 17, 1914
New York City

AS EVAN STEPPED off the train at Grand Central Terminal, the heat hit him first, then the noise. Both were oppressive. But he didn't care. Intoxicated by the sweep of his journey, he couldn't stop smiling.

With his duffel bag over his shoulder, he made his way through tall doors of bright brass into a cathedral of tiled archways and acres of polished marble floors. Standing beneath a vaulted ceiling painted like the evening sky, he looked up, turning round and round as he gazed at gilded stars and constellations, all the while buffeted by passersby—rushing past him in every direction.

"Wow! The Salt Lake City train station didn't look anything like this!" he shouted to no one in particular. "Wait a minute! Somebody made a mistake!" He pointed upward. "Look! Taurus and Gemini are on the wrong side of Orion—they're reversed!"

He lowered his gaze to the human tide that continued to flow swiftly about him like a raging river around a boulder. *I need to find a steamer for Europe,* he thought and searched the huge hall for an exit. *But first, I've got to get out of this train station!* He spotted a booth about fifty yards away crowned by a glowing brass clock. Beneath it, and also glowing, was the word INFORMATION.

He wove through the crowd, and reaching the booth, was surprised to see it occupied by a pretty young woman who appeared to be about his age. She was unlike any young woman he had ever seen in Utah. Sporting a sailor blouse with striped collar and black tie, her hair was loosely pulled into a soft bun at the back of her head, and she wore a monocle as she read a newspaper. But apart from the monocle, there was something familiar about her.

Of course! She looks like the Prudential Insurance calendar girl at the filling station!

She looked up, took off the monocle and smiled.

"Excuse me, miss . . ." he began.

"I can't hear you." She pointed to the electric fan beside her. "It makes a lot of noise, but it's as hot as heck in here—you'll have to speak up."

He stepped closer and asked, "Could you tell me how I can get out of here?"

"Out of *where?*"

"Out of this train station."

"*Train station?*" she laughed. "This is the Grand Central Terminal, and it's not called 'grand' for nothing!" She waved her hand. "This is only a small part of it."

"There's more?"

"And how! There are multiple levels with museums, restaurants, exhibitions, stores, an emergency hospital, an art gallery—even a movie theater." She smiled at him. "It's just dilly!"

He'd never heard the word *dilly* before, but figured it meant good.

"Do you really want to beat it?" she asked.

"What?" he leaned forward, unsure what she was asking.

"To skidoo . . . to leave?"

"Yes. I'm afraid so," he said and wondered when she got off work. She pouted. "You're not from around here, are you?"

"Is it that obvious?"

She wrinkled her nose and nodded.

"I'm originally from England, more recently from Utah—"

"Wow! I'd like to get an earful about that!"

He decided to ask. "When do you get off work?"

She raised her shoulders. "I kind of have a boyfriend . . . he's a simp, but still . . ."

"I understand." He took a breath. "So . . . how do I leave Grand Central Terminal? How do I *skidoo*?"

She laughed. "You'll find an exit over there. That leads out to 42nd Street." She leaned forward and added, "But . . . things change, so the next time you come this way, stop by and see me . . ."

"I will. Thanks!"

Evan shouldered his duffel bag, turned and made his way across the pink marble floor that sloped gently upward toward a wide arched doorway leading out of the terminal. As he neared the exit, he caught sight of a stand selling penny postcards and stamps.

Swell! I'll let Dad know where I am!

He looked over the available postcards, found one of the terminal's exterior, and bought it along with a green one-cent stamp. He began writing.

Dear Dad,

As you can see, I'm at Grand Central Terminal in New York— quite different from the train station in Salt Lake City! Sorry about leaving the way I did, but as I wrote in the note I left, I'm British and I can't be neutral about this war. Maybe the US can, but I can't. Once I get across the Atlantic, I'll write again.

Love,

Evan.

He dropped the postcard into a large brass mailbox set in the wall by the booth. Leaving the main concourse, he felt a surge of joy at having reached New York City. He found himself whistling "Brian Boru's March" as he passed into an adjacent hall illuminated by five huge chandeliers hanging from the high ceiling. Crossing that hall and still whistling, he left the terminal.

It was just as hot and noisy outside. Shielding his eyes against the sun's glare, he felt overwhelmed by the raw clatter of automobiles with blaring horns moving in a jagged torrent past the terminal. Among them were horse-drawn lorries that rattled by with the sharp clack of hooves on the gray concrete. Dark warehouses rose like a canyon wall, bordering the far side of 42nd Street, shouldering each other against a hazy sky.

Turning back, he looked up at the imposing facade of the terminal; Doric columns soaring upward in bas-relief beneath a massive pediment high above the street where a huge clock bounded by classic statuary announced the time as eleven thirty-five.

Whistling, he started down the street, duffle bag over his shoulder, head swiveling back and forth, he took in the barrage of sights and sounds. After a few minutes, he took off his fedora and wiped the sweat away from his eyes. He saw that the row of warehouses gave way to a ramshackle livery stable, and past that was a smoky huddle of shacks with cooking fires in what looked like a squatter's shantytown where goats grazed on tufts of dry grass. Then he froze. Looming high above the shacks was an impossibly tall and elegant building.

He stopped whistling as his jaw went slack. "Wow! How did they build *that*?"

He remembered the sheer canyon walls of his father's excavation site at Parowan Gap, and as he thought of his father, he was happy he'd sent the postcard and less guilty about how he had left. He resumed walking and whistling.

"Hey, you!" a man shouted from a stand selling soda water shaded by striped awning. "A pleasant tune you're whistling—know what it is?"

"I do," Evan said as he approached the stand. "'Brian Boru's March.'"

"So, you're Irish?"

"Scottish, actually."

"That's odd," said the man, scratching the stubble on his cheek with dirt-lined fingernails. "It's an Irish tune, but I suppose others enjoy it as well." He raised a glass. "How about we wet that whistle of yours with a nice cold drink? For two cents p lain?"

"Sure." Evan put down his bag and dug into his pocket. He picked out a worn Indian head cent and a shiny new Lincoln penny. "Are you from Ireland?" he asked.

"Indeed, I am," the man replied as he handed Evan a glass of soda water. "Came here for the work, though not *this* work." He pointed up at the tall building. "*That* work—the Met Life Tower. I helped build it till I hurt my leg and was cast out of heaven."

"It's safer here on earth, though," Evan said, holding the cold glass in his hand.

"Heaven paid better." The man wiped down the counter with a grimy rag and squinted at Evan. "You lookin' for work?"

"I am—as long as it's on a ship sailing for Europe."

"Are you *daft*? There's a *war* over there!"

"That's why I need to get back. I'm a citizen of England as well as a Scot."

"You don't sound Scottish, or English for that matter."

"Lost whatever accent I had after a few years here." Evan tilted the glass to his mouth, draining it in a few swallows. "May I have another, please?"

"Sure, son—and I'll throw in some lemon squash for free!"

"Thanks!" He slapped another two cents on the wooden counter.

"So, how is it that a Scottish lad came to know 'Brian Boru's March'?"

"It's a tune my father used to whistle. I also remember him singing it to put me to sleep when I was small."

"I love that tune," said the man. "Reminds me of home!"

"Why did you leave?"

"The mines closed. I came here like so many others—to seek my *fortune*!"

Evan felt a wave of sadness for him—far from home, injured and scraping by. "Could you write down the words for me in Gaelic and English?"

"Sure! Happy to do it!"

Evan put a shiny silver dime on the counter.

The man shook his head. "That's not necessary—"

"I insist."

"Alright, but in the bargain, you'll get another glass with lemon squash."

"It's a deal!" Evan gave him paper and pencil from his haversack, and enjoyed the cold drink while he watched the Irishman write as he sang quietly to himself.

"There you are! All done! Though I can't vouch for the spelling—not the Gaelic nor the English. But you'll be able to sing it to your *wee bairn*, as you Scots say!"

"When I have one!" Evan laughed. "Can you give me directions to the docks?"

"Still determined, are you?"

"I am."

The Irishman pointed. "Go cross-town west on 42nd Street—two, three blocks. Watch for the new library—beautiful building on your left, big lions, very impressive. Then head toward the 6th Avenue El—"

"The El?"

"Yeah, you know, the El—as in the *elevated railroad!* You take the 6th Avenue El downtown—five, six stops. Get off at 9th Street. From there you can walk to pier 39. That's where you'll find a steamer for Europe."

"Pier 39. Thanks, mister." Evan reached out and shook his hand. "Thanks for everything!" He heaved the duffel bag over his shoulder.

"Good luck to you, stócach! May the war be over before you get there!"

"I sure hope so," Evan said as headed down the street.

But he didn't mean it.

CHAPTER 22

August 24, 1914
Cedar City, Utah

CLIVE SLOWED to a stop beside an old picket fence, cut the motor and looked past a clutter of broken farm tools and rusting oilcans at the ramshackle house of Evan's friend, Mike Cope. As the motor rattled into silence, he could hear cicadas singing in the electric heat.

Evan had been gone for over two weeks.

Clive had hoped he would have been home before his seventeenth birthday on August 22, but that day had passed.

As he had done for the past few days, he'd left work early and been to the house. But Evan wasn't there—only the festively wrapped birthday gifts unopened on the living room table, and the cake Clive had purchased already stale. Confused and worried, he'd driven over to Mike's house to inquire.

Pulling a handkerchief from his breast pocket, he wiped the perspiration from his forehead and stepped out of the automobile. He walked up the dusty path to the front porch and knocked.

"Why, Professor Sinclair, how very good to see you!" Mike's mother smiled as she dried her hands on her apron.

"Good afternoon, Mrs. Cope." He touched the brim of his fedora. "Do you know when the boys are coming back home?" As he asked the question, he saw a cloud of apprehension pass over her face.

"But, Professor Sinclair, Mike came back two days ago."

Clive's breath caught. "Could . . . could I speak with him?"

"Certainly," she frowned. "I hope Mike hasn't done anything wrong . . ."

"No—nothing like that. I just need to ask him about Evan."

"Well, land sakes! You come right in and have a nice cold glass of lemonade. Mike's still asleep—all tuckered out since he got back, but it's high time he was up—been sleeping the better part of the day." She disappeared into the kitchen, then quickly returned and handed Clive a glass. "I'll go roust him."

The glass was cold, water beading down the sides. He held it against his forehead, feeling the coolness as his mind raced. *Where the hell is he? Did he decide to stay away for a few more days?*

"Hi, Professor Sinclair." Mike mumbled as he was prodded into the front room, blinking against the light, he'd clearly slept in his rumpled undershirt and blue jeans.

Mrs. Cope patted down her son's curly hair. "You have a nice talk with Professor Sinclair while I fix you some breakfast—or should I say lunch?"

Once she disappeared into the kitchen, Clive asked, "Do you know why I'm here?"

"Something to do with Evan?"

"Yes. Your mom says you got back two days ago, but he hasn't come home yet."

"What?" Mike's jaw dropped. "But, sir . . . he never came with us."

"He . . . *what*?" Clive couldn't believe his ears. "He wasn't with you on the trip?"

"No, sir. He told us you wouldn't let him go."

Clive's heart began to pound, and his hand shook as he put down the glass. "Evan left over two weeks ago Mike. I haven't seen him since."

"Gosh."

Clive took a deep breath. "Any idea where he might have gone? Any idea at all?"

"No . . . no, sir. I'm sorry . . ."

"Listen, Mike—if you hear anything, anything at all, you let me know, okay?"

"Sure, Professor Sinclair, sure. Gee, I'm sorry . . ."

As he opened the front door, Clive half turned and called, "Goodbye, Mrs. Cope. Thanks for the drink."

"You're more than welcome, Professor!" she called from the kitchen. "I hope we see Evan soon—such a fine boy!"

Clive got back into the motorcar. As a mounting fear gripped his heart, he asked himself, *Where could he be?* He tried to think what to do next. *Bob Pitney might know something!* He pressed the ignition button.

At the filling station, he was greeted by a pair of legs and scuffed brown boots extending out from beneath a shiny black car parked in the work bay.

"Be with you in a minute," a voice floated out from under the car.

"Bob, is that you under there?"

Pitney slid out from beneath the automobile, shielding his eyes, his overalls smeared with grease. "Hi, Perfesser Sinclair. How 'bout this automobile, huh? Ain't she a beauty?" Pitney climbed to his feet, smearing the black grease around on his hands with a greasy cloth. "This here's a brand-new Pierce-Arrow. Got *everything*—rear fuel tank, wire wheels, 'lectric starter—"

"Bob," Clive cut in sharply. "I need to ask you about Evan."

"He back already?" asked Pitney still looking adoringly at the Pierce-Arrow. "I bet he had a good ol' time at Moab and the Arches."

"Actually, he didn't go! I don't know *where* he went. That's why I need to talk to you. He's been gone over two weeks."

"Damn, if that don't beat all. Any idea where he went?"

"No, but did he say anything to you? Anything at all?"

"Not really," replied Pitney, shaking his head. "Just told me that he was goin' camping with his friends and wouldn't be back to work. I paid out his wage and that was that. He was a good boy, a good worker. Always on time."

"What about *before*? Do you remember *anything* unusual he may have said?"

"Well, let me study on that," Pitney muttered as he scratched the stubble on his face. "But it's hotter than hell and half of Georgia out here, Perfesser. Let's go inside—got a fan and an icebox in there. You wanna cold root beer?"

"Sure," answered Clive. It was damned hot, though the fear filling his chest was as cold as ice.

Once in the office, Pitney bent and reached into a dusty icebox in the corner. "Can't say that I recall Evan saying anything unusual. You know he was quiet-like, not much of a talker." Pitney pried the cap off two bottles and handed one to Clive.

Pitney took a drink, then sighed and stared at the desk. "When he wasn't out there with customers, he'd be sittin' right here with his nose in the newspaper. Readin'—all the time, readin'—'bout that war over there in Europe . . ."

As Pitney's voice droned on, Clive glanced at a calendar that hung on the wall over the desk. Looking closer, he saw cramped notes crowding the boxes through the first few days of August. *That's Evan's writing!* he thought and squinted through his spectacles. Along the bottom of the calendar, Evan had written a quotation that Clive had seen in the newspaper at the start of the war; *The lamps are going out all over Europe. We shall not see them lit again in our time.*

He saw that the last entry was on August 7, ending with the words, *British Expeditionary Force arrives in France.* He took a long swig of the root beer, draining half the bottle. *August 7 was just before he left! We had dinner together that night, and Evan mentioned something about the British Expeditionary Force buying their own tickets to cross the Channel, to reach the concentration point in France.* He heard Pitney's voice droning on.

" . . . come to think of it, that's all he seemed to talk about—that war in Europe."

That must be it. The thought exploded in Clive's brain. *He's probably already crossed the Atlantic and joined the British Expeditionary Force in France!* Feelings of helpless rage welled up in his chest. He took deep breaths and felt lightheaded.

Pitney spoke. "That's all I remember him talkin' about, Perfesser— the war, or as he called it—*the Great War for Civilization.*" Pitney burped and stood up. "Sorry I can't help ya."

"But you have, Bob. Thanks for the cold drink, and thanks for telling me *exactly* where Evan went."

"You mean . . ."

"Yes, Bob. He's gone to fight in the Great War for Civilization."

❋ ❋ ❋

Driving back to the house, Clive thought about all that needed doing before he could leave for Europe. *First thing is to contact anyone who can help me find Evan—anyone with connections in the War Office. Of course! David Hogarth and Ned Lawrence. I'll wire them now!*

He jerked the steering wheel around, scattering gravel and raising a cloud of dust as he turned and headed back into town, his mind churning with a growing mental inventory as he made plans to leave.

Afterward, I'll go to the university—they'll need to cover my classes and get word to the Ute that I won't be continuing the survey. Because, despite my misgivings about the war, my place is in England—especially with Evan over there.

Stopping at the telegraph office, he stepped out of the automobile and pushed the door closed. Once inside, he took the nub of a pencil, and standing at a worn wooden counter, jotted out a few words to his colleague and friend, David Hogarth.

EVAN'S GONE OFF TO WAR STOP NEED YOUR HELP TO
LOCATE HIM STOP ENGLAND IN FORTNIGHT

He wrote out the same message to Ned Lawrence.

Pausing to consider whom else to contact, he thought of Mervin, who was staying at the flat in Oxford. Taking another form, he wrote:

EVAN'S GONE OFF TO WAR UNSURE WHERE STOP SEE YOU AT
FLAT IN FORTNIGHT

He gave the forms to the telegraph operator and paid for their transmission.

His next stop was two doors away at the post office, where he filled out a form to forward mail to the Oxford flat.

He went back to the automobile and headed to the university. As he drove, his mind churned with thoughts about Evan, wondering where he was, how he was. He also realized how proud he was of him, Evan's initiative compelling his own action.

I only wish that he'd left a note!

At the university, he apprised the dean about the family emergency prompting his sudden departure. He was surprised and gratified by the dean's understanding and his offer to drive Clive to the railway station in Salt Lake City.

Heading back to the house, he felt calmer—his course of action set. All that remained was to pack up and leave.

He parked in the driveway and checked the mailbox. Empty— which meant that the postman either hadn't come yet, or that there was no mail.

He let himself in the front door, and stood for a moment,

remembering the familiar comfort of Evan's voice. His heart clenched at the sight of the birthday gifts on the living room table.

Relieved that he didn't need to worry about the house or the automobile that both belonged to the university, he was also gratified that the dean agreed he could leave all appliances and furnishings. That left only clothes and books to pack. He decided to start with Evan's things.

He pulled a steamer trunk out of the hall closet and carried it into Evan's room. The curtains were drawn, and it was relatively cool and dark. He lifted the trunk onto the bed, stepped to the window, parted the curtains, and raised the blinds, sending dust motes dancing in the ruddy evening sunlight.

Absently, he picked Evan's baseball glove off William Whiston's translation of *The Works of Flavius Josephus*. He sat on the edge of the bed, slipped the glove onto his hand, and putting it over his face, breathed deeply, smelling the sharp fragrance of the leather.

The house was very quiet.

He thought about the night Janet died, trying to separate his grief from the memory of Evan that night, trying to remember him. He recalled how hard it had been to leave the hospital, long after there was any reason to stay. He remembered Evan sitting in the empty waiting room, his face buried in his hands—how difficult it had been to comfort him—given his own grief and not knowing what to say. He remembered placing his hand on Evan's head, his surprise when Evan encircled him with his arms. Though only two years had passed since that night, Evan had been much smaller—his thin arms hugging him and not letting go. Clive swallowed hard as he remembered his hand on Evan's head, running his fingers through his hair, light brown, like Janet's, and streaked with sunlight.

He put the glove and book in the trunk.

He went through Evan's chest of drawers, packing up everything. He did the same with his desk and closet. Looking over Evan's room for the final time, he saw a newspaper under the bed. He bent down and picked it up.

It was a copy of *The Deseret Evening News* dated August 7. The headline shouted,

GERMANS SMASH INTO BELGIUM

He tossed the newspaper into the trunk, carried it into the front room and placed it on the divan. With a sigh, he put in Evan's birthday gifts.

Hearing the creak of the mailbox door, he was out the front door in time to see the postman ambling past the house. The sun had just set and the cloudless sky glowed crimson. Opening the mailbox, he found a single letter. He didn't need to check the sender's name to know whom it was from. He could smell the perfumed stationary.

Sad that there was nothing from Evan, he sat on the porch and began to read.

August 9, 1914

My Dear Clive,

I was pleased to receive your letter today here at Rounton, where I have fully recuperated from the exhaustion of my trip through the Syrian Desert.

Soon after returning home, I had the opportunity to report my findings about the desert Arabs to the Royal Geographical Society, and you'll never guess whom I met there! Our old chum from Oxford—Mervin Smythe! He had just returned from the University of Stuttgart, researching Teutonic archaeology, as is his compulsion. How he managed to extricate himself from Germany after hostilities began, God alone knows! He looks quite lost without you and misses you terribly. He's still crushed by Janet's passing and insisted I convey his profound condolences. Since he's staying at your flat in Oxford, he wanted me to let you know that most of the plants are alive and well.

After my talk at the Geographical Society, the Foreign
Secretary, Sir Edward Grey, contacted me. As I had hoped, my
sojourn among the tribes of Arabia has raised some interest
at the War Office. While it suits the Turks for the present
to remain neutral, suspicions are rife that they will soon ally
with our German cousins. Since I have witnessed the laxity of
Ottoman rule over the Arab tribes with my own eyes, it is clear
that we may be able to take advantage of this condition. Indeed,
the Turks themselves are quite concerned about an uprising of
the desert clans. Given this, Whitehall has finally shown interest
in my suggestion that we fully support the tribal chiefs of Arabia
in a revolt against the Turks. I have made the case that such as
Ibn Saud are most favorably disposed to British rule. I also have
it on good authority that Lord Kitchener and Henry McMahon
have made similar overtures to the Sharif of Mecca, Hussein ibn
Ali, and his son, Faisal.

Oh, to be a man at this monumental time! As a woman, I
can only counsel and cajole; but to be a man and lend an active
hand to the great Arab revolt—to play a part in granting self-
rule (under British supervision, of course) to the Arabs after 500
years of Turkish oppression! But as a woman, I know my place in
the world and in the Empire.

I also bring you warm regards from our dear friend, Richard
Doughty-Wylie. I first learned of your close friendship with
him when I met Richard and his wife in Constantinople just
before the Young Turk Revolution. At the time he was serving
as a British Vice Consul, and he regaled me of your adventures
together as young soldiers in China during the Boxer Rebellion.
When I wrote to him recently of you, he insisted I send you his
love and condolences. He is, indeed, so very fond of you! I should
also tell you that a very warm correspondence has developed

between Richard and I over the last few years, though we're
currently separated by unfortunate circumstance; he's been
posted in Ethiopia and will soon be deployed elsewhere.

For myself, I'll finish my report on Arabia for the Foreign
Secretary, and once done, travel to Boulogne to work with
the Red Cross in the sad business of listing the dead and
corresponding with their families.
We must all do our part.

> With warm regards to Evan,
> Your friend and colleague,
> Gerty

Clive looked back at the phrase Gertrude had written about
Richard—"a warm correspondence has developed between us." He
knew Richard well enough to know that something was afoot. Richard
was a ruggedly handsome sort, combining a striking physique with
kindness and bravery that women found irresistible. Even though
Richard was married, Clive knew where this "warm correspondence"
would lead, and he was happy for them both.

He also glanced at Gertrude's words in closing—"We must all do
our part."

She was right. He was glad to be returning to England.

The light was failing fast as dusk settled and a cold wind blew in
from the desert.

He went inside and decided to make a fire. Placing Bell's letter
on the low table by the divan, he knelt at the hearth and put down a
couple of logs but found that he had almost no kindling. He considered
going out to gather some but glanced back at Bell's perfumed letter.
That should make for a good accelerant, he thought and positioned it
with the other kindling among the logs. Taking a match from the tin,
he struck it, and flames sprang up.

He thought about the trip ahead—the road to Salt Lake City, the train to New York, and the ship to Liverpool or Southampton. He sat back on his heels and watched Bell's letter blacken and twist in the fire, the flames licking at the logs with orange tongues. He looked forward to volunteering for the war effort as soon as he returned. Once there, he'd also be in position to locate Evan.

A cinder snapped and a burnt ash, edged in glowing orange, floated out of the hearth. He watched in growing alarm as the bright ember settled under the divan. Turning onto his belly, he pulled down his shirtsleeve to cover his hand, reached under the divan and tamped it out.

As he remained prone on the floor, watching to make sure that the ember was out, he saw something else—a piece of paper.

He reached out and got hold of it.

Sitting up, he saw it was a page torn from a notebook with writing on it, but in the darkness, he couldn't make out the words. Moving closer to the hearth, he angled the paper to catch the firelight and read.

Dear Dad,

By the time you read this, I'll be far away . . .

CHAPTER 23

September 7, 1914
Villefranche-sur-Mer, Nice

TWO WEEKS OUT of New York, the *Sant Anna* stood at anchor off the Nice port city, the bright blue water of the Mediterranean lapping her bow.

Evan was among twelve stokers in a rowboat heading toward the beach. He and a young Spaniard, Fernando, each plied an oar, as the others faced landward, speaking excitedly in a cacophony of French, Italian, Spanish, and English. Having stopped at ports-of-call in Algiers and Naples, they were looking forward to another day of shore leave.

Beneath the bench where Evan rowed was his duffel bag. He would not be joining them on shore leave, nor returning to the *Sant Anna*. His voyage ended here and his journey to the front began.

In midmorning there was a cool wind off the water. As Evan rowed, he listened to the dip and splash of the oars and looked up at the *Sant Anna*, the French tricolor streaming from the main mast. When he had signed on in New York City as one of a hundred and twenty stokers, he had no idea what it meant to feed coal to the ship's bright furnaces in the unrelenting noise and heat of a boiler room. *As hot as hell and half of Georgia,* he thought, recalling Bob Pitney's favorite hot weather simile.

Thinking of Pitney, he remembered how he had accurately predicted the kaiser's rush to war with his homespun intuition—that he wouldn't have built up his navy if "he wasn't fixin' to use it." He also wondered if Pitney would be proven right in predicting the kaiser would someday live in the palatial hostel he had built on the Mount of Olives.

Reaching the shallows, he and Fernando shipped their oars and splashed out of the rowboat to help drag it ashore. Around them, the port city lined the crescent harbor. Turning his eyes to the bright umbrellas along the promenade, he yearned for a cold drink and a hot shower.

Both would have to wait.

"You sure you won't join us for a beer?" asked Fernando as they crossed the beach toward the promenade.

"No thanks," Evan replied. "I have a train to catch."

"What for?

"I told you—I'm heading to Paris."

"But that's too near the front!"

"*Exactly* why I'm going there."

"You're crazy!" Fernando swept a hand in the air. "Look at this place, Evan! Come with us. We'll drink beer and chase girls all day! After that, Marseilles for a whole *week* before we sail back to New York."

"A tempting offer, but . . . no. I've already collected my wages." Evan stuck out his hand. "It was great knowing you, Fernando. Have a cold one for me!"

"If you insist," Fernando smiled as they shook hands. Then he sprinted after the others, stopping to turn and shout, "Take good care of yourself, my friend!"

With the duffel bag over his shoulder, Evan turned toward Nice. Though carriages were available for rent, he preferred to walk the five miles to the train station. Keeping to the strand, he walked in warm sunshine beneath a cloudless sky, caressed by a cool breeze off the water, the blue Mediterranean stretching to the horizon.

He reached the Nice train station well after midday and checked the schedule posted on the door. The next train for Paris was the next morning, and a second-class ticket cost a fraction of the two hundred and fifty francs the purser had paid him.

He opened his duffel bag, found the French phrase book he'd purchased before leaving New York, and looked up the words he'd need to buy a ticket. He bought a one-way fare, and while still at the counter, asked the agent about an inexpensive hotel. He didn't understand the agent's directions to Hôtel Rossetti but followed his hand gestures, crossing a busy boulevard and dodging automobiles and carriages to reach what appeared to be the old section of Nice.

Wandering through a warren of narrow cobbled lanes, he asked directions from serial passersby, and eventually found himself standing in front of an antique building on a quiet lane. Tufts of dry weeds grew between rows of worn brick in wide gaps beneath crumbling stucco. The pale calligraphy on a faded sign read *Hôtel Rossetti*.

Pushing open the front door, he stepped onto the threadbare carpet of a lobby with stuffed chairs and old travel posters lining the walls. An elderly lady, regally perched on a cushioned chair near the empty front desk, smiled and nodded hello. Missing a few front teeth, she was draped with antique jewelry and a faded gown.

Turning her head, she called out, "François! Quelqu'un pour te voir!"

After a minute, an unshaven middle-aged man appeared behind the desk, his rumpled white shirt open at the collar.

As Evan approached, he asked, "Bonjour, Monsieur. Parlez-vous anglais?"

The desk clerk shook his head.

Using his high school French, he announced, "Je ne parle pas français."

That much was obvious.

He thumbed through the phrase book, wishing his father had tutored him in French rather than useless classical languages. *I could get a room easier in first century Rome,* he thought and attempted to ask, "Je veux une chambre . . . avec . . . avec . . . salle . . ."

"Perhaps I can be of some assistance," the woman said in heavily accented English. "Are you asking for a room with a private bath?"

"I am. Thank you!"

"They have no private bathrooms here, though every room has a wash basin and a chamber pot."

"That will be fine—how much for a night?"

The woman paused and seemed to contemplate Evan's blackened hands before asking, "Perhaps a hot bath as well?"

"Sure! That would be great."

"Combien pour une nuit avec un bain chaud?" she asked the clerk.

"Sept francs."

"I understand that—seven francs." Evan fished a handful of coins from his pocket and placed a few on the counter.

"You'll have hot water in about an hour," said the woman.

"I really appreciate your help, ma'am!"

"You're most welcome! We don't get many Americans here. They usually prefer the fancy hotels in the Promenade des Anglais."

"Actually, I'm English. I lived in the States for a few years and lost my accent."

"I lived in the States for a good many years, but obviously, I never lost mine."

The clerk placed a heavy brass key on the counter.

The woman handed it to Evan. "Number three—right next to the bath."

Evan took the key and was about to shoulder his duffel bag when the woman asked, "Pardon me, young man, but why did you travel here all the way from the States?"

"As I told you, ma'am, I'm English. I've come to volunteer for the British Expeditionary Force to fight against the Germans."

Her smile faded. "My dear boy, is there *anything* I can say to change your mind?"

"With all due respect, ma'am, I don't think so." He paused and added. "I leave for Paris tomorrow."

"How did you arrive here?"

"From New York—I was hired as a stoker on a Fabre Line Ship. I got off when we docked in Villefranche this morning."

"What an odd coincidence! I also used to work on Fabre Line Ships."

"Really?" Evan asked. "As a stoker?"

The woman laughed. "As a *dancer*—and *never* in the boiler room! For a few years the Fabre Line ran a service between Marseilles and the Grandes Antilles." She nodded up at a lithograph poster on the opposite wall. Turning her eyes back to Evan, she asked, "So, you arrived today and leave tomorrow?"

"Yes, ma'am."

"Then you must take advantage of your one night in Nice. And with this I can help." She leaned forward and whispered, "I operate a small escort service."

Evan was confused. "An escort service? For who?"

"Men—young and old and every age in between. When such men are lonely, or require female company at dinner, or just to . . . talk." She fixed Evan with her gray eyes. "What about *you*? Would *you* enjoy speaking with a lovely young woman later this afternoon, or this evening? Would you enjoy the company of a beautiful young woman before you go off to war?"

Evan's heart began to pound. "You . . . you mean *here* . . . at the *hotel*?"

"In your room, or wherever you like. You could go out with her to dinner, stroll along the promenade at sunset—whatever you choose."

"For . . . for how long?" Evan asked, excited at the idea of being with a woman.

"Whatever you desire—for the evening or all night—the choice is yours."

Evan drew a deep breath and steadied himself on the counter. "Is she pretty?"

"Very. And the young woman I have in mind has just arrived from Algiers and is about your age."

When Evan found his voice, he asked, "And you could arrange this?"

"I can, and for the right price, I will."

Evan fixed his eyes on the woman, his heart racing as he considered what she was proposing—that he pay to be with a woman. But it didn't seem right. He drew a deep breath. "Thanks, ma'am, but I think I'll just have a bath, take myself out to dinner, and go to bed. It's been a long day, and I have an early train for Paris."

The old woman smiled. "You're sure?"

"Yes."

"Have you ever been with a woman?"

"No," Evan said quietly and shook his head. "Which is one reason I don't want it to be like that . . ."

The old woman shrugged "If you change your mind, I will be right here."

Evan nodded his thanks and headed down the hall walking slowly, his heart racing.

CHAPTER 24

September 8, 1914
Boulogne-sur-Mer, Northern France

GERTRUDE BELL left her room at Hotel Meurice before dawn and hurried across the cobblestones of Rue Victor Hugo toward the beach. Beyond the low sea wall, dull gray sand yielded to a flat expanse of water stretching toward Dover where a smudge of silver marked the cloud-hidden sun. With a frigid wind off the water, she was grateful for her fur-lined parka, a souvenir from her mountaineering days in the Italian Alps. She was also grateful to have this time to herself. Pulling the parka close about her shoulders, she walked quickly along the beach.

Her early morning constitutional was a singularly important part of a day otherwise filled with long hours in the cramped Red Cross office. Every day crowded with names—names of the wounded, names of the missing, and names of the dead—names to be indexed and catalogued. Beyond the sheer weight of the names, was the sad chore of writing careful responses to anxious families—families desperate for word of a son, a husband, a brother. And beyond that, the hospital visits, where broken bodies lay in endless rows—men too wounded to be conscious, or too young to realize the full horror of a wounded life.

But not now. This was her time. Facing into the wind, she relished the simplicity of the empty beach and the unhurried tide beneath the gray sky.

Only three weeks had passed since she had arrived in France, joining Flora and Diana Russell—all doing their part for the war effort. But Gertrude was already anxious to leave. To be sure, work at the Red Cross was vital, but she found her old friends tiresome with their gossip. Besides, she'd already made a significant contribution to the work of the office, weaving scattered slips of paper into an ordered card index system. But, the main reason she wanted to leave was that she knew she could make a far more substantial contribution elsewhere.

"I should be at the War Office at Whitehall!" she shouted into the wind. "No British subject knows as much as I about the terrain and people of Arabia!"

She turned to watch the gulls, white and gray like scolding nuns, hovering and squawking at the water's edge. At low tide, a few fishing boats, abandoned by the water, lay tilted at odd angles, sails furled about their masts, anchors and buoys stranded and exposed, their lines like delicate strands of seaweed on the smooth wash.

Gertrude knew that her expertise would be vital when the war reached Arabia. She also knew that the Ottoman Empire would eventually join forces with the Central Powers. The kaiser would make sure of that.

She resumed her brisk walk down the beach and considered the inexorable German presence in the Ottoman Empire—gathering and growing for decades. She had witnessed it firsthand during her travels through Turkey, Arabia, and Mesopotamia, meeting German economic advisers and German arms dealers in Constantinople, German archeologists in Carchemish, and German railway engineers in Baghdad.

German interest in the Ottoman Empire had actually begun well before Kaiser Wilhelm II had come to power in 1888, but with his ascension, it had rapidly increased, especially when German banks offered to fund a railway from Constantinople to Baghdad with plans for branch lines to the Persian Gulf at Basra and into the Hejaz at Mecca.

Gertrude had witnessed the construction herself and knew the railway would give Germany significant penetration and influence in the entire region. And once Turkey entered the war with the Central Powers, Germany's control of the Ottoman Empire would be complete—as strong as the steel rails linking Berlin and Constantinople.

Her pace increased and, alone on the promenade, she shouted into the wind, "If British soldiers are to have any chance in the deserts of Arabia and Mesopotamia, they'll need my maps of the terrain, the springs and the wells! They'll need to know which Bedouin sheiks they can trust!"

She slowed her pace, annoyed by her lack of direct access to the War Office. She did a quick inventory of the men who might assist her in gaining access, livid with the knowledge that, as a woman, she had no choice but to work through men.

Pushing away her anger, she considered that Clive Sinclair would be very willing to advocate for her at Whitehall, if and when he returned to England. She also knew that Ned Lawrence would do the same. And David Hogarth, her friend Janet's older brother, would also sponsor her.

As she considered these men, she came to a stop. "Of course! There's also Richard! Though he's posted to Ethiopia, he's also well-connected at Whitehall!"

As her thoughts turned to Richard, she couldn't help but smile at how increasingly intimate their correspondence had become. In her last letter to him, she had been so bold as to suggest they meet in London between his deployments, which was likely in a few months. *I so hope he'll agree,* she thought as she increased her pace down the beach, wondering why her affections were so drawn to Richard, a married man. *Quite scandalous, really!* But beyond the fact that he was physically strong and handsome, she knew that he was the kind of man who, like her father, represented the unwavering patriarchy that was the iron of the British Empire. *Little wonder that I'm drawn to him!*

She paused to check her timepiece and saw that she should be heading back—back to the Red Cross office, and the work that waited for her—the card files, the hospital visits, and the letters of condolence. But, above all, the names.

She began running along the strand, the wind buffeting her, blowing back the hood of her parka, her hair free, blowing the names away.

☀ ☀ ☀

Nice
Côte d'Azur

Evan awoke to bright bands of sunlight shining through the shuttered windows. He sat up, yawned, and glanced at his wristwatch. *Half six.* Throwing off the blanket, he sat up and stretched his arms wide. Reaching down, he groped under the bed for the chamber pot.

The iron-frame bed occupied most of the small room, with a chipped white washbasin on a wooden stand by the window and a writing table and chair in the corner. A contorted effigy of Christ, his face upturned, hung on the wall above the bed.

Shirtless at the washbasin, Evan cupped his hands and splashed his face with cool water again and again. He lifted a threadbare towel from a peg on the wall and saw there was a door next to the window. Painted the same light green as the walls, the door was only distinguishable by a heavy burnished key resting in the lock. Turning the key, he pushed it open and stepped onto a narrow wrought-iron balcony, the air cool on his face.

The sun peeked between the low houses across the lane from the hotel. He wondered how he might appear to someone looking out from the shadows of those houses—like a cameo, perhaps, his pale body in the sunlight against the black of the doorway. He leaned on the railing, a smile on his lips. A faint lassitude hung at the edges of his mind like the sparse pink clouds that streaked the sky above the dark rooftops. He breathed in a lungful of morning air, then went back into the room.

Dabbing his toothbrush into the tin of tooth powder, he brushed his teeth, then rubbed some soap on his face and shaved off a sparse three-week-old beard with his double-edged safety razor. He rinsed his face, dried off, and dressed in blue denim pants and a clean white shirt. He shrugged into his brown leather jacket, stuck his French phrase book into a back pocket, and left the room.

The dim hotel lobby was deserted, though it still smelled of cigarette smoke. He was relieved that the old woman wasn't there, and glad he hadn't accepted her offer, with a fleeting sense of shame for even having considered it. He shook his head as he checked his watch. *It's not even seven, and the train for Paris leaves at nine—plenty of time for coffee.*

He pushed open the front door and stepped out onto smooth cobblestones. Moving quickly down the lane, he came to a sidewalk café where a waiter was setting out tables. He slowed to thumb through his phrase book. The waiter, who couldn't have been more than twelve, looked his way.

"Est-ce que je peux vous aider, monsieur?"

Though he didn't understand the question, he asked, "Café, s'il vous plait?"

"Certainement!" The boy gestured toward a table set in a patch of warm sunlight.

Hot coffee with rich cream and warm rolls with butter and preserves were soon on the table. He bit into a roll, leaning over the plate to catch the crumbs. Sighing, he took a long draft of coffee, savoring it, savoring the feeling that he was dreaming—with a whole hour until he had to leave for the train station. An eternity.

He wondered at the memory of pumping gas at the service station in the summer heat of Southern Utah, the memory of quarreling with his father about college. Now he did as he pleased.

He took another sip of coffee and flipped through his phrase book, rehearsing another question.

When a middle-aged man approached the table and placed down the bill, he was ready. "S'il vous plait. Quelle est la situation actuelle avec la guerre?" He hadn't seen a newspaper for two weeks and wondered where things stood on the Western Front.

"La gare?" The man raised his arm and pointed. "Descendez cette rue, tournez à droite au boulevard. La gare est à une distance de moitié par kilomètre."

"Excusez-moi?" It sounded like he was giving Evan directions to the train station. He tried again. "No—quelle est la situation actuelle avec la guerre?" He raised an imaginary rifle and made shooting sounds with his mouth. "La guerre," he repeated.

"You are asking me—how is the *war*?"

"Thank God! You speak English," Evan exclaimed. "Yes—I want to know what's happening on the Western Front. I want to volunteer."

"You are American?"

"No. I'm English. I'm going to Paris to volunteer with the British Expeditionary Force. Do you know where they might be?"

"I will make for you the map." Putting a clean paper place mat on the table, the man bent and drew a rough box with the stub of a pencil. "This is France. We are here in Nice. This is Paris. Many people in Paris, but the government, she has moved to here—Bordeaux."

He drew a long wiggly line from the dot that was Paris to the right, then down.

"This is a big river—the Marne. This short river is the Aisne. The soldiers of the Entente are here. Les Allemands, how you say—the Germans? They are over here. They have been stopped by the taxis."

"What?" Evan was sure he had misunderstood. "The *taxis* stopped the Germans?"

"The taxis of Paris bring soldiers to the Marne. They stop the Germans. They save Paris." With a final flourish, he tapped the map. "The soldiers of the Entente now fight the Germans at this river—the Aisne. Perhaps here you will also find the British."

The man grasped Evan's hand with both his own. "Thank you for giving your life for France!" he said and kissed Evan's hand.

Giving my life for France? The words shocked Evan as he reclaimed his hand.

The man took Evan's bill and tore it up. "You no pay! Please, order more food—no pay."

"You're very kind, thank you," Evan said, feeling queasy. "But I really must be going." As he pushed away from the table, the coffee cup tipped over, spreading a smooth brown stain over the map, obliterating the borders of France. "Sorry," he said as he stood up and stuffed several uneaten rolls into the pockets of his jacket.

On his way back to the hotel, the café owner's words kept returning. *Thank you for giving your life for France.*

Once in the room, he gathered his things in the duffle bag, left the room, and passed back through the lobby. The clerk wasn't there but the old woman was, regal in her moth-eaten gown. She waved to him from her perch beneath a faded travel poster.

"Au revoir, Monsieur!" She inclined her head elegantly, adding in accented English, "I wish you good fortune in your endeavors."

He nodded in response, consumed with the café owner's statement of gratitude. *Thank you for giving your life for France.*

Retracing his steps from the day before, he crossed the wide, tree-lined avenue, now empty. In the quiet morning, the war seemed very far away.

But not at the train station—there the air was electric with the din of a thousand voices echoing beneath the high-domed ceiling, and everywhere bright French flags in blue, white, and red.

Apparently, a train from Paris had just arrived. Evan made his way across the hall, duffel bag over his shoulder, jostled by the huge crowd streaming through the station—passengers arriving from Paris, struggling with suitcases and bundles, their eyes wide with panic. Among them were wounded soldiers with patched eyes, bandaged heads, arms suspended in slings, some limping on crutches, some on stretchers.

He thought about the café owner's words and wondered, *Why exactly am I here?*

As he looked at each of the wounded, his heart began to beat wildly, and his throat was gripped with an unfamiliar sensation. His white shirt, now soaked through with sweat, stuck to his body. It took a minute to recognize what he was feeling, and once recognized, another minute to acknowledge it.

I'm afraid.

Words of the café owner returned with each wounded soldier— *thank you for giving your eyes for France, thank you for giving your leg for France . . .*

He went out to the platform where the train idled and hissed. Taking off his jacket, he let the light breeze cool him. He breathed deeply, trying to quiet the horror rising in his chest, but all the while, the proprietor's words echoed in his mind.

He studied the people on the platform—clutches of families surrounding young recruits, who mostly looked about his age, though some were older reservists. The soldiers wore a hodge-podge of uniforms, dark blue tunics, blue-gray greatcoats, red trousers, blue linen overalls, short black gaiters with ankle boots. A few had haversacks replete with rolled blanket and mess tin.

As the minutes ticked by and the moment of departure drew near, Evan watched the goodbyes becoming more tearful and urgent. Hands that had been clutching small French tricolors let them fall to the platform to fiercely hold a beloved son, husband, father, brother, or lover with a fearful realization of a possibly final parting.

Evan looked down at the ticket in his hand, and asked, *Why am I here?*

He wandered down the platform toward a group of people in the shadows by an empty siding. He saw workers unloading narrow pinewood boxes—a long row already lined the platform. As he drew nearer, he heard the sound of weeping.

Lurching away, he made his way back to the platform, struggling to calm his breathing, trying to think clearly. *I've come too far to turn back.*

The train whistle shrieked.

A conductor shouted something in French that Evan didn't understand.

Soldiers pulled away from their families and began to board the train.

Evan drew a deep breath. *I don't have to decide now. I'll figure out what to do when I get to Paris.*

Stepping into a car, he moved forward, the train more than half-empty. He took the first compartment he could have to himself, pulled the door closed, sat on the upholstered bench seat, pulled down the window shade, and closed his eyes.

I'll decide when I get to Paris, he reassured himself again, and began to feel less anxious. *If I decide to stay, I stay. If I decide to go, I go. Whatever I choose. No one is telling me what to do—it's entirely up to me!* He began to calm down. But when the train lurched forward, the cold fear rose again. He opened his eyes and raised the window shade to see that the train was pulling out of the station.

He watched telegraph poles tick by as the outskirts of Nice gave way to open fields, then to rugged mountains. He dozed off but awoke with a start as the compartment door opened with a rush of noise.

"Billets, billets, s'il vous plait!" The conductor called, stepping halfway in.

Evan handed his ticket to the conductor. Looking out the window, he saw that the scenery had changed, the train now passing stone manor houses along a riverbank.

He divided the next several hours between leafing through his phrase book and watching the French countryside flick by the window. Whenever the fear crept back to tug at him, he reassured himself that he was just going to Paris.

The train stamped between crowding green hedgerows, past roads disappearing beneath shuttered archways of bending trees, past patchwork fields, bright meadows, dark tunnels, and high trestles over deep chasms. Evening drew on.

Hungry, he took the rolls from his jacket pocket and finished them as he thought about the restaurant owner, his voice filling the compartment.

Night fell and the panorama of the French countryside faded and disappeared. Looking out the window, all he could see in the dark glass was a reflection of his own face, the hollows of his eyes staring back at him—like a death's-head.

CHAPTER 25

September 9, 1914

Paris

SEATED AT A WORN wooden table in the center of an otherwise empty room, Evan looked up at Police Inspector Michel Gaudin. "I'm telling you for the tenth time—I don't *want* to volunteer anymore. I just want to go home."

"So," Gaudin said as he began to pace, "you've changed your mind."

Gaudin's English was excellent though his accent was pronounced. Evan guessed the Frenchman was about his father's age. He had thinning gray hair with what looked like a week's worth of stubble on his thin, doleful face. Gaudin drew deeply on a cigarette, the tip glowing red within a haze of smoke.

"That's right," said Evan. "I changed my mind." He looked down at the table, bare but for the inspector's cap. He studied the polished brass letters above the visor, *Préfecture de Police*. He wondered how much longer Gaudin would question him.

It had been four hours since he had failed to present any identification to two officers at the main Paris train station just after midnight and had been taken into custody. The officers hadn't been able to understand him, and he couldn't understand them, though he did recognize a couple of words they repeated—*saboteur* and *espionage*.

He looked up at Gaudin and asked, "Is it a crime to change my mind? Is that what this is about?"

Gaudin stopped pacing and looked down at Evan through half-closed, heavy-lidded eyes. "You know very well what this is about."

"As a matter of fact, I don't. But I *do* know my rights, and I demand to speak with the British consul."

"Nicht mit dem deutschen Konsul?"

"What? Do you . . .?" Evan sputtered. "Do you think I'm a German spy?"

Gaudin studied his cigarette and flicked off the ash.

"What do you *want* from me?" Evan asked, his voice rising.

"The truth would be nice."

"I've *told* you the truth."

"Perhaps you have. Perhaps not." Gaudin sat down behind the desk, exhaling the cigarette smoke in a weary sigh. "Put yourself in my place, Mr. Sinclair, or whatever your name really is. The Germans are on our frontier. We've pushed them back, but who knows for how long? Our central government has fled the capital, German saboteurs and sympathizers are everywhere, and *you* show up with your Aryan good looks and no identification papers. What am I *supposed* to think?" Gaudin shrugged. "My colleagues believe I'm wasting my time—that I'm being too *easy* on you because my mother was English. They say I should turn you over to our unit for special interrogation."

"I'm *talking*, aren't I? Go ahead—ask me whatever you want."

"Very well." Gaudin sighed, rubbing a hand over his face. "You claim that you traveled here from America, but you have no passport—"

"I already told you—I didn't *have* one! And nobody cared about a passport when I got hired to work on the *Sant Anna* out of New York."

"And there's this—you claim you're English but haven't a trace of an accent."

"I moved to America when I was fourteen, and I worked hard to lose my accent. It set me apart from other kids and I just wanted to

fit in. Look—I've shown you my high school graduation certificate."
Evan reached down for his duffle bag that lay on the floor by his chair.
"You want to see it again?"

"No. That could be easily forged—like the French language
notebook, supposedly from high school, which was almost
convincing—a nice touch." Gaudin sighed and put his fingers to his
chin. "You claim that you came to *volunteer,* but now that you're here,
you suddenly change your mind." Gaudin scraped his chair back with
a suddenness that startled Evan. "Why don't you tell me something
that makes *sense?*" He threw down the cigarette, crushed it out with
his boot, leaned over Evan and shouted, "Tell me why you're *really*
here!"

"But, I have!" Evan shouted back. "I've told you everything!"

"Everything?" Gaudin snapped a notepad out of his back pocket
and flipped through the pages. "Before you supposedly left England
with your parents two years ago, you were at a dig in Mesopotamia,
practically sharing the site with German archaeologists, and among
them, agents of the kaiser! And after *supposedly* living in America for
about two years, you materialize in France and *claim* you came to
fight on the side of the Entente. But now that you're here, you decide
that you want to go home—wherever *home* really is."

Gaudin waved the notepad. "And family? You claim that your
mother died and there's only your father, and someone you describe
as 'sort of an uncle'—Mervin Smythe. You should know that we
consider your *sort of uncle* to be a person of interest—"

"What? What does this have to do with Mervin?"

"*You* don't ask the questions here, I do!" Gaudin shouted and
lurched forward. "Tell me something of this *sort of uncle!*"

"Mervin? He . . . he and my dad were . . . students together
at Oxford. He teaches Northern European archeology . . ." Evan
stammered, trying to plumb his memory for details. "They've . . .
known each other for years—"

"Yes, yes," Guadin cut him off. "But according to our sources, Smythe has made quite a few trips to Germany recently. Why is that?"

"I told you! He teaches Northern European archeology—*German* archeology. It's only *natural* he would visit Germany."

"And how did you even arrive in Paris? You claim it was by train, but our officers didn't see you get off. They just observed you wandering around as if you were lost."

"I *was* lost."

"And no ticket. If you arrived by train, where's your ticket?"

"I must have left it on the train. I didn't think to keep it."

"And one thing more . . . when exactly did you change your mind about volunteering to fight for France?"

Evan drew a deep breath and tried to keep his voice from breaking. "At the Nice train station, I saw wounded. I saw coffins." He paused, adding in a whisper, "I was afraid." Looking up at Gaudin, he shouted, "I was afraid! Do you find *that* hard to believe?"

"No." Gaudin said quietly. "It's actually the only thing you've said that I *do* believe." Putting on his cap, he moved toward the door.

"So, I can leave now?" Evan asked as he pushed away from the table.

"I'm afraid not." Gaudin turned at the open door. "The enemy is at our gates, Mr. Sinclair, and frankly, *you* may be the enemy! We can't take any chances. I'm sending up officers to escort you for special interrogation."

He left and Evan heard the key turn in the lock. For a few seconds he stared at the door, his heart pounding. *I've got to get out of here!*

He jumped to his feet, ran to a window and stood on tiptoes to look out, past the iron bars. A flare hung in the night sky like a Christmas ornament, floating slowly downward. It made everything as bright as day, the shadows sharp on the ground. Beyond the police headquarters, there was an empty field and, at the far edge, a wood.

Along the street below, there was a hodgepodge of motorized

vehicles parked in a row—lorries of different sizes and a few buses. *That looks like a convoy.*

The low thunder of artillery shook the windows, coming from a distance, a hoarse bellow like the rutting black tail stags he used to hear in the high deserts of Utah. As he listened, he felt a strange calm, an unhurried focusing of the senses. *This is how I used to feel out in the desert—everything slower, clearer.* He stared at the trees beyond the field, then down at the convoy.

He turned at the sound of the door as it unlocked then opened.

Two policemen stood in the doorway. Each carried a rifle. One gestured and said, "You come now."

He stepped away from the window, picked up his duffel bag, and slung it over his shoulder. He was surprised at how calm he felt. It made no sense.

The men flanked him out the door, then down a dimly lit hallway. One whispered to the other. He tried to hear them, to understand what they were saying.

"Se dépêcher! Nous partons avec les camions dans une heure."

He knew that word—Camions were trucks—trucks leaving in an hour.

The other spoke, "Est-ce qu'on retourne à Nice?"

"Je souhaite que nous retournions à Nice," the other laughed. "Nous prenons les camions à l'avant . . ."

They were talking about the trucks, the ones in the convoy. It sounded like they were going to Nice . . .

Everything seemed to be happening slowly as they moved toward a stairwell at the end of the hall. He could hear the creaking leather of their boots, the tap and scrape of their steps on the stone floor, the slow jingle of keys. At the end of the hall, a large window bordered the stairwell, a window with no bars. Beyond the glass loomed the dark skeleton of a fire escape. He gripped his duffle bag, knowing what he was about to do.

The moment the guards turned toward the stairwell, he jerked the duffel bag off his shoulder and swung it round as hard as he could. It sent them sprawling, their rifles clattering away. Clutching the bag in front of his face, he lowered his shoulder and charged forward, diving through the window with a snap of breaking glass. He tumbled onto the fire escape—bright shards falling around him.

In a heartbeat he was on his feet, the street fifteen feet below. Gripping the duffel bag, he threw his body off the fire escape, keeping the thick padding beneath him, the bag's fabric against his face, the cool night wind before the jarring bump when he hit the ground. He rolled off, shaken but unhurt. He staggered to his feet.

From the landing above, the guards were shouting, one trying to lower the fire escape, the other aiming his rifle.

He began to run, the bag over his shoulder. He heard the crack of a rifle and a thin fountain of dirt rose at his feet. He raced down the street and out of the guards' line of sight, toward the convoy he had seen from the window, still illuminated by the single bright flare, now low in the sky.

The flare flickered and went out. In the darkness he reached out and felt about blindly. His fingers found the cold dew-covered metal of one of the trucks. He groped along it and felt canvas—the tarpaulin covering the cargo area. He jumped in, his duffel bag in one hand, tracing the edges of wooden crates in the darkness until he found a gap. He lurched into it and hunkered down, his breath roaring in his ears, his heart pounding.

Then came darting beams of light. Flattening down among the crates, he quieted his breathing. The street was alive with pounding boots and shouting, coming closer—then the sound of the canvas tarpaulin pulled back, the bright light of an electric torch igniting the cargo bed. He held his breath, and after a few seconds, the light disappeared.

There was a long stretch of silence, broken by the truck's motor rattling to life. Gears engaged. The truck moved, slowing, stopping, and turning. After a while, it accelerated and moved smoothly and steadily along. Cushioned by the duffel bag in the darkness, fatigue gradually took hold and he slept.

When he awoke there was daylight. He heard the drone of the motor and felt the lorry rocking from side to side. He checked his watch. It was just after nine thirty. He settled back and sighed, *Thank God! I'm on my way back to Nice! What was I thinking, anyway? Give my life for France? No thank you very much!*

Hungry, he searched through his jacket pockets, eating crumbs from the rolls he'd taken from the café in Nice. Then he lay back on his bag among the wooden crates.

How odd, he wondered, *that sense of calm I felt at the police station. What was that?* He let his eyes close and thought how Inspector Gaudin had challenged and frightened him, how he had made him recognize his fear. *And that made me stronger.*

With that thought, he yielded to the rocking of the lorry and the steady drone of the engine, and he slept.

CHAPTER 26

September 9, 1914

Mecca

Ottoman Province of the Hejaz

CLAD IN A DUSTY BEDOUIN ROBE, Faisal was seething with rage as he confronted his father. "Despite my deep affection for Turkey," he said in a voice dripping with sarcasm, "I will no longer serve her!" He pulled off his robe to reveal a khaki Turkish officer's tunic.

"What troubles you, my son?" Hussein asked as he rose from the divan.

"I would see the Arabs free of Turkish domination! Toward this end I will join the struggle for freedom!" He angrily undid the brass buttons of the tunic.

"*I* determine when that struggle begins," Hussein shot back.

"Why not *now*?" Faisal shot back as he paced along the embroidered carpet. "The day I left Damascus, twenty-one martyrs of al-Thawra were hung! I saw them die with my own eyes—twenty-one young men and women—dead because they believed in Arab independence!" He spat out the words and threw the tunic to the floor.

"My rash and impetuous son." Hussein glowered at Faisal from beneath his bushy eyebrows as he bent and lifted the tunic from the floor. "I believe this is called desertion."

"True, Father! I've deserted the Arabs—my own people! But, no more! I'm switching sides." Wearing a tan lambskin undershirt tucked into his khaki trousers, Faisal stepped to the washbasin and splashed cold water on his face.

"My son, I asked you to make *contact* with al-Thawra, not *join* it! This is not the time!"

"When *will* the time come, Father? When the fate of al-Thawra is upon *us*?"

"Your eyes are turned toward the bright dream of independence, my son. I, too, am committed to that dream," Hussein said as he settled himself on the divan.

"Then I am confused! You send my royal brother, Abdullah, a member of the Turkish Parliament, to secretly meet with the British in Cairo. You task me with fomenting a rebellion against Turkey, and at the same time have me ask Djemal for Arab self-rule. My head is spinning from all these contradictions!"

"Sit with me, my son, and I will explain." Hussein tapped the cushion next to him.

Faisal didn't move—his fists clenched in anger, his heart racing.

"Faisal!" Hussein commanded in a voice that brooked no dissent.

With an audible sigh, Faisal settled onto the cushioned divan. Leaning back, he pressed his hands over his eyes.

"First tell me, my son, who knows you are here?"

"No one."

"Are you certain? Turkish spies are everywhere."

"I left Damascus under cover of darkness and traversed Wadi Rum and the Hejaz on a purloined camel. I rode at night to avoid the Turks and the summer heat."

"Have you had anything to drink?"

"No. I came straightaway to you. I have yet to see my wife and children."

"You will see them soon. But first have a cool drink and we'll talk." He lifted a brass bell and shook it, the sound piercing the silence. "It is well that no one knows you're here."

"But they will, Father!" Faisal said and sat forward. He felt his anger ebbing away. "When Djemal learns that I have left Damascus, he will seek me here. Though I spoke flatteringly and delivered the letter to him from your hand, along with the many gifts you sent with me, I'm certain he harbors suspicions about my loyalties, especially after my request for Arab self-rule. It is only a question of time before his agents seek me here."

"But Mecca is far from Damascus. And besides," Hussein waved his hand toward the Great Mosque beyond the arched windows. "This is your city of refuge. No one knows the secret places of the holy precincts as well as you! Even as a small boy, you were able to hide from your mother and me!" Hussein smiled and asked, "How did Djemal react to the request for self-rule?"

Faisal rolled his eyes. "He said he would give it careful consideration."

"I suppose we cannot expect anything more at the present hour. Did you thank him for all he has done to maintain Turkish neutrality?"

"I did, Father—profusely, and begged him to continue avoiding entanglement in the European war."

"That is well . . ." Hussein left off speaking when the steward appeared. "Bring us iced violet sherbet."

"To hear is to obey, my master."

Once the door closed, Hussein turned back to Faisal, "When the Turkish Vali comes hither, making inquiry about you, I will disavow any knowledge of your whereabouts. Moreover, I will also disavow you! I will say that if you did anything to foment rebellion against the empire, it is also rebellion against me." He sighed and raised his shoulders. "Nonetheless, Djemal may doubt me, and to smooth away these doubts, I will make a noble gesture—an invitation to Medina to inspect the troops your brother, Ali, has raised in the Hejaz—"

"But, Father, these troops were raised for the *rebellion*!"

"Djemal has no way of knowing that. He has no spies among the

Bedouin since we are tightly bound together in loyalty by blood. He will be pleased to review Bedouin troops that he'll believe stand ready to join the Turks against the British at the Suez Canal—if and when that comes to pass."

"Excellent!" Faisal nodded, his eyes suddenly feral. "And once we have Djemal in Medina, we'll strike him down!"

"Strike down a guest?" Hussein shook his head. "Unthinkable! We never harm a guest, my son. Such a breach of the Bedouin laws of hospitality—"

"But—"

"But nothing! Though the Turks are godless transgressors in my eyes, we will never dishonor ourselves. We will host him in Medina. He will inspect the troops and return safely to Damascus, reassured of my loyalty. Furthermore, your brother Abdullah will remain in Constantinople as if nothing is amiss. All this will demonstrate our family's reliable allegiance, in spite of you—my prodigal and treacherous son." Hussein patted Faisal's knee and sighed. "I know you are confused by my actions, and as I've told you before, it is confusion I wish to create—this keeps the Turks off balance and encourages greater generosity from the British."

Hussein paused and added, "There is also this—your brother Abdullah's presence in Constantinople allows us to know the inclinations of Germany. They grow impatient with Ottoman neutrality because a full month has passed since the war began in Europe. It is whispered that the kaiser is furious and has sent more German advisers to Constantinople for the training of Turkish officers and troops."

"But if Turkey is still neutral, my father, why would the Germans commit advisers to a Middle East Front that doesn't exist?"

"Because the kaiser is determined that it *will* exist, and soon! He has instructed Enver Pasha to organize Turkish battalions in

Constantinople with German advisers. This is already happening—preparing to deploy them to the Hejaz."

"But it will take months for them to deploy."

"By rail, it will take only days."

"But the railway ends hundreds of miles from the Hejaz."

"That is no longer true. The German railway already reaches Medina."

"Wa'hiyat Allah!" Faisal exclaimed. "These iron rails cut through the flesh of our lands like an envenomed sword, spreading the poison of German power deep into our dominions."

"Your concerns are prescient and correct, my son. Indeed, your brother Abdullah has learned that plans are afoot to extend the railway to Mecca, and ultimately to complete the line from Berlin to Baghdad and Basra. Thus, the Ottomans will have access to the holy places, and the Germans will have access to oil for their war machine."

"Begging your indulgence, my masters!" announced the servant who entered with a tray. The iced violet sherbet you requested." Bowing with a flourish to the sharif, he extended the tray, and Hussein took a cup.

Faisal frowned and waved the servant away. "I cannot think about drinking now!"

"You must drink, my son! After your long journey, you must be parched, and I have much to discuss with you."

With a shrug, Faisal took a glass from the tray, raised it and said, "To your health, Father!"

"Thank you, my son." Once the servant was gone, Hussein continued, "With the railway and their spies, the Germans are even now maneuvering in our districts against the British. If Ottoman neutrality ends and they join with the Germans, an alliance between us and the British is vital, but it goes both ways: Without British aid, we have no rebellion, and without our support, the position of the

British in the Levant is doomed. Without our help, the British will not only lose the war, they'll lose their *empire*."

"So great is our power over the British?"

"Yes, my son." Hussein reached into his robe and produced a scroll. "Because of *this*—a personal message from the sultan, asking me to declare jihad from Mecca against the Triple Entente. If I refuse, it appears that the sultan himself will declare the Holy War from Constantinople."

"But, that cannot be done! All Islam knows that only *you* are empowered to declare jihad!"

"That is why the sultan seeks to use my office." He handed the scroll to Faisal. "Read aloud what that audacious son of a jackal would have me pronounce."

Faisal unrolled the scroll. "*Oh, Muslims! Obey the commands of the Almighty, who, in the Koran, promises us bliss in this and in the next world; embrace ye the foot of the caliph's throne and know ye that we are at war with Russia, England, France, and their Allies, and these are the enemies of Islam. The chief of the believers invites all Muslims to join in the Holy War. By this, the land of Islam shall be forever freed from the power of the infidels who oppress it. Know ye that the blood of infidels may be shed with impunity—except those to whom the Muslim power has promised security and who are allied with it.*"

Faisal handed the scroll back to his father. "There are indeed millions of Muslims within the British Raj, and millions more in Egypt. If they were to rise up in jihad, it would deal the British a mortal blow." He stood up and asked, "What does the sultan offer you in return for doing this?"

"Gold." Hussein sighed. "And another five centuries of servitude to the Ottoman Empire."

Though Faisal was feeling increasingly anxious, he tried to retain a veneer of calm in the presence of his father. He walked over to a window and looked out at the great square surrounding the black monolith of the Kaaba. "The sultan expects much and offers little, my father. Does he not understand you are Islam's greatest prince— the sharif of Mecca and guardian of the holy precincts?"

"I neither know nor care what the sultan understands. But I do know that this holy war he would have me declare is impious and dishonorable, and I will refuse to do it. Is it not written that Allah does not love aggressors? And besides, Jihad is a spiritual struggle, incompatible with an offensive war, and absurd with Christian Germany as the Turk's ally."

"But, Father, Germany may no longer be a truly Christian nation—"

"What are you saying? Of course it is."

"In Damascus, I learned that many Germans have turned away from the true God of Abraham and Ishmael, turning even from God's prophet, Jesus. It is said that, with the kaiser's blessing, many turn to pagan German gods."

"Preposterous!" Hussein exclaimed. "The kaiser fancies himself as Holy Roman Emperor and is thereby allied with the Roman Church. The kaiser not a Christian? Impossible! And what possible *advantage* is there for the kaiser to turn to pagan gods?"

"This isn't about advantage, Father, it's what the kaiser truly believes. His faith is based on supremacy of the German people under the protection of pagan German gods."

"But he made a Christian pilgrimage to the Holy Land and had himself crowned King of Jerusalem!"

"That is only because he seeks the power and the name of Jerusalem, my father. It is said that he wishes to reign from a pagan palace to be built within the sacred precincts upon the Holy Mountain, a palace that will stand in place of the Mosque of Omar!"

"Nonsense!" Hussein shot back. "The Turks will never allow it!"

"When the kaiser rules a German empire from the Rhine to the Euphrates, the Turks will be his vassals, and we will be his slaves!"

Hussein shook his head. "I hope that Djemal might yet succeed in keeping the Ottoman Empire out of this war! But from what I see now, it may not be possible." He fixed Faisal with his eyes and whispered, "Based on all we have discussed, my son, Djemal is likely aware of your contact with the Arab nationalists, and there is great danger to you here. I believe the time has come for you to disappear . . ."

"Disappear?" Faisal sat forward in disbelief, his heart pounding. "And my wife and little ones?"

"It is time for all of you to be secured somewhere safe."

"But where?" Faisal shouted. "Where might we find safe sanctuary?"

"I will secure a comfortable journey for your family to the far banks of the Red Sea. There they will be sheltered by our friends and cousins, the Tarabin Bedouin, and there they will wait in safety for you."

"But how long will I not be among them?" Faisal asked, saddened at the impending separation.

"That, I cannot tell you, but for the present, you will be sheltered in the bowels of the earth—here, within the deep catacombs beneath the holy precincts."

CHAPTER 27

September 10, 1914

Somewhere in France

HE TRUCK LURCHED and Evan awoke with a start. He had slept intermittently throughout the day, lulled by the droning engine, nestled among the wooden crates and cushioned by the pallet of his duffel bag. He raised himself on an elbow and saw that the sun had set, the sky streaked with crimson clouds. *Good! It'll be dark when we reach Nice, and I'll be able to get out of here without being seen.*

Looking through a gap between crates, he saw a red bus behind the lorry in the convoy, its headlamps painted over in black except for a small dull square of yellow light. He'd read about blackouts in the newspaper—*warlight* they called it—barely any light at all. A bend in the road gave him a glimpse through the side windows of the bus. He saw young soldiers his own age sitting shoulder to shoulder.

He settled back onto his duffel bag. Glancing at a crate next to where he lay, he wondered what was inside, but saw that it was nailed shut.

Reaching into his bag, he found his buck knife, and worked the blade under a wooden slat until it creaked open. He pushed aside packing rags and was surprised to see the wooden stocks of rifles.

That makes no sense—sending rifles to Nice—away from the front?

He lifted one out. It was a Remington. He tested the bolt action before putting it back. He began to feel uneasy and wasn't sure why— perhaps the prospect of getting caught when they reached Nice.

The truck bumped and rattled over a road that seemed narrow and very rutted, not the kind you'd expect between major cities. Over the rattling of the lorry and the droning of its motor, he thought he heard singing. He lay still and listened. It was unmistakable, the sound of men's voices coming from the bus. He recognized the melody of the "Marseillaise," the French national anthem. He began to hum along. Then he stopped.

Everything's wrong! The rifles. The soldiers singing. Even the direction of the sunset—especially the direction of the sunset! The thought exploded in his mind like a shell. *This convoy isn't going south to Nice! It's going north to the front!*

Over the sounds of the "Marseillaise" and the truck, he heard something else—a deep punctuation of thunder. As the minutes passed, it grew louder—deeper and heavier—like the hoarse barking of bullmastiffs.

Dogs of war—the memory from Shakespeare's *Julius Caesar* formed in his mind, assigned reading in senior English. "Cry, Havoc!" he said aloud, "Cry Havoc, and let slip the dogs of war." He felt fate closing in on him.

He heard the sharp crack of an explosion. Then another. And another. Ordinance finding its mark, steadily louder and steadily nearer, bright flames shining through the tarpaulin, the roar and snap of burning trees.

Clambering over the crates, he looked out the back of the lorry, no longer caring if anyone saw him. Bright orange flames were devouring a stand of trees just off the road. He saw the faces of the soldiers illuminated by the firelight, watching the trees burn.

The convoy rumbled away from the fire. Night took hold, darkness but for the pale headlamps of the bus. The woods grew quiet.

But not for long.

A high-pitched whistling filled the air. Evan ducked back into the truck as a sharp bellowing roar and burst of yellow flame ripped open the canopy of night. The lorry listed, the world spinning as the truck tipped onto its side, throwing him off his feet, crates shifting, pounding onto him, burying him beneath their weight—more explosions and the whining clang of metal, concussions of air pushing the breath from his lungs, setting his ears to ringing. Then, a sudden blow to his head and darkness closed in.

Minutes or hours passed.

He was awake but could see nothing. His head hurt, and he felt his right hand next to his forehead. He blinked his eyes and felt his eyelid move against his fingers. His eyes were open, but he couldn't see anything. He pushed back a wave of panic. *Of course I can't see— it's nighttime and I'm probably underneath the crates.*

He moved his fingers and felt his cheek, wet and sticky to the touch. His mouth tasted of blood. *How bad am I injured?* He took a deep breath and lay still, listening for any sound. But he heard nothing. A thought formed in his mind. *I should get out of here.*

He shifted about, relieved to be able to move his arms and legs. He felt the wooden edges of crates. Using his hands and feet, he pushed hard in every direction and found a crate he was able to move with his foot. Shoving it away, cool air flooded in. He lifted his head and saw light framed by the opening—flickering light of a burning fire. He managed to wiggle out feet first, dragging his duffel bag behind.

Once free, he tried to locate the bus full of soldiers. But there was only the skeleton of its frame engulfed by billowing black smoke, the empty windows pierced by tongues of flame.

With mounting horror, he stood by the remains of the lorry, looking at what remained of the convoy—burning buses and trucks. He looked for movement, listened for some sign of life, but all he saw were the banking flames, all he heard was the hiss and snap of the fires, and in the distance, the low barking of the big guns.

He stepped away from the lorry into a fog that seemed to blanket the ground, the air acrid with smoke, bitter on the tongue. With his duffel bag over his shoulder, he glanced back at the burning bus and shook his head. "Cry havoc," he whispered. Like an elegy.

The fog burned his eyes, and he was finding it hard to breathe. He began to run, slipping and falling among rocks and the jagged depressions of shell craters. He ran away from the creeping smoke, into the darkness among the trees. He kept moving, groping forward, dragging his duffle bag behind, into a thicket of bramble, scratching and holding him until he could go no further.

Sore and exhausted, he lay still. His throat hurt and his chest burned. He couldn't see anything in the darkness, but he could still hear the hoarse barking of the dogs of war.

"Cry havoc," he whispered as night closed over him.

CHAPTER 28

September 10, 1914

Montreux

Rhone Valley, Switzerland

THE DINING ROOM of Pension Bienvenue at the foot-hills of the Swiss Alps on the shores of Lake Geneva was filling up with the marooned British nationals.

"Let's take that vacant table toward the back," Weizmann said and led Vera and Benjy through the dining room.

"Your attention, everyone!" the British consul announced and tapped an empty water glass with a spoon. "Please find a seat. It's quite imperative that I address you without delay."

Amid the ensuing bustle, a dapper middle-aged Englishman approached Weizmann's table and asked, "May I join you?"

"Of course, Mervin! I was very much hoping we'd have the opportunity of seeing you before we return to England." During the month they had spent at the pension, Weizmann and Vera had gotten to know Mervin Smythe quite well.

"It certainly appears we may be finally leaving!" Mervin made an elegant bow in Vera's direction. "Frau Doktor," he said and sat next to Weizmann.

The Consul tapped the glass again, the sound cutting through the noise of cross conversations, and silence settled over the dining room. "Firstly," he began, "I'm happy to announce that we've received permission to travel by rail from Zürich to Paris!"

This was met with applause, which quieted as he continued speaking, "And from Paris we've arranged passage to Normandy and thence by ferry to Dover."

This was followed by another round of applause.

"But the first step of our journey," he continued, "begins at the Montreux railway station. We've hired taxis for everyone, and they'll be here within the half hour. Please, pack up your bags and we'll depart as soon as they arrive."

"Pardon me, sir!"

Weizmann was surprised to hear Vera call out.

She stood up and asked, "We're delighted to hear the news, but what has changed to allow us to travel?"

"The tide of battle has turned, my dear Dr. Weizmann," The consul replied. "A few days ago German troops were less than twenty miles from Paris, but they've been forced to retreat. We now have an opportunity to safely return home."

As others shouted questions in a general clamor for more information, the consul raised both hands. "Please! Time is of the essence! Prepare your luggage so we'll be able to leave on schedule! I'll provide more information at the railway station."

Weizmann stood up and extended his hand to Sykes. "Mervin, if you're ever in Manchester, we should share a glass or two of fine Scottish whisky."

"Speaking of whisky," Mervin smiled. "I found your distillery plans of great interest—for acetone, of course! Your innovation for manufacturing explosives will be a significant contribution to the war effort!"

"I'm hoping Whitehall will agree, and when we see each other in England, perhaps we'll raise a glass to the achievement of that effort."

"As long as it's not a glass of acetone!" Mervin said with a little bow to Vera. "Frau Doktor, it's been an honor."

Vera nodded, holding Benjy by the hand. "The honor has been ours, Professor Smythe. We do hope you'll pay us a visit in Manchester!"

"It will be my pleasure!" Mervin bowed again and stepped away.

Back in their room, Vera and Chaim made short work of packing. Once at the pension's front door, they boarded a taxi, and were soon on their way to the train station.

Weizmann sighed as he looked back at Lake Geneva framed by the Swiss Alps. *It's beautiful here, but I'm so glad to be leaving . . .* Turning to Vera, he said, "I do hope Mervin comes for a visit. I thoroughly enjoyed hearing about his research on Teutonic archeology."

"I was actually surprised by your level of interest," Vera replied.

"I was as well, but as a chemist and an admirer of Rilke—"

Vera laughed. "I just knew this would somehow involve your Rilke obsession!"

"Hear me out, darling. As a chemist, I was intrigued by Mervin's discussion about the ancient Teutonic notions of transformation involving the four basic alchemical processes associated with the four primordial elements—earth, water, air, and fire. Some of Rilke's poetry seeks to understand this alchemy as it pertains to the interaction of soul and spirit in what Rilke calls the *task of transformation*."

"My dear husband," Vera shook her head. "You're such a luftmensch! But that probably contributes to your ability to dream and innovate. My medical training requires a more *practical* view of the world."

At the railway station in Montreux, they boarded for the five-hour trip to Zürich. The route, by way of Interlaken and Lucerne, treated them to the beauty of the Alps and the Rhone Valley beneath a cloudless sky.

At Zürich Central Station, an attaché gave them their tickets for the train to Paris.

"How long will the trip take?" Weizmann asked.

"Normally twelve hours, though we expect delays with added stops and check points in France."

And so it was—a lengthy delay at the French frontier where border patrol agents examined the travelers' documents. Once in France, there were added stops at checkpoints, and delays when their train was banished to a siding, where it idled while other trains passed in both directions.

Concerned about the delay at one of these stops, Weizmann left the train and approached a conductor. "Excuse me, but why are all these trains being given priority?"

"The ones heading west are bringing French wounded to hospitals in Paris or repatriating French refugees from Alsace. The trains heading east are bringing reinforcements to the front, especially with the Battle of the Marne in full swing."

"The Battle of the Marne? What about the Battle of the Frontiers?"

"The Battle of the Frontiers has ground down to a bloody stalemate. The Battle of the Marne began four days ago—just east of Paris. At first, the Germans seemed unstoppable, which was why the government moved to Bordeaux. But the tide turned with the miracle of the Marne."

"What miracle?"

"When all seemed lost, a thousand taxis from Paris were organized under cover of darkness to take reinforcements to the front. Taxi drivers drove back and forth, day and night without sleeping. In the end they brought over five thousand soldiers to the front, and the Germans were beaten back. In this manner, they saved Paris and showed the Germans the sacred unity of the French people." The conductor smiled broadly. "How's that for a miracle?"

"Indeed! God willing, such unity will put an end to this German aggression!"

The train whistle shrieked, and Weizmann quickly boarded.

As the train resumed the trip to Paris, Weizmann told Vera and Benjy about the Miracle of the Marne, embellishing the story and stretching it out for more than an hour—if only to provide some respite from the tedium of the long trip.

After another twenty-four hours of checkpoints and rail crossings, they finally arrived in Paris. It was late at night and Benjy was asleep. Ordinarily, Weizmann would have been happy to carry him, but there were no porters to carry the luggage. They had to wake Benjy up, but in this they were only partially successful. Though upright, he was still half-asleep and completely disoriented.

"It's alright darling," Vera said softly as she guided him off the train. "We're at the station in Paris and you can go right back to sleep." She found a bench and soon had Benjy lying down with his head on her lap.

Weizmann fetched their tickets to Normandy from the consul's attaché. As he was returning to Vera and Benjy, he passed a French policeman who handed him a broadsheet. At first glance, it looked like a wanted poster—an artist's drawing of the faces of four men with large print at the top of the page, *AVEZ-VOUS VU CES ESPIONS ET SABOTEURS?*

He sat next to Vera who was stroking Benjy's head cradled on her lap.

"What's that?" she asked, looking at the broadsheet.

"The French police are offering rewards for information about these men, suspected of espionage or sabotage. Perhaps both."

"The young one looks rather out of place. What does it say about him?"

Weizmann squinted at the text and began to translate. "Evan Sinclair . . . escaped while being questioned by the Paris police on September 9 . . ." He paused and asked, "What's the date today?"

"The tenth, I think."

Weizmann looked back at the text. "Seventeen years old . . . suspected of espionage for the Germans." Weizmann froze, not believing his eyes. "Oh, my god!"

"What?" asked Vera.

"Under known associates it lists his father as Clive Sinclair . . ."

"Why is that name so familiar?" she asked.

"Didn't we hear him lecture at the Ashmolean a few years ago?"

"We did! He spoke about pre-Biblical flood stories from Mesopotamia. And if I'm not mistaken, you slept through much of it."

Weizmann laughed. "Clive Sinclair—that *was* him." He looked back at the paper in his hands. "It seems his son has gotten himself into trouble . . ."

"Maybe it was just a misunderstanding . . .he was only being questioned. Perhaps he's innocent."

"Innocent people don't usually run away from the police," Weizmann said as he continued to study the text under the drawing of Evan. "What's this?" he exclaimed. "Mervin Smythe is *also* listed as a known associate!" Weizmann looked up and began to scan the crowded landing, looking for him.

"What a bizarre coincidence!" said Vera. "Do you see him anywhere?"

At that moment, the train whistle cut through the noise of the railway station, the frequency rising as the train for Normandy approached.

Weizmann carefully folded the broadsheet and placed it in his jacket pocket. "We'll have ample time to speak with him about this on the train."

CHAPTER 29

September 15, 1914
Jerusalem

QUARANTINE at the sick house was over.

As darkness descended over the Old City, Gunter sat at the bottom of the steps leading down from the veranda, waiting for his daughter. He and Tirzah had been apart for a month—since just before Rachel's death—separated when they needed most to be together. But the separation may have saved Tirzah's life, sparing her from the dark reach of the smallpox contagion. Quarantine had done its part. Now it was finally over.

Tirzah, along with Rahman and baby Mahmoud had finished eighteen days of isolation at the Italian Hospital in West Jerusalem. Thereafter, they had stayed with David Nathanson and his wife, Sarah, in the new Jewish neighborhood of Nachalat Shiva.

Dr. Musayaf had come by earlier that day, instructing the Turkish sanitary guard to remove the barriers and warning signs. But the guard had delayed, and it was only after Gunter gave the man a sizeable bak'shish that the trappings of quarantine were finally removed, and the guard went away.

Gunter looked down the narrow lane of smooth cobblestones in the gathering dusk, watching for Tirzah. From the house above, he could hear the clatter of dishes as Fatima prepared for a special dinner to welcome everyone back.

Gunter had helped clean house during the day, moving furniture and hanging carpets over the veranda balustrade like pennants decorating a royal keep. He had especially relished beating the carpets, wielding the ornately scrolled bamboo wand with all his strength, smacking the carpets again and again, raising a cloud of dust with each stroke, beating away the memory of the smallpox that had disfigured and killed Rachel.

Since her death, he had heard her voice speaking in his mind. As he waited on the stairs, he heard her again.

My dear husband, you know that we're not truly apart, that you live in me, and I in you. This seeming separation is but for a little time, and then we'll be together in the Upper Jerusalem, and that will be forever . . .

Gunter drew a deep breath. *I'll grieve for you beyond the traditional thirty days of mourning, my darling, but I take solace in knowing that we'll meet again . . .*

Hearing the sound of footfalls in the lane, Gunter stood up and stared into the darkness beyond the furthest lamp. He could see them now, Rahman with baby Mahmoud in one arm, gripping a large suitcase with the other. And Tirzah, pale in the lamplight, a suitcase in her hand. Seeing him, she dropped it and ran forward.

"Fatima, they come!" Gunter called out and caught Tirzah up in his arms, spinning round as he hugged her—the softness of her cheek, the saltiness of her tears and his own, the joy of holding her. "You're more beautiful than I remember!"

"I missed you, Aba," she cried and clung to him fiercely. "And I miss Ima so much!" Her shoulders shook as she wept.

Rahman drew alongside. He put down his suitcase and placed his hand on Gunter's shoulder. "Hello, old friend."

Still holding Tirzah, Gunter covered Rahman's hand with his own. He nodded toward the veranda where Fatima waited. "Go ahead. I'll bring up your bag."

Holding Mahmoud in the crook of his arm, Rahman bounded up the steps.

Gunter took the bags, and with Tirzah, mounted the steps to the veranda. There they watched Rahman holding Fatima in his arms as Mahmoud, anxious in the darkness, climbed halfway over his father's shoulder and peeked back at his mother. Then his eyes brightened with recognition, and twisting in Rahman's arms, reached out for her.

"My love, my life!" Fatima cried, catching the baby up in her arms. She spun around in a little dance, weeping and laughing. Then, still holding Mahmoud, she brought Rahman into the embrace.

Though delighted by their reunion, Gunter's heart clenched at the emptiness Rachel's death had left in his life. He knew that for Tirzah, the loss was even sharper. Fatima apparently sensed Tirzah's pain and turned to her with Mahmoud still clinging to her neck.

She put an arm around Tirzah's shoulder and whispered, "I'm hugging you also for your mother, my dearest girl. She loved you so very, very much, and she would be so pleased to see us together again." Still holding Tirzah with one arm and Mahmoud with the other, she announced, "My dear ones, come to dinner."

As Gunter took a step forward, he felt Rahman tap him on the shoulder.

Apparently seeing the gesture, Fatima asked, "Aren't you two coming in?"

"Presently, my love, but I must first speak with Gunter. We'll be quick—"

"How quick?"

"Fifteen minutes."

Gunter heard an urgency in Rahman's voice, and saw that Fatima understood. She nodded and went inside with the children.

Gunter followed Rahman down a darkened hallway to his study. "Quite a relief to be back home, isn't it?"

"Not entirely . . ."

"What do you mean?"

"I'm overjoyed to see Fatima," he said and switched on a table lamp. "But it's not safe for us here."

"Because of the Turks? The Germans?"

"For the moment, they don't concern me. It's rather something that infects them which endangers us." As Rahman spoke, he pushed the door closed. Opening his valise, he lifted out a scroll and placed it on the table. "Look at *this*."

Gunter unrolled the parchment beneath a circle of lamplight. In a glance he took in the rough sketch depicting human figures and buildings with notations and transecting lines. "My God!" he whispered. "This is a copy of *The Ordination* from the second series of Poussin's *Seven Sacraments*! But, who made these measurements? It couldn't have been Walker—"

"It wasn't." Rahman's face darkened. "When Walker returned to Palestine last month, he was accompanied by Guido von List. You've heard of him?"

"I have." Gunter's heart sank as he stared at the parchment. "He did all this in less than a month?"

"Yes. He's also aware of the portal in the Tomb of Zechariah."

"What a *disaster*!" Gunter sighed as he released the edge of the scroll and it curled closed.

"How did this happen?" Rahman asked as he rested a hand on Gunter's shoulder. "You've always assured me that your father constructed a ruse to keep the portal safe—to make sure inquisitive eyes would look elsewhere—not here in Jerusalem."

"Obviously, it didn't work." Feeling deflated, Gunter sank into an upholstered chair on the other side of the desk. *I've lost Rachel, and now this . . .*

Sitting behind his desk, Rahman persisted. "You've never told me what your father did to misdirect people like List."

Gunter sighed out a deep breath and replied, "As you know well,

Europe's fascination with Jerusalem began with the Crusades."

"Indeed," Rahman agreed. "This has always been the challenge we've faced as Guardians of the Temple Mount."

"Yes, Rahman, and the high councils have always sought to protect the secrets by distracting the curious—making the seekers and treasure hunters look *elsewhere*."

Rahman nodded. "And for centuries the distractions worked well—El Dorado, the Fountain of Youth, Atlantis, the Grail Quest, the Chinese Seal of the Realm—"

"These ruses indeed worked," Gunter cut in. "But about thirty years ago, the council noted some determined and better-informed individuals in esoteric European circles. Such as these had developed an interest in *The Ordination.*" He leaned forward and reopened the scroll and pointed. "Particularly, the keys in Christ's hand, the Tomb of Zechariah, and the geometric arrangement of the painting—they all combined to hint at an entryway into the Temple Mount." He sank back in the chair and the scroll rolled closed.

"So, the council knew what was coming," said Rahman.

"Yes, and they began to prepare. They knew that this ruse would have to be truly ingenious, and indeed, it took decades to fashion. The site they chose was in Languedoc—the village of Rennes-le-Château."

"Perfect!" Rahman exclaimed, "with its already rich esoteric history!"

"Yes, and in addition to local legends of Knights Templar, the Magdalene, and the Grail Quest, there was the intrigue of the Albigensian Heresy and the legendary Cathar Treasure—the hoard of gold coins! All these aspects affirmed the council's choice of Rennes-le-Château as the site for the misdirection."

"But how did this involve your father?"

"He was central to the planning. Starting by identifying an old priest nearing retirement at the Rennes-le-Château church, my father found his successor—a young priest from a poor family named

Bérenger Saunière, unsuccessful in his first postings after ordination. When the old priest retired in 1885, my father arranged for Saunière to take his place.

"This was followed by the next phase of the plan—creating a forgery for Saunière to 'discover'—a Latin transcription of Gospel passages made to look of authentic antiquity—specifically, eighth century Vulgate. It contained a cipher—the Knight's Tour—with an ambiguous solution. My father brought the forgery to Rennes-le-Château and hid it in a hollow Visigothic pillar beneath the altar stone of the old parish church."

"And how would Saunière discover the forgery?" Rahman asked.

"My father presented himself to Saunière as the cardinal's representative from the Toulouse Diocese, charging him to renovate the church. He provided Saunière with detailed plans and funds for an extensive renovation—all supposedly from the diocese. A few weeks into the renovation, the forgery was *discovered* in the pillar and turned over to Saunière, who showed it to my father, seeking his advice—"

"And your father helped Saunière decipher the code?"

"That and more. He steered him into believing that the coded messages pointed toward another Poisson painting, 'The Arcadian Shepherds.' He actually took Saunière to Paris to see the painting at the Louvre."

"Why go to all that trouble?"

"It was important that Saunière see the painting for himself since it portrays a well-known local landmark—a tomb right outside Rennes-le-Château. In this way he connected Saunière with Poisson's painting and with the church. He also introduced another element for the treasure hunters—the legend of the Cathar treasure!"

"But how did he create that connection?"

"While in Paris with Saunière, my father went alone to taverns along Boulevard Saint-Michel in the Latin Quarter where he pretended to be drunk, ranting about the Cathar Treasure, Poisson's

Arcadian Shepherds, and the mysterious sudden wealth of Rennes-le-Château—"

"Just to plant the seeds," said Rahman. "Clever . . ."

"When they returned to Rennes-le-Château, my father told Saunière that the diocese required his complete silence—charging him to say nothing of the document, the coded message, or 'The Arcadian Shepherds' painting. And as compensation, Saunière would receive yearly installments for a total sum of six hundred thousand gold francs."

Rahman blew out a breath. "That's a lot of compensation! Where did the money come from?"

"From here—Egyptian and Roman gold coins from the Templar treasure chamber on the Holy Mountain—used to purchase French gold francs. My father stressed to Saunière that he would only receive the yearly trove of gold francs if he kept silent.

He also charged Saunière to use the funds extravagantly on other projects—such as the ornate tower with crenellated battlements in honor of the Magdalene—Tour Magdala."

Rahman smiled. "And with that ostentatious display, it was no surprise when rumors of treasure in Rennes-le-Château created a frenzy of speculation."

"Quite so. The rumors of hidden treasure combined with the region's history and theories about Poussin's *Arcadian Shepherds* to create a firestorm of interest among esoteric circles and treasure hunters everywhere."

"I'm not familiar with it. What was so compelling about it?" Rahman asked.

"It depicts Arcadian shepherds meditating over an inscrutable inscription on a tomb . . . Et in Arcadia Ego—Even in Arcadia, am I."

"What does that *mean*?" asked Rahman.

"In Renaissance art, Arcadia suggests an unspoiled paradise, and the phrase 'even in Arcadia am I,' suggests the inevitability of death. But beyond that, the painting's lines and angles created the impression of an intricately coded geometry. And taken with all the other elements, the ruse seemed to work—esoterics and treasure hunters flocked to Rennes-le-Château from all over the world, and most importantly, they turned *away* from Jerusalem."

"But, not List, and not Kaiser Wilhelm," Rahman said as he stood up.

Gunter sighed. "No one could have foreseen the kaiser's unique agenda regarding Jerusalem, which began with his pilgrimage to the Holy Land at the turn of the century. And now it appears his aspirations go beyond sitting on a throne on the Temple Mount. With the help of Walker and List, he wants what's hidden *beneath* that throne."

"That and the oil hidden beneath the sands of Arabia," Rahman said as he lifted the parchment from his desk.

Gunter noticed that Rahman's hands shook as he rolled up the parchment. "What troubles you?" he asked.

"Just this," Rahman replied and fixed his eyes on Gunter. "If List knows as much as he appears to know, he likely knows about *our* knowledge of these matters."

"Yes," Gunter said as he stood up. "And it's only a question of time before he comes for us. We should find sanctuary."

"But where?" asked Rahman. "We can't go to the tomb. List has posted Turkish guards there."

"How about the American Colony in East Jerusalem?" Gunter asked. "The compound is like a labyrinth, and I've known the founder, Anna Spafford, for years."

"Sounds promising."

"I'll speak with her tomorrow morning—I'm certain she'll agree."

Rahman opened the door. "But now, dinner! Afterward, I'll let Fatima know that we'll need to get packing, and why."

CHAPTER 30

September 16, 1914
The Hills near Dinant
German-occupied Belgium

"WELCOME BACK!"

The voice Evan didn't recognize spoke English. He winced as he sat up and saw that a gray blanket covered his legs. He was on a bare mattress in what seemed to be the remains of a room—one wall gone and half the ceiling open to the sky. A swath of sunlight fell across a floor littered with chunks of broken masonry. A few feet away, a boy about his own age, maybe younger, sat hunched against a wall of red bricks and cracked white plaster, watching him, a rifle across his knees.

Thirsty, he cleared his throat and asked for water in a hoarse voice he barely recognized.

The boy put aside the rifle, got to his feet, and went to a pail. He lifted out a dripping cup and handed it to Evan.

Nodding his thanks, he drank it down. His throat felt a little better. but confusion filled his mind and he wondered where he was. Stretching out his arm to hand back the cup, he saw a jagged tracery of scratch marks on his arm. Looking at his other arm, he saw the same pattern, and wondered how that had happened.

The boy returned to his seat on the floor against the opposite wall, the rifle across his knees.

Evan cleared his throat and asked, "Where am I?"

"*Now* you ask? You've been talking nonstop for two days."

"I have?"

"But you weren't making any sense."

He couldn't place the boy's accent. It sounded British and French at the same time. He rubbed a hand over his head, feeling a bandage. "I remember a truck . . ."

"That's where we got these Remingtons." The boy patted the rifle. "A good day for us."

"Us? Who *are* you?"

"My name is Emile. Your name is Evan Sinclair."

"How do you know that?" he asked, then noticed his duffle bag beside him on the mattress. "From something in there?"

"Yes—your high school diploma. But even before we found that, we knew."

"How?"

"Like I said, you've been talking a lot."

Evan tried to get up and a sharp pain jolted him back.

"You shouldn't try to get up."

Looking down, he saw that his chest and abdomen were bandaged. He lifted the tattered blanket and saw more bandages on his legs. "What happened to my pants?"

"We had to cut them away to clean you up." Emile stood and leaned the rifle against the wall.

Evan saw that the boy wore khaki breaches tucked into big clumsy boots. This made his lower body look stocky, even powerful, but his upper body, clad in a torn undershirt was slight, his arms white and thin, almost delicate. He stepped toward the mattress where Evan sat and crouched down.

"We found you near the wreckage of a train, and thought you were dead—tangled up in thorn brush and deep in a hedgerow. We couldn't get you out right away because we had to wait for the gas to clear."

"What gas?"

"Chlorine gas—the Germans have begun using it in some of their artillery shells. It took us an hour to get you out of the thorn brush. You were pretty torn up."

Evan's mind began to clear. He remembered the convoy, the fires burning along the road, the foul-smelling green smoke that made his eyes and throat burn, the shattered bus, and the helplessness as he lay trapped in the darkness, coughing, his chest burning.

"If you thought I was dead, why bother to get me out?"

"We can always use money and you actually had some. But what we really need are papers, and you had none—other than your high school diploma."

"You must have been pretty disappointed."

"We were." Emile nodded toward Evan's duffle bag. "We saw some kind of whip in there—what's that?"

"It's a Balearic sling—for throwing rocks."

"Sounds pretty useless—like your diploma." Emile smiled. "But, once we got you out of the brush, we saw you were alive, though barely."

"You keep saying we—where are the others?"

"Out looking for food. We ate everything we found in the pantry here and finished off the geese a few days ago."

"Are we in England?"

"England? Are you talking crazy again? This is Belgium, and every town within twenty miles is occupied by the Germans." Emile straightened up and looked down at Evan. "Why did you think we're in England?"

"Because of your English, you speak so well."

"My father's English—from Dover, and I spent a lot of time there with his side of the family. On my mother's side I'm Flemish, which is why I'm with the resistance." He stepped back to the wall and picked up his rifle. "But, why are *you* here? You're an American—"

"No. I'm English. I lived in America for several years."

"Cedar City, Utah."

"That's right. What else do you know about me?"

"That you're not German. Which is why you're still alive. But you still haven't told me the *one thing* we don't know about you. Why are you here?"

Evan looked at Emile as he considered what to say. He decided to keep it simple. "I came to fight on the side of the Entente."

Emile laughed. "There you go again. Talking crazy."

CHAPTER 31

September 20, 1914
Jerusalem
The American Colony

ANNA SPAFFORD left her daughter, Bertha, in charge of the soup kitchen and went to see if the next cauldron of lentil soup was ready. She traversed rarely visited limestone passageways and ramps within the compound to reach an old ancillary kitchen.

As leader of the American Colony, Anna was happy to provide sanctuary to Gunter, Rahman, and their families following the death of Gunter's wife, Rachel. They had arrived a few days before and were already settled in and helping with the colony's busy soup kitchen for Jerusalem's poor. Only Anna and her immediate family knew of their presence, and as far as Anna understood, the fugitives simply required a place to hide, with Gunter sought by German authorities for army service, and Rahman wanted by Ottoman authorities for a forced labor brigade.

Anna reached the old kitchen and saw Fatima stirring lentil soup in a copper cauldron. "Good morning, my dear, have you already added the dried basil and oregano?"

"I did, Mrs. Spafford. Would you like to have a taste?"

"I would, my dear, and please, call me Anna."

She took a spoon, and carefully tasted the hot soup, leaning forward to protect the white apron she wore over her pink blouse and long dark skirt. "Excellent! This batch is ready. I'll tell Jacob and Frederick to bring it out."

"Have we already met them?" asked Fatima.

"Briefly. Jacob and Frederick are my son and son-in-law. I'm sure you'll remember them when they come by to fetch the soup." Anna sighed. "Despite the rain, there's already a long line in the courtyard. I've never seen such a crowd!"

"It's the damned war!" Gunter said, entering the kitchen carrying a burlap sack. "Every day more men are taken away, leaving their families without support." He deposited the sack by the stove.

"Good morning, Anna," Rahman said as he also placed a heavy sack by the stove. "This is the last of the lentils."

Anna frowned. "If the crowd tomorrow is anything like today, we won't have enough. I'll send Jacob and Frederick to the souk for more."

"We'll also need more carrots, celery and onions," Fatima said and straightened her white apron. "Did you start the soup kitchen when the war began, Anna?"

"Heavens, no, my dear! We've been feeding the poor of Jerusalem for years—Arabs, Turks, Jews, Kurds, Armenians. Before the war we were feeding hundreds a day. Now it's in the thousands!" She rested her hand on Fatima's shoulder and added, "I'm so very grateful you're able to give us a hand!"

"It's our pleasure, Anna! We're pleased beyond words to help, and grateful for the protection you're giving us."

"We're in your debt!" Gunter added. "And if there's anything else we can do, we trust you'll let us know."

Anna smiled and turned to leave. "For now, Gunter, just put the lentils to soak."

✾ ✾ ✾

As Gunter watched her leave, he felt a stab of guilt. "Perhaps we should have told her about Walker and List . . ."

What's to tell?" asked Fatima as she put two rectangular pans on the counter. "According to what you've said, they've been in Jerusalem for over a month, and there's no evidence they know where we are. Why burden Anna with our anxieties?"

"I agree," said Rahman as he lifted a sack of lentils onto the counter. "She understands the clear danger we face from the Ottomans and Germans, and she's hiding us from them. Why worry her needlessly about Walker and List?"

"You're probably right." Gunter shrugged.

"How long have you known her?" asked Rahman.

"Forever!" Gunter replied. "I must have been about three when she and her husband, Horatio arrived here from Chicago. I have vague memories of visiting them with my parents at the place they rented near Damascus Gate. Horatio died from Malaria when I was ten, and I vividly remember his funeral on Mount Zion." Gunter sighed. "Since then, Anna has managed all the colony's affairs by herself—including the move into this compound.

"How old is she?" Rahman asked as he poured lentils into the pans.

"Seventy-two, and still going strong—the leader of a religious community who never proselytizes."

"She leads by example," Fatima stated and poured water over the lentils.

"She does," Gunter said. "With the soup kitchen, the hospital, the orphanage . . . she does more to spread the Gospel than a hundred overzealous missionaries—"

Gunter stopped speaking and held his breath, anxious at the sound of approaching footsteps. He exhaled when Anna's son Jacob and her son-in-law Frederick entered the kitchen pushing a wheelbarrow.

"Anna said you're ready with the next batch," said Jacob.

"Indeed, we are!" said Gunter.

"Thanks," said Frederick. "We really appreciate your help!"

"Please!" Gunter replied as he and Rahman helped load the caldron onto the wheelbarrow. "We're obliged to you for the protection and support we enjoy here."

"But it can't be easy," said Frederick. "Cooped up here day after day."

"Considering the risks out there," Gunter nodded at a shuttered window, "We'll settle for a little boredom."

Once they were gone, Rahman said, "Frederick's right. How long can we go on living in hiding like this?"

"My dear husband, we've been here less than a week, and you and Gunter have already been out to check on the portal. Did any Turkish guards even challenge you?"

"No one dares come close to *lepers*!" said Rahman.

"Your disguises work that well?" she asked.

"They do!" he replied. "Whenever anyone comes near, we pull the hoods of our robes over our heads and make noise with the rattles."

Fatima smiled. "I never thought being a leper would have such advantages . . ."

"No—only *pretending* to be a leper!" said Gunter as he stepped to the window and peeked out at the courtyard between the shutter's slats. "What a crowd! From here I can see Anna and Bertha in the tent doling out soup and . . ." He fell silent and leaned forward. After a long pause, he said, "That's strange!"

"What's strange?" asked Rahman.

"What's a fellow in a three-piece suit doing at a soup kitchen?" Gunter asked. "He looks more like someone going to tea at the Gezireh Sporting Club in Cairo!"

"Let me have a look." Rahman stepped to the window.

Gunter pointed. "There—at the edge of the tent, just folding up an umbrella."

"Oh, my God!" he whispered.

"You recognize him?"

"Of course! That's Montagu Walker!"

CHAPTER 32

September 21, 1914
Manchester, England

"CHAIM! I'M HOME!" Vera shouted from the foyer.

"I'm in Benjy's room! Why don't you join us?"

After a long day caring for mothers and their children at the Manchester public health service, Vera was anxious to see her own child. Reaching the doorway of her son's room, she stood silently for a long moment, watching Chaim and Benjy sitting on the rug, writing and drawing on large sheets of paper spread over the floor.

"This is Germany with its capital, Berlin," she heard Chaim say as he drew. "And this is France with its capital, Paris."

"What are you boys doing?"

"Hi Mummy!" Benjy looked up, beaming, then grew serious. "Daddy and I are talking about the war in Europe." As she took a step forward, he shouted. "Be careful! You almost stepped on Ireland!"

Pointing at France, she smiled. "Do you remember when we were in Paris?"

"I liked the park there very much! I especially liked the merry-go-round. That was *so* much fun!"

"Yes, it was!" she said with genuine enthusiasm. "That was the most beautiful merry-go-round I've ever seen!" Stepping carefully forward, she added, "I'll join you here in England!" She held out an envelope. "Here, darling—I stopped on my way home to pick up the mail they've been holding for us at the post office—you might want to see this right now." She fixed him with her eyes and added, "It's from Whitehall!"

Instead of taking it, Chaim asked, "Could you read it to me?"

Vera stepped away and opened the envelope.

"Look, Daddy! Mummy's standing in the Mediterranean Sea!"

"It's dated August 22—almost a month ago," Vera said and began to read. "*Dear Professor Weizmann, Thank you for your response to our appeal to British scientists regarding discoveries of possible military value. We are intrigued by your fermentation research that purports to produce large quantities of acetone.* This is wonderful, Chaim!" she exclaimed, and turned to Benjy. "May I sit next to Daddy in North Africa?"

"Certainly, Mum, but do be careful not to block the Suez Canal!"

"I promise to be careful if *you* go wash up for dinner."

"Yes, Mum!" Benjy said and ran off.

Vera continued reading. "*Please contact us with all dispatch to arrange for members of our scientific staff to come to your laboratory, review your notes, and repeat your experiments. Depending on their recommendations, we may invite you to the War Office in London to discuss implementation of a production program.* Looks promising." She handed the letter to Chaim and sat next to him.

He nodded as he scanned it. "Signed by Winston Churchill, First Lord of the Admiralty." He turned to her and said with a broad smile, "I might actually have the chance to make a significant contribution to the war effort!"

"It certainly looks that way." She rubbed his back and asked, "What does that mean . . . implementation of a production program?"

"Given England's dire straits, it's vital to implement any proposal that might benefit the war effort. A pilot plant would be built to evaluate production capabilities."

"Where would that be?" Vera asked, worried that he might need to spend a great deal of time away from home or that they might need to move.

"I'm not sure, but I know it could be set up in an existing distillery since the pilot plant basically requires large-scale distilling equipment—the same used for making whisky."

"Aren't there distilleries throughout England?" she asked.

"Indeed, there are."

"So, we won't necessarily need to move, will we?" she asked hopefully.

"I hope not, but the first step is to meet with Churchill." He got to his feet and reached down to help her up. "I'll cable him tomorrow morning. And speaking of cables, I received one this morning from Mervin Smythe, that nice chap we met in Switzerland."

"Did he make it back to England alright?"

"He did and wanted to apologize for not properly saying goodbye. Apparently, he went for a walk outside the railway station, got lost, and by the time he found his way back, the train had left the station."

"Such a dear absent-minded professor!" Vera laughed and shook her head. "It's a shame you never had the chance to ask him about that young Englishman on the broadsheet . . . what was his name again?"

"Evan Sinclair. When I see Mervin again, I'll be sure to ask him."

CHAPTER 33

September 21, 1914
Mecca
Ottoman Province of the Hejaz

FAISAL PEERED into the shadows beyond the wavering light of a torch set in the tunnel wall and saw what appeared to be a robed intruder armed with a rifle. With his heart pounding wildly, he raised his pistol and shouted, "Put down your weapon and step into the light!" His voice echoed in the catacombs beneath the Great Mosque.

In hiding since returning from Damascus almost two weeks before, he feared the Ottomans had found him.

"Faisal?" The voice was unmistakable.

"Father?" Faisal held the pistol steady, his finger still tensed on the trigger.

"Of course, my son!"

"Why do you come armed, Father?"

"What are you talking about?"

Faisal watched his father emerge from the darkness, leaning on a cane, which he had thought was a rifle. "I'm sorry," he said and quickly lowered the pistol. "It's just that I've been down here alone for so many days, I'm becoming unhinged!"

"It's unfortunately necessary, my son. The Turks have been scouring the precincts of the Great Mosque, indeed, all of Mecca, searching for you. Fortunately these catacombs are a secret known to very few."

"But, how much longer must I remain here?"

"Let us speak further in your apartments."

Faisal took his father's arm, and together they made their way through a rough-hewn limestone passageway. Faisal noticed that his father's limp was more pronounced than he remembered, and he appeared frail. Hussein's vitality and iron will had always inspired Faisal, but now he seemed old and weak.

They passed beneath a range of low stone arches covered in flaking white paint. Reaching a closed wooden door, Faisal drew a brass key from among his robes. Once through the door, he closed and locked it. The apartment was spare, lit by candles, lined by carpets, and warmed by a fire that burned in the hearth. Converted from a large cavern in the warren of secret passages beneath the Great Mosque, the shelves flanking the hearth were filled with books. He helped his father into an upholstered chair in the orange glow of the fire.

"You've found the accommodations comfortable, my son? The stored victuals have been to your liking?"

Faisal ignored the questions. "My father, this confinement is beginning to feel less like a temporary refuge, and more like a burial chamber! And the worse thing is that I have no idea where my wife and children are, and no idea what's happening in the world!"

"Your family is safe and secure, my son. As for the world above, sad to say, the war goes badly for England and her allies. The Germans advance on Paris, and in the east they've all but defeated the Russians." He raised his shoulders. "But all is not lost—the Austrians fare less well in the Balkans, and there is talk of America entering the war."

"And what of Turkey?" Faisal asked, "Have they joined with Germany?"

"They remain neutral even though the war began almost two months ago. Djemal appears to be prevailing over Enver Pasha."

"But for how much longer?"

"Who knows? Hopefully for the duration of the war."

"And what news from the British?"

"I continue to trade messages with McMahon and Kitchener, and they continue to convey vague promises of Arab independence, but nothing firm." Hussein shrugged. "I have no illusions about the British, my son; they will say anything to garner our support. Nevertheless, England's elusive language is more favorable to my ears than Turkish threats."

"What threats?"

"After I declined the caliph's request to declare the jihad from Mecca, a delegation from Enver brought me troubling directives— plans to blend away our language, to obliterate our customs. In short, I believe they wish to turn us into Turks, as they have attempted with the Kurds, the Jews, and the Armenians. There is also a law recently passed in Constantinople that requires full Arab conscription for the Turkish Army in the Hejaz."

"This is an outrage!" Faisal shouted. "How did you answer?"

"I informed them that Turkish laws are appropriate for Turkey, but the Hejaz is the land of God, abiding by the divine law of God and by the teachings of the Prophet. No other law can prevail in the Hejaz."

"You answered well, my father."

Hussein sighed. "I will continue sparring with them as long as I can, but as long as Turkish neutrality continues, I remain hopeful. For now, it remains expedient to camouflage our disaffection on all fronts with a curtain of politesse and compromise."

"But, Father, are we not inclined to revolt against the Turks even without assurances from the British, and even if Turkey remains neutral?"

"You must be patient, my son! Is it not said that haste is the invention of the devil? As I have told you, if the Turks remain neutral for the entire war, I am less inclined for rebellion. If they side with Germany, we will rise up for our freedom. But armed rebellion against a powerful enemy will require the help of a powerful patron. After all, it is with us as with any nation that dwells in the grasp of empire—we cannot conduct a campaign of defiance without help. Before we can even consider a rebellion, we will need clear guarantees of British support."

"Would that support be in the form of British guns and British gold arriving from Egypt at the port of Jeddah?"

"It would, indeed."

"But is Jeddah secure?"

"You are most sapient and keen of understanding, my son. That is precisely the issue I have come to speak with you about."

Faisal already understood the direction of his father's thoughts. "Would you have me go to Jeddah?

"Yes, my son, and soon."

Faisal paced the carpet as an anxious fear rose in his chest. "The risk of leading the Arab revolt troubles me, Father. What of my wife and children?"

"As I told you, they are safe.

"Where?" Faisal stopped pacing and faced his father. "Where are they?"

"Sheltered at the encampment of the Tarabin Bedouin in Nuweiba."

"Where is that?"

"In the eastern Sinai on the shores of the Gulf of Aqaba. The Tarabin are most loyal to our person and have sworn to shelter and protect them."

"But will I continue to be separated from them?" he asked, his voice rising.

"For the present, yes!" Hussein said sharply.

Stung by his father's rebuke, he was reassured when Hussein spoke again, his voice softening.

"Listen to me, my son. Since your trip to Damascus and Amman, the Turks regard you as an enemy, and it would have been only a matter of time until they would have sought to flush you out by leveraging the love you have for your precious ones. They had to be protected, and now they are."

"But when will I see them again?" Faisal asked as he sat on a footstool.

"Soon, but first, you are for Jeddah. You will leave this very night. I will avail you of my favorite and swiftest she-camel. She will carry you to the village of Hamra in the Wadi Safra. There you will unite the Bedouin tribes—the Howeitat and the Harb, the Utaybah and the Bani Khalid—all for the defense of Jeddah. And be assured," Hussein patted Faisal on the knee, "After you meet with the tribes, you will join your family in Nuweiba."

"That is well, my father." Faisal was relieved but saw that his father appeared troubled. "Is there anything else you wish to tell me?" he asked.

"Yes. My son. Since I have refused to declare the jihad against the British and French from Mecca, the sultan will soon declare it from Constantinople!"

"But surely, my father, Muslims will see that the Germans are behind this ruse."

"Some will, some won't. Remember—German propaganda has long portrayed the kaiser as a champion of Islam, also spreading the lie that he converted to Islam and is a devout Muslim—Hajji Wilhelm they call him, the great Muslim Emperor of Germany!"

Faisal shook his head. "The kaiser shamelessly uses religion to enhance his power—whether he's masquerading as a Muslim or as the Christian Holy Roman Emperor. But, as I heard in Damascus, his only true religion is a pagan self-worship committed only to the supremacy of the Germanic race under his leadership."

"So, my son, let us hope that the Arabs will remain true to Islam, and to the Prophet with his bloodline through *us*. Let us pray this will put the lie to this counterfeit call to a false jihad. In the end, our goal is freedom for the Arab people—freedom from the Turkish yoke, and freedom from German hegemony. And if we rise up in rebellion, it will be in the name of the Prophet." Hussein sighed. "And with help from the British."

"And when will the Arab revolt begin?"

"Again, my son, that depends—if Turkey joins with Germany, it will come soon. If they remain neutral, we'll bide our time . . ."

"But, Father, I must know what to tell the Bedouin."

"Tell them to remain in readiness. Tell them that when the hour arrives, we will have access to British guns and British gold. In the meantime," Hussein smiled. "You will remain sheltered with your wife and children in Nuweiba, and I will send for you when the time is right."

"However, my father, it may prove impossible to rise against the Turks if they are in alliance with Germany, even with British support.

"*Impossible?*" Hussein shook his head. "It is written that for those who struggle for freedom, the difficult is easy, and the impossible just takes a little longer."

CHAPTER 34

September 22, 1914
Oxford

CLIVE AWOKE to the shriek of the steam whistle as the train slowed. He pushed open the window dressings and saw it was morning. They were pulling into a large station, which he suspected was Oxford—confirmed by a conductor shouting, "Oxford! Oxford General Station!"

He drew a deep breath, relieved that the journey was over—across America and across the Atlantic. He descended to the platform, lit by the first rays of the rising sun. His steamer trunks and suitcases rattled toward him on a cart pushed by two porters.

"Those would be mine!" He handed them each two shillings. "Please transfer them to a cab for Marston Street, number 32. Thanks so much."

He followed them out onto the street, struck by the stillness and nearly complete absence of people. He'd never seen Oxford Station so deserted.

After the porters loaded his luggage into the boot of a black Ford taxi, he got in.

"The boys mentioned Marston Street, Number 32—that correct, guv?"

"Yes, it is."

The taxi pulled away and twenty minutes later, they turned onto the street. Nearing the house, his breathed out a sigh—*I never imagined this homecoming without Janet, but I imagine Mervin will be there, and I so hope Evan has been in contact with him—or that he might be there!*

As the driver and Clive carried the first steamer trunk up the steps to the flat, the front door opened, and Mervin beamed. "Welcome home, old chum! Welcome home!"

"It's so good to see you, Mervin!" Clive said as they shook hands warmly. "Is Evan here?" he asked, hoping with all his heart he was.

"Sorry, old chum . . ."

Once Clive's luggage had been deposited in the foyer and the taxi had rattled away, Mervin turned to him. "But, I do have *some* news! As I was making my way back from Switzerland about ten days ago, I passed through the train station in Paris where the police were handing out a broadsheet—"

"The police?" Clive cut in, suddenly anxious.

"Yes, old boy, but let me explain since I believe the whole affair was a *colossal* misunderstanding. The broadsheet displayed four suspects, and Evan was one of them, though I must say, the artist's sketch did *not* do him justice. Nevertheless, it was unmistakably Evan. It said that he had escaped while being questioned by the Paris police."

"Questioned by the *police?*" Clive couldn't believe his ears. "On what charge?"

Mervin shrugged. "Of being a spy or a saboteur. It also stated that he claimed to be English, though he had no valid identification."

"Do you have a copy of it?" Clive asked, his heart pounding.

"No."

"Did it say anything else?"

"Not really . . ."

Clive put a hand over his chest, trying to catch his breath. "I need a drink!"

"Capital idea, old boy, but first thing in the *morning*?

[240]

"I mean tea—a strong cup of tea!" Clive said as he lurched toward the kitchen.

"I'll whip up some builder's brew," said Mervin. "Have a seat in the parlor. You look like you're about to collapse!"

Clive exhaled loudly as he sank into what had been his armchair. The sitting room, now bathed in morning sunlight, overlooked the front garden. His mind crowded with memories of Janet and Evan, moments with them in this very room. From where he sat, he could see that most of the perennials appeared to have survived. *That's all well*, he thought, *but what of Evan?* He shook the memories away as Mervin entered with a tray.

"So, that was it? The broadsheet?" Clive took a mug and added milk and sugar.

"Basically, yes."

"Clive took a long drink, put down the mug and got to his feet, pacing as he spoke. "So, as of ten days ago we know that Evan was alive and in Paris. That's bloody good news! He eluded the Paris police, and now the question is—where did he go? Could he be trying to get back to England? Did he manage to volunteer?" He stopped pacing and shouted, "I've got to find him!"

"What's your plan?" asked Mervin.

"First, I'll find the nearest induction center and activate my commission. Then I'll go straightaway to the War Office in London and begin to look for him. I'll start by contacting the French police and see if he's back in their custody. If he is, I'll find a way to go to Paris and clear up this misunderstanding."

"And, if he's not?"

"I'll find a way to stay at Whitehall and continue to search for him." Clive shrugged. "With my experience at digs throughout the Levant, I'm sure I'll be able to serve there at some capacity . . ."

Mervin raised his eyebrows and asked, "But, you're not too . . .?" he began.

"Old?" Clive laughed. "For combat, perhaps, but I'm sure they'll find *some* way for me to contribute. After all, Mervin, we must all do our part!"

❀ ❀ ❀

The Pilgrim Road between
Mecca and Jeddah

Camels weren't sure-footed in the dark, but Faisal had no choice in the matter. His father had insisted he leave Mecca well after sunset on a moonless night. For the sake of secrecy, not even the slaves knew of his journey to Jeddah.

The little she-camel was fitted with a saddle of the finest Nejd leatherwork, richly inlaid with metal tissues and hung with plaited fringes in many colors. She was the best riding camel his father possessed. However, the beautiful saddle was invisible in the darkness, as was the pilgrim road, causing the camel to slip and stagger.

Faisal traveled alone, wrapped in a cloak against the icy fingers of the night air. Pausing to look up at the sharp points of the winter stars, he knew it must be well after midnight for them to banner the late summer sky.

Between the cold and lurching mount, sleep was impossible. Besides, he was too excited to sleep. After centuries of living in the iron grasp of the Ottoman Empire, Faisal was proud to have a role in helping the Arabs throw off the yoke of Turkish oppression. He finally had a task worthy of his dreams—to gather the Bedouin tribes of the Hejaz into an army that would someday rise up against the Turks—perhaps, someday soon.

After a few hours, the sky lightened toward dawn and the stars faded. The camel's footing became steady as the road grew visible to the eye. He looked out over the desert, and his heart swelled at the perfect crescents and sweeping dunes of pure white beneath the gunmetal sky.

He was certain that, if put to the test, the Bedouin army would be victorious. With their bravery, speed, and knowledge of the desert, they would carry the revolt all the way to Damascus!

The sun rose and the particles of sand on the road shone clean and polished, green schist and black basalt catching the blaze of sun like small diamonds in a reflection so fierce that Faisal couldn't endure it. He pulled his *keffiyeh* forward to shut out the light. Quickening the pace, he peeked out, searching for a place to water the camel. He also knew that it would be prudent to leave the road before it became crowded with pilgrims and Turkish patrols.

He cut across the gentle rise of a flat basalt ridge and found that the white sand over the harder stratum was like a pile-carpet—perfect for the camel's running.

Hills of sand rose and fell, and the morning grew warm as the sun rose, the pilgrim road now far behind him. On either side, windswept dunes stretched to the horizon. He crested a dune and came upon a verdant wadi, sharply marked with clean beds of sand and an occasional large boulder brought down by a flood. The cool shadows of the shaded banks were welcome relief, as were the many green broom bushes—useless as pasture but restful to the eye. Following the wadi, he passed patches of sagebrush and an occasional acacia tree. As the sun rose over the shoulder of the eastern dunes, he came to a palm grove and urged the camel forward, knowing he would soon find water.

Other Bedouin were here, some drawing water from a well. From their robes he saw that they, like him, were of the Harb tribe, though of different clans; he was of the Bani Salem, and they were of the

Masruh. The two clans were now at peace, united in their common hatred of the Turks.

As he neared the well, many nodded a greeting, and he greeted them in kind, because the Bedouin, though divided into clans and tribes, were truly one people—no more separate from one another than the fingers of a hand. And like a hand, he knew that when the time was right, the separate fingers would draw into a fist, and together they would smite the Turks. Together they would gain their freedom.

CHAPTER 35

September 22, 1914
London

AS CLIVE APPROACHED the War Office building, he paused to smooth his officer's tunic and tug down on his Sam Browne belt. After looking up at Whitehall's soaring ionic columns, he headed up the granite steps. It was just past noon, though Clive's day had already been quite full; after disembarking in Southampton early that morning, he'd reached Oxford by train, reunited with Mervin at the flat, then re-enlisted in Oxford and received his commission and uniform with instructions to report to MO-4. And now, after a short train ride to London, he was reporting for duty.

He pushed open the heavy doors and was greeted by a rush of noise filling a grand hall of marble and Yorkstone, abuzz with swarms of uniformed personnel. Needing directions, he tapped a soldier on the arm. "Excuse me . . ." he began.

The soldier snapped to attention. "Yes, sir. What might I do for you?"

"I'm to report to the MO-4 map room. Could you direct me?"

"Yes, sir." The soldier pointed toward a crowded alcove. "Take those stairs to the second floor, turn right down the corridor, and the map room is first door on your right."

Clive nodded at a deserted broad marble central staircase leading up to a well-lit landing, and asked, "Don't those stairs lead to the second floor?"

"They do, sir, but they're not for general use." He smiled and added, "The grand staircase is only for field marshals and charwomen!"

"Thanks—I certainly don't fit either category." Clive headed into the alcove where he was jostled by soldiers moving up and down the narrow iron steps. Reaching the second floor, he searched the landing but didn't see any corridor.

"I say, sir, are you lost?"

The voice came from close at hand, but looking about, he saw no one. Then he looked down. There was a Boy Scout looking up at him. A very short Boy Scout.

"Yes, quite lost." Clive smiled. "I'm to report to the MO-4 map room."

"I'll show you, sir." The boy turned smartly and led the way.

"Do you scouts work here at the War Office?" Clive asked as he followed the boy across the crowded landing.

"We're volunteers, sir—mostly as messengers and guides—that sort of thing. We must all do our part, you know!"

The boy led him into an arcade ringed by marble columns. "The map room, sir."

Before Clive could thank him, the boy had run off. Clive straightened his tie and knocked on the door.

"Come!" shouted a voice from within.

Clive pushed the door open.

An oval table dominated the wood-paneled room with a high-beamed ceiling and tall windows lining the far side of the room. Muted sunlight shone on the brown hardwood floor, and strands of light bulbs hung like ropes of bright pearls over the table.

A slight young man with tousled blond hair, dressed casually in an open short-sleeved shirt beamed at Clive from the far side of the table.

"Professor Sinclair! How very delightful to see you!" Thomas

Edward Lawrence called out and quickly made his way around the table.

"Ned," Clive took Lawrence's hand, then pulled him close. "My dear boy!" He recalled that Lawrence was short, but he had somehow expected him to have grown since their last meeting. Still, he could feel the sinewy power of his small frame. Stepping back, Clive saw that he wore civilian clothing. "Aren't you with the military?"

With a bemused smile, Lawrence shrugged. "Sort of . . . in order for me to work here, they've made me a second lieutenant on the Special List—whatever that means."

"No matter! How long has it been? Three years?"

"Indeed so, Professor."

"Dispense with that *Professor* rubbish."

"Is that an order, sir?"

"Absolutely!" Clive pointed to the three bath stars affixed to his shoulder epaulette. "I outrank you, and I will be obeyed."

"And if I slip up, Captain, will you have me flogged?"

"That depends—"

"On what?"

"On whether you'd consider flogging punishment."

Lawrence laughed and his fair skin flushed red. "I'm not sure I understand . . ."

"Your penchant for self-scourging, Ned! As I recall, you used to sleep on a hardwood floor, refusing a bed. And you've pushed yourself on bike treks and hikes for thousands of miles, often during the summer heat! Need I continue?"

"Guilty as charged, sir. I do enjoy a certain extremity of experience."

"So, tell me, Ned, which of our old mates is about?" Clive asked and tossed his peaked officer's cap on the table.

"Newcombe, of course, and Leonard Woolley, who got himself

stuck in an artillery unit in France and is desperate to transfer out. Gertrude *should* be here but isn't. Instead, she's wasting her talents doing secretarial work at the Red Cross in Boulogne." Lawrence drew a deep breath and his smile faded. "I'm so very sorry about Janet," he said softly.

"Thank you, Ned." Clive stared over the table, pretending to look at maps. He remembered the last time they had seen each other; the photograph Lawrence had taken at the train station in Mesopotamia; Evan—an obedient and cheerful boy, Janet—pregnant with the brief life that would take her own. He had lost them all: Janet, the baby and possibly Evan. A heavy grief pressed down upon him, and he drew a deep breath—to fill it with air and lift it away.

He turned to Lawrence. "Janet was so very fond of you, Ned."

"I know. I felt the same toward her—both of you, really—like my own parents." Lawrence left off speaking as he leaned on the map table next to Clive. When he spoke again, his voice was low. "My feelings toward my mum and dad have always been a bit complicated." He cleared his throat. "Anyhow, since I received your telegram, I've been looking forward to seeing you!" He placed his hand on Clive's shoulder. "Your cable mentioned that Evan had gone off to war. Any news?

"Only that he was leaving to fight *in the great war for civilization!*" Clive made quotation marks in the air. "That was six weeks ago. Not a word since."

"Any idea where he is?"

"Not exactly, but Mervin had some news when I saw him this morning at our flat in Oxford. You remember Mervin Smythe, don't you?"

"He's not an easy person to forget—even if one tries! What did he have to say about Evan?"

"He'd seen a broadsheet in France about ten days ago to the effect that Evan was wanted by the Paris police on suspicion of sabotage and espionage."

"*What?*" Lawrence exclaimed. "That's insane!"

"Apparently, the whole thing was just a misunderstanding since Evan was traveling with no identification. And, with the German Army at the gates of Paris . . ."

"Is there any way to contact the Paris police?"

"That's exactly what I plan to do from here at Whitehall, and if necessary, I'll go there myself, and—"

Clive turned as the door swung open with a rush of noise from the stairwell.

An officer strode purposefully forward, his brush moustache twitching, his hands held smartly behind his back. He fixed Clive with his eyes. "I'm Colonel W. Coote Hedley, commander of MO-4, and you are?"

Clive snapped off a salute. "Captain Clive Sinclair, sir, reporting for duty."

Lawrence straightened his slouch a little and made a desultory attempt to salute.

"Welcome aboard, Captain Sinclair!" said Hedley, ignoring Lawrence and returning Clive's salute. "Tell me, Sinclair, how do you like it?"

"*Like* it, sir?" Clive wasn't certain what he meant.

"The building, man! The War Office building!" Hedley took in the structure with a sweep of his arm. "They say it's in the Renaissance style, but some scamps," Hedley narrowed his eyes at Lawrence, "in mock deference to our former Sovereign, call it Edwardian Baroque. But by whatever name, how do you *like* it?"

After a moment's hesitation, Clive replied, "I like it fine, sir."

"And well you *should,* for this is your home now." He turned to

Lawrence, frowning as he looked him up and down. "Lieutenant, you certainly have an *interesting* notion of military discipline . . ."

"Sir?" Lawrence smirked.

"Your *uniform?*" Hedley exclaimed. "Along with your commission you *were* issued a uniform, were you not?"

"I assumed it was for special occasions and otherwise optional."

"And why would you consider your uniform optional?"

"Well, sir, since I was made second lieutenant on the Special List, I considered that the *usual* protocols don't apply to me."

"Oh, I assure you, they *do*. The special list merely designates that you have no particular regimental affiliation. Please see to it that you appear in uniform throughout the rest of your duty with us here, which, hopefully, won't be much longer."

"How's that, sir?" Lawrence asked, showing what appeared to be genuine surprise.

"You're to be transferred to Cairo, Lawrence. Apparently, Hogarth feels your particular talents will be put to better use there, and he's probably right." He waved a hand over the table. "I must admit that your maps of Sinai and Syria are first rate. And I know a thing or two about maps." Hedley puffed out his chest. "I headed the Geographical Society ordinance survey in '98, and our group was the first to introduce lithographic printing. The very first!"

Lawrence shot Clive a quick grimace as Hedley prattled on.

"Yes, my good man, I know quality work when I see it, and, putting all your eccentricities aside—which isn't easy, mind you—you do a capital job, a capital job, sir!" Hedley turned his attention back to the maps. "There's only one problem . . ."

"What's that, sir?"

"Too many pages!" Hedley began scooping up sheets of paper. "Four, five, six . . . six sheets for Syria? This won't do. I want you to reduce this to a three-eighths map. That should tidy things up and bring it down nicely to two sheets. Do that, and I'll sign your transfer. Then you can beetle off to Cairo . . ."

"Delightful, sir, but what of the maps for Mesopotamia?"

"Sinclair will take that over. From what Hogarth tells me, he'll handle that job quite nicely." He tossed the pages onto the table. "There it is then—two sheets for Syria and be double quick about it." He turned to leave, adding, "And I should need that by *tomorrow*—first thing in the morning."

"Happy to do it, sir. I rather enjoy working through the night. But what's the awful sweat?"

"Don't you *know?*" Hadley asked in a low voice.

Lawrence shook his head.

"The Turks, man," Hedley hissed. "The bloody Turks are very likely to jump in with the Krauts—more likely by the day. And with a front in the Levant, our men will need to know *every* detail of the terrain. Their very lives will depend on it!" He glared at Lawrence, pointing at him for emphasis. "*First* thing in the morning."

"You'll have it, sir." Lawrence met Hedley's determined gaze with his own.

As Hedley turned to go, Clive stepped forward. "Colonel, I do hate to trouble you, but it's about my son . . ."

"Your son?"

"I believe he may be serving in the European theater, but I've lost contact with him." Clive had no intention of telling Hedley about the suspicions of the Paris police.

Hedley sucked in a deep breath and fixed Clive with his eyes. "Did he go off and volunteer without telling you?"

"He did, sir—for the BEF, and just turned seventeen."

"What can I do?" he asked, his voice softening.

"I just want to know where he is, sir. An old friend of mine was certain he'd seen him in Paris a fortnight ago. I request your permission to speak with anyone here who might help me find him."

"I'll do better than that." Hedley smiled. "I'll take you myself."

Clive followed Hedley from the room with a quick wave to Lawrence.

They entered a corridor of closed doors with opaque panels of amber glass. Hedley moved forward in long strides with Clive nearly running to keep up.

Opening one of the doors, Hedley wheeled into a large office, charging past banks of desks surrounded by wooden filing cabinets. The air was hazy with cigarette smoke and rang with the clatter of typewriters. Hedley rapped on the opaque glass of a door neatly lettered with the name "Major-General Charles Callwell."

"Come!" a voice thundered from within.

Hedley opened the door and leaned in. "Sorry to barge in on you, old boy . . ."

"Hedley! How very grand to see you! Come in!"

"I do hate to impose," Hedley began as he drew Clive forward and stepped into the cramped office.

"Stuff and nonsense, man! Come in!" Callwell, a robust officer with a red face and a well-waxed curly moustache, rose from behind a cluttered desk.

"Captain Sinclair is a new man in my division . . ."

Clive snapped off a crisp salute.

Callwell off-handedly saluted back. "Of course, as you were, Sinclair." He waved his hand at two straight-back wooden chairs. "Do have a seat and tell me what this is about."

Hadley settled into one of the chairs and replied, "Sinclair believes his son went off and volunteered for the BEF, sir, but he hasn't the foggiest where the boy is."

"Yes, yes. We've had quite a bit of that sort of thing." Callwell leaned forward and patted the papers covering his desk. "Where's that bloody pencil gone?" he muttered. "Ah, here we are. What's the lad's name then?"

"Evan Sinclair, sir."

Callwell wrote the name in large clear letters. "And no idea where he is?"

"Only that he was sighted in Paris about two weeks ago and that he was keen to serve in the BEF."

"That's a start. Anything else?"

"Actually, yes, sir. I'd hope to take it upon myself to check other avenues; such as the British diplomatic mission in Paris and the Paris police—"

"The Paris police—whatever for?"

"To report my son as a missing person."

"Reasonable, I suppose, if we can't otherwise locate him." Callwell lifted a brass bell from his desk and shook it. "I'll get my best man on this."

The office door opened, and a young soldier stepped in and snapped to attention.

"Give this to Henderson. Tell him that I should like this young man located with all dispatch. Start with BEF new recruits. And please bring Captain Sinclair to my secretary, Miss Johnson." Turning to Clive, he said, "The woman is unbelievable! She's able to contact anyone on the planet by telephone or cable. You can rest assured that she'll be a great help in finding your boy." He extended a large hand. "Good luck then, Captain."

Clive, momentarily confused, caught himself in mid-salute. "Thank you, sir." He abandoned the salute and shook Callwell's hand.

"We'll let you know as soon as anything turns up with the BEF." He waved the sergeant away. "Off you go now, Sergeant, chop-chop!"

Clive and Hedley followed the sergeant out the door and into the outer office. There, Hedley patted Clive on the back.

"I'll leave you here, Sinclair. Good luck finding your boy."

"Thank you, sir."

After Hedley strode away, the sergeant guided Clive to one of a dozen secretaries working at their desks. "This is Miss Johnson, sir."

"Thank you, Sergeant." Clive turned and bowed his head to the matronly woman. "Miss Johnson," he said, "I'm Captain Clive Sinclair. Major-General Charles Callwell suggested I speak with you about finding my son."

"I'll be happy to help in any way I can, Captain," she gestured toward a wooden chair next to her desk. "Have a seat and tell me about your boy."

CHAPTER 36

September 29, 1914
Manchester

O N A DREARY MORNING, Chaim Weizmann stood in
one of the private cubicles within the university's telephone center,
waiting for Asher Ginsburg's weekly call from London. His timepiece
said it was almost the appointed time—nine o'clock. Through the
single smudged window of the cubicle, he looked out at the All Saints
Church burial ground where a heavy mist clung to the earth like a
dirty shroud beneath the cold gray sky.

Turning, he pushed the door closed and pulled back the chair set
before a wooden desk, empty but for a black candlestick telephone.
He sat down and stared at the telephone. *I don't even feel like talking
today—my spirits are as bleak as the view. The war is going poorly for
the Entente—badly on the Western Front and worse in the East. And the
situation for the Jews of Russia is increasingly precarious . . .*

The sharp ring of the telephone cut through his thoughts. He
lifted the receiver off its perch, held it to his ear, and heard the
operator's voice.

"Professor Weizmann—I have Asher Ginsburg on the line."

"Thank you. Put him through, please," he said into the mouthpiece
on the telephone's black stand.

He heard a clicking sound as the call was connected.

"Chaim! Vus machst a yid?" Ginsburg playfully greeted him in
Yiddish.

Weizmann imagined his old friend's eyes, smiling at him through his wire-rimmed spectacles. "Not well," he replied in English.

"What's the matter?" Ginsberg asked. "Are you ill?"

"No."

"Vera and Benjy are well, I hope."

"Everyone's fine."

"*You're* not!"

I'm sick with worry about the war, Asher. If the Germans win, they'll hold the keys to Palestine."

"And we've certainly cast our lot with the Entente, haven't we?" Ginsburg's voice floated into his ear. "But the Zionist Central Committee has made every effort to appear neutral—"

"Their attempts fool no one!" Weizmann cut in. "Besides, there's no longer any room for the supposed neutrality of small nations—not at times like these. You're either with the Triple Entente, or with the Central Powers." He frowned and added, "If only we had an envoy with favorable access in Constantinople—"

"Excuse me? Didn't you just say that one must be on one side or the other?"

"I know what I said, but after almost two months, Turkey remains officially neutral! Who knows? Perhaps they'll stay neutral—maybe even side with the Entente. We should keep our options open."

"And what would you propose to offer the Turks?"

"They remain in desperate financial straits, and if we had the right envoy, we could use this moment to our advantage—paying them handsomely for parcels of land in Palestine and paying them again to allow Russian Jews to immigrate and settle on that land. We simply must get the Jews out of Russia. If the war continues to go badly there, I fear they will be blamed, and pogroms will begin—"

"However," Ginsburg cut in, "if Turkey enters the war with the

Central Powers, giving them money would be like giving it to the kaiser!"

"That's true. But so long as the Turks remain neutral, we *can* deal with them, and with sufficient inducements, they might allow large numbers of Russian Jews into Palestine to settle on land we've purchased there."

"Who's on the land now?"

"Probably Arab peasantry, but I refuse to argue with you about this, Asher! You must understand how I think. As a scientist, I ask questions and solve problems. If the problem is a lack of acetone for munitions production, I ask, how can acetone production be increased at little cost? I've solved *that* problem. Now the problem that concerns me is the fate of Russia's seven million Jews. Again, as a scientist, I ask the question—how can we get them out of Russia and resettled in Palestine?"

"Chaim, I completely understand and share your concerns, but it will only create negative conditions for our brethren in Palestine if we don't take the feelings of the local Arabs into account."

"There's no time for that!" Weizmann snapped. "They've lived like serfs under the Turks for centuries. We can't solve their problems. We can only try to solve *ours*!"

"Granted," Ginsburg shot back. "But, we must do all we can to coexist, to build bridges with them."

"We have no time to build bridges with Arabs when the Jews of Eastern Europe are about to be slaughtered!"

"Chaim, I'm concerned about the Arabs *precisely* because I'm committed to our survival as a people, *precisely* because I wish to see a physical and cultural reawakening of Jews in Palestine with the rebirth of Hebrew as a living language! To do so, we must avoid the creation of some terrible version of 'Had Gadya' in Palestine—"

"What's that supposed to mean?"

"Cause and effect, Chaim. As we recite every Passover, the 'Had Gadya' parable is a chain reaction injury; the water puts out the fire, that burned the ox, that gored the dog, that bit the cat, that ate the kid . . ."

"Please, Asher! What's the relevance?"

"What you propose creates one problem as you solve another!"

"But the situation for the Jews of Eastern Europe is too pressing—we must get them out and answer the question: how might they be resettled in Palestine?"

"You're asking the wrong question."

"What in your opinion is the *right* question?" Weizmann asked, his voice rising.

"Listen to me Chaim!" Ginsburg's voice pleaded in his ear. "For centuries, the Jews of Eastern Europe have lived with changing conditions—from good to bad, to terrible, to good, and so forth—like a deadly carousel going around and around. If we ignore the Arabs of Palestine in our haste to create a Jewish homeland, we'll cause great friction between our peoples. After all, the Arabs aren't responsible for what we suffer in Europe! When Jewish migration into Palestine occurs, as we hope it will, the lives of the local Arabs will be affected, for good or ill. We must do all we can to reach out to them in cooperation and friendship. Otherwise, I fear we'll be getting off a deadly eastern European carousel only to get on an equally deadly one in Palestine."

For Weizmann, the image struck home. He remembered the carousel in Paris and the lines from Rilke . . . *in this bright land that lingers before it perishes* . . .

He shut his eyes and sighed. "You're right, Asher. We should try to build a bridge between us and the Arabs of Palestine. But whom do you see on the other end of that bridge? With whom do you propose we speak?"

"I don't know, Chaim, but at least that's the right question."

Weizmann listened intently, expecting Ginsberg to continue speaking. But hearing only silence, he feared the call had been disconnected. "Hello! Hello!" he called into the mouthpiece.

"I'm here, Chaim. I was just thinking, and I believe I might have an answer to the question—how might we find an Arab partner with whom we might cooperate in developing Palestine? It's like this—if Turkey remains neutral, we convince them to sell us land in Palestine and allow Jews to settle there without displacing local Arabs."

"But, how would you propose to do that?"

"We start with tea."

"Tea?" Weizmann wasn't sure he'd heard Ginsburg correctly.

"Yes. Call it tea diplomacy. As you know, Chaim, before Ze'ev Wissotzky died, he hired me as his office director in London, and since then, we've expanded—with branches in France, the US, and Canada. Wissotzky is now the largest tea company in the world . . ."

Weizmann pressed the receiver to his ear, making sure he heard every word.

"I can send a Wissotzky representative to Djemal Pasha in Damascus, supposedly as an emissary for our tea interests. Under the pretense of selling tea to the Ottoman Empire, we'll create a framework for money transfers—paying Turkey generously for land purchases in Palestine *and* for allowing Jewish immigration to those lands!"

"Sounds promising, but how does this do anything for local Arabs?"

"We've seen reports in the press about Arab nationalists in Damascus, so . . . while our tea envoy is there, he'll secretly contact these Arab nationalists about finding a negotiating partner to discuss Arab-Zionist cooperation. What do you say?"

"I say yes!" Weizmann felt a surge of hope, and the heaviness of his melancholy began to lift. Looking out the window, he saw that the sun had broken through the clouds, and the mist covering the church burial ground was gone. Bringing the mouthpiece close, he added, "If and when your tea envoy discovers who might be our Arab partner, I'll provide an official letter from the Zionist Organization. Would that be acceptable?"

"I'm counting on that, Chaim!"

CHAPTER 37

September 30, 1914
The War Office at Whitehall
London

A WEEK HAD PASSED since Clive had begun working with Lawrence in the map room, and since he'd cabled the Paris police about Evan.

At the end of a long day of work, there was a knock at the door.

"Come!" Lawrence called out.

A Boy Scout stepped in and announced, "I have a cable for Captain Sinclair!"

Clive came quickly forward and took the buff-colored envelope. "Thank you."

"You're welcome, Captain. I'm also to tell you that Colonel Hedley would like a word with you."

"I'll be there forthwith."

The scout turned smartly and marched away.

Clive tore open the envelope and read the cable aloud for Lawrence to hear.

FROM: PARIS POLICE PREFECTURE

FRENCH MINISTRY OF THE INTERIOR

TO: CAPTAIN CLIVE ROBERT SINCLAIR

WAR OFFICE AT WHITEHALL, LONDON

THIS IS TO INFORM YOU THAT AN INDIVIDUAL BY THE NAME

OF 'EVAN SINCLAIR' WAS BRIEFLY HELD AND INTERROGATED
AT PRÉFECTURE DE POLICE DE PARIS BUT DEPARTED
WITHOUT PERMISSION. THERE IS NO PERSON UNDER THAT
NAME IN OUR CUSTODY AT THIS TIME.

"That's it?" asked Lawrence.

"That's it," said Clive. "I guess I'm relieved, but I still don't know where he is." Putting on his cap, he turned to leave. "I wonder what Hedley wants—perhaps he's got some news."

"If he does, I hope it's good," said Lawrence.

"Whatever the case, I'll request permission to travel to Paris. I want to speak to whoever interrogated Evan. It might give me a clue where he may have gone."

Reaching Hedley's office, he knocked. "Captain Sinclair to see you, sir!"

"Come in!" Hedley's voice boomed out.

Clive entered, Evan uppermost in his mind.

"Have a seat." Hedley nodded at the chair across from his desk, and asked, "Did the cable you received concern your son?"

"It did, sir." Clive unfolded the cable and handed it to Hedley. "As you can see, the Paris police interrogated him, but he's not in their custody."

"So, you still have no idea where he is . . ."

"That's the size of it, sir. I should like to request leave to travel to Paris in order to speak with the interrogating officer—"

"No need for that, Sinclair. After you requested permission from General Callwell to contact the Paris police, I decided to reach out to them myself . . ."

"You did, sir?" Clive was pleasantly shocked.

"Yes. I obtained the name of the officer who interrogated your boy from the French Ambassador to the Court of St. James. The name of the chap is Police Inspector Michel Gaudin, and I took the liberty of cabling him—explaining exactly what you had told me—that Evan had simply run off to volunteer for the BEF, and this rubbish about being a German spy is just that—rubbish! I also indicated that you're actively looking for Evan while working at MO-4, and you'd appreciate any information about his whereabouts."

Clive felt a rush of gratitude and a glimmer of hope. "You received a response?"

"Just now, which is why I summoned you. Inspector Gaudin goes into a good deal of detain—filling a full four pages of teletype—longest cable I've ever seen. I'm certain you'd like to read every word of it." Hedley pushed a beige folder across his desk. "Have at it."

Clive's heart raced as he read Gaudin's cable, which included notes from the interrogation. It appeared that Evan had arrived in Nice by working on a ship out of New York, and had traveled to Paris, where he was arrested since he hadn't any identification papers. He quoted Evan as saying that he had become afraid after seeing wounded soldiers and coffins in France, no longer wanted to volunteer, and wanted to return to England. Guidin finished by stating that Evan had managed to escape from the police station before being processed, and his whereabouts were unknown. But given the clarification provided, Guidan no longer harbored any suspicions about him and considered the matter closed.

Clive heaved a deep sigh, closed the folder and pushed it back to Hedley.

"No. You keep it." Hedley cleared his throat and asked. "Where do you think he is?"

"I don't know, sir. Evan had certainly been keen to join the BEF, but according to this, he may have changed his mind."

Hedley nodded. "And if he had gone to Maubeuge to join the BEF, we would already know about it—it's only a hundred and fifty miles from Paris and he had more than two weeks to make the trip."

Clive raised his shoulders. "And if he had returned to England, he would have gone to our flat in Oxford and my friend who's living there, Mervin Smythe, would have contacted me . . ." Clive fell silent and frowned.

"So, what now, Captain?"

Clive stood up. "I'll keep making inquiry with the Red Cross and the BEF, sir, and hope he may yet show up at our Oxford flat. With Miss Johnson's help, I already filed a missing persons report in France, and with your permission, I'll have her file another for Great Britain."

"Permission granted, Captain. Good hunting!"

"Thank you, sir." Clive stood up, saluted and left Hedley's office. He headed toward Miss Johnson's desk wondering, *Where the hell could he be?*

CHAPTER 38

October 29, 1914
East of Tervate
Occupied Belgium

"A RACE TO THE SEA?" Evan balanced on a tree branch, reaching for a shrapnel-scarred apple among the bare branches. "What's *that* supposed to mean?" He wore his haversack even while climbing the tree. He liked the way it felt on his back—a reminder of his treks through the high desert in Utah. In addition to his Balearic sling, he kept his high school diploma tucked into a waterproof oilskin bag Emile had given him to keep it dry.

"The race to the sea is just that," Emile replied as he stood on the muddy ground below, monitoring Evan's progress toward the apple. "The war on the Western Front now hinges on who will control the ports on the North Sea—the Germans or the Entente."

Nearly a month had passed since Flemish partisans had rescued Evan from a thicket of thorn bush and a low-lying cloud of chlorine gas. While his skin lacerations and lungs had healed, Evan, like the rest of the group, now suffered from chronic hunger.

"Why is it so important who controls the North Sea ports?" Evan asked, edging further along the branch.

"Everyone knows that it's the Germans' last chance for a quick victory. And without a quick victory, they'll have none. They can't win a long war, and they know it."

The light was dying, the sun low in the sky beneath a bank of scarlet clouds. In the twilight, the farmhouse next to the ragged orchard looked even more forlorn—scorched masonry blocks lay scattered on the ground among broken roof tiles with two rooms gaping open to the sky.

As Evan inched his way along the branch, he was struck by how quiet it was, and realized he could no longer hear any sounds of artillery. "Why are the German guns silent?" he asked.

"They probably took a break for dinner."

Evan paused to listen, then asked, "Why isn't there any birdsong?"

"You just noticed? The birds have been gone for months. Don't you wish *you* could fly away?"

"Sure do." Evan stretched out his hand, but the apple was still out of reach. "So, if the Germans lose this race to the sea, they lose the war."

"That's the size of it." Emile took a step forward. "Try shaking the branch."

Evan rocked the branch, but the apple remained firmly attached. "I have another idea." Evan climbed back down the tree. "I should have done this to start with." He took the sling out of his haversack and began to rotate the weighted end. Releasing it with a few feet of slack, the sling wound around the branch holding the apple, which snapped off and fell to the ground.

"Excellent!" Emile exclaimed and picked up the branch, removed the apple, wiped off the mud, and took a bite. While he chewed, he continued talking. "The Germans know we can slow them down enough to make them lose the race to the sea. That's why they fear us." He handed the apple to Evan.

"The Germans fear a few starving partisans?" Evan took a bite and handed it back to Emile.

"There are thousands of groups like ours—exactly what the

Germans wanted to avoid—a strong resistance." He took another bite and handed it to Evan.

After taking a big bite, Evan gave Emile what was left and asked, "You really believe we'll make a difference?"

"I'm certain we'll make a difference!" Emile polished off the apple, core and all.

"That's what I came for," Evan said and returned the sling to the haversack. "To make a difference! I want to help stop the Germans from reaching the sea."

Emile smiled. "The Germans don't know it yet, but the sea might come to *them*!"

"What do you mean?"

"Come, I'll show you."

The evening light was fading as Emile led Evan at a brisk pace up a hill. Reaching the top, he pointed. "See the lowlands around the Yser River? That's the polders that King Albert has decided to flood."

"How?" Evan asked as he looked down at the darkening meadow dotted by clumps of weeds and pools of water, stretching out toward a bend in the winding river.

"You have to open sluice gates at high tide and close them at low tide. If you do it right, you turn the polders into a swamp, which will put two miles of muddy water between the German army and the port cities. That will stop them completely."

As Emile spoke, Evan saw two partisans trudging up the hill.

Emile waved. One of them spoke to Emile in Flemish, and a dark cloud crossed his face. "This isn't good," he muttered.

"What did he say?"

"The engineers sent to help us open the sluice gates at Noordvardt were killed and there are no replacements."

"Can't someone else to do it in the morning?"

"No. It has to be tonight. There will be a full moon and flooding the polders requires the right tides. Come on," he said. "We must decide what to do."

Evan followed Emile into the house as the German artillery started up again—a distant thud of howitzers.

They filed into what had been a large room, with most of the ceiling gone and open to the sky. A low fire burned in the hearth.

Hendrik Geeraert was speaking in Flemish. He had been a history teacher in Louvain before the war. In his late twenties, he was the oldest and their leader.

"What's he saying?" Evan whispered.

Emile translated for Evan in whispered fragments. "He's telling us how bad things look. German reinforcements are pouring in . . .mostly by train, with more artillery. They've reduced Diksmuide to rubble. Belgian troops are almost out of ammunition. They've left St. George and crossed the Yser. But that's the plan—to cross the river and flood the polders—the only way to stop the Germans from reaching the sea. But the engineers are dead, and the sluice gates of Noordvardt must be opened tonight."

Using a piece of charcoal, Hendrik began drawing on the wall next to the fireplace. Evan recognized the undulating line of the Yser River.

"He says that we're below that bend in the river, near Tervate, which is full of Germans. A few kilometers to the west are the Noordvardt sluice gates. That's where we're going tonight."

Hendrik begam began drawing something else on the wall.

"These are the sluice gates and the lever that opens and closes them. The gates are closed with the lever like that, and it takes two people to move the lever to the open position. Once the gates are open, we need to make sure the Germans can't close them."

Hendrik bent down, picked a hatchet off the floor and held it up.

"He says that once the gates are open, we'll chop off the lever."

Hendrik looked over the room and asked, "Vragen?"

"He's asking for questions."

A partisan stood up. "Wanneer gaan wij?"

"When do we go? When it's dark." Emile translated the question and answer. "Someone is asking about German patrols spotting us under the full moon. Hendrik says that it should be dark enough with the clouds. Someone asks what happens if the sky clears."

Evan watched Hendrik draw a deep breath and reply, his voice low and urgent.

"He says that flooding the polders is vital. It could save Belgium and defeat the Germans. He knows it will be dangerous, but we must try. Hendrik says that he'll go to open the sluice gates, but he needs a volunteer to go with him . . ."

Emile stopped translating and stood up. "Ik zal met u gaan!"

At first Evan didn't understand what had happened. There was a rush of activity with everyone speaking at once in Flemish. He saw Emile, stripped of his ragged shirt as he was being shown maps. Evan was again struck by how thin and white his body looked in the firelight, his arms so thin. Then Emile and Hendrik were dressed in black, and their faces smeared with mud. They left the house with Evan and the others following behind.

A silvery glow in the overcast sky marked the cloud-hidden moon. Hendrik was right; with cloud cover, it was very dark. The pastureland beyond the hedgerow sloped away beneath a shroud of darkness, the farmhouse a faint, spectral whiteness.

As his eyes accommodated, he could see the moving silhouettes of the partisans.

"Listen to me, Evan."

He heard Emile's voice at his side, felt his hand on his shoulder.

"I'm going with Hendrik now. You'll stay with the others. He wants everyone to remain a few hundred meters behind us." Emile drew someone forward. "This is Kerel. He speaks good English. You stay close to him, okay?" Emile patted Evan on the back as he turned to go. "Behave yourself till I get back."

Evan watched Emile disappear into the darkness.

※ ※ ※

With the German Fourth Army
West of Roeselare
Occupied Belgium

Kaiser Wilhelm was unhappy. He had come with his staff to the forward command post to personally conduct the conquest of Ypres and seal Germany's victory in the race to the sea. For the occasion, he wore his favorite dress uniform, studded with medals and hung with gold braid. But victory required that they take Diksmuide, which would secure the French ports of Calais and Dunkirk for Germany. But if they didn't take Diksmuide, they would lose the race to the sea.

Wilhelm was also unhappy that the alliance with Turkey hadn't materialized. "We've been at war for three months and the damned Turks are still being coy," he muttered in the darkness of the command bunker. "And after all we've done for them!"

"What's that, Your Excellency?" someone asked, loudly enough to be heard over the roar of the howitzers bombarding Diksmuide.

Wilhelm turned to see his war minister, General Erich von Falkenhayn. From an aristocratic but impoverished family, he had impressed the kaiser with his bravery during the Boxer Rebellion, and over the years he had been promoted quickly through the ranks.

"I'm furious with our tepid Ottoman friends," the kaiser shouted in reply. "They're still sitting on the fence despite the damned alliance agreement we signed with them just before the war began in August!"

"True, sire, but General von Moltke didn't stipulate any military action on their part—"

"That dotard!" the kaiser spit out the words, then looked at Falkenhayn. "How would you like to replace him as chief of staff?"

"Your Excellency! I would never presume to replace or even criticize General von Moltke—he's been my master and mentor—"

"Of course, General! It's proper you should feel that way." Wilhelm knew that, despite his lip-service of loyalty to Moltke, Falkenhayn would love to be chief of staff. He considered how to resolve the frustrations that vexed him, starting with the Turks. *Let's see what Falkenhayn can do if properly motivated . . .*

"Tell me General, do you have any ideas how we might convince our Turkish friends to get off the fence?"

"I might at that, sire."

"I'm listening," the kaiser prodded.

"Very well, Your Excellency. You may remember that after we signed the alliance agreement with them, the British predictably took offense and cancelled delivery of two battle cruisers they had just built for them—"

"Yes, I remember!" Wilhelm cut it. "And as replacements of what the British denied them, I gave the Turks two of our battle-ships."

"You did, indeed, sire—the *Goeben* and the *Breslau*. Both became part of the Turkish Navy with Turkish names, flags, and registry. *However*, even now German officers and German sailors still train and instruct the Turkish crews on all aspects of the ships' maintenance and care."

The kaiser's eyes grew large. "You're telling me that these two battle cruisers are still commanded and partially crewed by Germans?"

"That's exactly what I'm saying, sire. With your order, we could send them through the Bosporus into the Black Sea—"

"Yes!" the kaiser exclaimed. "And we'll have them bombard Russian installations along the Black Sea coast."

"Is that an order, Your Majesty?"

"It is! Send a cable immediately! And once those Turkish warships attack Russia, I'll contact the Turkish ambassador in Berlin with our congratulations to Constantinople for joining the Central Powers against our enemies. And, for that matter, General, congratulations to you as well!"

"For what, sire?"

"You're my new chief of staff!"

※　※　※

Once Falkenhayn left to cable the order, Wilhelm felt better, and though it was late at night, he wasn't at all tired. Looking over Diksmuide, he was pleased to see fires burning throughout the city. Suddenly, however, the howitzers fell silent.

What the hell? He thought and shouted the name of the local commander, "General von Württemberg! Albrecht! Where are you my dear cousin?"

"What is it, Your Majesty?" Albrecht asked, as he emerged from the shadows of the command post. A cousin of the kaiser, he commanded the German Fourth Army.

"Why is it that I no longer hear the artillery?" Wilhelm canted his head with his right hand to his ear as if listening. "Did I order the artillery to cease firing?"

"No, Your Excellency. We always stop at midnight."

"Why?"

"For the crews to rest, sire, and for the guns to cool so they can be cleaned."

"Interesting! How long does it take for the guns to cool and be cleaned?"

"About four hours, my royal cousin."

Kaiser Wilhelm opened his timepiece. "In that case, resume firing for two more hours. That should give the crews plenty of time to do their work before dawn."

"But sire—"

"I want Diksmuide reduced to rubble!" Wilhelm snapped his timepiece shut and smiled. "Do I make myself clear, Albrecht?"

"Of course, Your Excellency." Albrecht cranked a field telephone and gave the order. Then he turned to Wilhelm, clicked the heels of his shiny black boots, and made a little bow. "A splendid idea, sire! They won't be expecting a continued bombardment."

"They also won't be expecting *this*." Wilhelm handed Albrecht a dossier.

While Albrecht read, Wilhelm surveyed a wall map of the Western Front with small flags indicating the battles at hand, though his mind was filled with other thoughts.

How I detest the dreary cold of Flanders and yearn for the warmth of the Holy Land! Once we end this business in Europe, I'll bargain with Cousin George—my terms, simple and generous—he'll keep his throne in Westminster, and I'll gain mine in Jerusalem where I'll reign as Holy Roman Emperor! He'll have Egypt and India, and I'll have Arabia and Mesopotamia. I'll propose that we share the Suez Canal, and together, Britain and Germany will rule the world! And with my capital in Jerusalem, I'll possess an unassailable fortress upon the Holy Mountain, and finally, my place in the sun!

"The dossier is very well-reasoned, Your Excellency. However, we've already used shells filled with tear-producing gas and they weren't effective."

"I fear you misread the dossier, Albrecht. It doesn't speak of *tear*-producing gas, rather *chlorine* gas." Wilhelm smiled beneath his formidable moustache. "Hoechst and Bayer have been producing chlorine gas as a by-product in their dye manufacturing for years and just throwing it away! Now we're putting it to good use! We've already conducted some operations in occupied Belgium with marvelous results!"

"Interesting, sire! As a better tear-producing gas?"

"No, dear cousin. Chlorine isn't a tear-producing gas at all." Wilhelm put his arm around Albrecht's shoulders and squeezed. "You see, I don't want the Belgians to cry, I want them to die!"

CHAPTER 39

October 29–30, 1914
No Man's Land
West of the Yser River
Belgium

THE FLEMISH PARTISANS crossed the polders in single file, moving slowly in relative darkness, the full moon hidden by heavy clouds. In the half-light, they were able to avoid the ditches and canals, the wide puddles, and patches of bramble. As expected, the German artillery stopped at midnight, and perfect silence fell over the moor.

Evan was sore and tired after walking for what seemed like hours. He thought about his mother buried in Utah. He wondered how his father had reacted to his note and postcard. *As soon as I'm able I'll write and let him know how I am—*

With a suddenness that made him start, the German artillery began to roar again.

The column stalled in confusion—partisans bumping into each other.

"What's happening?" he asked Kerel as lights flashed along the eastern horizon and thunder rolled over the flood plain.

"I'm not sure. They always stop at midnight. We're worried they know what we're planning."

"But, they're not shooting at us," said Evan, "They're bombarding Diksmuide."

"So it appears," Kerel replied.

"Do you think Hendrick and Emile are already at the sluice gate?"

"We'll find out when we get there."

The column began moving, the roar of the big guns buffeting the air.

Suddenly, the clouds parted, and moonlight flooded the polders, reflecting off still water in ditches and puddles. Now exposed, the partisans stopped and hunkered down.

"This is very bad! We must hide in those bushes." Kerel pointed.

"Are we near the gate?" Evan asked as he crawled along in the mud next to Kerel.

"Yes. It's about a hundred yards—"

The sudden clatter of a machinegun sounded close at hand. Gripped with terror, Evan pressed his body down into the folds of soft earth.

"They're not shooting at us!" Kerel shouted. "They're shooting at Hendrick and Emile at the sluice gate."

They crawled into the shelter of the brush, and Kerel pointed. "There's the machinegun nest!"

Peeking through the brush as the partisans spoke in harsh whispers, Evan saw a cubical enclosure surrounded by sandbags and open to the sky. As the gun fired, light flashed through narrow slits between the bags and gray smoke rose in the air.

Kerel nodded toward a partisan looking through field glasses on a nearby bluff. "He says Hendrick and Emile are hiding within the concrete walls of the sluice gate, but they can't reach the lever without being seen. We've got to stop that gun."

"How?"

"Sylvain has a grenade. He'll throw it when he's close enough."

In the bright moonlight, Evan could see Sylvain crawling toward the machinegun nest. When he was about twenty feet away, he rose quickly to his knees and drew back his arm. Rifle fire flashed through the narrow slits of the nest. He fell forward and the grenade detonated a few feet from where he lay.

Evan's breath stopped as he looked at Sylvain's still body and the grenade's gray smoke drifting away toward a nearby stand of poplar trees. A wave of sadness washed over him. Then determination.

The machine gun continued firing, raking the sluice gate.

Evan looked back at the poplar trees bordering the polders. About a hundred feet away, their yellow leaves shone brightly in the moonlight with deep shadows beneath them. He shifted his weight and noticed that the ground under him was covered with smooth stones, like a dry riverbed. Like Utah. "Now, what?" he asked Kerel.

"I'm not sure." Kerel appeared to listen to another whispered conversation between the partisans. After a moment he turned to Evan.

"Now, we try again—this time with a pistol from the bushes closer to the machine gun. The shots might distract the Germans long enough—"

"But they'll see where the shots are coming from," Evan cut in.

"Yes, but it might give Hendrick and Emile enough time to open the gates."

"I've got a better idea." Evan picked up a smooth black stone and held it up.

"You want to throw rocks at the Germans?"

Evan nodded.

"Are you crazy? You can't get close enough."

"I won't be throwing with my arm. I have a sling in my haversack."

"But you have to stand up to use that, and they'll see you!"

"Not if I can get over to those trees." Without waiting for a reply, Evan began to crawl.

The machinegun continued to fire at regular intervals, reassuring Evan that Emile and Hendrick were probably still alive.

Halfway there, he heard someone screaming. He paused and

turned his head. One of the partisans was on his knees, about thirty feet from the nest, yelling and firing uselessly at the sandbags until rifle fire erupted from the nest and he fell forward.

Evan continued crawling and reached the shelter of the trees. He could see nothing in the darkness but felt dry leaves beneath him covering smooth stones. The machinegun continued firing, stopping about every minute to reload.

He stood up, pulling the sling from his haversack. He crouched down and groped for a stone. Finding one of the right size and shape, he placed it in the apex of the sling and looked out from the darkness to the brightly lit plain. He saw the machinegun firing out of the nest, as clear as in daylight, the sound muffled among the trees.

They'll never know where these are coming from, he thought and estimated that the gun was about two hundred feet away, gauging the distance in reference to the ball field in Cedar City—about the distance from the outfield to home plate.

He began to spin the sling, making a few tentative rotations to make sure there were no low branches in the way. Then he spun it faster and faster until he released the lower strap, and the stone flew out of the darkness.

He watched it fall about twenty feet short.

He tried again and came closer.

As the machinegun clattered, he worked more quickly, and soon found the mark. One stone after another arced down into the nest, interrupting the salvos and eliciting cries of pain and angry cursing.

Aimless small arm's fire erupted from gaps between the sandbags as Evan hurled one stone after another.

"If it's a distraction we need, I think we have it," he muttered with satisfaction.

But suddenly, he heard a few shots tick off a nearby tree.

"Looks like they figured out where I am!" Groping in the darkness, he moved to his right until he felt the thick trunk of a large poplar.

There he resumed his offensive, unleashing about a dozen rocks.

When a blast of machinegun fire ripped through nearby trees, he flattened himself behind the thick poplar, his heart racing as a hail of bullets scattered leaves and splintered wood, raking back and forth.

Good! I managed to get their attention away from the sluice gate, he thought as he crouched down and gathered stones, stuffing them into his pockets. He realized that he was afraid, but at the same time, he felt profoundly calm, his hands steady.

Once the machinegun stopped, he stepped around the thick poplar, unleashing stones until they started firing at him again, the bullets leaping through the trees. After repeating the pattern several times, he returned the sling to his haversack and waited for the firing to stop. When it did, he bolted to his right, groping and stumbling between the trees. When the shooting started again, he threw himself to the ground. They were now firing into the wood far behind him.

As the machinegun salvos continued, starting and stopping, he was up and then down, moving among the trees, in a wide arc back toward the partisans.

He reached the edge of the wood and lay prone on the soft earth, clinging to the hollows in the mud. Turning his head, he looked out at the polders, bathed in moonlight.

He saw the flash and smoke of the machinegun, still firing wildly into the wood.

And something else—the flood plain was shining in the moonlight.

The water was rising.

CHAPTER 40

October 30, 1914
Four kilometers south of Ypres
Belgium

ONCE THE MACHINEGUN nest flooded, the shooting stopped, and Evan waded through the water to rejoin the partisans on higher ground.

The Germans manning the gun tried to surrender, but the partisans weren't taking prisoners.

Evan was among those who found Emile's body, listing in the water by the sluice gate, still clutching the wooden control lever. He carried him out of the water, surprised by how light he felt in his arms. He laid him on the dry ground covered by the smooth stones, the bullet wounds in his chest washed clean by the water. Looking down, he saw how small he was—just a boy, really.

Hendrick's body had been carried by the water and was recovered thirty feet away from the gate. Riddled with bullets, it took a while to get him free, his body so entangled in the brush.

They buried Emile and Hendrick, along with the two other partisans killed during the night, in a single grave.

They decided to reach Diksmuide rather than remain in German held territory. Building a raft from wooden boards taken from the machinegun nest, they used the long wooden sluice gate lever as a pole and maneuvered into the current. They floated south toward the glow of the fires burning in Diksmuide. Reaching the Ypres-Yser canal, the raft moved easily, and they reached the outskirts of Ypres before dawn.

Now in territory controlled by the Entente, they pulled the raft into a stand of trees beneath a railroad embankment that ran above the river. In the darkness, Evan sensed that the partisans seemed relaxed but wary.

"Why are we still hiding?" he asked Kerel.

"The British Expeditionary Force is arrayed along the ridge above us. In the dark they might mistake us for Germans and shoot us. We'll show ourselves in the morning, and we want you to do the talking."

When dawn broke, they climbed up the embankment, leaving their supplies, salvaged weapons, and ammunition with the raft. Kerel had fashioned a flag of truce by tying his dirty white shirt to the sluice gate lever.

Evan, carrying his haversack, and Kerel waving the white flag, led the way.

"We're Belgian partisans!" Evan called out as loudly as he could.

"Stop right there, Hun!"

An English soldier in khaki drab and puttees stood above them on the lip of the embankment, aiming his rifle. "Get your arse over 'ere, Cobber!" he called out. "I 'ave me a nice collection of alleymen 'ere!"

Evan raised his arms and moved forward. "Wait. You don't understand . . ."

"'Alf a mo', if you please, Heine!"

"Please! You've got to listen to me!" Evan shouted.

"Talk the King's English like a Yank, do you?" The soldier pointed his rifle at Evan. "Spent time in the States, 'ave you? You Heine bastard!"

Looking at the barrel of the rifle, Evan froze. From the cockney slang he knew the soldier was an east-end London boy.

The partisans moved forward, their hands in the air. The white shirt on the pole fluttered in the wind. "We are free Belgians!" one called out in heavily accented English.

"Per'aps you are, Kamerad. Per'aps not. All I know is that you've come from the direction of Kaiser Bill's Fourth Army!"

Evan and most of the partisans stopped, but a few continued forward. Evan saw the soldier's finger tighten on the trigger.

"Stop, I say! Stop or I'll shoot!" the soldier shouted and swung the rifle wildly back and forth. "Stop right there!"

Another soldier appeared at the top of the embankment, also aiming at them.

"Please, no shoot! We are friends! We are friends!"

The soldiers were panicking, mistaking the partisans' Flemish accent for German.

Evan was certain that he could reason with them. He raised his arms higher and stood on the embankment. "Please listen to me! I'm English! Please—"

He stopped speaking when he heard the crack of the rifle and felt a blow to the chest. Like he'd been hit with a rock.

"Please," he said again, then paused as a puff of blue smoke rose from the muzzle of the soldier's rifle. "I'm English."

The partisans stood very still on the slope, on either side of Evan.

Evan turned his head to the left, then to the right. He saw that the partisans were looking at him. He also saw that the soldiers weren't moving, their rifles motionless. He looked at their faces, their jaws slack.

Everything was still. Only Kerel's white flag moved, fluttering in the wind.

Evan motioned with his hand and whispered, "We're partisans."

Now his chest burned, and it hurt to breathe. He looked down and saw blood spreading over his muddy shirt.

More words formed in his mind, but he chose not to speak. He had to concentrate.

He had to decide what to do next. He sat on the sloping ground and closed his eyes.

Feeling dizzy, he lay back, and felt himself sliding—down the embankment toward the water.

✿ ✿ ✿

Boulogne-Sur-Mer, France
Office of the Red Cross

Gertrude Bell emptied the canvas mailbag onto the table. With each passing day the pile seemed larger, growing with the mounting casualties on the Western Front.

As they did every morning, Gertrude and the Russell sisters began by sorting the deluge of anxious inquiries as to the fate of a missing husband, a father, a son.

As Gertrude shook the last letters from the bag, Diana Russell came alongside and stared at the pile over her pince-nez. "My dears! How will we *ever* get through them all? We simply *must* have more help."

"Sorting is the easy part, though, isn't it?" Gertrude said as she took her seat at the table. "For me, the hard part is writing letters to next of kin."

"I so agree," Flora said as she and Diana took their seats at the table. "A truly sad and difficult chore—like the hospital rounds."

"But we certainly don't need to be reminded how crucial our job is, do we, ladies?" Gertrude said and heaved a sigh. "Especially when one considers the sacrifices our brave boys are making!" She shook her head and opened a velvet box where she kept her letter opener, actually a small scimitar with a gilded hilt, a treasured memento from a Baghdad bazaar. She sliced open an envelope. Another workday had begun.

The sorting of letters usually went quickly because only a cursory perusal was required to establish the missing soldier's troop designation. Nonetheless, as Gertrude scanned the first letter, she was drawn along by the elegant cursive.

Dear Sir or Madam,

I'm writing to enquire as to the whereabouts of my son, Albert Birch, No. 525839, a private in III Army corps, Fourth Division. My Albert is nineteen years old, and his last letter home was dated 9 September. I am including a photograph in the hope it will assist you in locating my boy. I pray he is well. Any information you might provide will be vastly appreciated.

With gratitude, hope, and unceasing prayer,

Margaret Birch

Gertrude sighed as she studied the photograph of the young man posing in uniform, his smooth face turned to the camera, his eyes wide. "Where are we putting Third Army, Fourth Division?" she asked.

Flora pointed a red-lacquered nail toward a box on the floor between their chairs. "That one, my dear, and I strongly suggest you work a bit more quickly. There's so very much we must do today!"

Gertrude bristled as she placed the envelope in the box. She found Flora difficult, though they had once been quite close while working together in England's antisuffrage movement, that is, before Flora switched sides to join Diana in the prosuffrage movement. But with the war, that struggle had been pushed to the side. Nonetheless,

Gertrude found Flora irritating—especially the way she overdressed. This morning she wore a touring hat lavishly bedecked with silk, netting, lace, feathers, and flowers—more suited for an afternoon promenade than for the work at hand. Her blouse was equally impractical with mutton sleeves so puffy, she often knocked letters off the table.

They sorted for another hour without speaking.

"Here's a sad one," Flora said, breaking the silence.

Gertrude looked up to see Flora shaking her head, but only slightly so as not to disturb her hat. "What is it?" she asked, knowing that she was dying to tell them but required prompting.

"This father doesn't know his son's divisional designation, and he's not even sure the boy is actually *in* the BEF! Have you *ever?*" She handed the envelope to Gertrude. "Here, my dear. That box is behind you."

Gertrude took the envelope and turned to toss it among those with insufficient information, but the handwriting caught her attention. She looked closer.

Clive?

Flipping the envelope over, her suspicion was confirmed— *Captain CR Sinclair, MO-4, The War Office at Whitehall, London.*

Her face flushed. She looked to see if Flora or Diana had noticed. They hadn't. She stuffed the envelope into her pocket, knowing that Evan must have gone off and enlisted. She was pleased that Clive was back in England and couldn't wait to read the letter and answer it personally. Then a thought came to her that lifted her spirits. *At Whitehall, Clive could advocate for my transfer to MO-4!* In this frame of mind, she worked quickly.

When the stack of letters was almost gone, Flora began chatting about the war news. "This race to the sea is *desperately* important, my dears. They say if Germany seizes the North Sea ports, we'll have to evacuate this office, and far worse, the hospital!"

"Much as I want to return to England," said Diana, "not under *that* circumstance!"

"What's *this*?" Flora cut in as she unfolded a sheet of stationary. "Dearest Gerty?" She looked at the envelope she had just opened. "Oh, Gertrude, I'm so very sorry. This would seem to be addressed to you!"

She held the letter out to Gertrude who, blushing crimson, shot out of her chair.

"Thank you, Flora," she said. "I know where to file this one." Still blushing, she stuck the letter in her pocket. Knowing it was from Richard, she was vexed it had ended up among the Red Cross mail. Anxious to read it, she nodded at the table. "We're almost done here, so I'll go do the hospital rounds."

"But Gertrude, you did rounds yesterday! It's simply not fair for you to suffer two days in a row."

"I'm happy to go again!" she said and bolted from the office.

As the door closed, she heard Flora speaking in a shocked voice with Diana.

"I *do* wonder why she's in such a *state* . . ."

Gertrude hurried down Rue Victor Hugo toward the BEF hospital, her heart racing. Stepping into an alcove, she took Richard's letter from her pocket.

Dearest Gerty,
I shall be leaving Addis Ababa in four months for London to
receive new orders. I would that you join me there. I assure you,
Lillian will not be with me.

As she read, she could hear his voice, feel his touch, his mouth on her lips . . .
What I wouldn't give to have you with me. I should not want to

talk. I should make love to you. Would you like it, welcome it,
or would a hundred hedges rise and bristle and divide? But we
would tear them down. You will be in my arms, alight, afire!

Until then, my dearest love,

Richard

Gertrude took a deep breath and put the letter back in her pocket.

Taking the letter Clive had sent, she read his impersonal inquiry about Evan—the words spare, yet so full of pain. She imagined she could feel his anguish in the movement of pen on paper, in the careful folding of the note. He had included a photograph—the two of them standing in front of a petrol station surrounded by empty desert, Clive's arm around Evan's shoulders.

She decided that, after hospital rounds, she would go back to the office and check the card file for any mention of Evan. *I'll answer Clive this evening—with news of Evan if there is any, or with the promise to make further inquiries throughout the Red Cross organization. I'll also ask him about putting in a good word for me at MO-4 . . .*

Leaving the alcove, she walked toward the hospital, elated about the letter from Richard. She imaged his letter floating to her out of Africa—his yearning and ardor rising above the sad tide of letters filled with anxious despair. She drew a deep breath and set her jaw, refusing to be dragged down by the unhappy human toll she struggled with every day, resolved not to drown in it. With thoughts of Richard, she walked on and felt that she was floating—weightless in love— thrilled that he wanted to spend his leave with her, thrilled to finally be with him beyond the chaste love of written correspondence.

CHAPTER 41

October 30, 1914
Jerusalem

"THE ONLY THING MORE BEASTLY than this weather is Guido von List!" Montagu Walker muttered as he stood in the driving rain, holding up a lantern with one hand and clutching his parka closed with the other. Following List down a muddy path through the Kidron Valley, Walker squinted at the wall bordering the Temple Mount—the huge blocks of limestone like sarcophagi, faint in the half-light and the rain. "Herr von List," he shouted over the storm.

"What is it *now*?" List jerked his head around with reptilian speed.

"The Temple Mount is *this* way!" Walker raised his lantern in the direction of the walled city. "The path you're taking leads nowhere."

"Quite the contrary," List replied, lamplight glinting off his glasses. "My research points to another way to access the chambers within the Temple Mount."

"With all due respect, sir, I've had some experience—"

"Your *experience*?" List spat the words out and lunged toward Walker, reaching him in two strides. "You call that disaster of yours, *experience*? You found *nothing* and nearly got yourself lynched! What we learn from your *experience*—"

The old man's words were lost as lightning split the clouded sky and a loud crack of thunder echoed through the valley.

"But this is absurd!" Walker persisted. "Why not take a direct approach?"

"Because your *direct* approach leads directly to failure," List shouted as another bolt of lightning flashed along the city wall. "As a *scientist*, I take a *scientific* approach. I have a working hypothesis and we're here to test it. Now come along!"

This is insane! Walker thought and didn't move. "What's your hypothesis?"

"My study of Poisson's painting points to a secret portal into the Tomb of Zechariah that will allow us to access the Temple Mount—"

"A secret portal? That's idiotic!" Walker cut in. "Zachariah's Tomb is solid rock and more than a hundred yards from the Temple Mount. It's also on the opposite side of the valley! And if there were a secret portal, don't you think people would know about it?"

"People *don't* know about it, you imbecile! That's what makes it a *secret*! And if you were doing your damned job, those who know of the portal would be in our hands!"

While they had been arguing, the rain stopped. The clouds had parted, and moonlight filled the valley. List pushed back the hood of his robe—his wild white hair surrounding his head like a preternatural aura. A cold chill gripped Walker's heart as he saw the apparition that was List. He tamped down his rising fear and grumbled, "It's not like I haven't *tried* to find them . . ."

"Trying isn't good enough! You have their names and photographs—how can you fail?"

"I'll find them alright but getting them to talk will be another matter."

"You needn't worry about that," List whispered as he stood in front of Walker, his eyes invisible with moonlight reflecting off his glasses. "You've already proved your squeamishness in that sphere. Just find them and bring them to *me*!"

List's ominous tone and his spectral appearance filled Walker with dread. He looked away and pointed down the valley. "Well . . . you wanted the Tomb of Zechariah? There it is!" To his relief, List turned to look.

The giant funerary monument loomed above them, caper brush sprouting on its sides, the pyramid shaped capstone shining after the heavy rain.

And in the silence, Walker heard something—a dull rattling coming from the northern reaches of the Kidron Valley behind them. As he listened, the sound of rattles grew louder.

"What's that infernal sound?" List shouted.

"Lepers," Walker replied and stepped past List toward the tomb. "Follow me unless you'd rather share the road with them."

※ ※ ※

"Walker!" Rahman whispered as lamplight illuminated the face of one of the men at the Tomb of Zechariah. "We haven't seen anything of him since you identified him at the American Colony soup kitchen a month ago."

"Anna was clearly able to disabuse him of the notion that we were there," Gunter whispered in reply.

"So, it appears," Rahman replied. "But who's the one with the wild hair?"

"Guido von List—an Austrian occultist and purveyor of Nordic-German racial supremacy. I've seen his photograph in German newspapers."

Dressed in hooded robes, they continued limping slowly down the Kidron Valley in the moonlight, shaking their rattles. After passing Zachariah's Tomb, they limped to an olive tree off the path, its thick trunk so twisted it seemed to writhe in the moonlight. They looked out from behind the tree, watching the lamp circle the tomb.

"Are you surprised he found it?" Rahman asked.

"Not when you consider that he's been studying Poisson's painting."

"Do you think Walker's clairvoyant from last time had a hand in this?"

"Aleister Crowley?" Gunter shook his head. "No. He's in New York, trying to get the US to support Germany in the war. But *someone* is guiding him."

Rahman held his breath as the lamp disappeared behind the tomb. When it reappeared, he exhaled. "We know one thing about their hidden guide—if he knows about the portal, he knows about us."

CHAPTER 42

November 4, 1914
Hampstead, London

IN ANTICIPATION of his morning meeting at the War Office, Chaim Weizmann had left Manchester the day before and spent the night at the London home of Asher Ginsberg. Up before dawn, he'd bathed, put on his best three-piece suit, and sat in the library to review his research notes—the best way to calm himself, though he felt anything but calm as his mind raced with thoughts.

This meeting is pivotal in so many respects—the effect it will have on my career, the potential influence for the cause of Zionism, but above everything, the implications it holds for the war effort! Simply put, my method for large-scale acetone production will give Great Britain the ability to produce the munitions it needs to win this war!

In the slumbering silence of early morning, the word *munitions* reminded him of Ginsberg's frequent scolding—*must our aspirations for a homeland be distilled through the making of munitions?*

Though equally committed to helping the Entente win the war, and to creating a Jewish homeland in Palestine, Weizmann had his own doubts about the morality of his contribution to munitions production.

My dilemma is very much like that of Alfred Nobel, he thought as he considered that Nobel had also struggled with similar feelings after gaining wealth and fame through his discoveries of dynamite, gelignite, and blasting caps. Late in life, Nobel had been appalled at reading his own premature obituary titled, "The Merchant of Death is Dead." The obituary was mistakenly published by a French newspaper when it was actually his brother, Ludvig, who had died.

But Nobel was so shaken by the specter of such a legacy that he decided to endow five yearly grants recognizing contributions in the sciences and arts to those who brought benefit and peace to mankind—Nobel Prizes as they were now called.

Weizmann's thoughts were interrupted by Ginsburg's cheerful greeting as he shuffled toward the kitchen in his favorite slippers and robe. "Good morning, Chaim! How about a nice cup of tea?"

"Thank you, Asher." Weizmann tucked the papers into his valise and followed Ginsburg into the kitchen.

"Why are you studying? Are they going to give you an exam?"

"I give exams, Asher. I don't take them." Weizmann laughed. "I was just reviewing research notes . . ."

"When do you leave for your meeting?"

Weizmann checked his pocket watch. "My taxi to Whitehall will be here in fifteen minutes."

"Good. Let me hear what you'll be telling them," Ginsburg said as he set water to boil on the stove, then pried the top off a floral tea tin.

"Like a rehearsal?" Weizmann asked.

"Yes! I want to hear what you have to say."

"Alright." Weizmann sat at the kitchen table. "I began studying fermentation because I was interested in the production of synthetic rubber—"

"Because of what King Leopold did in the Congo?" Ginsburg asked, cutting in.

"Yes," Weizmann replied. "I was appalled at the human cost of harvesting natural rubber! The mutilation and massacre of Africans in forcing them to collect rubber was monstrous! I was looking for a way to end that horror by eliminating the need for natural rubber—specifically, with a method to produce isoprene that I could polymerize into synthetic rubber. But, in order to produce isoprene, I needed a method to produce isoamyl alcohol, which I *thought* was a by-product of alcoholic fermentation. I hoped to find a bacterium that would produce the isoamyl alcohol by the fermentation of sugar—"

"Stop right there, Chaim," Ginsburg said as the kettle began to whistle. He cut the fire on the stove and turned back to Weizmann. "Who are you meeting with at Whitehall?"

"Mr. Winston Churchill, the First Lord of the Admiralty."

"Is he a chemist?"

"No."

"Will he be carrying a weapon?"

"Certainly not!"

"I'm relieved to hear that, Chaim, because if Mr. Churchill is armed, and you start talking about isoamyl alcohol and bacterium and by-products, he might shoot you!" He paused to pour hot water into the teapot. "Look, the War Office chemists already reviewed your research, they reproduced your results and made their recommendation. Churchill will only have one question for you: when can you begin acetone production?"

"So, I should keep it simple."

"Your life may depend on it!" Ginsburg put out everything for tea and sat at the table. "Now, there's something I need to speak with *you* about—"

"Are you going to nag me about leveraging munitions production for support of a Jewish homeland?"

"You mean like this?" Ginsburg began rapping a spoon against the teapot. "Hak mir nisht keyn tshaynik?"

Weizmann couldn't help but laugh at Ginsburg's literal demonstration of a popular Yiddish expression, "Don't bang a teapot at me," which meant, "Don't nag me."

"Chaim! Give me some credit. I know how much your scientific work means to you, and I understand its importance for the war effort. Trust me, I'll find another time to nag you about my moral misgivings. For now, I want to talk to you about the idea we discussed on the telephone—my tea envoy to Damascus!"

"You have some news?" Weizmann asked, excited. "Did the envoy speak with Djemal about paying the Turks for allowing us to purchase land in Palestine and for Jewish settlement?"

"No—that's off the table after Turkey joined the Central Powers."

"What?" Weizmann was stunned. "When did that happen?"

"Haven't you heard? A few days ago Turkish ships attacked Russian installations on the Black Sea."

"Oh, my God—I didn't know! I've been so preoccupied about this meeting . . ."

"The Ottoman Empire is now allied with Germany in the war against Great Britain, and we cannot have any financial dealings with them. *However*, as we discussed, my envoy was already in Damascus and met with members of the Arab secret societies. They showed him something called the Damascus Protocol, which commits the Arabs to support Hussein in a revolt against the Turks—if Great Britain agrees to provide the revolt with weapons and gold, and most importantly— if Great Britain accepts the concept of independent Arab states in what is now Ottoman West Asia."

"Which includes Palestine!" Weizmann smiled and stirred cream and sugar into his tea. "But what about finding an Arab leader interested in Arab-Zionist cooperation—the bridge we've been hoping for between us and the Arabs—"

"Sharif Hussein *is* that bridge, Chaim." Ginsberg paused and his smile faded. "But, the *actual* leader of the revolt was to have been one of his sons, Prince Faisal."

"Excellent!" Weizmann exclaimed with mounting excitement. "I'll write Faisal on behalf of the Zionist Organization—"

"I said *was*, Chaim." Ginsberg cut in. "Faisal has disappeared, and no one seems to know where he is, or even if he's still alive. He was last seen more than two months ago in Damascus when the Turks executed twenty-one Arab nationalists by public hanging. There's been no sign of him since . . ."

"But, couldn't he just be in hiding?"

"It's possible, I suppose."

"If he is, wouldn't his father, Hussein know how to reach him?"

Ginsburg shrugged. "So, address your letter to both of them, and if Faisal is still alive, Hussein might connect you with him."

A horn blared out in the street. Weizmann picked up his valise and went to the front door. Seeing the taxi waiting, he turned to Ginsburg. "When I get back from Whitehall, I'll write that letter, and we'll hopefully begin to build that bridge!"

※　※　※

"Welcome to the Admiralty, Professor." A scout guide said and nodded at the door. "His Lordship's office is inside."

Weizmann thanked him, opened the door and stepped in.

"How may I help you, sir?" a uniformed officer asked from behind a desk.

"I'm Professor Weizmann, here to meet with His Lordship, Winston Churchill."

"He's expecting you." Turning, he led the way through a warren of cubicles and tapped on a door panel of opaque glass. "Professor Weizmann to see Your Lordship."

"Come in!"

Weizmann entered a well-appointed office where a dapper man stepped from behind a large desk. He came forward, hand extended. He wore a dark jacket over a high-collared white shirt with a black bowtie. His brown hair was sharply parted on the left, his movements were quick, his manner engaging.

"I've been looking forward to meeting you, Professor!" Churchill beamed as they shook hands. "Please, have a seat." He motioned toward one of two leather armchairs facing the desk.

Weizmann set down his valise and settled into one of the armchairs, pleasantly surprised to see Churchill sit next to him in the other, rather than going back behind his desk. "I'm most honored to meet Your Lordship."

"Please, Professor, dispense with *Your Lordship*—Winston will do nicely."

"In that case, you must call me Chaim."

"So I shall!" Churchill sat forward. "Chaim, the issue before us is this: we have a severe shortage of acetone, which, we require for making cordite, the explosive we employ in all our artillery and naval guns. Without cordite, we would have to make far-reaching changes in our big guns—reinforcing breeches to withstand higher pressures—an impossible task. That is our *problem*, and we're asking you to *solve* it." Churchill fixed Weizmann with his piercing gray eyes. "We need thirty thousand tons of acetone. Can you make it?"

Thirty thousand tons! Weizmann felt a tremor of terror at the size of the request, but responded calmly, "I'm a research chemist, Winston, not a technician. I've succeeded in making a few hundred cubic centimeters of acetone at a time in my lab. However, with the right equipment, I'm confident that I'll be able to produce a ton of acetone. After that, I'll multiply it by any factor you choose."

"How can we make that happen?" Churchill asked.

"Once I establish the scale of bacteriology for the process," Weizmann replied, "it's only a question of distilling, and for that, I'll need the expertise of a brewing engineer from one of the big distilleries."

"Done! Anything else?"

"I would naturally require the government's support to obtain all necessary equipment and support staff."

"You shall have all you require! We're ready to construct a pilot plant where you'll be able to refine all aspects of production and train your staff."

Feeling encouraged, Weizmann plunged forward. "We also need a reliable source of starch. In England, that would be wheat. We can only produce large quantities of acetone if we have enough wheat."

"*That* could be problematic." Churchill sat back in the armchair. "We're dealing with significant grain shortages, and I imagine you'd require large amounts of wheat."

"I would, though there is another option—maize from America."

"If the Germans don't expand their U-boat campaign, that *might* be possible. Is there any other source we might access?"

"Not really. I've tested other possibilities—from Indian rice to Australian eucalyptus to horse chestnuts—they're all suboptimal."

"You've clearly researched the issue!"

"That's what I do, Winston. Every scientific process involves trial and error. It's the only way we learn what works and what doesn't."

"Indeed! One of my father's favorite sayings was that success consists of going from failure to failure without a loss of enthusiasm!"

"Yes! And if *you* supply the starch, *I'll* supply the enthusiasm—and the acetone!"

"Very good! We'll work on securing a steady supply of wheat and maize. As to the pilot plant site, we've selected the Nicholson gin factory in Bromley-by-Bow."

"Would that be in Manchester?" Weizmann asked hopefully.

"Hardly, my good man! It's right here in London—East London, actually; not far from the East India Docks on the Thames—the major brewing center of England!"

Vera won't be happy about this! Weizmann thought and drew a deep breath. "Winston, I'm one hundred percent committed to meeting the goal of acetone production, but my wife and son—"

"Chaim, I'm aware of your family situation. I'm a family man, myself! Be reassured, for the present, we have no need for your full-time presence in London, though we expect you'll give us three or four days a week to get things started. Over the coming months, we'll help you relocate—with housing, a good school for your son, and a comparable or even better medical position for your wife."

"Thank you, Winston. I can't wait to get started!"

"Indeed, there's no time to waste," Churchill said and stood up. "We have an automobile waiting to deliver us to the pilot plant, where a brewing engineer will be present to discuss modifications." Churchill motioned toward the door. "Shall we?"

CHAPTER 43

November 7, 1914
British Expeditionary Force (BEF) Field Hospital
Boulogne-Sur-Mer, Northern France

ONCE EVAN REALIZED he was awake, he tried to sit up, and found that he couldn't.

What the hell?

He turned his head and saw that he was in a long white tent filled with about twenty beds arranged in two rows. To his right was a figure almost completely encased in plaster bandages. Two thick auburn tubes ran from both sides of the man's chest to two bubbling bell jars that stood on the floor by his bed.

Okay. I'm in a hospital.

Looking down, he was stunned to see a thick auburn rubber tube rising from among white bandages covering his own chest. *Oh God!* Panic clawed at his throat, his heart pounding. *How bad am I hurt? Am I going to die?*

He again tried to sit up, but a sharp pain stabbed through his chest. Lifting his head, he saw a wide leather belt cinched across his abdomen, pinning his arms to his sides. He struggled to free his arms but quickly gave up. He found that he could move his legs, though they also seemed to be tethered. He let his head fall back and lay still, his heart pounding wildly.

The air was edged with the sharp smell of disinfectant—a hospital smell. He recalled the last time he'd been in a hospital—in Utah when his mother died. He wondered if he was going to die.

He looked up at a bare light bulb above him, closed one eye, then the other, relieved he could see clearly with both. He realized it was daytime since the light bulb was off, but light filled the tent.

Okay, what do I know? I'm injured and in a hospital tent. I'm not paralyzed and I'm not blind. But I don't know where I am or how I got here . . .

But, in the time it took to draw a breath, he remembered.

He remembered the thin trail of blue smoke rising from the barrel of the English soldier's rifle on the embankment. He remembered the polders flooding, the avenging water in the bright moonlight. He remembered slinging smooth stones at the Germans from within the shadows of the poplars. He remembered Emile at the sluice gate, and he remembered that Emile was dead.

Time to find out where I am . . .

"Hello?" he called out.

"Good morning!" came a voice in the lilting accent of the Indian sub-continent.

Evan turned his head to the left and found himself looking into the brown eyes of a handsome, dark-skinned man with a khaki turban who was lying on his stomach. The man flashed a bright smile. "Good morning," he said again.

Evan cleared his throat and asked, "Where am I?"

"A BEF field hospital in France," the man said. His head rested on folded brown hands, cushioned by a white pillow. He continued to smile.

"What are you smiling about?"

"I am happy to see that you are not dead, Mr. Evan Sinclair. And I am pleased to make your acquaintance."

"How do you know my name?"

"Everyone knows your name. The Flemish partisans told us of your heroic exploits in the flooding of the polders."

Evan lay back and closed his eyes. "So, it worked . . ."

"Oh, it worked quite well. The German advance has stopped. Indeed, they've pulled back to Roeselare."

Evan turned his head and opened one eye. "And you are . . .?"

"Rissaldar Pratab Gupta of the Jodhpur Lancers!"

"Pleased to meet you, Rissaldar."

The man made a little laugh. "Rissaldar is my rank. In the Indian Army, rissaldar is something like a lieutenant. Please, call me Pratab."

"Okay, Pratab. What time is it?"

"Close to eleven—quiet time—after ward rounds when the staff takes a break before they give us lunch."

"How long have *you* been here?"

"About a week, like you."

"What?" Evan's breath caught. "I've been here for a week?"

"Yes."

"And I just woke up *today*?"

"At least you *woke up*! Not like our friend there, the *soldier in white* we call him. They're not expecting him to ever wake up. They were also wondering about you, Evan Sinclair. You were in pretty bad shape."

"Please, just Evan."

"They say you lost a lot of blood and had a collapsed lung and a concussion. They've been checking on you a few times every day, trying to wake you up. Do you remember?"

"No. I only remember dreaming, or bits of dreams." He felt something on his nose and struggled to free his hands. "Pratab, the leather belt doesn't let me move my arms. Could you unbuckle it?"

"Sorry. I can't reach it."

"What's on my nose?"

"Not *on* your nose, *in* your nose."

"What do you mean?"

"That's how they've been feeding you—through that tube. Like the gentleman on your right."

"Feeding me through a tube in my nose?" Evan grimaced and managed to shift his body toward Pratab. "Take it out, will you?"

"I shouldn't do that. I will call for a nurse."

"Okay—go ahead."

"Hello? Hello?" Pratab called out. When there was no response, he shrugged. "Like I said; the staff is on a break."

"Can *you* take it out?

Pratab shook his head.

"Please! You can see that I'm awake. It's really bothering me!"

"Alright, I'll try, but only if it comes out easily. I won't pull hard. If it doesn't come out easily, I won't do it. Agreed?"

"Sure."

Pratab stretched out his right hand and took hold of the tube.

Evan winced as he felt the adhesive pull at his nose. Then he felt an odd sensation in his chest and gagged as the tube came out. He coughed, then smiled. "Thanks!"

"Want to keep it?" Pratab waved the glistening rubber tube for Evan to see.

"No thanks." Evan fixed his eyes on Pratab. "Where were you wounded?"

"Outside Ypres on the Meninx Road. We were attached to Allenby's Cavalry—"

"No." Evan cut in. "I mean, where on your body, were you wounded?"

"In the back."

"Your upper back?"

"No, my lower back."

"How low?"

"Oh, quite low . . ."

Now it was Evan's turn to smile. "Pratab, were you shot in the ass?"

"If by the word *ass*, you are referring to the buttocks, then yes. Specifically, the right ass." Pratab paused and asked, "You're an American?"

"No. English."

"But you speak like an American."

"I lost my accent when I lived in the States."

"Where did you live there?"

"In Utah. Why?"

"Because if you lost your English accent in Utah, then I shall go there and find it. If you won't be using it, I should like to have it."

"For whatever it's worth, I think you sound fine."

"No. I don't sound *fine*. I sound like a sepoy of the Raj speaking English. If I am to be a proper English gentleman, I should *sound* like one. I have always desired to be truly English. Indeed, it is for this reason that I volunteered to serve. What about you? Did you volunteer to join the Flemish resistance?"

"Not exactly . . . well . . . it's a long story."

"We have a long time." Pratab rested his chin on his hands. "I want to know—"

He left off speaking as a nurse approached, pushing a rattling cart down the aisle between the two rows of beds. An energetic matron with steel-gray hair and spectacles hanging from a cord about her neck, she came to a stop at Evan's bed.

"Well, someone's awake today." She lifted a tray from the cart and placed it on the bed. "Good morning, Mr. Sinclair. I'm the Ward Sister—Claire Johnson."

Evan could hear the rustle of her clean, white uniform. Lifting his head, he saw that the tray held shining metal instruments, rolls of gauze, balls of cotton, ampoules, and a few evil-looking syringes with long needles.

She bent down and turned a crank, moving Evan into a sitting position.

"Time for lunch?" he asked hopefully.

"Not quite." She picked up a syringe. "This is morphine—for the pain."

"But I'm not in any pain!"

"You will be," she said with a smile and lifted the sheet off his left thigh.

He smelled the alcohol and felt the coolness of the swab on his thigh before the sharp jab of the needle. "Ow!" he whined. "Why did you do that?"

"Time to change dressings."

"What dressings?"

"The one on your chest and that one." She pointed at his head. "Your turban . . ."

Evan nodded toward Pratab. "Wrong patient—he's the one with the turban."

Pratab laughed. "You too, Sahib. It is what you English call *going colonial.*"

"But why is my head bandaged?"

"You had a nasty encounter with a rock after you were shot, Mr. Sinclair."

"How nasty?"

"Pretty nasty—a skull fracture and concussion." Johnson began pulling strips of adhesive tape off his head. "We thought we might lose you."

"From the concussion?" Evan asked.

"No. From the chest wound. We lose most of you boys to septicemia—infections with bacteria in the blood."

Evan watched the nurse's arms moving in hypnotic circles as she unwound the bandage from his head. "Could you also free up my hands?"

"Perhaps, after I'm done."

"What about the chest tube? Can that come out?"

"That's for the doctors to decide."

"When will that be?"

"During rounds this evening." Johnson reached over and placed a roll of bloodied gauze on the tray. She looked at Evan and raised an eyebrow. "I notice that your feeding tube appears to be missing."

"It came out," Evan offered.

"All by itself?"

Evan nodded. He was feeling the morphine beginning to work. "I sneezed and it just popped out."

"It's true, Nurse Johnson. You can see for yourself." Pratab pointed down at the floor between the beds. "It's right here."

"That is such a shame, Mr. Sinclair. I was so looking forward to sharing some delicious, puréed stew with you."

But Evan wasn't listening. Heaviness settled over his eyes, and he let them close.

❄ ❄ ❄

"Good morning, Nurse Johnson." Gertrude Bell attempted a smile as she addressed the Ward Sister just inside the hospital tent door. "I'm terribly sorry we're not able to come by daily, but we've been overwhelmed with the number of wounded."

"No need to apologize, my dear. We're all overwhelmed—running just to keep up."

Gertrude looked out the tent door at several large white tents pitched in the field hospital grounds. "You've certainly increased bed space, but are the men comfortable in these tents?"

"Quite so, Miss Bell. With extra blankets and kerosene stoves, the tents are positively toasty." She stepped forward. "Shall we begin?"

Gertrude hesitated. "Yes, but before we review the wounded, I should identify the dead, but no one seems to know where they're being kept now."

Johnson sighed. "My dear Miss Bell, didn't you hear? The dead are no longer coming here. They're being buried in Flanders—by the thousands."

For a moment, Gertrude couldn't speak. Placing a hand on the nursing station counter, she steadied herself, then asked, "But, how are they being identified?"

"Many aren't—they're known only to God. That's what they put on the crosses—*Known Only to God*." She stepped around her desk, "Let's begin."

"Certainly." Bell drew a deep breath and nodded as she followed the Ward Sister.

Johnson pushed a metal rack with patient charts down the long aisle between the two rows of beds. The cart lurched and squeaked on its small wheels. The metal chart holders swayed and clicked against each other.

Stopping at the bed of each BEF soldier, Johnson consulted the charts to convey the information Gertrude required to inform next of kin of their condition.

They reached an Indian soldier with a khaki turban, who, unlike most of the other wounded, was lying on his stomach.

The sister lifted a chart from the rack. "Rissaldar Pratab Gupta of the Jodhpur Lancers, attached to General Allenby's Cavalry—sustained a penetrating bullet wound to the right buttock on the Meninx Road outside Ypres, 27 October. Expected to live."

Gertrude entered the information in her notebook as the nurse pushed the cart along, passing the bed of a young soldier who looked vaguely familiar. A single chest tube rose from heavy bandages covering his chest and his head was wrapped in gauze. He seemed to be sleeping.

Moving past the young soldier, Johnson stopped the cart at the foot of the bed occupied by a soldier completely encased in plaster bandages. She pulled a metal file from the rack and nodded toward the soldier in white. "*This* poor young man—"

"Excuse me, Claire," Gertrude cut in and motioned with her pencil at Evan. "What about that one?"

"Not one of yours, my dear. He was with the Flemish resistance."

CHAPTER 44

November 8, 1914
British Expeditionary Force (BEF) Field Hospital
Boulogne-Sur-Mer

MAJOR RICHARD HOWDEN led the BEF surgeons on predawn rounds, verbally sparing with them before the day's surgeries. As he had done on rounds for years at Guy's Hospital in London, Howden wore a gray tweed jacket over his green operating room tunic.

Their progress through the ward was heralded by the clatter of the metal chart rack with its gray steel chart holders. It rattled to a stop by the bed of Pratab Gupta.

"Rissaldar Gupta," Howden said as he lifted out a chart and flipped it open. "How is the butt of our bad humor this fine morning?"

"Not very well, sir." From his prone position, Gupta turned his head to see the doctors. "I had a good deal of pain and chills during the night."

God! Please not another septicemia! Howden thought as he handed the chart to a young doctor in the entourage. "Let's have a look at that wound," He snapped on a pair of rubber gloves. "Those joining us for the first time should know that Rissaldar Gupta served with the Lahore Division, which joined Allenby's Cavalry in holding the Messines ridge against thousands of Germans. It's because of men like him that Ypres is still in our hands. Unfortunately, he was wounded in a regrettable anatomical region." Taking scissors and a surgical clamp from a sterile tray, he removed the bandage covering the wound with swift precision. Without looking up, he asked, "Captain Hollingsworth, what do you make of the fever chart?"

The young doctor frowned as he peered at it. "Could it be malaria, sir?"

"Good Lord, man! When you hear hoof-beats, why do you imagine zebras? This wound is the source of the fever!" Howden parceled a wad of discolored gauze into a metal bowl. "Tell me what you smell."

Hollingsworth leaned forward and warily sniffed the air over the metal bowl. "Nothing, sir."

"And what does that tell you about the offending organism?"

"Staphylococcus?"

"Correct!" Howden patted Gupta on the shoulder. "We'll clean that up for you, Rissaldar."

Stepping away from Gupta's bed, Howden gathered the half-dozen doctors and nurses in a tight circle and whispered, "Gupta's infected wound is worrisome—there's a significant risk of septicemia. Any thoughts about how we might offer him something beyond soap and water?"

"Bromine or mercury, sir?" asked Hollingsworth.

"No. Both too painful and damage healthy tissue. Better options?"

"Carbolic acid?" someone suggested.

"That's worth a try! Lister used it as a disinfectant in the operating theater fifty years ago." He turned to Johnson. "Ward Sister, please clean Gupta's wound and pack it with one-part carbolic acid and four parts boiled linseed oil."

"Yes, Doctor." She left rounds and went to the nursing station.

Howden shrugged. "I trust we'll someday have specific agents for these nasty bugs. For the present, we do the best we can."

He lifted another chart off the rack and stepped toward Evan's bed. "Young Mr. Sinclair somehow snuck into occupied Belgium, joined the Flemish resistance, and was wounded in the flooding of the Polders—a rather significant turning point of the war. He was one of our sleeping beauties until yesterday, when he awoke!" He smiled at Evan. "We're so glad you're finally able to join us! How are you feeling?"

"Quite well, sir! But I'd like to get the chest tube out so I might move about."

Howden dropped into a crouch to examine the water-filled bell jar on the floor next to Evan's bed. "No air leak," he murmured. Standing up he saw that the Ward Sister hadn't returned, so he turned to a Volunteer Aid Detachment nurse in the entourage. Squinting at her nameplate next to the VAD badge on her white tunic, he read, "Miss Sharon Meehan."

"Yes, Major?" the young woman replied.

"Please clamp Mr. Sinclair's chest tube." Howden glanced at Evan and saw him looking at the young nurse. "You don't mind if Miss Meehan fills in for our Ward Sister, do you, Mr. Sinclair?"

"Not at all, sir!" Evan exclaimed.

"We'll keep it clamped for the next twenty-four hours and see how you fare." He leaned forward and examined Evan's well-healed head wound. "If your lung heals as well as your head, we'll soon pull the tube."

❋   ❋   ❋

Augusta Victoria Hostel
Jerusalem

Montagu Walker had just managed to fall asleep when the door of his bedchamber shook with a salvo of knocking, followed by the gruff voice of a Turkish guard.

"Mr. Walker, Herr von List would speak with you."

"Coming!" he called out, then muttered through clenched teeth, "Damn him! It must be past midnight!"

His quarters were Spartan, though he did have a coal-burning parlor stove that made the frigid Jerusalem nights tolerable. In the orange light of the stove's glowing grate, he located his slippers and threw on his robe.

Damn him! he thought as he headed toward the library, where List worked and slept. His slippers made no sound on the smooth travertine tile floor. *What's so bloody compelling to roust me from my bedchambers at such an ungodly hour?*

But he knew why. They were at an impasse, and List blamed him for failing to acquire the two adepts who could help them access the Tomb of Zechariah.

Two months had passed since List's analysis of Poussin's painting, *The Ordination*, indicated an entryway to the Temple Mount by way of the Tomb. But the portal remained hidden, and List's mood blackened with every impatient cable from the kaiser.

Reaching the library, Walker found the door slightly ajar, and peeked in. List, wearing a long dressing gown, was silhouetted against a fire burning in the hearth, staring up at the working copy of Poussin's painting.

Walker silently entered the room. Standing at a deferential distance, he cleared his throat. "How may I be of service, Herr von List?"

By way of a reply, List handed him a cable. "Read it aloud, please."

The large black type was easily legible in the firelight.

THE HOLY ROMAN EMPEROR AND KING OF JERUSALEM, KAISER WILHELM II IS ALARMED BY WORDS OF ILL-OMEN FROM HIS FUTURE CAPITAL. WORD HAS IT THAT YOU HAVE NOTHING TO SHOW FOR MONTHS OF WORK. THIS IS UNACCEPTABLE. MUST WE REMIND YOU THAT YOUR VERY SURVIVAL IS--

List snatched the cable away. "I cannot recall the kaiser ever expressing himself so bluntly."

"We're doing all we can, sir."

"Are we?" List's features twisted into a snarl. "Mr. Walker, the kaiser brought you here for the express purpose of using your connections with the local apelings to our advantage. During your previous sojourn in Jerusalem you hosted lavish parties and supposedly cultivated contacts among the Turkish police, army, and business community. Where are these contacts, Mr. Walker? How have you failed to acquire the two adepts, B'Shara and Wertheimer?" List brought his face closer, his eyes glittering in the firelight beneath the gray thicket of his eyebrows. "Your continued failure to acquire them does our fortunes grave harm!"

Walker couldn't decide which of List's features was more overpowering—the fetor of his breath or the dark malevolence of his voice. Either way, he felt a growing dread enveloping him. "What more can I do?"

"You were given their identities and photographs weeks ago. What have you done with the information provided by our colleague?"

"What colleague?" Walker shot back, his voice rising. "I've never even met—"

A blow from List's fist snapped Walker's head to the side, followed by another that sent him staggering backwards.

"Do not *dare* address me with that tone again!" List shouted, then quickly turned his back and faced the hearth.

Shaken, Walker dabbed blood from his nose with the sleeve of his robe. He watched in growing terror as List took hold of a cast-iron poker and began stirring the glowing coals in the hearth. His heart beat wildly as he wondered, *What can I say to calm him down?* After a brief hesitation, he said, "I'm extremely sorry, Herr von List. I will be more respectful in the future and do whatever I can to advance our cause."

Walker watched List lift the poker from the fire, its pointed tip a bright orange. Frantic with fear, he saw List raise it up, seeming to admire the glowing metal, then he leaned it against the hearth.

"Your apology is accepted," List said pleasantly. "Please, have a seat!" he nodded toward two chairs that faced the hearth separated by a small round table.

Once they were seated, List spoke again, "You have all the tools required to complete your task, Walker. You must simply use them properly. If the Jew Nathanson knows the whereabouts of the two adepts, *we* must know what he knows!"

"But, Herr von List, we tortured Nathanson for weeks! I'm certain he has *no* idea where they are hiding, and no knowledge about the portal."

"I'll grant you that," List said quietly. "Where is he now?"

"Home. After we released him, he was admitted to the Italian Hospital in West Jerusalem where he recovered. He was discharged this morning."

"You are correct in stating that Nathanson cannot tell us what he does not know, but his *travails* might bring the rats out of hiding . . ."

"I'm not sure I understand . . . we tortured him to the point of death."

"So you did." List turned and looked at Walker, his eyes shining like glowing coals. "But why stop with *him*? He has a family, no? A wife? An infant son?"

Walker nodded silently. He remembered his friend, Clarence Watson, the expression on his face as the pistol discharged, the sound like the slamming of a door.

There was no going back.

"I'll see to it first thing in the morning—"

"No. You will see to it *now*."

"In the middle of the night?"

"*Precisely* when they won't be expecting it! Have a few soldiers *immediately* secure Nathanson's home and keep them there. You will follow with more guards and a lorry to collect the family and bring them to me . . ." His voice trailed off as he stood up and again took the iron poker and stirred the coals. "Tomorrow morning you will see to it that word is spread throughout Jerusalem, that Nathanson, along with his wife and child will be tortured to death unless we acquire Wertheimer and B'Shara." He turned to Walker and smiled. "Do I make myself clear?"

"Yes, Herr von List," he replied evenly, though beneath his robe he was sweating.

List waved the iron poker toward the door. "Now, go."

"Yes, sir." Walker left the suffocating warmth of the study. *Damn him!* He thought with a flash of anger. *How dare he strike me and order me about? I have half a mind to tell him to go to hell!*

Instead, he ran out of the hostel to the barracks tent where the Turkish soldiers were billeted. Lighting the way with his electric torch, he thought, *I'll have those two chaps who speak English make the Nathansons stay put. I'm glad I insisted on having some Turks who actually speak English!*

Having relied on the two before, he knew where to find them. "Mustafa! Yusuf!" he hissed loudly and shook them awake."

"What? Came a sleepy voice. "What is it?"

"Get up! I have a very important task for you. Get dressed, bring your rifles, and meet me at the main gate in three minutes!"

Returning to the hospice entryway, Walker found it deserted apart from clouds of moths that fluttered against two buzzing electric lamps that bathed the gray stone with yellow light. Hearing footsteps, he saw the two soldiers emerge from the shadows.

"What is it, sir?" Mustafa asked.

Walker quickly repeated List's instructions.

"Is that the apartment building across from the Persian Consulate?" Yusuf asked.

"Yes. The flat is on the ground floor. Make certain to keep them there—Nathanson, his wife, and child. I'll be along within the half hour in a lorry with a few soldiers to bring them here."

"Didn't we finish with Nathanson?" asked Mustafa.

Walker fixed him with his eyes. "Do you really have to ask?"

CHAPTER 45

November 8, 1914
Nachalat Shiv'a
West Jerusalem

AVID NATHANSON knelt by the tub, bathing his son, Isser. The light of a single candle augmented the bright orange grate of the parlor stove filling the bathroom with a warm radiance. But a sidelong glance at the stove's glowing grate sent a sickening jolt stabbing through David's brain—the raw memory of the glowing tip of the iron poker burning his skin. He crushed his eyes shut, pushing the pain away. Opening them, he looked down at his son and smiled. He was home.

How fortunate I am! He gently sponged soapy warm water from Isser's delicate skin. *What a blessing to hold him in my arms again!* He whispered a prayer of thanksgiving in Hebrew, "Blessed are you, Lord our God, Ruler of the world, who kept me alive, who sustained me, and who enabled me to reach this moment!"

After a week recuperating at the Italian Hospital, he was beginning to feel more like himself. Apart from a few missing teeth, healing burns, and fading bruises, he looked much the same as he had before the ordeal. But the torture had left an open wound in his soul, and like the burns and bruises, he prayed that wound would also heal.

His wife, Sarah, entered with a white towel over her arms. "Are you finished?"

"We just need a rinse."

Sarah lifted a pitcher from the floor and carefully poured warm water over Isser's plump body. Then David placed him in Sarah's arms, and she wrapped him in the towel.

Isser kicked his legs free as he gummed a small fist, looking up at his mother with bright astonished eyes.

The sight of his wife and son filled David's heart with joy, and he silently repeated the blessing of gratitude.

Drying his hands, he asked, "Are you ready to go?"

"Yes. Are you?" Sarah asked and carried Isser into the bedroom.

"Almost." He checked his timepiece. "Gunter will be here at two a.m. We have twenty minutes to close up the house."

"But, how did Gunter and Rahman know to come here on the evening of the day you left the hospital?" she asked and placed Isser on the bed.

"Jerusalem is a small town—everyone knows everything," he said and closed his valise. "They would have come earlier in the day, but they only go out when it's dark to avoid the German and Ottoman authorities."

"I didn't even recognize them!" Sarah said as she patted Isser dry with the towel. "They looked like lepers with those ragged hooded robes and the rattles!"

"It's the only way they're able to go out, and only at night." Seeing that Sarah was staring at the healing burns on his arms, he rolled down his sleeves. "I'm just grateful they invited us to join them in hiding—wherever that is . . ."

"But why are we still hiding? You told me the Turks were finished with you."

"It's not the Turks that worry me, Sarah. Most of them didn't hurt me. Someone else was guiding them, asking the questions, and directing the torture."

"But, who?"

"I don't know. A few of the Turks only *pretended* to torture me— telling me to scream as if I were in pain."

"So, not all the Turks were monsters."

David nodded. "Two guards in particular protected me at every opportunity— treating my wounds and sneaking me bits of food and chocolate. I don't know if I would have survived without them."

"But, you're worried they'll bring you back for more questioning— aren't you?"

"Yes." The thought terrified him. "Thank God we're getting out of here."

※　※　※

"I'll drive," Yusuf Kemal said as he opened the car door and stepped onto the running board. "You do the hand crank and light the headlamps."

"Alright." Mustafa Kadim nodded. But only if I get to drive on the way back."

"Agreed. Let's go!" Yusuf settled into the driver's seat. Once the automobile was ready, he guided it onto the road toward the northern reaches of the Kidron Valley.

"Do you think they'll be at the house?" Mustafa asked.

"I hope not," Yusuf said, shifting into low gear as the road ascended. "That way we won't have to lie when we tell Walker they were gone when we got there."

"Mustafa exhaled loudly. "What are we going to do if they're still there?"

Yusuf shrugged. "Whatever we can to get them out!"

The Mercedes picked up speed, moving toward West Jerusalem.

※　※　※

Sarah was wrapping Isser in a blanket when three soft taps at the front door shattered the silence as if they had been explosions.

She caught up the baby in her arms, her heart pounding. "Could that be Gunter already?" she whispered, panic rising in her voice.

David glanced at his watch. "No. It's too early—"

She could hear the fear in his voice as three more taps sounded at the door, lightly but insistent. She watched in terror as David, his hands shaking, opened the door. Her breath caught. Two Turkish soldiers filled the doorway, and each carried a rifle.

Stifling a scream, she clutched Isser close and stumbled backwards. The baby's blanket fell to the floor.

The soldiers stepped through the door with their heavy boots.

One of them whispered to David. "Do you remember us?"

They've come back for him! The thought screamed in her mind. She held Isser closer, wanting to pick up the blanket to cover him, but afraid to move. She saw that David was staring at the soldiers, his mouth agape.

He doesn't know what to do! Shaking with fear, she watched as David moved toward them. Crushing her eyes closed against the tears, she was about to scream when she heard David speak. "How good to see you again!"

What? She opened her eyes and saw David shaking hands with them. She also realized that they were speaking to each other in Hebrew.

One of them stepped toward her. She flinched and stepped back.

The Turk picked Isser's blanket off the floor and held it out. "Please," he said in Hebrew. "It's very cold outside and you must leave quickly."

Dumbfounded, she looked at David who stood next to the other Turk, a hand on his shoulder. As if in a dream, she heard David ask,

"Are they coming to take me again?"

"They're coming to take *all* of you," replied the soldier.

Sarah couldn't believe her ears—hearing David and the Turkish guards speaking in Hebrew, hearing what they were saying.

The soldier checked his timepiece. "They'll be here with a lorry in about fifteen minutes. They must not find you here."

"David!" Sarah stepped forward. "Do you know these men?"

"Yes!" He motioned toward them. "Mustafa and Yusuf—these are the Turkish guards who protected and helped me."

"There's no time for this," Yusuf cut in. You must leave *now*."

"We will," David grabbed the suitcases that stood in the foyer. "Someone's coming to take us with an automobile. We'll be gone in a few minutes."

"Perfect!" Mustafa said. "You have someplace safe to stay?"

"Yes," David replied and moved toward the door.

"Good. Let's go."

Sarah watched Yusuf pick up a suitcase and quickly leave the flat with David. She followed with Isser in her arms, wondering if she was dreaming, hoping it wasn't a nightmare. *God willing, we'll get to safety!* She silently prayed.

Once outside, Sarah saw that the deserted lane was shrouded in total darkness beyond the small halo of a lone streetlamp. The night was cloudy and very cold. She pulled the blanket closer around Isser, thankful he was asleep.

"Lock the door," she heard Mustafa whisper to David.

"Why?" David asked as he fumbled for his keys.

"The house should be locked before we break in to look for you."

David locked the door and handed the keys to Mustafa.

"No. You keep them. It's your house."

As she watched and listened, Sarah began to understand that the

Turkish soldiers were there to help them. "Are you going to follow us?" she asked.

"How? We never saw you," said Yusuf. "We'll tell them that we found the house locked and empty."

"What if they ask the neighbors?" David asked.

"What neighbors?" Yusuf nodded up at the dark windows. "When is the automobile coming?"

"Any minute now."

"To the house?"

"No. Two blocks up Jaffa Street."

"Good," Mustafa said. "Now go, and may God watch over you."

Sarah stepped toward the soldiers. "Thank you! We'll never forget your kindness. May God bless you!"

The Turks nodded in reply. One waved goodbye.

Sarah and David walked quickly away as a light rain began to fall. But, after a minute, and still within sight of the house, Sarah froze. "What's that?" Her breath caught as an automobile with bright headlamps came from the direction of East Jerusalem. "Could that be the lorry?" she gasped.

"No. It's an automobile."

Sarah saw it slow down as it passed the Turkish soldiers, almost stopping, then speeding up. David stepped into Jaffa Road as the automobile approached. In the glare of the headlamps, he raised a hand and signaled the driver to stop.

Sarah recognized Gunter von Wertheimer through the glass, his mouth agape as he stared back at the soldiers. "What the hell is—"

"Don't ask," said David.

Sarah cradled Isser in her arms and got into the back seat as David quickly stowed the luggage in the boot. He got in next to Gunter and pulled the door closed.

The auto slid along Jaffa Road as the rain increased.

Sarah realized that she'd been holding her breath. She exhaled, kissed her sleeping son's head, and whispered, "The guardian of Israel neither slumbers nor sleeps."

❋ ❋ ❋

Yusuf and Mustafa stood in the shadows beyond the wavering light of the kerosene streetlamp, watching the automobile disappear up Jaffa Road. The rain was falling faster.

"Okay my friend, time to do what we came for," Yusuf stepped back to the flat, and with the butt of his rifle, struck the door. The sound exploded in the silent darkness. "Open the door, Nathanson!" he shouted in Turkish. "We know you're in there!" He struck the door again, then turned to Mustafa and whispered, "Your turn."

"Open the door or we'll break it down!" Mustafa shouted. "This is your last chance!" He kicked at the door, which splintered along with the doorjamb.

The rain increased, coming down in sheets.

By now, candlelight was shining in windows throughout Nachalat Shiv'a.

"Okay, we woke up the neighbors," Mustafa said, squinting at Yusuf through the downpour. "Let's get out of the rain!"

They burst in, shouting as they pretended to search for the Nathansons.

❋ ❋ ❋

Jaffa Road to the American Colony
Jerusalem

"Weren't those Turkish soldiers?" Gunter asked as he gripped the steering wheel, straining to see the road through gaps in the rainwater streaming over the windshield between the steady beating of the wiper blades.

"They were," David replied, "but there's nothing to worry about from those two. They saved my life when I was at Augusta Victoria, and they just helped us get away before they could bring us back there . . ."

"We were worried about that—that List and Walker would bring you back."

"*Who?*" David cut in."

"Agents of the kaiser. Did you really believe it was the Turks interrogating you?"

"I never saw anyone there *but* Turks, but who are these agents of the kaiser?"

"No doubt you've already heard of one of them—Montagu Walker—the treasure hunter who excavated on the Temple Mount a few years ago . . ."

"I remember that," Sarah said from the backseat. "It was in all the newspapers."

"And the other one?" asked David. "Another treasure hunter?"

"Guido von List is something far more sinister. It was actually List who was directing your interrogation and torture. He's the real reason we wanted to get you away."

"And just in time," said Sarah, and Gunter felt her hand on his shoulder. "Thank you for coming when you did—a few minutes later might have been a disaster!"

David nodded. "Your punctuality was a lifesaver!"

"You needn't thank me for punctuality. I'm a German—I can't help it!"

"But where are we going?" asked Sarah.

"The American Colony, and we're almost there."

"There's room for us there?"

"Plenty of secure and hidden spaces. There's also the advantage of American neutrality in the war—neither Germany nor the Turks want to give the US an excuse to join the Entente. So far, that's kept List at bay."

"The American Colony?" asked Sarah. "Is that where you've been hiding?"

"Yes," Gunter replied as he maneuvered on a particularly muddy section of road, waiting for the next question, which he knew was coming. And sure enough, David broke the silence.

"During the interrogations, they kept asking me about you and Rahman. Why?"

"List believes we know something . . ." Gunter paused, unsure how much to tell David. " . . .about ways to access hidden chambers within the Temple Mount."

"Do you?"

"No," Gunter lied. "But some scholars believe there are hidden channels into the Temple Mount—Clive Sinclair, for example. He used to go on and on about it."

"I remember him arguing that point," said David. "About some underground aquifer from the pool of Bethesda into the bedrock beneath the sacred precincts."

"And if you think *that's* far-fetched," Gunter said, "List believes the true passageway begins at the Tomb of Zechariah!"

"They asked about that, and I told them it made no sense—the tomb is solid rock and it's on the wrong side of the Kidron Valley. Where did List get that idea?"

"From a painting."

"I believe I saw it—human figures, buildings, transecting lines, angles, arcs . . ."

"What you saw was List's working copy of Poussin's *The Ordination*. Do you recall anything that looked like the Tomb of Zechariah?"

"Now that you mention it, yes. And in the center was a figure—Jesus, I suppose . . ."

"Do you recall what Jesus is holding in his hand?"

"A large key."

"That's the reason List is looking for us. He believes *we* have the key."

CHAPTER 46

November 9, 1914
BEF Field Hospital
Boulogne-Sur-Mer

EVAN WAS DREAMING that the doctors were crowding over him, blocking out the light, the air sharp with the smell of disinfectant as they tugged on his chest tube, pulling it out with a jagged metallic sound.

Starting awake, the grating noise continued in the darkness, the hospital tent lit only by a weak light burning at the nurses' station. He patted his chest and found the tube still in place, first to his relief, then his disappointment. Listening to the sound, he realized it was coming from Pratab's bed frame.

He must be shaking from fever, Evan thought and asked, "Are you okay?"

"No." Pratab's breathing was quick and ragged. "Could you take me outside?"

"What are you talking about?"

"I'd like to see the night sky, the stars . . ."

"I'll call for the nurse," Evan said, concerned about Pratab's apparent delirium.

"Please don't. They'll just give me a sponge bath. Please, take me outside."

"You know I can't. I still have the chest tube."

"Oh, yes. I thought it had come out. Perhaps I just dreamed it."

"I had the same dream," Evan replied. The bedsprings continued to squeak with Pratab's shaking chills "I should really call for the nurse—"

"Not yet," Pratab said sharply, then drew a deep breath. "Talking to you makes me feel better. Tell me, Evan, do you like the poetry of Longfellow?"

"I suppose . . ." Evan replied hesitantly.

"What's your favorite of his poems?"

"'Paul Revere's Ride' is pretty good." Evan felt that Pratab seemed lucid.

"Any others?"

"Not really. They made us read 'Evangeline' in school, but I hated it."

"Me, too," Pratab said and laughed weakly. "Longfellow's epic poems do go on and on. My favorite, though, is 'The Occultation of Orion.'"

"Never heard of it."

"I committed some of it to memory. Might I recite the final lines for you?"

"Sure." To his relief, Evan noted that Pratab's voice was stronger, and his bed had stopped squeaking.

" . . . *from sphere to sphere the words re-echoed down the burning chords, Forevermore, forevermore, the reign of violence is o'er!*"

"Nice, Pratab, but you and I know that 'the reign of violence' is far from over."

Pratab sighed, then whispered, "I *so* wish I could see the Summer Triangle . . ."

"How do you expect to see the *Summer* Triangle in the *fall*? And in the Northern Hemisphere? What's so special about it, anyway?"

"The Summer Triangle is part of the ancient Vedic constellation of Acvattha, the sacred fig tree, and the three bright stars of the triangle are said to mark the first footsteps of Vishnu in the sky—the gateway to heaven. On summer nights back home, I would often sleep on the roof, and I could see how the Milky Way swept through the sky, inviting me along, inviting me to travel in the footsteps of Vishnu." Pratab paused and said, "Please call for the nurse now, Evan."

Alarmed, Evan called out, and the nurse was soon there—the pretty nurse who had clamped his chest tube. The bright beam of a battery-powered torch illuminating the floor at her feet. "Nurse Meehan, Pratab isn't feeling well!"

Reaching out, she placed a hand on his forehead. "He's burning up." Since he was already lying prone, she was easily able to place the rectal thermometer.

"Ouch! The wound hurts quite a bit now, nurse."

After a few minutes, she checked the thermometer.

Evan saw her eyes widen. "Does he have a temperature?" he asked.

Making no reply, she hurried back to the nurses' station.

A minute later, he heard the clatter of small wheels on the wooden floor and two orderlies appeared with a gurney.

In the erratic light of the nurse's torch, Evan caught a glimpse of Pratab's face, glowing with perspiration. He heard him say, "Perhaps I can convince these gentlemen to take me outside . . ."

Evan's heart sank. He had often heard the word *septicemia* spoken by the doctors, and he had seen the way it sprinted ahead of them, confounding their skills, and claiming many young soldiers. As the orderlies moved Pratab onto the gurney and wheeled him away, Evan called out, "Hey, Pratab! I'll see you later."

Alone in the darkness, he couldn't sleep. He asked Nurse Meehan for morphine, which was ordered as needed for pain. After the shot his thoughts strayed back to what Pratab had said about the Summer Triangle and the gateway to Heaven. He drifted into sleep remembering nights when he had slept out in the Utah desert beneath a sky crowded with stars.

Throughout a night spent in the numbing embrace of morphine, he was dimly aware of lights going on and off, of people coming and going. When he finally woke up to the brightness of late morning, he found that he was lying on his right side.

How is that possible? He looked down and saw that the chest tube was gone.

Looking up to his right where the soldier in white had been, the bed was neatly made and empty.

He turned to the other side.

Pratab's bed was also neatly made. And empty.

❀ ❀ ❀

Whitehall War Office
London

Darkness had fallen over London and a dozen bare light bulbs illuminated the map table as Clive and Lawrence bent to the task of filling the empty stretches of Mesopotamia with springs, wells, hills, wadis, and islands of human habitation.

"I say, Ned, shall we take a break for dinner?" Clive asked as he straightened up.

"I thought you'd never ask," Lawrence replied and stretched. "Considering that neither of us have recently been there, I think we're doing a smashing job!"

"But we both know who needs to be here to finish this—"

Lawrence shrugged. "We've nagged Hedley for weeks to bring Gertrude aboard. What else can we do?"

Clive took his cap off the table. "Despite Hedley's long experience with the Geographical Society, his behavior is inexplicable. Gertrude has addressed the Society on several occasions *precisely* on the subject of

Mesopotamia! She has current firsthand knowledge of the geography and knows many of the current Bedouin sheiks!"

"It's painfully clear that Hedley has a problem with the fact that Gertrude is a woman, and a brilliant one at that!"

"Damn it, Ned! Given the fact that the Turks are in this now, we should go above Hedley—straight to Major-General Callwell—and do it together before you leave for Egypt!" Clive felt Lawrence's hand on his shoulder and turned to see his enigmatic smile.

"Let me speak with Hedley. I'll make him an offer . . ."

"What do you have to offer?"

"Just this—if he brings on Gertrude, I *won't* complain to Callwell."

"Will that work?"

Lawrence nodded. "I'll appeal to his vanity—that Gertrude's appointment will be heralded as a bold and brilliant decision!"

"Good!" Clive put on his cap. "Now I have an appetite for dinner. Let's go!"

As they went out the door, Lawrence asked, "Any news of Evan?"

"No. I did receive a note from Gertrude at the Red Cross in France, reassuring me that his name isn't among the wounded or dead. Also, I've had Evan listed as a missing person in France, England, and the US. Plus, I continue to monitor the BEF. But, so far—nothing! I have no bloody idea where he is, and it's driving me mad!"

"But, at least here, you have access to as much information as possible."

"That's why I'm staying."

"And here, you'll be able to work with Gertrude when she comes aboard!"

"No," Clive said as they descended the stairs in the narrow stairwell. "Once you leave, I'll put in for a transfer. I don't have any more to contribute at MO-4, but with Turkey in the fray, I'll find some interesting assignment on the Middle East Front!"

"Funny how that finally happened!" said Lawrence as they left the stairwell. "After three long months of staying neutral, Turkey suddenly sends their battleships to attack Russian positions along the shore of the Black Sea!"

Clive stopped Lawrence with a hand on his shoulder. "You know those weren't really *Turkish* battleships, don't you?"

"What are you talking about? Of course, they were."

"It's like this, Ned, while the two battle cruisers did have Turkish registry, they were both commanded by German officers with a fair number of German crew—still training the Turks."

"How is that possible?" asked Lawrence as they headed toward the officer's mess.

"Those were the two battleships Kaiser Bill gave Turkey to replace the two England had built for the Turks but didn't deliver . . . you know, in retaliation for that agreement the Turks signed with Germany just before the war began."

"So," Lawrence smiled. "Kaiser Bill gave the Turks a shove!"

Clive nodded. "Otherwise, they may have stayed neutral for the duration."

Lawrence laughed. "I'm surprised he didn't do it sooner, considering his impatience and short temper. But, at least this way, we have our Middle East Front!"

CHAPTER 47

November 10, 1914
The American Colony
Jerusalem

ANNA SPAFFORD had yet to speak with the Nathansons since their arrival at the American Colony.

She simply hadn't the time.

Her usual administrative duties, in addition to Thanksgiving preparations, had consumed every moment—all the more challenging with a kerosene shortage and greater demands on the soup kitchen from the growing number of Jerusalem's poor.

Night had fallen and Anna hadn't yet changed out of her daywear—a tailored jacket over a pale blouse with a long dark skirt. The clock on her mantelpiece said it was nine thirty. *If I'm going to speak to my new guests today, it must be now,* she thought, lit her lantern and blew out her candle.

Raising her lantern, she navigated the labyrinth of intersecting corridors, arched passages, and descending stairwells to finally reach a dark and empty drawing room, which served three separate rooms in a hidden subterranean part of the compound.

With a scarcity of candles, most colony residents fashioned lamps from sardine tins; each having a hole for the wick and another for sesame oil. Finding a few of these in the drawing room, she lit the lamps, then tapped on the door of the room shared by Gunter and Rahman.

Gunter opened the door, his face illuminated by the lamp in his hand. "Good evening, Anna. Is everything alright?"

"Quite alright, thank you." She saw that both men had been working at the room's small table, Rahman still writing by the light of his lamp. "I'm sorry to disturb you, but I'd like to speak with everyone, especially the Nathansons."

"Wonderful!" Rahman said and put down his fountain pen. "They've been looking forward to that!"

Within a minute, all were assembled in the drawing room— the Nathansons sat together on a settee, their infant son sleeping in Sarah's arms.

Anna moved her chair toward them. "On behalf of myself and my family, I want to welcome you to the American Colony. Are your accommodations satisfactory?"

"Oh, yes! Mrs. Spafford!" said Sarah. "We can't begin to thank you for your protection and gracious hospitality."

"Please, Sarah, call me Anna."

"We don't know how we can ever repay you—" David began.

"Put aside such thoughts, my dears. This is why the American Colony exists!"

"We were wondering about that, Anna," said Sarah. "Why did you leave a comfortable life in the United States to come here?"

Anna smiled and settled back in her chair. "A full answer to that question might prove too taxing for you at this late hour. Even the short version . . ."

"If it's not too taxing for you, Anna," said Gunter, "I believe we'd all appreciate hearing your story—whatever version you prefer."

"Very well!" Anna began. "My Horatio and I married in 1861—a simple wedding since it was during the American Civil War. Horatio was already a successful Chicago lawyer, and our life together moved in positive directions over the next decade; we purchased a cottage at Lake View, we were blessed with four beautiful daughters, Horatio became a church elder and director of the Presbyterian Theological Seminary of the Northeast, and his law practice flourished.

"However, the following decade brought us great misfortune, starting with the Great Chicago Fire of 1871, which destroyed our home and real estate investments. Two years later, we were determined to visit friends and family in England and booked passage. Since Horatio was busy with work, we determined that I would travel with our four girls, aged between eighteen months and twelve years, and Horatio would follow a few weeks later.

"But tragedy struck; our steamship collided with an iron sailing vessel and sank, and . . . our four little girls . . . perished . . ." Anna paused to compose herself, her eyes glistening with tears, which she dabbed away with her handkerchief.

"My dear Anna—how devastating," Sarah said, and with Isser in her arms, she leaned forward, trying to stand.

Anna motioned Sarah with her hand to stay seated. "Thank you, dear Sarah, but allow me to finish." Anna drew a deep breath and continued. "We were indeed devastated—not only by our heartbreaking loss, but also by the cruelty exhibited by many of our friends at church. At the time, the Puritan foundations of our Presbyterian faith held that sickness or sorrow was the result of God's retribution for sin, and some confronted us with questions as to what sins Horatio and I had committed to bring about such a tragedy. As you might imagine, this compounded our sadness. We consulted with our friend, the evangelist, Dwight L. Moody, who counseled us to simply become busy helping those who had also gone into the depths of despair. By bringing comfort to them, we might overcome our own sadness.

"Following his advice, we devoted ourselves to philanthropic work with Chicago's destitute. Other church members who had known loss joined us. We overcame our sadness by helping others; and became known as the 'Overcomers.'

"During those years, Horatio and I were blessed with two more children—Horatio Jr. and two years later, our daughter, Bertha. As we continued to care for our children and for those who needed our help, we began to feel restored, as did the other Overcomers. We came to view our sorrows not as punishment but as *opportunities* to overcome and serve—to show God's love for others even in the valley of weeping, and to make it a place of springs. In this we felt we were simply following the example of Christ, of whom Isaiah prophesied—*a man of sorrows, and acquainted with grief.* However, Horatio and I didn't realize, we would yet experience more grief."

Anna paused again and pressed her handkerchief over her eyes. "At the age of four, Horatio Jr. died of scarlet fever. This tragedy was held up by some at church as further proof of our sinfulness. They also accused us of belonging to a new and heretical sect. But we knew that what we were doing wasn't new and wasn't heresy. We were simply following the example of Christ.

"We were asked to leave the church, which we did, along with the other Overcomers. At that point we felt that the sorrow that drew us together, also drew us to Jerusalem—as my Horatio wrote to our group. *Jerusalem is where my Lord lived, suffered, and conquered. It is where I'll learn how to live, suffer, and especially to conquer.* So, in 1881, we came here, and that is why we've remained—to simply love the Lord God with all our hearts, and to love our neighbors as ourselves."

Anna looked at Sarah and smiled. "That's the short answer to your question, my dear. We came here to create a Christian community of selfless giving—to silently reflect the love of Christ for the people of Jerusalem—Muslims, Jews, Christians, those of any faith and those with none.

"My Horatio died from malaria in 1888, and I've carried on with our mission. The colony has thrived, and new members have joined us from America and Sweden."

Anna drew her chair closer, fixing David and Sarah with her eyes.

"These are dangerous times for us all, as you know all too well. I've heard what David endured at Augusta Victoria, and I want you both to know that you'll be safe here." She put her hand on Sarah's knee. "This is your city of refuge—your ir miklat. Only my children and I will know of your presence—the rest of the colony will never know." She searched their faces. "You do understand the need for absolute secrecy, don't you?"

"We understand completely, Anna," said David. "We know the relentless and wicked nature of those who are searching for us, and we're relieved beyond words that you're willing to give us shelter."

Gunter stood up and said, "We appreciate your support more than you can know, Anna. However, you must realize the full extent of the threat we pose to you and your family."

"I'm well aware of the danger posed by the Ottoman and German authorities, Gunter, as well as Mr. Walker's penchant for mischief . . ."

"They are no longer our main concerns, Anna. The real danger comes from another agent of the kaiser—Guido von List."

Anna felt a chill. "Who's *that*?"

"An Austrian occultist who has endeared himself to the kaiser with his theories of Germanic-Nordic racial superiority he calls Armanism. It links German and Nordic people to a glorious Teutonic heritage of Blut und Boden—blood and soil. List is here to realize the kaiser's dream to be King of Jerusalem, and also seeks to realize his own vision of Germanic ethnic superiority once the kaiser sits upon a throne on the Temple Mount—to rule the world from Jerusalem."

"Really, Gunter! I've long heard such silly notions from deranged individuals—"

"It's gone well beyond that. Under the kaiser, this is becoming Germany's new nationalism, and List will stop at nothing to further it. This is why sheltering us puts you and your family in peril. List believes Rahman and I have secret knowledge that will allow him to achieve his goals."

"Do you?" she asked.

Gunter shrugged. "So, he believes. To be sure, Rahman and I have excavated around the Temple Mount for years, and List will stop at nothing to capture us and force us to divulge these supposed secrets. That's why David was tortured, and why we requested that the Nathansons might be sheltered here—a request you generously granted."

"I was honored you asked me and happy to agree."

"Thank God you did, Anna. Because List intended to bring David, Sarah, and the baby to Augusta Victoria the very night we brought them here—to force us out of hiding by torturing them!"

"Oh, my God!" Anna's hand went over her heart. "I didn't realize . . ." Her blood felt cold in her veins.

"This is the danger you and your family now share for sheltering us, Anna. You must know this. And knowing this, you must tell us if you prefer that we leave and seek shelter elsewhere—perhaps, in one of the Arab villages on the Coastal Plain, or in one of the Jewish settlements in the Northern Galilee. This doesn't have to involve you. Tell us what you would have us do."

For a long minute Anna didn't speak. When she did, her voice was calm and resolute. "Horatio and I came here as Overcomers, and I speak to you now for both of us. Our purpose *then* was to do God's work in this world, and that's our purpose *now*. Thank you for telling me about the risks. We're honored to remain true to our purpose. That's why we came and why we stay. And we're grateful to you, to all of you, for the opportunity to demonstrate that living faith and that abiding love." She smiled and added, "I want you to stay."

With faces streaked with tears, Sarah and David stood up and thanked Anna.

Gunter watched as she gathered the two of them in her arms and stood, like an angel with outstretched wings, holding them.

CHAPTER 48

November 15, 1914
Mecca
The Holy Precincts

SUMMONED BY HIS FATHER from Nuweiba, Faisal was anxious to hear the reason. He had traveled over a thousand miles by camel, and completed the journey under cover of darkness, reaching the holy precincts before dawn. He accessed his hidden apartment in the catacombs of the Great Mosque, enjoyed a hot bath followed by twenty minutes of quiet prayer. And now, as he navigated the empty passageways up to his father's chambers. Here, he felt uneasy—Ottoman sympathizers could be anywhere.

He knocked and waited for an anxious minute. He was about to knock again when a key turned in the lock and the heavy door creaked open.

The steward bowed. "Welcome, O prince! Your royal father will be most pleased to see you. Will you have coffee, sire?"

"No, thank you," Faisal murmured and stepped through the foyer to a window where he looked out at the Kaaba, still in shadow. The rising sun ignited the tops of the seven tall minarets looming over the arcade. He drew a deep breath, tasting the morning air, happy to be back in Mecca, though saddened to be far from his wife and children, still sheltering in Nuweiba.

He turned at the sound of a familiar voice.

"My son, I am so very pleased you arrived safely from your long journey!"

"My beloved father!" Faisal was relieved to see his father no longer looking frail, but regal in his dark robe.

Hussein kissed Faisal on each cheek. "Sit with me, my son, and I will hear your report." He gestured toward the divan.

Faisal arranged his white robe and sat down. "I have much to impart, my father. Did you receive my brief messages?"

"Yes, and I was pleased to see your discreet and judicious use of our trusted retainers who hid the messages well, sewing them into the hems of their garments or hiding them in sword hilts or shoes. But those were but short missives. I would hear a full accounting from your own lips. Please, my son, tell me of your journey."

"Where to begin?"

"Does the poet not instruct us to begin at the beginning?"

Faisal leaned forward, hands clasped and elbows on his knees. "After leaving here, I was carried by your little she-camel through the night to a luminous morning and a warm welcome at the oasis outside Jeddah, where our Bedouin brothers of the Bani Salem and the Masruh were gathered. I found that we were as one in our hatred of the Turks, may Allah utterly reject them. All swear allegiance to your lordship and await your signal to rise up and gain our freedom from the Ottoman yoke of oppression."

"What numbers might we expect from Bedouin in those regions?"

"About eighty thousand men, and each mounted on camel or war horse."

His father gave him a rare smile. "I am pleased to hear that you were afforded the honor you deserve—in your own right and as my son. The Bedouin are, indeed, our most trusted allies, sharing sacred bonds of blood as descendants of the Prophet and as proud warriors of the Hashemite house." Hussein patted Faisal's knee. "Please, continue!"

"Telling them I would return when the time of uprising was at hand, I took my leave and went north, slipping past Turkish outposts through Aqaba to Taba. From there a day's ride brought me to Nuweiba, where I was pleased beyond words to find my wife and children living happily under the protection of the Tarabin Bedouin." Faisal smiled. "Like a *dream* to finally be among them in one large tent on the shores of the Red Sea; to be with my beloved wife, to play with my little ones in the warm water, and to dine with our Tarabin hosts. Though part of me hoped that time would never end, I was gratified to receive your summons, knowing it meant the time of the revolt is coming."

"Indeed, my son, but tell me, did you also represent our cause to the Tarabin and other Bedouin of the Sinai?"

"Of course, Father. Our Tarabin brothers invited other tribes to meet with me—the Awlad Said and the Bani Hassan—swelling our ranks with another thirty thousand mounted warriors. Now, all we require is British support."

"And we shall have it!" Hussein held up a sheet of buff-colored paper. "This cable from Kitchener arrived two weeks ago."

Faisal took the paper and read aloud;

```
LORD KITCHENER'S SALAAMS TO HIS EMINENCE SHARIF
HUSSEIN IBN ALI,
IT MAY BE THAT AN ARAB OF TRUE RACE AND A DIRECT
DESCENDANT OF THE PROPHET SUCH AS YOUR LORDSHIP WILL
ASSUME THE KHALIFATE AT MECCA AND GOOD MAY COME BY
THE HELP OF GOD OUT OF ALL THE EVIL THAT
IS NOW OCCURRING.
IF THE SHARIF OF MECCA IS WILLING TO ASSIST GREAT
BRITAIN IN THE COMING WAR, WE WILL RECOGNIZE
AND RESPECT YOUR SACRED OFFICE, AND GUARANTEE
```

THE INDEPENDENCE, RIGHTS, AND PRIVILEGES OF THE
KHALIFATE AGAINST ALL FOREIGN AGGRESSION, IN
PARTICULAR THAT OF THE OTTOMANS.
I CONCLUDE BEGGING YOU TO ACCEPT MY SINCERE RESPECT
AND BEST WISHES,
HORATIO KITCHENER, FIELD MARSHAL
1ST EARL OF KHARTOUM
SECRETARY OF STATE FOR WAR

Faisal handed back the cable. "We have long awaited these words, my father—the promise of British gold and British guns!"

Hussein nodded. "We now have in writing what McMahon and Kitchener have been saying for months. This cable is the pact between our person and Great Britain, and it comes not a moment too soon, for the Turks have joined with the Germans in the Great War and the sultan has declared the jihad from Constantinople, hoping to arouse the Muslims of India and the Nile basin against the British."

Faisal gave a snort of disgust. "When Muslims see the scarlet Hashemite Banner at the vanguard of an Arab rebellion, this will expose the sultan's illegitimate call to holy war."

"That is my hope. The Turkish sultan is cynically manipulating the zeal of the faithful, and I, myself must put the lie to this brazen and fraudulent notion of holy war."

"How?" A feeling of anxious uncertainty caused Faisal to frown.

"I will appeal with respect and affection to the better inclinations of all Muslims, be they Sunni or Shia. Is it well said that, when you shoot an arrow of truth, you should dip its point in honey! We will soon declare the revolt, and it is my expectation that millions of Arabs will rally to our banner and our righteous cause—from North Africa to Mesopotamia, from Syria to the Horn of Africa!"

"Yes, Father! And with such a multitude and God's help, along with the support of Great Britain, we will prove masters of the Ottoman Turks!"

"However, my son, it is manifestly clear that we will *also* require support to withstand the challenge of our chief rival in Arabia, Ibn Saud. He and his followers may go so far as to ally with the Turks and betray the Arab rebellion just to spite me!"

"How might we grapple with this challenge?" Faisal asked.

"In addition to British support, we will make common cause with unlikely allies—other disaffected peoples who have suffered beneath the Ottoman yoke—an alliance of the wretched—Arabs, Armenians, Assyrians, Kurds, and Jews."

"Regarding the Jews, Father, I know that the Zionists are attempting to make inroads in Palestine. They have tried to curry favor with the Ottomans and the Germans. Now, they are putting all their efforts to make an alliance with the British."

"They're also reaching out to *us*!" Hussein exclaimed and produced a folded paper from his robes. "This letter came to me last week, from one called Chaim Weizmann—a Zionist Jew and a chemist, now working with the British. It came to me by way of a discreet emissary from the largest tea company in the world, founded by a Russian named Wissotzky, one known as the *tea king of Russia.*"

Faisal laughed. "I did not realize that the czar shares power with a *tea king!*"

"So it appears," said Hussein with a rare smile. "Please read and translate."

To his Excellency Sharif Hussein ibn Ali, with respect and salutations,

I, Chaim Weizmann, greet you in peace on behalf of the Zionist Organization. In the hope that the Central Powers will be defeated in the current war and the Ottoman Empire undone, I

*write to you in recognition that an independent Arab state may
be created in West Asia.*

*Insofar as Your Excellency is Islam's greatest prince and
guardian of the holy places, and believing you and your son,
Faisal, will be leading a rebellion of the Arabs against the Turks,
I wish to offer, on behalf of the Zionist Organization, any
assistance you may require to achieve success.*

*In offering our support, I am mindful of the racial kinship
and ancient bonds existing between the Arabs and the Jewish
people. In this spirit, I offer to meet with you, or your son, at any
time and place of your choosing to discuss our common cause
and our mutual aspirations—for Your Lordship, an independent
Arab state—for us, an independent Jewish homeland.*

*Desirous to create a good understanding between us, I look
forward to hearing from your eminence.*

With all respect and admiration,
Professor Chaim Weizmann
General Zionist Council

Hussein nodded at the paper in Faisal's hands. "The Jews are
certain that the Entente will win the war and the Ottoman Empire
will be broken into pieces. They turn to us as lords of the land—
hoping they might receive a portion thereof as a homeland of their
own."

Faisal handed the letter back. "How will you respond, my father?"

"I would you assist me in this, since an alliance between us and
the Zionists might prove useful."

"How would you propose to meet with Weizmann?"

"*You* will meet with him as my proxy, Faisal, perhaps in the British
protectorate of Aden. As for the British, we will reply that we will
help them win the war in return for their support of an independent

Arab state along the lines of the Damascus Protocol."

"Agreed, my father. What else would you have me do?"

"I would that you return to Jeddah and prepare the Bedouin troops of the Hejaz for battle. You should also send for the Bedouin of the Sinai."

"I will, my father, yet there is one thing I would ask of *you*."

"What is that, my son?"

"I would implore you to place Kitchener's cable in your safe. For countries, like men, are sometimes forgetful. The British may someday require a reminder of promises they have made."

CHAPTER 49

November 15, 1914
BEF Field Hospital
Boulogne-Sur-Mer

ON SUNDAYS there were no early rounds, and it was midmorning when the light bulbs, strung down the center of the long hospital tent, began to glow. Evan had been awake for hours, thinking about the letter he wanted to write to his father.

In Pratab's bed to his left, there was now a heavily sedated French corporal. Evan sighed. Despite being filled with the newly wounded, the tent felt terribly empty.

The rattle of small wheels over the wooden floor announced a cart with magazines pushed by an orderly wearing white shirt and trousers. He stopped at the foot of Evan's bed.

"You want something to read, mate?"

"Do you have any *Argosy*?"

"I do!" The orderly bent and shuffled through the magazines. "Here we are—*Argosy All-Story Weekly*." He handed the dog-eared magazine to Evan.

"Thanks." Evan winced at the cover, which featured a swarthy, muscular, and bare-chested man carrying a beautiful blond woman in his arms. She was either sleeping, unconscious, or severely ill. The title read, "Red Darkness. Somewhere Between Night and Eternity."

"May I have some stationary and a pencil?"

"You don't want the magazine?"

"Not to read—it's a good surface for writing."

"Here you are, mate." The orderly handed Evan a sheet of buff-colored paper and a stub of a pencil. "Anything else?"

"Actually, yes. Could you write a letter to my father for me?"

"Sorry!" The orderly laughed. "You'll have to do that yourself!"

Evan stared at the blank paper as he fingered the pencil in his hand. What could he say after not having written for three months? But he knew he needed to do it—to feel connected to someone, and his father was the place to start.

He began by apologizing for the way he had left home and went on to describe all that had happened since he had left New York—but in sparse enough detail so as not to incur the wrath of the censors. Then he added a final paragraph in present tense.

I'm looking forward to being with you and telling you what I've seen so far in this war. If you're still in Utah, that won't be soon, and it may be months before you get this letter, if you get it at all. But I'm hoping you've left the US and are now in England since, once I'm discharged from hospital, I'm planning to go to our place in Oxford and check in with Mervin. I'm hoping you'll be there too.

I have to close now since the ward sister is coming to change my dressing—for the last time, I hope. On the other hand, I'm delighted to see that the sister is accompanied by a very pretty Voluntary Aid Detachment nurse.
Wish me luck.

With my apologies and with love,
Evan

❄ ❄ ❄

"Top of the morning to you, Mr. Sinclair!"

"And a good morning to you, Ward Sister. Are you here to torture me again?"

"Of course, though I fear for the last time." She stepped quickly to the bedside with Sharon Meehan beside her. "I'll be instructing our VAD nurse, Miss Meehan, so your suffering might provide some educational value." She reached down and tore off adhesive strips securing two squares of gauze—one over the surgical site, the other over the chest tube site.

"Ow!" Evan winced.

"You didn't really want those chest hairs, did you, Mr. Sinclair?" Johnson asked.

"Actually, I was rather attached to them." Evan angled his head, trying without success to see the healing wound sites. "How do they look?"

Johnson peered through her pince-nez and nodded. "Good." Stepping to the side, she made room for Sharon. "Here, Miss Meehan. What do you think about Mr. Sinclair's wound sites?"

Sharon bent forward. "Both look clean—no swelling or redness."

"Good. Let's proceed with the extraction of these two sets of Donati mattress sutures." She took a pair of forceps and scissors from the metal tray and handed them to Sharon. "You'll need to lift the knot with the forceps, snip the suture loop beneath it, then simply pull it out."

"Can't you just leave them in?" Evan asked hopefully. "Won't they just . . . disappear?"

"Miss Meehan, please correct Mr. Sinclair's misconception regarding this type of suture."

"Certainly, Ward Sister," Sharon bent low over his chest. As she spoke, he could feel her touching one of the wounds. "These nonabsorbable skin sutures of cotton thread must be removed once the wound has healed—usually, after about a week."

"Ouch!" said Evan. "Did you get it out?"

"That was the first one." She looked at him and smiled, "Three more to go."

Evan felt the forceps on his skin again as she continued speaking. "When the surgeon, Mr. Howden, removed the bullet from your chest, he repaired the damaged tissues internally with absorbable suture material—catgut."

"Ouch!" Evan said again. "Are you done now?"

"Only two more!"

"So I have cat guts inside me?" he asked with genuine concern.

Sharon shook her head. "They're only called catgut, Mr. Sinclair. They're actually made of collagen from sheep or goat intestines sterilized with carbolic acid."

"Why doesn't that make me feel better? Ow!" He winced.

"And one more," she said and bent close.

Evan saw her blue eyes focus on the suture, saw how she lightly bit her lower lip in concentration, her mouth inches from his skin. And when she pulled out the last suture, he felt a certain pleasure in the quick pain.

"Are you done now?"

"I am!" she said and dropped the forceps and scissors into the metal tray.

"Well done, Miss Meehan!" the Ward Sister exclaimed. "A fine procedure and a good job with patient education."

"What now?" asked Evan.

"Miss Meehan will clean the skin, put on small adhesive bandages, and you'll soon be on your way."

"On my way? Where?" he asked.

"To England, my boy!" Johnson leaned forward and added in a whisper, "On a hospital ship in a day or two, provided you don't spike any fevers." She turned and headed back to the nursing station leaving Sharon at the bedside.

Evan's heart began to pound as he tried to think of something to say to her. He was thankful when she spoke first.

"I'm so happy for you, Mr. Sinclair, but sad you'll be leaving," she pouted as she cleaned and bandaged his wounds. "I had so hoped we might get to know each other . . ."

"I feel the same way," he said. "I also wanted to thank you for helping out that night with Pratab—getting him quickly into the operating room."

"I'm so very sorry we lost him. And soon, I'll be missing you!"

"Who knows, perhaps I'll develop a fever and stay."

"I hope *not*! But, before you leave, I'll give you my address, so we might remain in touch." She smiled and returned to the nurses' station.

Turning his attention back to the letter to his father, he carefully checked for errors in spelling or passages his father might consider poor syntax. Before he was halfway through, he heard footsteps on the tent's wooden floor.

Looking up, he saw Major Howden moving down the center aisle. He was alone—without the usual entourage of junior surgeons and nurses. As usual he wore a tweed coat over his surgical scrubs. He looked as if he had slept in them. Slowing his pace, he came to a stop and stood at the foot of Evan's bed. Instead of a chart, he had a folded newspaper in his hand.

"Good morning, Evan. How are you feeling today?" he asked quietly.

"Very well, sir, thank you, but how are *you*?" He was surprised at how subdued Howden appeared.

"Passing well," Howden nodded at the bed previously occupied by Pratab. "You miss him, don't you?"

"Very much, sir."

"So do I." He sighed. "Pratab, and all the boys we've lost

here." He turned halfway round, his eyes passing over the rows of the wounded. Seemingly in a daze, he whispered, "They shall not grow old . . ." He swallowed hard and sat on the edge of Evan's bed, putting the newspaper next to him on the blanket.

For a long minute neither spoke. Evan turned the words over in his mind, *They shall not grow old—what did he mean by that?* He saw that Howden's eyes were red-rimmed, and he looked tired. "When will you be rounding today, Major?"

"After lunch. We always round late on Sundays, and we especially needed a break today, operating as we did till about five this morning." He turned his head and looked at Evan. "I should imagine you're anxious to go home."

"If you're referring to England, sir—yes, I am. I heard from the Ward Sister that the hospital ship is due to sail soon."

"It's quite an undertaking—over four hundred wounded plus medical staff," Howden whispered. "But do be quiet about it—U-boats in the Channel, you know."

"I understand."

"What will you do once you're discharged?" asked Howden.

"I'll go straightaway to Oxford to see if my dad is back from America. Then I want to get back in the fight."

"With the Flemish resistance?" Howden asked with a little smile.

"I think not. I'm hoping to join the BEF."

"I may be able to help with that . . ." Howden said softly, almost to himself as he looked at Evan, then added, "But I should think you've had quite enough of mud."

"I'll go wherever I can help."

"I won't have a hand in sending you to the Western Front, Evan— not after all you've been through—not after what I've seen."

"What about the Middle East?"

"A promising idea." Howden stood up and looked down at Evan. "The road to that front begins in Cairo. I know someone at Whitehall, and I'll see what I can do."

"But I have no papers, sir."

"Here—take mine." He pushed his newspaper over the coverlet to Evan. "*The New York Times*, no less."

"Thanks, sir, but not exactly the papers I need." Evan sighed. "I feel a bit guilty about not joining the fight here in Europe—"

"Rubbish!" Howden said sharply. The Western Front has been reduced to bloody trench warfare with thousands dying every day for *nothing*!" He waved his hand over the rows of beds. "The boys newly come tell of cowering for weeks in muddy trenches with rats and vermin, with senseless charges into machine gun fire and barbed wire, with constant artillery bombardment, chlorine gas, and frigid rain. If you want to go into *those* killing fields, you'll do it without *my* support!"

Taken aback by the vehemence of Howden's response, Evan shrugged. "But there's no *action* in the Middle East, sir."

"There will be," Howden whispered. Then he turned and left the tent.

Once he was gone, Evan took the newspaper Howden had left on his bed. It was dated November 2, 1914, and much of the front page announced the entry of Turkey into the war on the side of Germany. In particular, a quotation of the kaiser caught his eye. "Among my many titles, 'King of Jerusalem' is the most precious to me, and soon to be made fully manifest in alliance with the Ottoman Empire."

Bob Pitney was right, thought Evan. *The kaiser is fixin' to move into his palace in Jerusalem . . .*

Shaking his head, he saw that the lower part of the front page featured a poem, "For the Fallen," written by someone named Laurence Binyon.

He began reading.

They shall not grow old, as we that are left grow old;
Age shall not weary them, nor the years condemn.
At the going down of the sun and in the morning,
We will remember them.

As he read on, he thought of his mother and of Emile and of Pratab, and after several stanzas, the words blurred, and he couldn't read any more.

CHAPTER 50

November 17, 1914
BEF Field Hospital
Boulogne-Sur-Mer

AWAKE BEFORE DAWN, Evan sat on the edge of his bed in the slumbering darkness of the hospital tent. Though he couldn't see the soldiers in the beds around him, he could hear the unhurried sounds of their breathing and snoring. As he waited for rounds to begin, he wondered if any had died during the night.

Finally, the bright string of lights along the center of the tent went on, followed by the racket of steel pans and instruments coming from the nurses' station—the discordant music of Ward Sister Claire Johnson, preparing for surgical rounds. At the same time, orderlies and nurses spread out through the tent, recording the soldiers' vital signs. Among the nurses was Sharon Meehan.

He saw her advancing down the line, watched her move with an easy grace, her figure striking above and below her tapered waist. Locks of hair the color of burnished gold escaped from beneath her white head cloth. She approached his bed, and his breath caught as she fixed him with her calm blue eyes. She smiled and held up a thermometer.

"I hope that's an *oral* thermometer," he said.

"It is now," she replied and placed it beneath his tongue.

Bending low, she whispered, "Good morning, Mr. Sinclair."

"Isn't it time you called me Evan?" he mumbled around the thermometer.

"How are you feeling today . . . Evan?" she asked and laid her fingertips lightly on his wrist to check his heart rate.

"Okay."

"Are you sure?" she asked, a smile on her lips. "Your heart rate seems a bit elevated." She wrapped the blood pressure cuff around his upper arm, and whispered, "I know all about your heroic story, but no one seems to know how you ended up with the Flemish resistance."

"Long story."

"A long story I'd very much like to hear," she said and positioned the earpieces of the stethoscope. She took a measurement, her hand on his arm as she pumped the bulb. The cuff tightened, then eased as she deflated the cuff, his pulse pounding in his arm. She slipped the thermometer out of his mouth and recorded his blood pressure and temperature. "Lovely!" She put aside the stethoscope and unwound the cuff. "Everything is perfectly normal, except for your elevated heart rate."

"Which is your fault."

"You Americans . . ." she blushed.

"I'm not an American, Sharon. I'm English—just lived in the US long enough to lose my accent. But I love yours."

"Do you? And where would you say I'm from?"

"West Country," he paused and added, "Somerset, I should think."

She laughed, and he saw the flash of her even white teeth. "Can you be more specific?"

"Bristol."

"Close enough." She gave his hand a gentle squeeze then turned to place his chart in the rack.

Rounds began as Major Richard Howden led the charge

into the ward with the other doctors, with the nurses bringing up the rear. Dressed in his usual tweed jacket over an operating room tunic, Evan was relieved to see Howden looking rested and energetic. Gone was the weary sadness of the day before.

The entourage moved from bed to bed, drawing nearer as the minutes passed. He caught Sharon's gaze when she looked his way, and when she smiled, his heart pounded. He found himself wishing he could stay in the hospital longer.

The chart rack rattled to a stop by his bed.

"Mr. Sinclair." Howden opened Evan's chart. "Are you ready to leave us?"

"You tell me, sir."

"Any pain or chills during the night?"

"None, sir."

"Good! Let's have a look at that head wound."

Evan leaned forward.

"Looks good." Howden rested his hand on Evan's shoulder and settled him back. "And now the chest wound and tube sites." Howden removed the bandages. "Nicely healed as well. Alright, then—for the next week, I want you to wash both wounds with soap and water, and change bandages daily."

"So, I'm being discharged, sir?"

"Tomorrow, my good man! That is, if you remain afebrile. I've already sent a letter of introduction and recommendation to the military secretary at Whitehall."

"Whitehall, sir?"

"The War Office—a beautiful new edifice at the corner of Whitehall and Horse Guards Avenue."

"But sir . . . won't I be joining the BEF in Cairo?"

"That will be determined at Whitehall. They'll have my letter verifying your identity and informing them of your contribution to the war effort in the polders! I also made a copy for you. So, if you get any cheek at Whitehall, I suggest you show your copy to Lloyd George, the chancellor of the Exchequer."

"How will I find him?"

"His office is at Parliament. Lloyd George knew my father, and I'm certain he'll help you join the BEF in Egypt."

"Thanks very much, sir!"

"Godspeed to you, Evan." Howden turned and led the way to the bed across the aisle, shouting, "Onward Christian soldiers!"

As Sharon passed Evan's bed, she dropped two folded pieces of paper on his blanket. He unfolded one and read the elegant cursive.

A Book of Verses underneath the Bough,
A Jug of Wine, a Loaf of Bread—and Thou
Beside me singing in the Wilderness—
Oh, Wilderness were Paradise enow!

With a touch of sadness, he recalled his mother reading him this and other quatrains from Fitzgerald's translation of the "Rubáiyát" by the Persian poet, Omar Khayyám. He had continued to read the Rubáiyát after her death, committing about a dozen quatrains to memory, and this was one of them. His heart ached as he reread the familiar words, remembering his mother.

Looking at the second piece of paper, he saw that she had written her address; Sharon Anne Meehan, Cloud House, The Avenue, Bath 2, Somerset, England

He looked up at her, still on ward rounds. When their eyes met, she smiled and blushed. With a stab of regret he knew that he'd likely be leaving the hospital the next day. Then he remembered Howden's words . . . *if you remain afebrile.*

For a few seconds, he considered falsely elevating his temperature. He knew of a number of methods—rubbing the mercury tip rapidly back and forth on the bed sheet to create friction, drinking very hot tea before the measurement . . . *What am I thinking?* He felt ashamed that he was entertaining ways to stay in the hospital when there weren't enough beds for the mounting number of wounded.

But he was sad he was leaving and might never see her again. He reread the quatrain, then placed the papers in the top drawer of the table by his bed.

※　※　※

With the German Fourth Army
West of Roeselare
Occupied Belgium

Chief of the general staff, General Erich von Falkenhayn was becoming accustomed to the kaiser's tirades. With the initially swift German advance stymied by the flooding of the polders, Wilhelm was given to frequent fits of rage. As he ranted and paced back and forth in the war room, Falkenhayn held his tongue and thought, *It's all I can do to navigate these narrow straits between the Scylla and Charybdis of the kaiser's raging ego and our increasingly dire strategic position in the European war . . .*

"This is completely unacceptable!" Wilhelm shouted as he paced next to the large map on the war-room table, festooned with small flags and wooden blocks of armies and artillery. "You assured me that France would have fallen by now, yet here we are—stagnating for months—a war on two fronts with no end in sight!"

"As you know, Your Excellency, it was my predecessor, Moltke, who weakened the Schlieffen Plan —"

"Of course! It was I who retired the old fool!"

Wilhelm's dress uniform, hung with medals and gold braid, shone in the firelight as he paced along the map, muttering, "All went so *well* in the beginning. We took Liège, we captured Charleroi, Mons, Antwerp . . ." His voice trailed off as he stared at the map.

"All true, sire, but once our advance was blocked by the flooding of the polders, here," he tapped the map with a long wooden pointer. "We face a new reality—Yser is a stalemate and some of the general staff believe it is no longer possible for us to win this war. They raise the notion of a diplomatic solution—"

"Tell them to save their breath!" Wilhelm shouted and grabbed the wooden pointer. "I will never accept defeat. Do you hear me? Never!" Agitated, Wilhelm paced along the map. "Be quiet now, General! I require time to think."

Giving the kaiser a wide berth, Falkenhayn retired to a desk in the corner of the war room and watched the kaiser pace as he muttered and stared at the map. After a time, he stopped pacing and shouted, "General von Falkenhayn!"

Hurrying to his side, he saw the kaiser jab the pointer at the Eastern Front.

"We'll simply reverse the Schlieffen plan! We'll redirect our main attack against Russia! Instead of breaking the French on the Western Front, we'll break the Russians in the east." He slapped the pointer down on Russia with a loud retort. "That's it then—we'll make our main European effort here! Accordingly we'll transfer forces and join with our Austrian brothers and our Ottoman allies to quickly eliminate the Russian threat. And we'll also direct our attentions here." He tapped the Suez Canal.

"But, sire, how can we spare any troops for the Middle East? We're already dividing our efforts between the two European fronts—"

"It won't require any troops!" The kaiser cut in. "In the Middle East we now have the armies of the Ottoman Empire at our disposal, and we have General von Kressenstein as liaison to the Turks. Kressenstein and his staff will plan and lead a Turkish invasion force across the Sinai and take the Canal!"

"It's risky, sire."

"Perhaps not as risky as you suspect, General!" The kaiser smiled. "As you may know, we've been conducting a campaign throughout the Levant for years—convincing the Arabs that I converted to Islam following a secret trip to Mecca—*Haji Wilhelm*, they call me, defender of the one true faith!" Wilhelm's shoulders shook as he laughed.

"Fascinating, sire, but how does that contribute to crossing the Sinai and defeating well-entrenched British forces in Egypt?"

"My dear General, perhaps you're unaware that the sultan has called for a holy war against the infidel English and French. When the Ottoman armies attack the Suez Canal, thousands of Egyptian Muslims serving with the British will rise up against them! In this manner, we'll take Cairo and perhaps drive the British from Egypt!" He slapped Falkenhayn on the back. "Be of good cheer, General! We'll not only establish our military superiority in the Holy Land, but we'll also draw British and French forces away from the Western Front. By early next year we will have neutralized the Russians in the East, established our claim to the Holy Roman Empire in Jerusalem and, with the English and the French weakened in the West, we'll move ahead to final victory!" He tossed the wooden stick back at Falkenhayn. "Any questions?"

"Just this, Your Excellency, since we've lost the race to the sea, the British Navy will be able to freely resupply their troops in France."

"I've an answer for that as well! As you say, we've failed to reach the sea at the key Channel ports. Therefore, we will simply gain control of the sea in another fashion."

"Excuse me, sire, another . . . another fashion?" Falkenhayn stammered.

"Yes." The kaiser pointed at the coast. "We will reach the sea by going *under* it."

"Your Excellency? Do you mean—"

"Yes, my dear General. Unrestricted U-boat warfare!"

"Even in the English Channel?" Falkenhayn asked in disbelief.

"Especially in the English Channel!"

CHAPTER 51

November 18, 1914
BEF Field Hospital
Boulogne-Sur-Mer

"WERE YOU PLANNING to walk out of here wearing only a revealing hospital gown?" asked Ward Sister, Claire Johnson.

Evan laughed and looked at the folded pair of pants and a shirt, topped with a pair of socks at the foot of his bed. "Thank you, but . . . no shoes?"

"Didn't know your size. Once you're dressed, go to the storeroom—there are plenty of shoes and more clothing there for you to choose from. I also set aside a nice big valise." Johnson nodded in the direction of the nursing station at the far end of the tent. "You'll also find your copy of Dr. Howden's letter to Whitehall on the counter."

"That's wonderful—thank you! But do I really need a big suitcase? I have a perfectly good haversack."

"That's fine for a few things, like that whip you insist on keeping, but hardly adequate for the clothing and other items you'll need."

"All these *items*—were they lost or abandoned?"

"Neither. Just left behind . . ."

For the first time, he heard sadness in her voice and glimpsed something behind her usual mask of cold efficiency. *How difficult it must have been for her since the war began—day after day, taking care of badly injured young men, and watching so many die.* He fixed his eyes on hers and nodded, affirming his understanding and his admiration.

"Time to get dressed," she said with a little smile, which quickly faded. She took a deep breath and rose to her full height. "Feel free to rummage about in the storeroom and take what you need." She turned and went back to the nurses' station.

Evan slipped into the clothing she'd left for him—trying not to think of who had worn them before. Wearing tan trousers, a white linen shirt, and a pair of gray wool socks, he padded down the aisle. At the nurses' station, he found a brown envelope and a burlap suitcase.

Johnson was standing off to the side, readying medications for distribution. He cleared his throat and asked, "The storeroom?"

"In there." She motioned toward a closed door behind the station.

"Thanks." He pushed open the door and stepped into the darkened room. Before the door settled closed, he saw a string hanging from the electric light bulb. He pulled it and the light clicked on.

"Wow!" he whispered and looked over shelves filled with neatly folded clothing, orderly personal items, and coats on hangers lining the far wall with about two-dozen paired boots and shoes beneath them on the floor.

He picked out boots that looked his size, tried them on, and found they fit well.

Kneeling by the canvas suitcase, he released the two latches and opened it up. Setting to work, he filled the valise with trousers that looked his size, underwear, and a few shirts and socks. Among the coats, he found a brown leather jacket. He tried it on and found it fit him perfectly.

Among a clutter of safety razors in a wooden box, he saw a straight razor. The orderly who had shaved him that morning had used one, and he recalled that his friend, Mike Cope, had always favored a straight razor, and had let Evan use it a few times. Though he only needed to shave once or twice a week, he loved the ritual of it—sharpening the bright blade on a leather strap, whipping up lather in a shaving mug, brushing the white lather onto his face, and carefully drawing the razor over his skin. Looking through the box of shaving supplies, he found everything he needed including a shaving mug with a thick layer of dry soap at the bottom. He put it all in the valise.

Two knocks on the storeroom door broke the silence.

"Just a second!" he called out as he closed the valise and secured the latches. "Okay, Nurse Johnson, I have everything I need!" He opened the door.

But it wasn't Johnson at the door. It was Sharon Meehan, her blue eyes shining with tears. She stepped into the storeroom and pushed the door closed.

"Evan, it would surely kill me if I had no hope of seeing you again," she said and dried her eyes. "You'll write, won't you? Please say you will."

"Of *course*, I will."

She took a step toward him. "It's just that . . . I've become so very fond of you."

"I want us to stay in touch, Sharon," Evan said and put down the valise. "I'm pleased you're here now, because I wanted to tell you how wonderful it was to read those lines from the 'Rubáiyát' you wrote!" He smiled and raised his shoulders. "I can't believe it's just a coincidence! That's one of the dozen or so quatrains I love and know by heart!"

"Me, as well!" She clapped her hands.

Hesitating, he took a step toward her, but hit his head on the light bulb, which swung wildly back and forth, light and shadow shifting over the shelves of clothing.

Before he knew what was happening, she was holding him in her arms, her face upturned, her mouth against his. The softness of her lips and the fragrance of her took his breath away. He stepped back and, smiling down at her, raised his hand and steadied the swinging light bulb. Then, cradling her face in his hands, he held her gaze for the space of a deep breath, and kissed her again. Then, drawing her close, he whispered another quatrain.

> *"Awake! For Morning in the Bowl of Night*
> *Has flung the Stone that puts the Stars to Flight . . ."*

And to his delight, she finished the verse.
> *"And Lo! The Hunter of the East has caught*
> *The Sultan's Turret in a Noose of Light."*

He kissed her again, then sighed. "I *will* write to you, Sharon. I promise I will, and when all this is over, I'll see you again . . ."

"Oh, yes!" And then we'll have the luxury to read all one hundred quatrains together!" She put her hands on his chest, rose up on her toes, brushed her lips on his, and kissed him again. Then she sighed, straightened her white head cloth, stepped out of the storeroom, and flashed a quick smile before the door closed.

He stared at the door for a long minute, his heart pounding, excited by her touch and the bond he felt between them. Then, as one wakes from a dream, he shook his head, took the valise, and stepped out of the storeroom.

An hour later, Evan sat in the dim light of a gently-rocking lorry with about a dozen other young men bound for Calais to take ship across the Channel. He reached beneath his leather jacket and fished a folded piece of paper from his shirt pocket, squinting at Sharon's address in the weak light.

He touched his lips, still able to taste her kiss on his mouth. *I hope those first kisses won't be our last,* he thought and refolded the paper. He placed it, along with the lines from the "Rubáiyát" she had written out, in the waterproof oilskin bag Emile had given him, and with a sigh, he put the bag in his haversack.

He realized that he didn't know Sharon well, but he knew that he loved the sound of her voice, her sense of humor, and their shared love of the "Rubáiyát." He smiled and thought, *there's also her slender body, the curve of her breasts, her lovely face, and the softness of her lips.* He had already learned how war erased lives and carved down good moments to nothing. He hoped that someday he might have many good moments with Sharon.

He exhaled loudly and looked down at the heavy tan boots he'd selected in the hospital storeroom. The leather was quite supple, and the soles showed hardly any wear. He wondered about the boot's previous owner, about the roads he'd taken, about his last road. *And what about mine? What roads will these boots take me down?*

He lifted the tan valise onto his lap. It was practically new and nicely constructed from wood and burlap. The latchets, leather straps, and studs showed little wear. Clicking open the latchets, he tipped open the lid, removed the manila envelope from the upper compartment, slipped out Howden's letter, and read it silently.

November 15, 1914
Major-General Charles Callwell
Military Secretary at Headquarters
The War Office—Whitehall and Horse Guards Avenue, London

My dear Major-General Callwell,
I'm writing about one Evan Sinclair, a British subject who wishes to join the Expeditionary Force in Egypt. Having given medical care to young Sinclair, wounded while helping the Flemish resistance flood the polders, I can attest to his integrity, his intelligence, and his bravery. Indeed, had he been enlisted with

*British or Commonwealth armed forces, an argument might be
made that he should be awarded the Victoria Cross for gallantry
in the face of the enemy.*

*Now that his wounds have healed, I'm able to attest to his
health and fitness for service, and I'm hoping you'll be able to
honor his request to serve the Empire on the Middle East Front.*

With gratitude and with my humble duty,
Major Richard Howden, MBChB Chief of
Surgery, British Expeditionary Force Field
Hospital, Boulogne-Sur-Mer, France

He slipped the letter back into its envelope and put it into the
waterproof oilskin bag with Sharon's address and the quatrain. He
put the bag in his haversack, which he placed on the floor between his
feet. Then he closed his eyes.

As the lorry rolled and jolted along the rutted roads bordering the
French Atlantic coast, he remembered another lorry—the harrowing
ride in the convoy with the red bus behind and the young soldiers
singing, and the devastation that followed.

Shaking those thoughts away, he recalled some Latin text his
father had forced him to memorize—words of Seneca from *The Mad
Hercules.*

Quis hic locus, quae regio, quae mundi plaga?

What place is this, what region, what quarter of the world?

And as he drifted toward sleep, wearing the boots and clothing of
unknown dead men, the words echoed in his mind.

He felt very much like Hercules, waking from a trance after
unknowingly destroying all he loved—waking with a torrent of
sadness and disoriented horror. But for Evan, it wasn't like that at
all—rather a disoriented joy in the strange new world he was creating.
And having broken free from the stifling connection with his father,

he was now able to love him with the freedom of not being his son, of not being anyone's son.

He opened his eyes and looked at the row of sleeping soldiers slumped against each other on their bench seat across from his. And as the lorry gently rocked, speeding toward the English Channel and the waiting ship, Evan whispered words of wonderment,

What place is this, what region, what quarter of the world?

TO BE CONTINUED IN:

Crossroads of Empire.

CHARACTER LIST

PLEASE NOTE: historical figures are listed in all-capital letters and departures from actual historical detail are noted in *italics*.

AHMED DJEMAL PASHA (1872–1922)
Ottoman military leader and one of the Three Pashas—the Young Turks who ruled the Empire during WWI. He favored entering the war on the side of the Entente but was overruled by Enver Pasha.

BELL, GERTRUDE (1868–1926)
British archeologist, writer, traveler, and political officer central in shaping British policy during and after WWI.

B'shara, Rahman–Fatima and Mahmoud
Arab archeologist at École Biblique, Jerusalem, his wife and infant son.

CALLWELL, MAJOR-GENERAL CHARLES (1859–1928)
Director of Operations and Intelligence during World War I at the War Office at Whitehall.

CHURCHILL, WINSTON (1874–1965)
First Lord of the Admiralty in the Asquith government, tasked with overseeing Britain's naval effort when WWI began.

Cope, Mikel
Evan Sinclair's high school friend in Cedar City, Utah. (Fictionalized after Mikel Cope, author's high school friend in Oakland, California who worked at the actual Bob Pitney's filling station).

DOUGHTY-WYLIE, LIEUTENANT COLONEL RICHARD (1868–1915)
British Army officer and diplomat, who died at Gallipoli and was recipient of Victoria Cross for his service at Gallipoli, as well as the Ottoman Empire's

Order of the Medjidie for his humanitarian service to Turkey during the Balkan Wars.

FAISAL BIN HUSSEIN BIN ALI AL-HASHEMI
(1885–1933)

Third son of HUSSEIN BIN ALI, SHARIF OF MECCA, born in Mecca and educated in Constantinople. Historically, met TE LAWRENCE in Wadi Safra, 1916 and met CHAIM WEIZMANN with LAWRENCE at a British/ Arab encampment in the Mountains of Moab overlooking the Dead Sea in June, 1918. *(In book, Faisal's meeting with Lawrence moved to Nuweiba in the Sinai, January, 1915, and his meeting with Weizmann and Lawrence moved to Aden, May 5, 1915).*

FALKENHAYN, GENERAL ERICH VON
(1861–1922)

Chief of the German General Staff from September 1914 through August 1916.

Geeraert, Hendrik

Leader of a group of Belgian partisans

GINSBERG, ASHER ZVI HIRSCH (1856–1927)

Better known by his Hebrew penname, Achad Ha'am (meaning "One of the people"). Ginsberg was a Talmudic prodigy, Hebrew essayist, and one of the earliest and most prominent Zionists in the Russian Empire. Known as the founder of "cultural" Zionism that stressed the rebirth of the Hebrew language and the centrality of Jewish ethics in settling Palestine with respect for the rights of the indigenous residents of the land.

Gupta, Rissaldar Pratab

A wounded soldier of the Raj who befriends Evan Sinclair at the BEF hospital in France.

HEDLEY, COLONEL W. COOTE (1865–1937)

Commander of MO-4, British Intelligence, Geographical Division

Howden, Major Richard

Chief surgeon at the British Expeditionary Force Field Hospital, Boulogne-sur-Mer, France

HUSSEIN BIN ALI AL-HASHIMI, SHARIF OF MECCA
(1854–1931)
Leader of the Banu Hashim Bedouin tribe and direct descendent of The Prophet. As sharif and emir of Mecca, he declared the Great Arab Revolt against the Ottoman Empire in June, 1916. Self-declared King of the Hejaz from 1916 to 1924.

Johnson, Claire
Ward Sister at the field hospital of the British Expeditionary Force at Boulogne-sur-Mer in northern France.

KAISER WILHELM II, GERMAN EMPEROR AND KING OF PRUSSIA (1859–1941)
According to German historian, Thomas Nipperdey, Wilhelm was " . . .superficial, hasty, restless, unable to relax, without any deeper level of seriousness, without any desire for hard work or drive to see things through to the end, without any sense of sobriety, for balance and boundaries, or even for reality and real problems, uncontrollable and scarcely capable of learning from experience, desperate for applause and success . . ." On November 9, 1918, having lost the support of the military, and with a revolution underway, he abdicated his throne and fled Germany for Holland, where he died on June 4, 1941.

KAISERIN AUGUSTA VICTORIA OF SCHLESWIG-HOLSTEIN (1859–1921)
Wife of Kaiser Wilhelm II.

Kemal, Yusuf and Kadim, Mustafa
Two twenty-year-old Turkish friends, graduates of the high school section of the American Robert College of Istanbul, the oldest continuously operating American school outside the US. Given their English language skills, the two were drafted into the Turkish army and assigned to service at Augusta Victoria Hostel in Jerusalem.

LAWRENCE, THOMAS EDWARD (1888–1935)
Known as "Lawrence of Arabia," he was a British archaeologist, scholar, soldier, spy, and writer. He helped lead the Arab Revolt with Faisal and brought Faisal together with the Zionist leader, CHAIM WEIZMANN.

LIST, GUIDO VON (1848–1919)
Austrian occultist and novelist who expounded a revival of the religion of the ancient German race and in 1910 suggested the swastika as a symbol for all anti-Semitic organizations. Active in Austria and Germany during the war, he oversaw publication of his books promoting ultra-nationalism and Germano-Nordic racial supremacy. Died in Berlin on May 17, 1919. *Von List's life is fictionalized in the book to the extent that he never traveled to Jerusalem and never worked with the historical Montagu Parker.*

Meehan, Sharon
Twenty-year-old Volunteer Aid Detachment (VAD) nurse who befriends Evan Sinclair when hospitalized at BEF hospital in France.

Nathanson, David (with Sarah and Isser)
Jewish archeologist at École Biblique, Jerusalem, his wife, and infant son.

NEWCOMBE, STEWART FRANCIS (1878–1956)
British army officer who served the Empire in South Africa, Sudan, Egypt and Arabia. Mapped the Sinai and Negev deserts with T. E. LAWRENCE and LEONARD WOOLLEY in dual capacities of mapping and espionage of the Ottoman Empire's capabilities in advance of WWI. Organized the Military Intelligence Branch in Cairo, was sent to Gallipoli to command an Australian division of Royal Engineers, followed by action in all theaters of the Great War.

Pitney, Bob
Owner of filling station in Cedar City, Utah. (Fictionalized after filling station owner in Oakland, California).

Russell, Flora and Diana
Sisters who worked at the Red Cross office in Boulogne-sur-Mer at the start of the war, tracking the dead and wounded from Western Front, joined there after a few weeks by their friend, GERTRUDE BELL.

Sinclair, Clive Robert
Professor of Near Eastern languages and Archeology, Balliol College, Oxford. Father of Evan.

Sinclair, Evan William
Sixteen-year-old son of Clive Robert Sinclair.

Smythe, Mervin
Colleague of Clive Sinclair, Professor of Teutonic Archeology with academic appointments at Universities of Oxford and Stuttgart.

SPAFFORD, ANNA LARSEN ØGLENDE (1842–1923)
Norwegian-American woman who, along with her husband, HORATIO SPAFFORD, emigrated from Chicago in 1881 with a dozen other Presbyterians, settling in Jerusalem. There they were joined by Swedish Christians, and established the American Colony, where they engaged in philanthropic work for the people of Jerusalem regardless of their religious affiliation and without proselytizing.

SPAFFORD, HORATIO GATES (1828–1888)
Prominent American lawyer and Presbyterian church elder who established the American Colony in Jerusalem with his wife ANNA SPAFFORD. He wrote the hymn "It is Well with My Soul" following the tragic deaths of their three-year-old son from scarlet fever followed by the death of their four daughters by drowning on a transatlantic voyage.

VESTER, BERTHA SPAFFORD (1879–1968)
Daughter of ANNA and HORATIO SPAFFORD, born in Chicago after family tragedies (see SPAFFORD, HORATIO). Bertha served the American Colony as an educator, nurse, and provider of social services. She assumed primary administrative responsibility for the colony upon the death of her mother ANNA SPAFFORD in 1923 until her own death in 1968.

VESTER, FREDERICK E. (1869–1942)
Husband of BERTHA VESTER and manager of the American Colony Store just inside Jaffa Gate—a commercial, charitable, and educational enterprise.

VESTER, HORATIO FREDERICK (1906–1985)
Son of BERTHA SPAFFORD VESTER and FREDERICK E. VESTER. He was doted on by DJEMAL PASHA when he visited the American Colony during the early years of the war.

Walker, Montagu

Soldier, adventurer, and treasure hunter, Walker barely escaped with his life after excavating the Temple Mount in 1911, returning to Jerusalem under the kaiser's patronage three years later. In the book, Walker is the fictionalized version of MONTAGU PARKER, a British aristocrat and soldier who truly did serve in the Boer War, searched for treasure on the Temple Mount in 1911, and escaped Ottoman authorities on the yacht of CLARENCE WILSON. *But, unlike this fictional version, the historical Montagu Parker did not return to Palestine, but went on to fight in WWI and was decorated with the Croix de Guerre. He inherited title of Fifth Earl of Morley in 1951 with the death of his older brother and died in England on April 28, 1962.*

Watson, Clarence

Young aristocrat, Boer War veteran, and yachtsman, he is a friend of and collaborator with Montagu Walker. They were discovered excavating the Temple Mount for treasure in 1911, and managed to escape the mob and Ottoman authorities, sailing away from Palestine on Watson's yacht. *Clarence Watson is a fictionalized version of the historical CLARENCE WILSON (just as Montagu Walker is a fictionalized version of the historical MONTAGU PARKER).*

WEIZMANN, BENJI (1907–1980)

The eldest son of CHAIM and VERA WEIZMANN, he was born in Manchester, England, settled in Clonlara, Ireland, and became a dairy farmer.

WEIZMANN, CHAIM (1874–1952)

Russian-born biochemist and Zionist leader, he met with FAISAL and TE LAWRENCE to work toward Jewish-Arab cooperation in Palestine. Weizmann's development of a biochemical fermentation method to produce acetone was central to England's ability to produce munitions during WWI. Weizmann would serve as Israel's first president from 1948 until his death in 1952. *The actual meeting between Weizmann and Faisal facilitated by LAWRENCE portrayed in book as taking place on May 5, 1915 in Aden, actually took place in southern Transjordan in June of 1918.*

WEIZMANN, VERA (1881–1966)

Russian-born physician and Zionist activist who married WEIZMANN, CHAIM in 1906 and soon thereafter settled in Manchester, England, where their first son, BENJI, was born in 1907. Vera received her English medical license in 1913 and directed a public health clinic for mothers and infants.

Wertheimer, Gunter von (with Rachel and Tirzah)

Archeologist at École Biblique, Jerusalem, of German Lutheran Templer parentage. His wife, Rachel is a Yemenite Jewess and linguist, and Tirzah is their fourteen-year-old daughter.

WOOLLEY, LEONARD (1880–1960)

British archaeologist who worked with Lawrence at the excavations in Carchemish, then on the desert survey that yielded their report, *The Wilderness of Zin*. All the while they reported crucial geographic and Ottoman-German movements to British Naval Intelligence.

ACKNOWLEDGMENTS

I want to offer my profound gratitude to all those who read the manuscript in its various forms and offered their comments and encouragement. Foremost among them is Bill Gottfried, in whose memory the book is dedicated. Bill was an early beta reader who suggested that a ponderous two-hundred-thousand-word version constituted a clear and present danger to anyone reading in bed.

Special thanks are also due to the long-suffering members of my critique group, Critical Mass—Margaret Dumas and Claire Johnson, there from the very beginning to the final beta reads. Without their relentless and merciless attention to detail, this book could not have been written.

I'm also indebted to fellow authors, Annamaria Alfieri and Matt Coyle for their support and friendly encouragement.

Special thanks are due to my loving wife, Teri, who gave me the time and space to weave multiple storylines into a sweeping tapestry while she was stitching together spectacular quilts.

I also wish to thank John Koehler of Koehler Books for bringing *Wages of Empire* in from the cold, Becky Hilliker for cleaning it up, and Christine Kettner for giving it proper attire.

SUGGESTIONS FOR
FURTHER READING

Anderson, Scott. *Lawrence in Arabia: War, Deceit, Imperial Folly and the Making of the Modern Middle East.* New York: Doubleday, 2013

Bell, Florence, ed. *The Letters of Gertrude Bell.* New York: Boni and Liveright, 1927

Fromkin, David. *A Peace to End All Peace – The Fall of the Ottoman Empire and the Creation of the Modern Middle East.* New York: Avon Books, 1989

Garnett, David, ed. *The Letters of T.E. Lawrence.* London: Jonathan Cape LTD., 1938

Haythornthwaite, Philip J. *The World War One Source Book.* London: Arms and Armor Press, 1992

Lawrence, T.E. *Seven Pillars of Wisdom: A Triumph.* New York: Doubleday & Company, Inc., 1935

MacDonogh, Giles. *The Last Kaiser: The Life of Wilhelm II.* St. Martin's Press, 2001

Mack, John. *A Prince of our Disorder: The Life of T.E. Lawrence.* Cambridge and London: Harvard University Press, 1976

Manchester, William. *The Last Lion: Winston Spencer Churchill – Visions of Glory.* New York: Dell Publishing, 1983

Morris, James. *The Hashemite Kings.* New York: Pantheon Books, Inc., 1959

Sicker, Martin. *Between Hashemites and Zionists: The Struggle for Palestine.* New York: Holmes & Meier, 1989

Spafford-Vester, Bertha. *Our Jerusalem: An American Family in the Holy City.* Jerusalem: Ariel Publishing House, 1950

Van der Kiste, John. *Kaiser Wilhelm II: Germany's Last Emperor.* The History Press. Cheltenham, UK, 1999

Wallach, Janet. *Desert Queen: The Extraordinary Life of Gertrude Bell.* New York: Anchor Books, 1999

Weizmann, Chaim. *Trial and Error: The Autobiography of Chaim Weizmann.* New York: Harper & Brothers, 1949

Woolley, C. Leonard and Lawrence, T. E. *The Wilderness of Zin: Archaeological Report.* London: Palestine Exploration Fund by Harrison and Sons, 1915

Printed in the USA
CPSIA information can be obtained
at www.ICGtesting.com
CBHW010320220224
4593CB00009B/184